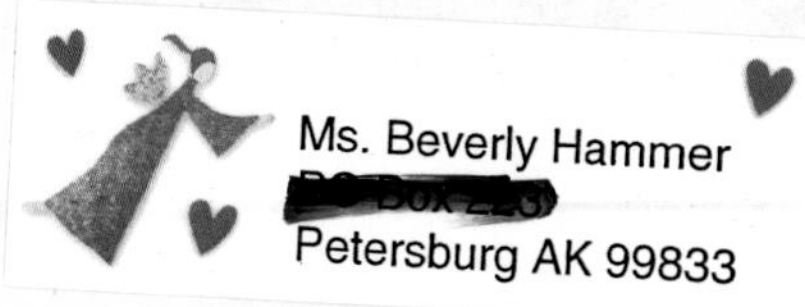
Ms. Beverly Hammer
Petersburg AK 99833

W9-BGQ-587

Elizabeth's Journey

A Novel

Shirley A. Stephenson

AuthorHouse™
1663 Liberty Drive
Bloomington, IN 47403
www.authorhouse.com
Phone: 1-800-839-8640

First published by AuthorHouse 9/23/2009

ISBN: 978-1-4389-9175-7 (e)
ISBN: 978-1-4389-9174-0 (sc)

Library of Congress Control Number: 2009908941

Printed in the United States of America
Bloomington, Indiana

This book is printed on acid-free paper.

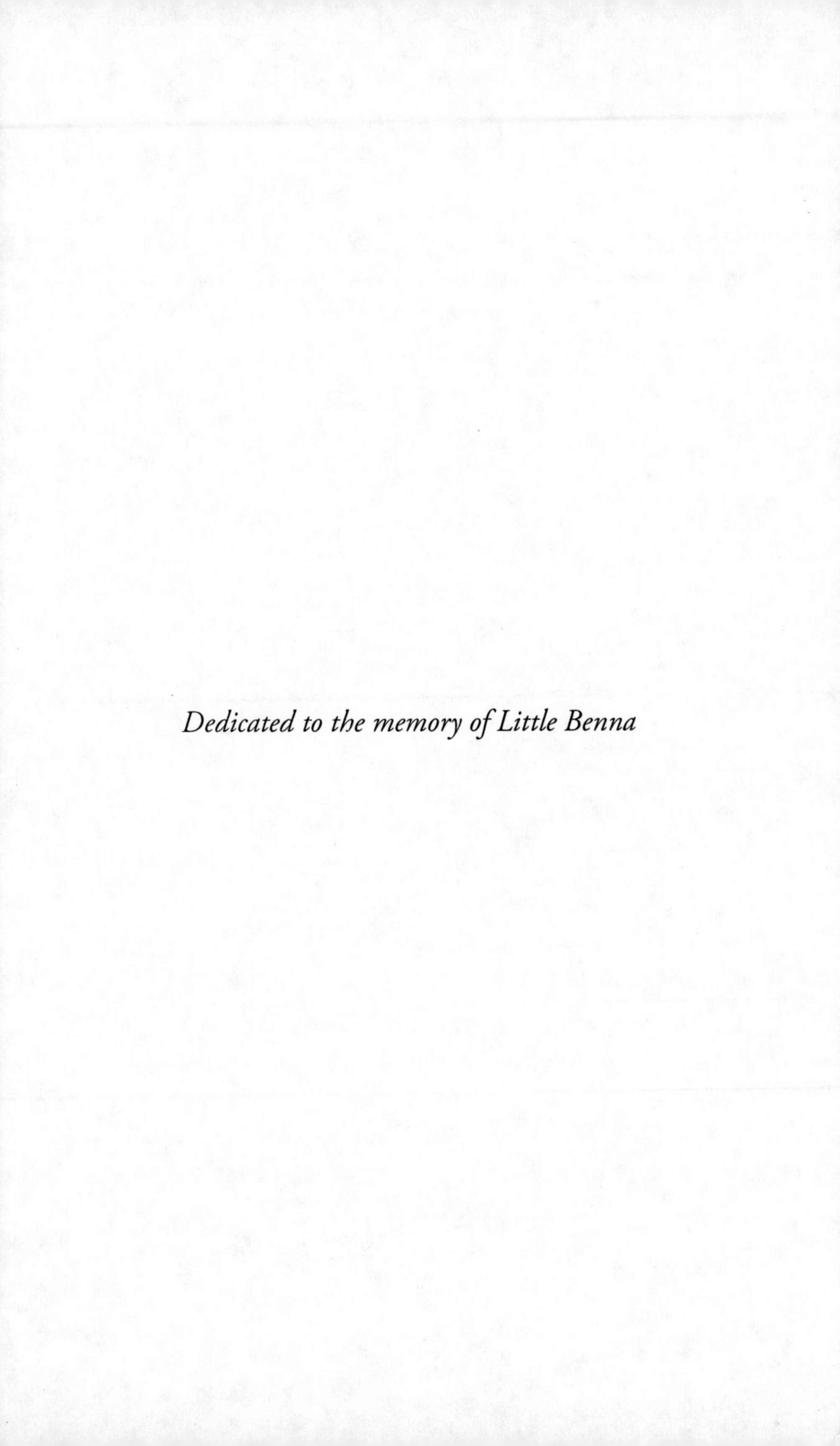

Dedicated to the memory of Little Benna

Preface

This is a historically accurate work of fiction based upon a true story. Sources of historical events include family histories, local legends and vintage newspapers. Since historical characters are best equipped to describe the events of their times, the names of Elizabeth's family members, merchants, fishermen and their boats are, for the most part, factual. All of the major characters are deceased. The conversations ascribed to these individuals are, of course, imaginary. News travels quickly in small towns, however, and it's possible the conversations took place as presented.

In summarizing the contents of hundreds of vintage newspapers from the microfilm collection of the Alaska State Library, I included only those events of which Elizabeth would have had knowledge – through personal experience, by reading the very same newspapers or through conversations she may have had or overheard. A small number of imaginary characters has been placed among the genuine participants of events in history. You, Dear Reader, are entitled to know what is fiction and what is historical fact:

Illinois 1906-1912

- Elizabeth's cousin Ella and Albert Roger's tutor master machinist Herr Braun are imaginary characters.
- The Orpheum Theatre and Westward Supper Club in Evanston and the Clayborn Hotel in Chicago are imaginary.
- Mr. Lingren and his daughter Rose are imaginary characters. The second bride in Elizabeth's wedding picture is unidentified.

Illinois/California 1912-1918

- It is uncertain whether or not Elizabeth's brother-in-law Joe Roger was a physician and the product of his father's first marriage.
- The surfing exhibition at Ocean Beach, CA is fictitious; however, a Hawaiian surfer is known to have given such demonstrations farther up the coast.
- There is no documentation that Albert Roger worked on the development of Balboa Park for the Panama-California Exhibition. However, given his occupation as a machinist, it is likely he would have been employed there along with hundreds of other men recruited for the project.
- A postcard from Sweden addressed to the Mount Olive Ranch in Alpine, CA is the only clue that Elizabeth spent time there. The Smith family and their hired hand are imaginary.
- The actual location of Albert Roger's janitorial job in Evanston, IL is unknown.

Alaska/Illinois/Alaska 1918-1922

- The twin peaks of Ripple Rock in Seymour Narrows, British Columbia were blasted out on April 5, 1958 in the world's largest non-nuclear peacetime explosion.
- Carl Roger suffered a gunshot wound to the head at the hands of his partner ten months before Elizabeth arrived in Alaska Territory. The timing, location and provocation for the shooting were changed to make a more compelling story. The name of Carl's partner was also changed.

- ❖ It is unknown whether or not Mrs. Ballance was employed at the seafood cannery; however, most of the town's women worked there during the season.
- ❖ It is unknown whether or not Elizabeth suffered from the "Spanish Flu." Nevertheless, more than three hundred cases were reported before the epidemic subsided.
- ❖ The name of the local agent for the "Rechickening France Committee" was changed. Ole' Willie, porter on the Great Northern Railway, and Mrs. Henderson, employee of the Hotel Arctic, are imaginary characters.
- ❖ There is no documentation that Carl Roger purchased the property at the north end of Wrangell Narrows during the town site trustee's sale of 1920.
- ❖ It is not known whether or not Mrs. Mathis was on the welcoming committee for the visiting Shriners in the summer of 1920.
- ❖ The purpose of Carl's trip to Seattle in 1921 is unknown. The author assumed it was to discuss the business of the hotel during the 1920-1921 depression.
- ❖ Elizabeth's visit to the Patten's fox ranch was most likely to their farm on Akusha Island rather than to their earlier venture on Storm Island.

Chapter 1

February 4, 1918 – Over breakfast, Elizabeth asked, "Is it my imagination, or did the ship just slow down?"

"No, it slowed," said Carl, looking out the window. "We just passed Cape Lazlo and the captain needs to time our arrival at Ripple Rock at the highest possible tide. Time to get ready for the lifeboat drill."

Passengers assembled on the top deck and donned life vests just as the *Jefferson* entered the south end of Seymour Narrows, British Columbia. It was cold out on deck and Elizabeth gagged on the acrid smoke swirling from the steamer's single stack. She joined the line forming before her assigned lifeboat.

The water moved fast in the narrow passage between Vancouver and Quadra Islands. The dolphins that had been glancing off the submerged bow quickly vanished.

"There's an underwater mountain up ahead," Carl said. "Ripple Rock is actually two peaks that are only nine feet below the surface at low tide. The best time to navigate the narrows is at high-water slack tide. Any other time, you risk being caught in a whirlpool and dragged under. Many shipwrecks have taken place in these waters."

The water beneath the ship turned turbulent and a large whirlpool appeared off the port bow. The big ship slipped sideways toward the whirlpool despite the captain's efforts to steer a straight course. The steamer shuddered as the propeller hit air pockets in the roiling water.

Suddenly, they shot ahead, released by the current's strong grip. Captain Nord straightened out the ship and they continued north up the channel.

Elizabeth realized she had been holding her breath. "Is there more?" she asked.

"No, that's the worst of it," replied Carl. "Let's go below and warm up."

They lined up with the purser for lunch seating and watched the passing scenery. There were no more settlements and the tide ran rapidly. At Johnstone Strait, Elizabeth spied a pod of killer whales. Their tall, stiff dorsal fins skimmed the surface wet and black. Occasionally, one raised out of the water far enough to see the white markings on its side. They paid the ship no heed and continued their search for food in the cold, dark water.

Chapter 2

August 1905 – Elizabeth's first ocean voyage was thirteen years earlier when she and her guardian, Uncle Emil, emigrated from Sweden. They were deposited at the Ellis Island processing center where her uncle's name was changed from Bror Anders Emil Scheutz to Emil White. Elizabeth remained Johanna Christina Elizabeth Johnson, although the spelling was changed from the Swedish *Jonasson* to the Americanized *Johnson*.

Elizabeth's mood was sullen as the train left New York. She still couldn't believe her aunt and uncle divorced after nineteen years of marriage when Aunt Emma refused to follow him to America. Elizabeth wished she could make the train turn around and take her back to her friends. But, her guardian and his sister, Elizabeth's mother, gave her no choice in the matter. She was being delivered to a house full of strangers in a strange country.

The Pennsylvania Special left New York Penn Station, crossed the Hudson River and reached Newark Penn Station in less than an hour. They followed the setting sun through cities with strange sounding names before the train labored up the eastern slope of the Allegheny Mountains. Elizabeth watched the fading scenery as long as she could stay awake but finally retired to the sleeper car. The *clickety clack* of the wheels put her to sleep instantly.

The next morning, the landscape had changed to rolling farmland. During breakfast, they passed cornfields and herds of dairy cattle. They spent the day in the observation car where a small boy distracted her from her worries by running the center aisle as fast as he could without losing his balance in the swaying coach. Everyone was relieved when he wore himself out and settled down for a nap.

The train crossed into Indiana and stopped at Fort Wayne Station. Their car transferred to the Chicago, Rock Island and Pacific Railroad and headed northwest toward Lake Michigan. Elizabeth felt herself getting farther and farther from home.

"How much longer, Uncle Emil? Do you think they will remember me? I was only four years old when they left Sweden. Will they make fun of my English?"

He just laughed and told her to stop worrying. Finally, they pulled into Chicago's Union Station. "Look, Lisa," he said. "There's your Mamma. And could those be your brothers Karl and John? My, how they've grown."

Elizabeth peered through the smudged window at the group standing on the platform. Her mother looked smaller than she expected. And the photographs they had received over the years did not prepare her for how tall Karl and John really were.

Elizabeth slowly followed Uncle Emil down the steps where there was much hugging, hand shaking and back thumping. Everyone talked at once. Her brothers collected their baggage and the group boarded a commuter train for the short trip to Evanston. Mamma explained that Papa was at work and Elizabeth's sister, Helen Ida, was at home looking after the children.

"Home" was a crowded two-story house on Ridge Avenue. Elizabeth met her new brothers and sisters amid noisy confusion: twelve-year-old Elmer; nine-year-old Paul; seven-year-old Alice and six-year-old Ruth. Clarence, the baby, was two years old. Her thirteen-year-old cousin Julia also lived with them. Her sister, Helen Ida, was three years younger than Elizabeth and had been a baby when the family left for America.

Later that night, after the parade of aunts, uncles and cousins had left, Mamma entered the room Elizabeth shared with Helen Ida and sat at her bedside. She stroked her hair and said, "Welcome home, Lisa. I'm so happy to have all my family together again." She kissed Elizabeth's cheek and slipped quietly from the room.

Uncle Emil stayed for a week before moving to Rockford and a position with Hess & Hopkins Leather Company. There, he rented a room at a boarding house for gentlemen.

As eldest daughter, Elizabeth was expected to help with the children, cleaning, laundry, sewing and cooking. Working around the house together, she was struck by how alike she and Mamma were. They were both petite – though Elizabeth was a little taller – and stronger than they appeared. They both wore size five shoes and shared the Scheutz-family nose that drooped slightly at the tip. Elizabeth wore her light brown hair in a short Marcel wave parted on the left and combed low on her forehead. She could see she'd have to let her hair grow if she were to fit in with the American style. Mamma told her she was more mature than American girls her age and more level-headed.

Papa was a stern man with too many mouths to feed. A broad mustache hid the lower part of his face and sometimes his pale blue eyes stared without expression. Mamma was the only girl who wasn't afraid of him. He was especially strict with Julia whom he sent to collect the coal that fell off passing freight trains and fetch his pails of beer from the tavern on the outskirts of town. He thought formal schooling was wasted on girls and didn't quite seem to know what to make of Elizabeth.

Mamma taught Elizabeth to bake bread and they took turns keeping the family larder filled. After kneading the dough, Elizabeth let it rise beneath a clean white cloth, punched it back down with her fist, shaped it into loaves and let them rise one more time before putting them in the oven. After baking, she drizzled melted butter on the still-warm loaves to keep the crusts soft. The aroma of freshly baked bread was a constant presence in Papa's house.

The women kept busy preparing meals and filling Papa and Karl's lunch pails. The men left early each morning for their construction jobs where Karl was learning the carpenter trade.

Helen Ida was only too happy to share child-tending duties with Elizabeth. The baby was going through the "terrible twos" and required constant watching. Ruthie was a scamp and although she was only six, she schooled Elizabeth in American English.

One night before going to sleep, Elizabeth whispered, "Helen Ida, are you still awake?"

"Um hmm," said Helen Ida.

"I don't understand something about Julia."

"What about Julia?"

"Is she our cousin, sister, or what?"

"Both, I think."

"How can that be?"

"Well, her mamma is Aunt Alma who lives in Rockford. And I'm not really sure who her father is."

"But Aunt Alma is married to Uncle Karl. Isn't he Julia's father?"

"I think Julia was born before Aunt Alma and Uncle Karl ever met. No one talks about it, but I think her father could be our Papa."

"What do you mean?"

"Well, when our family came over from the old country, Papa came first together with our brother Karl and Aunt Alma. She's Mamma's youngest sister, you know, and would have been seventeen or eighteen years old. Mamma came a year later, bringing me and our brother John. You stayed in Sweden with Uncle Emil and Aunt Emma. When we got to Evanston, Aunt Alma had given birth to Julia."

"And nine months later, our brother Elmer was born?" asked Elizabeth.

"Yes."

"So within a year of coming to this country, Mamma had two new babies to raise – Julia and Elmer?"

"I think so."

"*Uff-da.*"

Elizabeth was curious about her new surroundings that were so different from Ödeshög. Evanston was much larger than she was accustomed to. Both towns were located near water – Lake Vattern in Sweden and Lake Michigan in Evanston.

Northwestern University sat on the lakeshore and occupied the eastern side of town. The college had been there for more than fifty years. Storekeepers were friendly and there were many young people – especially students.

Many beautiful homes in Evanston were owned by wealthy people escaping the congestion of Chicago. Papa said Chicago had tried to annex Evanston three times and voters rejected them every time.

For her eighteenth birthday, Mamma took Elizabeth shopping in Chicago. Chilly October winds whistled off Lake Michigan. The city was crisscrossed by shipping canals and elevated railways. Papa said it was known as *the city the Swedes built*, because Swedish carpenters helped rebuild the city after the Great Fire of 1871. He said the fire destroyed more than 18,000 buildings and killed many people.

Some of the buildings on State Street were twelve stories high. They stood shoulder to shoulder, solid brick and granite monuments built to withstand fire and storm. Electric trolleys ran down the center of the street, sharing space with horse-drawn freight wagons, runabouts and an occasional automobile. Broad sidewalks were filled with pedestrians hurrying about their business, being careful where they stepped when crossing the street. Elizabeth and Mamma spent the entire day in the city and never left Marshall Field's department store.

Elizabeth joined her sister and cousin Ella as they watched a baseball game at the church picnic. This sport was new to her and Ella explained the rules as the men took turns swinging a wooden bat at a ball thrown to them by a player standing in the middle of the field. Ella said everyone was crazy about the Chicago White Sox and Chicago Cubs. Both teams were expected to compete in the World Series.

A sturdy young man with wavy blonde hair strode to the batter's box and prepared for his turn at hitting. He glanced directly at Elizabeth and grinned, flashing strong white teeth. She blushed and lowered her gaze as Helen Ida and Ella teased her. She hurried back to the Lutheran ladies' food tables, not even waiting to see if he hit the ball.

Later, Ella told her his name was Al and he lived in Chicago. He came to Evanston on weekends to visit friends.

Elizabeth saw the brash young man again at a summer dance. Music from the community hall drew Elizabeth and Uncle Emil inside where dancing couples whirled around the floor.

People of all ages were there – little girls in dresses covered by frilly white aprons, young people glancing shyly across the hall at one another, and their parents standing in small groups or taking their turns on the dance floor.

The hall was decorated in red, white and blue bunting and smelled of floor polish and tobacco. The floor boards gave a little with the weight of the dancers. A punch bowl stood on a corner table covered with a lacy white cloth.

Helen Ida and Julia seated Elizabeth between them along the "girls' side" of the hall. Elizabeth felt everyone's eyes appraising the new Johnson girl. She must have passed, because a seemingly endless stream of young men asked her to dance. She danced the two-step and waltz until her toes could tolerate being stepped on no longer.

In the far corner, a group of youngsters scandalized their elders by dancing the Cake Walk. The backward-bending, high-stepping strut had recently made its way up the Mississippi River from New Orleans.

As Elizabeth sat down to give her feet a rest, she heard a voice ask, "May I have this dance?"

She looked up into the teasing blue eyes of the young man she had seen playing baseball. He introduced himself as Albert Roger and led her into a lively polka. He was an excellent dancer. They barely stopped to catch their breath, danced a Schottische together and then a waltz.

Uncle Emil watched as they whirled around the dance hall, her feet barely touching the floor. When the musicians played a waltz, he cut in and admonished Elizabeth for letting Albert monopolize her dance card. "You should meet as many people as possible, Lisa," he said.

Not all of Elizabeth's activities were occupied by helping Mamma at home. Occasionally, there were swimming parties and carnivals.

A small cove just north of campus was a favorite swimming spot for locals and students. The crescent-shaped beach was covered with small pebbles. A rope swing dangled from a branch on a large tree jutting out over Lake Michigan's chilly waters.

On one summer day, the beach was littered with blankets, towels and picnic baskets. Elizabeth, Ella and Helen Ida took turns smearing lotion on each other as they soaked up the sun. Albert Roger was there along with Helen Ida's boyfriend Earl. The rest of their crowd was spread out on the beach or swimming near the shore.

"Oh look," Helen Ida said, "Al is going to dive from the swing."

They watched as Al swung out over the water and let go just as the rope swing reached its apex. He gave a loud "whoop" as he dove headfirst into the swimming hole's deepest part.

The knotted rope continued to swing back and forth in smaller and smaller arcs. Frayed ends beneath the knot flared out like a twirling dancer's skirt as the rope untwisted. The water's surface began to smooth over.

Someone said, "He hasn't come up yet." People began to move toward the water.

Suddenly, Al broke through the surface like a breaching whale. Sunlight glistened off his tanned muscular body as he waded, laughing, to shore.

"Leave it to Al to scare everybody," said Earl.

Later that day, after the sun had set, they huddled around a campfire on the beach. The boys were still showing off, telling raucous stories and singing drinking songs. Several times, Elizabeth caught Al looking at her.

The circus arrived and Elizabeth and cousin Ella walked down the midway enjoying music from the calliope, the shouts of the carny barkers and shrieks of delight from excited children.

Ella tugged at Elizabeth's arm as they passed Madame Cézanne's fortuneteller's tent.

"C'mon Lisa, let's go in and have our fortunes told. Maybe we'll find out we're going to meet a tall, dark and handsome stranger."

"Oh, I don't know Ella, I really don't believe in those things."

"I don't either," Ella replied, "but it'll be fun anyway. Let's just see what she has to say. I'll go first."

They entered the tent and Elizabeth waited in a small dingy room while Ella stepped behind a beaded curtain where Madame Cézanne sat before her crystal ball.

The waiting room was dark and smelled of incense. Elizabeth sat on one of four straight-backed chairs lining a wall draped with dark fabrics. A worn Oriental rug with intricate patterns covered the earthen floor.

Ella came through the curtain, a big grin on her face. "That was fun. You're next."

Elizabeth passed through the curtain and a puffy-faced old lady motioned her to a chair across the table. She wore a purple turban with a fake diamond in the center knot. She didn't use her crystal ball but instead took Elizabeth's right hand in hers and turned it palm side up.

"You have a very long lifeline," she said, tracing her index finger across Elizabeth's palm. "You will live a very long time. I see a long journey over water and I see two little girls in your future." She paused, looked directly into Elizabeth's eyes and added, "That will be five cents."

When Elizabeth told Ella what the fortune teller had said, she replied, "Wow, all she told me was I would attract lots of beaus. I could have told her that."

Elizabeth was nervous as she prepared for her first date with Al. He had invited her to see *The Great Train Robbery* playing at the Orpheum.

She wore her best Sunday dress with white sandals. Papa answered his knock on the door and the men talked while she collected her purse and gloves. Al held the door for her as they left, turned, and shook hands with her father.

"I'll have her home by ten," he said.

At the theater, they sat off to one side rather than joining their friends. Al held her hand as they watched the "Hole in the Wall Gang" rob a Wyoming train. Sound effects were provided by the theater manager hidden behind the screen. In the final scene, a bandit pointed his gun directly at the audience and pulled the trigger. Everybody screamed, ducked and then laughed at their folly. Elizabeth found it thrilling while Al was more intrigued with the movie-making process.

Holding hands, they walked slowly home in the twilight and talked and talked and talked. Al told her about his parents and brothers. He had been expected to join his father in the butcher business in Sweden. Instead, the three boys followed one another to America where each pursued a separate calling. One was a chef at a Seattle hotel and the other was a doctor in San Diego.

Elizabeth told Al how abandoned she had felt when her family left her in Sweden and came to America without her. Uncle Emil and Aunt Emma didn't have any children, so her parents gave them Elizabeth. Her Papa only sent for her when Mamma needed help with the children and the household chores.

Al told her about his apprenticeship to master machinist Herr Braun in Chicago. It was a four-year program of study and supervised experience. When finished with his apprenticeship, he would be a certified journeyman machinist qualified to work anywhere.

Elizabeth watched expressions play across his face as he described calculating dimensions and tolerances, understanding the effects of heat treatment on metals, and making machinery and industrial equipment on the spot to keep production moving. She understood very little of this but was caught up in his enthusiasm.

"Metal is to a machinist as wood is to a carpenter like your Papa, Elizabeth," he said.

His blonde eyelashes curled at the tips and a dimple on his chin moved as he spoke. This was a quieter, more thoughtful Albert that he kept hidden when out with their friends. He spoke earnestly of his hopes and plans.

Elizabeth liked this more serious side of Al.

Al and Elizabeth spent many happy hours together. In summertime, they had picnics in the park, rented paddle boats and explored the college campus. In winter, there were ice-skating parties, hay rides with their friends and campus lectures to attend.

Without a conscious commitment, they had become a couple. Elizabeth hadn't met anyone she'd rather spend time with and, as far as she could tell, he wasn't seeing anyone else either.

His kisses were sweet and tender and Elizabeth was in heaven when she was in his arms. Their silences were just as comfortable as when they were together on a dance floor. Julia teased Elizabeth that her head was in the clouds where Al was concerned.

Elizabeth's brother John asked, "So, when are you two getting married?"

She couldn't believe he would ask such a personal question, and in front of Al.

Elizabeth glanced at Al and quickly replied, "That's something we don't talk about."

"Oh," said John.

Three months later, Al invited her for dinner and dancing at the Westward. The supper club was softly lit with candlelight and the dance floor cozied up to the band. They danced before and after a meal of braised tenderloins and fresh vegetables.

She was thoroughly enjoying this new experience when Al covered her hand with his and said, "I love you, Elizabeth. Will you marry me?"

This was so unexpected that Elizabeth wasn't sure she had heard correctly.

"What?"

"Will you marry me?"

"Oh Al, yes."

"I'll ask your father's permission tomorrow. It's too late to get him up tonight. How does an April wedding sound to you?"

"It sounds wonderful. Oh, I can't think. You'll be finished with your studies by then?"

"Absolutely."

Papa gave his blessing and Elizabeth moved through her daily activities in a daze. Al had a standing invitation to Sunday dinner and he started calling Elizabeth *min lilla Svenska* – my little Swede. Her brother John said, "It's about time."

Al completed his training, becoming a fully qualified journeyman machinist. Herr Braun gave him a Gerstner toolbox as a graduation present. Made of golden oak, it would hold a full complement of journeymen's tools as Al acquired them. He showed her how each drawer was lined to provide a moisture-free environment for the proper storage of his precision tools.

Al continued to work on jobs with Herr Braun until the wedding. They hadn't decided where to settle down but Elizabeth would follow him anywhere.

One evening before the wedding, Helen Ida knocked softly on Elizabeth's door. "Lisa, can I talk to you?" she asked.

"Of course, come in. I'm writing thank-you notes for the beautiful gifts we've received. I'll mail them after the wedding. Why Helen Ida, you're crying. What's the matter?"

"Oh Lisa, it's terrible and I don't know what to do."

"Nothing could be as bad as all that. Tell me."

"Earl and I . . . well. We're in a family way."

"Oh, my. Have you told Papa?"

"No. No one. Papa would kill me and I don't know what he'd do to Earl."

"How far along are you?" asked Elizabeth.

"Four months."

"How does Earl feel about this?"

"He wants to do the right thing," said Helen Ida. "We've been keeping company for a long time and have talked about getting married someday, just not this soon."

"Helen Ida, you have to tell Papa."

"I know. But I don't want to spoil your wedding. Promise you'll tell no one and we'll tell Papa afterward – it's less than a month away and I'm not showing yet."

"I promise," said Elizabeth. "But what can I do for you? How can I help?"

"Just having someone to talk to is a great relief. Thank you, Lisa. I'm going to miss you when you move out."

April 6, 1912 dawned cool and overcast. The winter snow had melted and spring was in the air. Everywhere there were signs of new beginnings – in the budding trees, flowering plants pushing their heads above the soil and robins singing in the fields.

Papa had found a way to save money on Elizabeth's wedding by sharing expenses with his friend Mr. Lingren whose daughter Rose was also getting married. Al and Elizabeth didn't really mind a double wedding, although they didn't know the other couple very well.

Julia, Elizabeth's maid of honor, helped her dress in the church basement. Her silk organza wedding gown came from Marshall Field's. The slightly flared skirt was ankle length and dozens of covered buttons climbed up the back. A wreath of satin flowers anchored the full-length veil.

"You're beautiful, Lisa," said Julia. "I'm so happy for you."

Helen Ida poked her head into the room. "Everyone is seated. It's time. Oh Lisa, you look so pretty."

Julia preceded Elizabeth into the corridor where Papa was waiting. He didn't say anything – just gave her arm a squeeze as they followed Julia and the flower girl down the aisle.

Al was standing straight and serious. She thought he looked so handsome in his dark suit, white shirt and white bow tie. Uncle Emil stood beside him as best man.

When they reached the men, Papa removed her arm from his and slipped it into Al's. Papa sat down in the front pew next to Mamma.

They waited as the other bride and groom marched down the aisle until they were also standing before the altar. Elizabeth was so nervous, it seemed as if she were watching the ceremony from afar. Julia lifted Elizabeth's veil and smoothed it back.

Pastor Swanson intoned, "I now pronounce you man and wife. You may kiss the bride."

The wedding party formed a reception line and greeted well wishers as they moved into the community hall. Everyone said what an attractive couple she and Al made.

Elizabeth's parents and siblings, including her brother Karl's new family, made a happy clamor as they moved among their friends and neighbors. Herr Braun and his wife joined the celebration and all created a din of laughing, talking and clinking glasses.

The musicians played a lively tune as Al whirled her around the floor to the accompaniment of clapping hands and stomping feet. Soon, everyone was dancing. Time seemed to speed up. Elizabeth barely recalled her father and Uncle Emil making toasts, she and Al cutting the wedding cake and tasting the buffet delicacies. She wished she could slow everything down so she could savor every detail.

Glancing across the room, she saw a tall stranger in the doorway. Something about him seemed familiar. The wedding party continued with its happy chatter, barely noticing his presence. Julia knelt to buckle the flower girl's shoe. Al grabbed her arm and said, "Elizabeth, look. It's my brother Carl all the way from Seattle."

He propelled her toward the door for introductions. Carl took her hand in his two large ones and said warmly, "It's a pleasure to meet you, Elizabeth. My brother is a lucky man. I'm sorry I missed the ceremony. The train was late."

His hands were soft with fingernails as clean as a surgeon's. Like Al, his blue eyes and fair complexion hinted at his German heritage. He was taller than Al and where Al's blonde hair was wavy, his brother's was straight.

After polite small talk, Elizabeth left Al to catch up with his brother and found Julia at her elbow.

"Who is that man?" Julia asked.

"Al's brother Carl. He's the head chef at the New Washington Hotel in Seattle. His train was delayed and I want to give Al a chance to visit with him."

Later, Al told her Carl was seeking business opportunities in Alaska.

The party was still going strong when Elizabeth and Al slipped away to her parent's house to change into traveling clothes. They were going to San Diego for their honeymoon.

Chapter 3

February 5, 1918 – Elizabeth was seasick. She should have skipped dinner. They were crossing the unprotected waters of Queen Charlotte Sound during the night. She awakened to a rolling ship and climbed down from the top bunk to look out the window. She couldn't see a thing – just darkness and a sense of disorientation. She crawled into the lower bunk; *maybe the ship won't feel so unstable down here.* It didn't seem to make much difference. *How could a ship roll this much without tipping over?* She hung onto the side of the bunk and watched as her trunk slid across the floor from one side of the cabin to the other.

She finally fell into an exhausted sleep after what seemed like hours of plunging and rolling through the sea. When she awoke, the ship was no longer bouncing and daylight peeked through the salt-streaked window. She tidied herself and her cabin and found Carl in the lounge, looking concerned.

"That was a rough crossing, Elizabeth. How do you feel?"

"Like I just found my sea legs. And I'm hungry."

"Then breakfast it is," he laughed. "And I don't think there'll be a line."

The ship made a hard left turn at Boat Bluff and entered Tolmie Channel. They passed narrow, steep-sided fjords forested with western hemlock, spruce, firs and cedars. Carl told her more about their fellow travelers.

"Mr. Leines over there, now he skippers the boat *Laddie* for the local cannery," he said. "She's a handsome boat, newly built and they use it as a tender."

"What's a tender?" Elizabeth asked.

"It's a boat the cannery owns or hires to buy fish directly from fishermen on the fishing grounds. That way, the fishermen can keep on fishing while the tender takes the catch into the cannery for processing. The tender also brings supplies and water to the fishermen on her return trip."

"Mr. Leines is also working on repiling the cannery docks and warehouse," Carl continued. "The fellow sitting at that table by himself is Mr. Peterson. He has the boat *Peggy*. And Charles Norberg, you met his wife, has the gasboat *Flyer*. He's also a director of the local bank. One of the Hungerford boys is also on board this trip. They have a logging camp near the Indian village of Kake this season."

Elizabeth passed the afternoon in the lounge in the company of the other women. Carl was deep in conversation with a group of men across the room. She caught snippets of war and fishing news. Carl smiled across the room at her as he refilled his pipe every now and then.

In late evening, the ship slowed before entering narrow Grenville Channel. Carl said these waters were full of logs and other hazardous debris. It was a gloomy and lonesome-looking stretch of coastline and they hadn't seen another boat for hours. Captain Nord stopped by and Carl introduced Elizabeth.

"Welcome aboard, Mrs. Roger," he said. "I understand you'll be making your home in Petersburg. Alaska needs strong women to keep these rascals civilized," he chuckled, looking at Carl. "Come to the bridge in the morning and I'll show you your new home on the navigation charts."

"Why, thank you Captain, I'd like that," she replied.

During the night, Elizabeth was awakened by the ship's whistle and she felt the engines slow. Looking out her window, she saw another steamer, the *City of Seattle,* pass in the opposite direction. The two ships passed so close she could make out the captain on the well-lit bridge waving as he pulled the cord for an answering whistle. The *Jefferson* resumed speed and she fell back asleep to the steady throb of the engines.

Chapter 4

April 1912 – After the wedding, Elizabeth and Albert took the commuter train to Chicago and the Clayborn Hotel near the Polk Street Station. Elizabeth was still surprised Albert had chosen her to marry – the popular young man could have had any girl he wanted. She guessed he preferred "old country" values to those of flighty American girls when it came to his wife.

She was certain she was the only twenty-four-year-old Swedish virgin in America. It had reached a point during their courtship when she would have given him even that, but he was always careful that they didn't go too far.

Now they were married. Al swooped her off her feet and carried her across the threshold. They took turns slipping into their night clothes in the tiny lavatory and snuggled into bed.

"I love you, *min lilla Svenska*," he said.

"I love you too, Al."

Their night clothes were soon on the floor.

Early the next morning, Al left to see about their tickets and give her some privacy. She tried to wash the blood stains from the sheets; she didn't want the chambermaid to see them. She hadn't expected the marriage act to be painful. Oh, it was wonderful too, but where there's blood there's bound to be some pain. That would probably go away with time.

At least they'd been spared the humiliation of a shivaree. Karl and Jenny's friends had kept them up most of their wedding night with singing, shouting and banging on tin kettles. And unlike her brother, Elizabeth and Al didn't have to face their friends' knowing smirks the next morning.

A knock on the door, and Al poked his head in. "Are you hungry? There's a restaurant at the station."

They crossed the street to breakfast an hour before the train was to leave for California. Al had reserved a private compartment with barely enough room in which to turn around. They were giddy with excitement as they boarded the Atchison, Topeka and Santa Fe and watched the station's clock tower recede in the distance.

Elizabeth felt like she could fly. She was finally released from her father's household, accountable only to her new husband. At times, she had felt like an indentured servant.

Now they were free from family obligations and setting off in their own direction. She was nobody's chambermaid now. As she gazed at her handsome husband, Elizabeth was filled with hope and excitement that great things were in store for them. She loved the freedom of not knowing where they would settle. There would be time enough to make that decision after the honeymoon. She just knew they could make it anywhere and their choices were limitless.

They traveled southwest through Illinois and Missouri and arrived in Kansas City in time for supper. It felt good to get off and stretch her legs on the broad platform. They finished a light meal in the depot restaurant just as the conductor called, "allll aboard."

The view through the window in the morning was as flat as far as they could see. "The Great Plains," Al explained. "We passed through Kansas last night. We'll be crossing the Rockies in Colorado soon."

From the sightseer lounge, they watched the scenery change from flat land to mountains as the train began its slow climb to Raton Pass – 7,588 feet above sea level according to the travel brochure. A spring storm had left snow piled at the entrance to the summit's half-mile-long tunnel.

The train picked up speed as they descended into New Mexico. This was America's famous Southwest. Elizabeth searched the landscape for cowboys and Indians but the only Indians they saw were women selling baskets, blankets and beads at the depots they passed.

They arrived in Albuquerque and everyone got off while the train was serviced. The passengers moved toward a young man beating a metal gong at the entrance to a Harvey House restaurant. The brakeman had teletyped the passenger's menu preferences ahead so their meals were waiting even as they were being seated.

One of their traveling companions explained that the waitresses were called "Harvey Girls" and lived above the restaurant. The girls were recruited through advertisements placed in eastern newspapers and they served the traveling public with the arrival of each Santa Fe train. They were dressed in long-sleeved black dresses covered by white wraparound aprons with two pockets and a large bow tied at the waist.

The meal was served on fine China and included French coleslaw, roast sirloin of beef *au jus*, Fred Harvey whipped potatoes with beef gravy, Santa Fe asparagus, fresh baked rolls, Charlotte of peaches with whipped cream, a cheese and fruit assortment and a beverage. Everything was hot and delicious and they began re-boarding less than an hour after their arrival.

The train traveled through Arizona during the night and crossed the Colorado River into California at daybreak. They peeked into yet another Harvey House at the high desert town of Barstow. This one was called *Casa del Desierto* and included a hotel and ballroom used by the locals for dances and other social events. The surrounding countryside was arid, with blowing sand and sagebrush.

The landscape turned greener on the other side of Cajon Pass and they stepped off the train into the light floral scent of citrus blossoms in Fullerton in mid afternoon.

"Look at all the orchards, Al. Are those orange trees?" asked Elizabeth.

"Yep, and avocado, too."

"And palm trees," she said. "They're so tall and skinny, why don't they topple over?"

"Don't know. Deep tap roots I guess."

In Fullerton, they transferred to the Santa Fe's "Surf Line" and headed south to San Diego. It wasn't long before they got their first glimpse of the Pacific Ocean. Tiny waves glistened in the sunlight like twinkling diamonds.

The train passed within one hundred yards of the surf at San Clemente. Seagulls floated motionlessly above towering cliffs. The passengers pressed against the windows on the train's right side, marveling at the rugged beaches and wide expanse of blue water.

They rolled to a stop at San Diego's Grand Union Depot just as the sun sank into the ocean, coloring the sky with orange and yellow afterglow. Balmy breezes surrounded them with the scent of night-blooming jasmine. Palm trees swayed in the breeze, silhouetted against a darkening sky. Ah, paradise.

Al's brother Joe and his wife Anna loaded them into their car for the ride to their home on Pueblo Street. Joe was fourteen years older than Al, the product of their father's first marriage.

He was shorter than Al and his closely cropped hair, full mustache and pince-nez spectacles gave him a dignified demeanor befitting a doctor.

Anna was gregarious and funny. Fifteen years younger and two inches taller than her husband, her smiling face was framed by a thick shock of short red curls. She tucked Elizabeth's arm into hers saying, "Come with me Elizabeth. The men will see to the luggage. Oh, we are going to have such fun."

Exhausted from their journey, Elizabeth and Al slept late the next morning and awakened to the aroma of coffee wafting up the stairs. Anna heard them stirring and called out, "Come on down you sleepy heads, coffee's on. Joe's with a patient and he'll join us for lunch. Come tell me all about your travels."

For three weeks, they explored San Diego with Joe and Anna. Streetcar wires created an overhead lattice above "N" Street as they rode downtown for window shopping. Nobody appeared to be in a rush and they didn't miss Chicago's hurried pace. On weekends, they went to the beach or picnicked along the coast road.

Every morning, invisible songbirds held choir practice in the Ficus tree outside the bedroom window. The sun shone daily and the air smelled fresh and clean. They were always aware they were never far from water – either the sheltered depths of San Diego Bay or the white-capped Pacific Ocean. Many homes were built in the Spanish style – with arched entry ways, stucco walls and red-tiled roofs.

Anna insisted on introducing them to Mexican food at *Mamacita's Cocina*. "We'll order for you," she said, upon seeing their blank expressions after reading the menu.

Anna ordered tamales, enchilada rancheros, chili rellenos, refried beans and tortillas. The enchiladas looked like Swedish pancakes stuffed with meat and sprinkled with cheese. Very tasty.

"Now try this," Anna said, placing tamales on their plates. "No, no, you have to remove the outer layer of corn husks first."

The pale fingers of corn meal-covered pork spiced with chili peppers, onions and garlic didn't look very appealing but they were willing to try anything new. The first few bites were satisfactory, but not exceptional. Suddenly, Elizabeth felt her neck and face flush and glanced at Al to see beads of perspiration on his brow. They both reached for their water glasses as Joe and Anna laughed uproariously.

"I'll bet you don't have this kind of food in Chicago," Anna said. "*Mamacita* makes the best tamales in town. You can tell because they hurt so good."

A letter arrived from Mamma telling them that Helen Ida and Earl were married in a ceremony at home two weeks after Elizabeth's wedding. Helen Ida was having a difficult pregnancy and their baby was due in August. They also received a postcard from Uncle Emil with a picture of him and his boardinghouse companions attempting to play croquet on a bumpy lawn. Uncle looked every inch the businessman in his dark suit, white shirt and conservative tie. His three younger companions were coatless with sleeves rolled up to their elbows. All four men stood hatless beneath a dull, gray sky.

One evening near the end of their stay, the men disappeared into Joe's office and didn't emerge for two hours. Anna and Elizabeth chatted about the day's activities over coffee until Joe and Al rejoined them and they all headed upstairs for bed.

That night, Al turned to Elizabeth and said, "How would you like to make our home in San Diego? It's a growing town with lots of potential, we love the climate, and Joe tells me there's demand for men with my skills. He says I could find work through the local International Association of Machinists as I get established. I think I could become an important man in a town of only fifty thousand people, Elizabeth."

"It all sounds wonderful, Al. You know I'd follow you anywhere. Where would we live?"

"We'll find a place to rent until I get established," he replied. "Are you sure you won't miss your family too much?"

"You're all the family I need."

"Then it's settled. We'll start looking for a place tomorrow."

Anna was ecstatic when Elizabeth told her the news. Joe recommended they look for a house near the union hall so Al could commute easily. They scoured listings of homes for rent in the *San Diego Union* and found a house on a narrow lot on 18th Street. It had a covered front porch for sitting out on warm evenings, and best of all, it was less than a mile from Joe and Anna's. Al registered with the local union and wired Herr Braun to send his tools from Chicago.

Al rode his bicycle to the union hall every morning with his lunch pail tied behind the seat. As the new man in town, he was the last to be hired but found work most days with established machinists who took him along on their jobs. Elizabeth cooked, kept house and planted a vegetable garden in the small back yard. Anna and Elizabeth visited often and she and Joe took them sightseeing on weekends whenever Al wasn't working.

Early one Saturday, Joe and Anna picked them up to view a surfing exhibition at Ocean Beach. A man from Hawaii had arrived from up the coast where he'd been demonstrating the lost art of surfing while standing up. He was advertised as, "the man who can walk on water."

Their shoes sank in the soft sand as they walked toward the crowd gathered near the water's edge. Sand dunes covered with pickle weed and golden dodder gave way to fine silt deposited by the nearby San Diego River. Sandpipers poked the wet sand revealed by the receding surf, then scurried up the beach to avoid incoming waves. A conga line of brown pelicans skimmed the wave tops. The Pacific Ocean stretched to the horizon.

A small group of men helped a dark-skinned man carry an eight-foot surfboard into the water. "That surfboard weighs over two hundred pounds," said Joe.

They watched as the Hawaiian knelt on the now floating board and paddled seaward. Green water poured over his head and shoulders as he paddled through three sets of breakers. He continued paddling beyond the turbulence until he was a distant spec.

"Are you sure he's coming back?" Anna joked.

"What's he doing now?" Elizabeth asked.

"Just sitting there," Joe replied. "Waiting for the right wave, I guess."

A murmur moved through the crowd as the small man stood and his board began moving toward shore. He folded his arms across his chest as the board picked up speed. When he reached the breakers, he unfolded his arms, bent his knees and steered the board diagonally across the face of the waves, feet and ankles buried beneath churning white foam. Everyone applauded as he hopped off in knee-deep water and the board shot ahead, sliding onto the sandy beach like a wet seal.

Elizabeth received a letter from Mamma in late August. Helen Ida had given birth to a baby boy. Papa bought a lot on Cleveland Street and had begun building a house for the family. He worked on it between paying jobs.

Al brought home good news just before Christmas. "Elizabeth," he said, "it looks like I'm going to have more work than I can handle for the foreseeable future."

"How's that?"

"The city is building a great park in which to host a year-long exhibition commemorating the opening of the Panama Canal," he said. "They're calling it the Panama-California Exhibition and it's scheduled to open in Balboa Park on January 1, 1915."

"That's two years away," said Elizabeth.

"Exactly," replied Al. "It'll take that long to put up the buildings, prepare the sites, bring in water and electricity, build a bridge over Cabrillo Canyon and extend the trolley lines. They need every machinist, engineer and carpenter they can find. There will be several on-site machine shops and I'll be supervising one of them."

Christmas in California was idyllic – the first December Elizabeth and Al had known without snow. The temperature never dropped below 48 degrees and the closest thing to snow was a few rainy days. Stores were decorated with imported evergreens and Elizabeth and Al were amused to see palm trees outfitted in Christmas lights. The only thing to mar Elizabeth's happiness was news from Mamma that Helen Ida's baby had died. He was born sickly and was only three months old when they lost him.

Al worked long hours at Balboa Park. Exhibition organizers erected 100 four-person bunkhouses and a small hospital for workers who lived on site. Al moved his machine shop as each new building went up – the Administration Building was followed by the California and Fine Arts buildings.

They were adopted by a gray, long-haired cat Elizabeth named Tut-son. She sat in Elizabeth's lap, swatting at her knitting needles while they waited for Al to come home in the evenings. Elizabeth crocheted a handbag in pale silver with a satin lining and tortoise shell clasp. Anna admired it and asked Elizabeth to make one for her too. She helped pick out the thread – settling on a deep maroon color.

Elizabeth sent a postcard to Mamma to let her know they were well, hoping she recognized Elizabeth and Albert in the picture on the front. They were dressed for an evening out. Elizabeth was seated on their front steps with Tut-son on her lap. Al stood on the porch, one hand on his hip. He wore a dark suit, white shirt and dark tie. Shade from his Bowler hat obscured his face but not the thick mustache he had grown since they were married. Elizabeth's hair was swept up and pinned high on her head. She wore a blue taffeta dress with three-quarter length sleeves and a full skirt. Matching slippers peeked from beneath the long skirt. The bodice was cut low with a wide collar that draped over her shoulders. The necklace Al gave her for Christmas circled her bare neck. She loved how the seventy luminescent pearls felt so cool and smooth against her skin.

Mamma wrote back with news that Julia had married her young sweetheart Chester and moved to Maywood where he worked at the metal manufacturing plant.

Al was making good money and spending lavishly. He bought Elizabeth more hats and dresses than she could wear. Their social life, however, was curtailed by the long hours he put in at Balboa Park. He bought a car – a used Model T Runabout – and was like a little boy with a new toy. The car was a very dark, almost black, shade of blue. He polished it constantly and found excuses to drive them everywhere.

Work on the Cabrillo Canyon Bridge commenced in the spring of 1914. It was an impressive sight – forty feet wide and one hundred twenty feet high supported by seven graceful arches. The first car that drove across contained Assistant Secretary of the Navy Franklin D. Roosevelt, San Diego's mayor, and the president of the Exhibition.

In June, they were shocked when Germany invaded Belgium following the assassination of the Austro-Hungarian archduke Ferdinand. They followed the war news carefully. Al's parents were born in Germany and he had many relatives there.

Elizabeth's family also had ties to Germany. In 1716, Bohemian authorities forbade one of her great grandfathers from taking his glass-blowing skills out of the country. So he was smuggled out in a wine barrel and taken to Kungsholms Glassworks in Sweden. He started the Swedish branch of the family after leaving his parent's home in what later became Germany and Austria.

In August, Britain declared war on Germany and Al and Joe spent many evenings following developments. The men were concerned that with Britain in the war, America would not be far behind. They all hoped matters would be settled before it came to that.

The buildings in Balboa Park were ready one month before the Exhibition was to begin. On Christmas Eve, President Woodrow Wilson pressed a telegraph key in Washington, D.C., turning on every light in the Park and setting off a fireworks display. The entire city turned out to celebrate on the Isthmus, a fun park and pleasure street of carnival rides and vaudeville shows.

San Diego's rainy season and a national recession kept fair attendance low during the first three months of the Exhibition. On a clear day, Al gave Joe, Anna and Elizabeth a guided tour by electriquette – a wicker-bodied electric cart. He proudly described the work he contributed to each building and Joe and Anna were entertained by his "behind the scenes" anecdotes. While Elizabeth admired the artisans' workmanship, she found the highly ornamented Spanish-Renaissance style buildings far too fussy for her Scandinavian tastes.

The landscaping, however, was breathtaking. The park was perched atop a high mesa swept by trade winds. Mature trees planted at great expense gave a feeling of permanence. Lush gardens of shade-loving clivia and bird of paradise descended into the canyons. Red bougainvillea, orange bignonia and lavender and white clematis climbed the walls of the buildings. Blackwood acacias lined the El Prado pedestrian walkway. Pergolas provided cool shade, even on the Home Economy Building's second story. Bush fowl, guinea hens and peacocks roamed freely beneath the stern gaze of Balboa astride his muscular horse in the Plaza de Panama. It was impossible to tour the entire six hundred-acre site in a single day, leaving many exhibits for future visits.

Special events took place at the Park all year long. These included horseback riding exhibitions, Organ Pavilion concerts, military parades, airplane stunts, parachute jumping, outdoor balls and fireworks. A battleship squadron arrived in the harbor and Thomas Edison and Henry Ford were among the visiting dignitaries.

Elizabeth and Al's attendance at these events dwindled the longer Al was out of work. They had been blissfully ignorant of the recession as long as Al was busy on the Exhibition. But it caught up with them when the work was completed and the temporary workforce assembled for the project added to the labor-force glut. Al left each morning for the union hall and Elizabeth didn't see him again until evening. He said he and the other men spent their time playing cards and waiting for work. Lately, though, he'd been coming home smelling of beer.

Elizabeth finally confronted him and he raised his voice at her for the first time in their marriage.

"What do you want from me Elizabeth?"

"It's just that — ."

"I'm trying to find something, but there just isn't any work."

"But — ."

"And I'm not the only one in this situation."

"I could look for work at a downtown store, Al," she said quietly.

"No wife of mine is going to work. I'll figure something out."

Al sold the car and resumed riding his bicycle to the union hall. Elizabeth stretched the food budget by making stews with carrots, potatoes and onions from the garden and cheap cuts of meat from the butcher shop.

They didn't see Joe and Anna as often as before, but one day Elizabeth heard Anna's familiar "Yoo-hoo" at the door and the two women sat down at the kitchen table for coffee.

"Joe and I are concerned about you two, Elizabeth," said Anna, "and we want to help out."

"Thank you, but you know Al would never allow that. I suggested I could get a job but he's too proud to let me work. Don't worry. We'll be all right."

"I was afraid of that," said Anna, "and have an idea he just might accept. What if you were to make more of your beautiful handbags and we display them for sale in Joe's waiting room? I just love the purse you made for me and get compliments on it all the time."

"That might be something Al wouldn't object to," said Elizabeth. "Are you sure Joe wouldn't mind?"

"Not at all. You'll be doing all the work."

So Elizabeth spent the summer making purses and growing vegetables while Al kept looking for work. He found an occasional odd job but nothing steady. Her handbags sold well and she crocheted everything from large shopping totes to dainty evening clutches.

Chapter 5

February 6, 1918 – Elizabeth and Carl climbed the steps to the bridge of the *Jefferson*.

"Good morning," said Captain Nord, "come right in. This is the pilot, Mr. Olegreen."

The pilot smiled hello as he turned the ship's wheel. The cramped bridge had windows on three sides and was perched atop the same deck that held the lifeboats. One window was open, letting in frigid air. Captain Nord showed them the throttle marked *Stop, Stand By, Slow, Half and Full.* It was set on *Full Ahead.*

"Now step over here to these charts," said the captain, "and I'll show you where we are. We're in Chatham Sound just a little north of 'Rupert," he said, pointing to a map stretched out on a glass-topped table.

"We've been in Canadian waters most of the trip, and we'll cross over into U.S. waters right here at Lord Rocks in a few hours. Then, we'll travel across Dixon Entrance to Revillagigedo Channel that will take us through these islands and into Ketchikan. We may get some weather crossing Dixon where it's exposed to the outside, but it won't be anything like crossing Queen Charlotte."

"When will we reach Ketchikan?" Carl asked.

"Around four o'clock this afternoon."

"And how long will we be there?"

"Just long enough to offload and take on water and northbound passengers – an hour or two, at most."

"From Ketchikan," the captain continued, "we'll travel up Clarence Strait, passing between Prince of Wales and Etolin islands. At Zarembo Island, we'll turn northeast and head into Wrangell, which sits at the tip of Wrangell Island and is the closest town of any size to Petersburg. It's near the mouth of the Stikine River, the jumping-off point for travel to the Canadian goldfields. We'll spend about an hour there before leaving for Petersburg. It'll be quite early – around five in the morning, but you can get off and walk around a bit."

"Leaving Wrangell, we'll turn northwest into Sumner Strait and then north through this channel between Woewodski and Mitkof islands. We'll follow Wrangell Narrows for twenty miles or so to Petersburg, which sits at the northern tip of Mitkof Island. The Narrows separates Mitkof from Kupreanof Island and is a navigational challenge due to its twenty-foot tides."

Elizabeth stared at Mitkof Island on the map. It was shaped like a tear drop. "How big is the island?" she asked.

"About twenty-three miles from north to south and sixteen miles across at its widest point," replied the captain.

"What's on the other side of the island?"

"Some truly beautiful country. If you follow Frederick Sound around the east side of the island, you'll reach Le Conte Glacier. It's the southernmost tidewater glacier in the territory and drops its bergs directly into the sea. In the spring, ice bergs from the glacier are carried into the Narrows by the tides. Another navigational hazard for us, but quite a sight nonetheless."

"Are there any other settlements on the island?" Elizabeth asked.

"Nothing permanent. We'll pass Scow Bay about three miles down the Narrows from Petersburg and there are a few fish and logging camps, but they're seasonal. And there's the Indian village of Kake near the north end of Kupreanof Island. It used to be a summer fishing camp but it's a growing settlement now. We put in there sometimes in the summer months."

"The forestry service and the territory have been working on a road from Scow Bay to Petersburg for the last few years but keep running out of money or road-building weather," Carl added. "They've cleared about 4,000 feet down to blue clay which they'll cover with gravel or sand. They still have to remove stumps from the ungraded parts of the road. It'll probably be finished this year or next. And they already have a telephone line running into town."

"How big is Scow Bay?" Elizabeth asked.

"They have two canneries, a cold-storage operation, a sawmill, ship building and a one-room schoolhouse," said Carl. "It's smaller than Petersburg and it'll be good when the two are connected by road."

"I think Southeastern is the most beautiful spot on earth," said Captain Nord, "and once you get the hang of it, you will too. We carried more freight in and out of Petersburg than ever before last year, and this year we expect to be even busier."

"Thank you, Captain, for the geography lesson," said Carl.

"My pleasure," he said. "Always happy to help a newcomer learn the lay of the land." He shook their hands as they left the bridge. "And I'll let the purser know that the Hotel Wester is under new management. Passengers bound for Petersburg often ask him where to stay."

Chapter 6

October 1915 – Joe and Al retired to Joe's office to smoke their pipes and discuss the war. A stalemate continued on the Western Front and it didn't seem like the war would ever end. Anna and Elizabeth visited until Al collected her for the short walk home. "Give it some thought," Joe said, "and let me know if you're interested."

"What was that all about?" Elizabeth asked as they walked through the fading light.

"Joe has a patient he's been treating for a broken arm," said Al. "The man has an olive ranch thirty miles from here and he's looking for a dependable couple to look after it while he goes back East. His father's ill and they'll be gone for six months or so. Joe wanted to see what I thought about it before recommending us."

"You want to be an olive rancher?"

"It's better than starving. And there may be more jobs available in San Diego next summer."

Joe introduced them to the rancher, Walter Smith, the next day. He was a big man with a weather-creased face from spending most of his time outdoors. He was in town to get his cast removed and meet with buyers for his crop.

The men worked out an arrangement for Al and Elizabeth to manage the ranch while the Smiths were away. Mr. Smith wanted them to move in immediately so he could show Al what needed to be done in his absence.

"Call me Walt," he said, shaking Elizabeth's hand. "I'm sorry the missus isn't here to meet you but she's busy packing for the trip. I know she'll like you and will be pleased to have you run her house while we're away."

Two days later, they boarded the San Diego, Cuyamaca and Eastern Railway at Ninth and "N" streets. Joe and Anna accompanied them on the train that climbed from San Diego through Lemon Grove, La Mesa, El Cajon, and Santee to Lakeside. Elizabeth was amazed at the change in climate – from palm trees and ocean breezes to pine trees and mountain streams in just two hours.

Walt told them about Alpine as the train rattled along. "We're two thousand feet above sea level," he said. "The air and water are so pure that a fellow named Arnold built a hotel for people coming to the mountains to improve their health. Arnold also started the regular stagecoach service between Lakeside and Alpine. Before that, Alpine was just a stage stop for the Cuyamaca Mountain mines."

They disembarked near the Lakeside Inn and boarded a four-horse stage for the eleven-mile journey to Alpine. The terrain was mostly uphill. They passed rolling hills of sage brush and chaparral, deep canyons with eucalyptus, oak and sycamore trees, and grassy meadows dotted with huge granite boulders.

As the stage approached Alpine, Walt pointed south and said, "The Galloway's live down in that valley. They grow raisin Muscat grapes. Below them in Harbison Canyon is a big apiary operation. They've got nearly two hundred bee hives, last I heard."

The horses trotted down Alpine's main street to the stage stop. Elizabeth glimpsed a schoolhouse, town hall, combination general store and post office, and a tavern. Frank, Walt's hired hand, met them with the wagon. "Frank agreed to stay on while we're away so long as he doesn't have to do his own cooking and laundry," Walt laughed.

Frank drove the wagon to the Mount Olive Ranch where they met Walt's wife Sally and their five-year-old son, Todd. Joe and Anna helped Elizabeth and Al get moved in and Frank drove them back to the stage stop for the return trip to San Diego.

After breakfast the next morning, the men took Al on a tour of the ranch while Sally showed Elizabeth her daily routine. Soon, Elizabeth was feeding chickens and learning where they liked to hide their eggs. The vegetable garden still had some pumpkins and winter squash.

"This garden won't need any attention 'til spring," said Sally, "and we'll be home by then to turn it over and replant. The greenhouse garden is another matter, though, and you'll be able to pick some nice vegetables even in winter. Just keep the plants watered, especially Walt's truncheons." She showed Elizabeth long rows of foot-long olive tree limbs buried in soft soil. Green shoots appeared above the soil and she said they would be ready for planting in the orchard after two years.

As they moved through the chores, Sally explained that her father-in-law was ailing back East and Walt's parents had never met their grandson. "We don't like to leave," she said, "but winter is the best time for us to be away. Our busiest times are spring planting and fall harvest. I'm so glad you and your husband were available to look after the place while we're gone."

The Smiths left early the next day and Al, Frank and Elizabeth established an easy routine. They were up at cockcrow and Elizabeth prepared breakfast while the men milked the lone cow and turned out the two wagon horses. Elizabeth found baking bread in Sally's coal and wood stove to be a challenge. The first loaves came out lopsided because the oven was hotter on the side next to the firebox. She soon learned to rotate the loaves when they were partially cooked.

The men maintained the irrigation system, ranch tools and equipment. Frank said the people who planted the first olive trees had to carry pails of water from Viejas Creek at the foot of the mesa to water the trees. The ranch had seen many improvements since then. Most of the harvest was in but the remaining fruit needed to be picked and delivered to town for shipping to San Diego where Walt had prearranged a sale with a produce man.

Joe and Anna visited from San Diego and Anna was so taken with ranch living that she insisted on staying a week to help pick the last of the fruit. Joe laughed, shrugged, and returned to his practice in San Diego without her.

Anna and Elizabeth looked a sight in their "farmer's togs." They dressed in baggy bib overalls, white blouses with rolled-up sleeves and neckerchiefs. They tucked their hair up beneath wide brimmed straw hats. Their black work boots laced to the ankles and were covered in red dust even before they reached the orchard.

The women helped place burlap around the base of the trees to catch the olives the men knocked down with long poles. The olives from a single tree ranged from bright green to deep purple. Frank explained that the trees produced a large crop one year and a small crop the next. This was a small crop year. He also instructed Anna and Elizabeth to roll down their sleeves and put on gloves to protect their skin from the rough bark and foliage.

The crop was shipped to Lakeside on the stage and then by express to San Diego. The horses dragged a harrow through the groves to return debris to the soil. The next harvest would be in ten months.

Joe returned to the ranch to take Anna back to the city. He reported that the Liberty Bell from Philadelphia was visiting the Exposition. It was accompanied by a military escort and displayed on a special platform in the Plaza.

The nights turned cold as Christmas approached. Elizabeth made a pact with Frank that she would prepare a turkey dinner, including plucking the feathers, if he killed the bird. They feasted on roast turkey, giblet gravy, cranberry sauce, mashed potatoes, winter squash stuffed with stewed raisins, green beans and sourdough biscuits with Sally's strawberry preserves. The last pumpkin from the garden made two large pies.

Frost threatened the trees in January. Al and Frank spread straw around the trees for insulation and the frost melted by midday. One evening, they were amazed to step outdoors into a dusting of dry, fluffy snow. It had come so quietly they hadn't even heard it. It too, was gone by noon.

The war news still was not good. The British started conscription in early February, drafting men between the ages of eighteen and forty-one for military service. That's all that Walt and Al talked about whenever they returned from town. That, and whether or not America would be entering the war soon. Al thought they would; Frank wasn't so certain.

Spring brought heavy rains and flooding. The earth turned muddy and the creek below the plateau became a fast-moving river tumbling boulders the size of houses. One hundred-year-old oak trees slipped into the water. The roaring waters tumbled down the mountains all the way to San Diego and the ocean. The railroad track between Lakeside and Foster washed out. Melted snow from higher elevations combined with the rain to wash out more than one hundred bridges in San Diego.

The men pruned the dormant trees between rain squalls, removing cross branches within the canopies to let in light. "It's important to prune lightly," Frank explained. "Shortening branches that have born fruit will develop new sprouts to bear next year's crop."

Al received a wire from Walt. His father had passed away and they needed to stay longer to settle his affairs and prepare his mother to move to California. Could they stay on for three more months? Al wired back, "Yes."

The days turned sunny and warm. The olive trees blossomed with delicate, cream-colored flowers. The spring rains produced an abundance of wild flowers. Indian paint brush and lupines brightened the slopes. Golden poppies and yellow monkey flowers blanketed the highlands. Honeybees busied themselves in the fragrant sage.

The men turned over the vegetable garden and planted the same assortment the family planted each spring – carrots, peas, radishes, lettuce, zucchini, tomatoes, onions and potatoes. Anna arrived for another week-long stay. Fortunately, she loved gardening.

One evening, they rode into Alpine for a summer dance. Horses were tied to hitching rails and to the eucalyptus trees around the town hall. People came from as far away as Lakeside to have a good time and catch up on the latest news. Al and Elizabeth were introduced to the Virginia Reel and before long, they were do-si-do-ing and sashaying around the hall. The musicians stopped at midnight and everyone enjoyed sandwiches, coffee and cake. It seemed the rooster was up earlier than usual that morning.

In early July, Al and Elizabeth left the ranch in Frank's hands and traveled down the mountain to San Diego. Al wanted to assess the job market and line up work. Elizabeth was anxious to see if there were any houses available in their old neighborhood.

Evidence of the devastation from the spring storms was everywhere. The Sweetwater Dam had been breached and the Lower Otay Dam washed out. Passengers on a Santa Fe train marooned north of the city had been rescued by sea launch. Muddy waters covered farms and ranches and homes slipped off their foundations. Troops had been sent into the flooded areas to protect people and property. Dried mud and debris still covered many areas.

Elizabeth noticed women were showing a bit more ankle and made a note to raise the hems on her dresses. She restocked her knitting yarns and crochet threads from the wide selection at Marston's Department Store.

"The news is not good, Elizabeth," Al said. "The men at the union hall tell me the floods and lack of tourists set the city back in the time we've been away. Bandits are harassing Americans along the Mexican border and fewer people are traveling due to the war in Europe. If anything, San Diego's job market is worse than before we left."

"What do you think we should do?" asked Elizabeth. "The Smiths will be home any day now."

"I think it's time to return to Evanston," replied Al. "There are more jobs available there and we know more people."

Al and Elizabeth returned to the ranch and packed their belongings. Frank waved goodbye from the stage stop as they traveled down the mountain to meet the Smith's train. At the depot, Al helped load Mrs. Smith's household goods onto a wagon for transport to the train to Alpine. The men visited Walt's bank and Al received payment for the three extra months they had managed the ranch.

In the morning, Joe and Anna saw them off at the new Santa Fe Depot. "Promise you'll come back and visit us real soon," said Anna.

"We'll try," Elizabeth replied. "I'll let you know when we get settled."

They waved goodbye as the train slowly left the station, retracing the route Elizabeth and Al had taken four short years earlier.

Chapter 7

February 6, 1918 – Elizabeth and Carl joined the passengers in the *Jefferson's* lounge and watched the passing scenery. The sea turned rough as they sailed across Dixon Entrance into Alaskan waters, but she was accustomed to the ship's roll by then and barely noticed. Heavily forested mountains shouldered their way to the sea. Intermittent snow and rain fell from skies heavy with dark clouds. She spied something odd among the dark trees and asked Carl what it was.

"A totem pole," he said. "If you watch closely, you'll see others from time to time."

"Who made them?" she asked.

"The natives. Tlingit or Haida, I don't know which. You can tell their clan by looking at the figure on the very top. See, that one's a raven. I've also seen eagles, bears and beavers. Some of these totems are very old – they're made from cedar trees that last a very long time."

"Where are the people who made them?"

"They move around, following the salmon and herring runs," said Carl. "There's a lot of them in Kake, the Indian village Captain Nord mentioned. And a few live in every town."

The silent sentinel faded into the forest as the ship slowly passed.

By late afternoon, they had seen more whales and a herd of deer on the beach. Bald eagles hunkered on craggy tree tops. The shores were blanketed with snow that stopped at the tide line. The feeling of solitude and gloom began to lift as they neared Ketchikan. Other boats appeared on the water and homesteads dotted the shoreline as they approached the town.

Elizabeth finally set foot in Alaska Territory! Ketchikan's dock was slippery with slush and footing was treacherous. She'd grown so accustomed to the ship's motion that the ground beneath her feet seemed to keep moving. It was dark in the early evening and they didn't stray too far from the dock where freight was off loaded and new passengers boarded for the trip north to Juneau. Carl pointed out the Standard Oil dock in the distance where a tank steamer was loading oil and distillate for delivery to smaller stations and canneries. They slipped into the New York Café on Front Street for a quick cup of coffee. Carl told her the city of more than five thousand people had five fish canneries. The *Jefferson's* whistle called them back and Elizabeth settled in for her last night aboard ship.

They arrived at Wrangell's snug harbor early the next morning. Diffused ice crystals hung in the still morning air, creating a halo effect around the dock lights. Carl said thousands of miners had traveled through Wrangell on their way up the Stikine River during three different gold rushes. More freight was unloaded and no new passengers came aboard.

Chapter 8

July 1916 – Elizabeth and Al arrived in Evanston tired and dusty from their trip. It was good to see the family again. Papa had built a magnificent three-story house. Mamma and Papa lived on the top floor. The second story was divided into bedrooms for children still living at home and a small apartment where Elizabeth's brother John lived with his family. Two first-floor apartments provided rental income.

Al took a janitorial job at the university, working nights so he could search for machinist's work during the day. They rented a small house on Hinman Avenue a few blocks from Lake Michigan.

Elizabeth's sister Ruthie spent more time at Elizabeth's house than at Papa's. Ruthie had matured into a real beauty with large, expressive eyes beneath high, dark eyebrows. At seventeen, she had several beaus and asked Elizabeth's sisterly advice on each one.

One summer day, they arranged a picnic at the lake with Ruthie and Elizabeth's twenty-one-year-old cousin Victor. It was a pretty day – a few puffy clouds lingered in the bright blue sky. A soft breeze took the edge off the humidity. Everyone was in good spirits.

The sand was warm beneath their bare feet as they carried their picnic supplies across the beach crowded with squealing children enjoying their summer vacations. Seagulls called to each other overhead.

Al and Victor dashed into the water and Victor won their race to the raft anchored offshore. They were both strong swimmers. Ruthie and Elizabeth strolled down the beach, wading in the cool water and collecting driftwood and polished stones. They were shocked to see how far they'd gone when they finally turned back.

Al and Victor were stretched out on the beach blanket, the unopened picnic basket between them. "It's a good thing you came back when you did," said Victor, "we were just about to break into this lunch."

They enjoyed fried chicken, potato salad, fresh baked bread, apples, cheese and lemonade and slipped into a state of drowsy well being. Elizabeth was thinking about the sheer bliss of a perfect day when Al said he wanted to go for one more swim before they packed up. Victor said he was done swimming and Al trotted down to the water and swam to the raft.

They watched Al hoist himself out of the water and prepare to dive. Other beachgoers were watching too. Al raised his right arm above his head, waved, and dove head first into the water.

The water smoothed over and someone said, "He hasn't come up yet." People began moving toward the water.

Victor cast Elizabeth a worried glance as he rose to his feet. "Don't worry," she said, "he's done this before. He can stay under water for a very long time."

Victor joined several men in knee-deep water. "There he is," someone shouted as Elizabeth breathed a sigh of relief. But then she caught a glimpse not of Al swimming strongly from the depths, but a lifeless form floating just beneath the surface. The men swam out and carried his limp body to the beach.

"Stand back, I'm a doctor," a stocky little man shouted. The crowd fell back, giving him space. Elizabeth watched from the crowd as the doctor worked to revive Al. "It's no use, his neck is broken," he said.

Elizabeth heard a roaring in her ears as though the lake had become a raging storm. She saw mothers pulling their children away from the crowd looking down on Al's still body. She saw the doctor's anguished expression looking at her and at Ruthie over her shoulder. And then, she neither heard nor saw anything.

Elizabeth awakened in the shade of an elm tree overlooking the beach. She was wrapped in blankets and Ruthie was rocking her in her arms. Her teeth couldn't stop chattering. A group of men stood in a cluster across the beach. Victor was there – he'd changed out of his bathing costume – and Al's lifeless form was covered by a blanket. "We'll get you home just as soon as Victor finishes with the authorities," Ruthie said.

Victor handled all the arrangements; he notified Al's parents in Sweden, his brothers in San Diego and Seattle and Herr Braun in Chicago.

Elizabeth saw herself from a distance moving trance-like through the inquest. Cause of death was determined to be "Injuries due to a fractured dislocated neck produced by a dive into water and striking bottom." Her husband was laid to rest at Memorial Park four days later.

Mamma wanted Elizabeth to move into their home but she preferred to stay at the house Al had provided. Ruthie moved in with her for the time being.

The strain of the tragedy caught up with Elizabeth late one night when she awoke sobbing uncontrollably. She was both angry and incredibly sad. She felt as though half of her had been chopped off. She and Al had such a bright future. It wasn't fair that such an intelligent, vigorous man was taken in his prime. She punched her pillow over and over; tears streamed down her face and dripped off her chin. She heard a soft knocking at her door and Ruthie was there, sitting on the edge of the bed comforting her. "It's good to let it out, Lisa," she said. "We've been so worried about you." Elizabeth cried and cried until empty and fell into an exhausted sleep.

Elizabeth got reacquainted with her family as summer faded into fall. They finally convinced her to move into her father's house so she didn't have to pay rent on the Hinman house. Elizabeth agreed it was a good move while she figured out what to do with herself.

Her brother Elmer married his fiancée Minnie in January. Their wedding was at the same church where Elizabeth and Al were married. Pastor Swanson had been replaced by Pastor Hope, but everything else was unchanged. Stained glass windows filtered the winter light and the oak pews were polished to a soft, glowing sheen. It was a beautiful ceremony.

So far, America had stayed out of the war raging in Europe. However, in March, newspapers around the country reported the interception of a shocking telegram sent from the German minister Zimmerman to his United States' ambassador. The letter outlined a plot whereby, if the United States did not stay neutral, Mexico would join Germany with the understanding that, after the war, Germany would help Mexico reconquer lost territory in Texas, New Mexico and Arizona. And, if the outbreak of war with the United States became certain, Mexico should invite Japan to join the plot.

In April, America declared war on Germany and set June 5 as the date for all men between the ages of twenty-one and thirty, inclusive, to register for army service. Some marched into recruitment offices and enlisted at the first opportunity. Their mothers, wives, sweethearts and sisters were weepy with worry. Elizabeth's brother Paul wanted to volunteer and Mamma tried to talk him out of it. A feeling of uncertainty and upheaval was everywhere.

Elizabeth received a letter with an unfamiliar postmark from her brother-in-law Carl. He had taken over management of a small hotel in Petersburg, Alaska and invited her to move north and help him run it. He could handle cooking at the restaurant but needed help with waitressing and housekeeping duties. Since Elizabeth had lost a husband and he had lost a brother, he hoped she would see this as an opportunity to move on with her life. That is, unless she had made other plans.

Elizabeth showed the letter to Ruthie. "You can't move to Alaska, Lisa," she wailed. "I'll never see you again. What if Carl gets called into military duty? And are there even any respectable white women up there?"

"I don't think it's as primitive as that," Elizabeth replied. "Carl's only two years younger than Al, so he's safe from military conscription. With Albert gone, there's really nothing for me here. I have no illusions and I'm not afraid of hard work. And this time, I know I'm going to be the chambermaid."

Elizabeth and Carl exchanged several letters and agreed to meet in Seattle. She packed the Louis Vuitton trunk, a wedding gift with a history from Carl. Presented at the 1909 Alaska Yukon Pacific Exhibition in Seattle, it rolled easily on recessed castors and a wide leather strap buckled in the front. Three gleaming brass latches held the lid in place and the center latch had a large lock. The spacious interior held two stacking shelves lined with pink felt. The trunk practically shouted that it was eager for adventure.

Elizabeth packed some of the wedding gifts she and Al had received. Aunt Emma's reversible afghan with broad wine, rust and tan stripes went in first, providing padding for the more delicate items. Aunt Emma had used a combination of crochet and Swedish embroidery stitches, finishing it with a thin green border. Heavy cut glass crystal bowls were next; each carefully wrapped in soft cloth. An intricately carved candy dish on an eight-inch pedestal presented a particular packing challenge. Elizabeth held it to the light and admired rainbows gleaming from the deeply-scored surface.

She wrapped lace doilies, linen napkins and crocheted potholders around delicate bone China coffee cups and saucers in different shapes and patterns. Her favorite was a gold-rimmed, fluted cup decorated with tiny red roses. The cup handle was gold and the saucer had a matching ridge of gold around the rim. She wondered if such delicate items were even available in Alaska Territory.

Skeins of yarn and crochet thread went in next together with her knitting and crochet needles. She tucked family photographs of Albert, Uncle Emil and Aunt Emma, Mamma and Papa, and her brothers and sisters into a box of stationary. Then she carefully packed her silver-backed hand mirror, comb and brush set so they would not be damaged during the move.

She packed her wardrobe last. Warm gloves, stockings, union suits, nightclothes, dresses, hankies, aprons and two pairs of shoes fit snugly in the top of the trunk. These were items she thought she might need during the trip. She planned to wear her winter coat and carry her rain bonnet, jewelry and cosmetics in her handbag.

Elizabeth said goodbye to her family amid tears, hugs and promises to write. She thought Mamma and Papa were privately relieved to be rid of their "problem" daughter. Her brothers John and Clarence and sister Ruthie accompanied her to Chicago and put her on the Great Northern Railway to Seattle.

Fourteen-year-old Clarence was especially excited about her destination. "I wish I was going with you Lisa," he said. "I'd like to see those Eskimos, igloos and polar bears. When I get out of school, I'm going to come see you."

John said, "You look good without those widows' togs, Lisa. Take good care of yourself and when Clarence is old enough to make the trip, I'll come along with him."

Ruthie gave her a big hug, and neither of them could speak without crying. Elizabeth watched the group getting smaller and smaller as the train pulled away from the station.

Elizabeth reflected on her life as the train made its way over the Burlington Route. She was thirty years old with nothing more than the items in her luggage and the money Uncle Emil insisted she take for the trip. And she was on her way to a frontier outpost of strangers. That is, everyone was a stranger except Al's brother Carl, but she barely knew him. She'd never felt so alone before. But what did she have to go back to? She'd put on a brave front for Ruthie's sake but deep down, she was just as nervous about this move as Ruthie. There was no turning back now and Elizabeth was determined to make a go of it. She took a deep breath and turned her attention to the passing countryside.

The tracks followed the banks of Lake Michigan and they arrived in Milwaukee by suppertime. This was the land of German immigrants, manufacturing and shipping. The tracks turned west and they passed dairy farms and shivering livestock before crossing the Mississippi River. Elizabeth retired to the sleeper car and tossed fitfully through the night. She awoke when they stopped for coal and water in St. Paul. It was much too early to get up so she stayed in her bunk listening to the sounds of the train being serviced.

By daybreak they were traveling across northern Minnesota, a land of frozen lakes and forests, and arrived at Fargo, North Dakota by late morning. She overheard another passenger explain that Fargo was in the heart of the Red River Valley and named for the founder of the Wells Fargo Express Company. Boarding passengers stamped snow off their boots and rubbed their cold hands together as they settled in for the westward journey.

They traversed North Dakota and reached Minot in time for supper. Elizabeth joined the passengers who disembarked to stretch their legs while the train was serviced. It was bitter cold and light was fading fast in this northern latitude, but it felt good to get some fresh air. Just west of Minot, the train crossed the Gassman Coulee on a high-level trestle. Snow-covered wheat fields stretched across the great plains as far as the eye could see.

She slept much better the next night and awoke refreshed as they pulled into Shelby, Montana early the next morning. The passengers got their first view of the Rocky Mountains between Shelby and Browning. How different they appeared from the mountains she and Al had seen in Colorado. These were covered with snow that looked like it never melted. The Canadian border was only twenty-five miles away. A high trestle took them across Two Medicine River to the Glacier Park Station where ten-thousand-foot mountains were obscured by clouds.

The train crossed the Continental Divide and followed a low pass through the mountains. Snow was piled high on both sides of the track, obscuring the view until they arrived at Whitefish in early afternoon. Idaho was a blur and they crossed its fifty-mile panhandle in no time at all. They continued on to Spokane, Washington where Elizabeth strolled through the depot before retiring for her last night aboard the train.

She was up before dawn as they entered the Cascade Tunnel beneath Stevens Pass east of Everett. She tried to imagine what the tunnel would have been like before it was electrified a few years earlier. They descended the western slope of the Cascades and arrived in Everett in time for breakfast.

Only two hours to go. Elizabeth packed her belongings, freshened up and peered from the window as the train skirted Puget Sound and stopped at the dock in Edmonds. Small islands dotted the Sound and the air was filled with the scent of freshly cut lumber. They finally left for the one-hour journey to Seattle, passing waterways traversed by fishing boats and tugboats towing rafts of logs. Heavy rain was falling as the train arrived at Seattle's King Street Station.

She spied Carl right away, standing tall near the back of the crowd. Rain dripped off his hat brim as he stooped to give her an awkward hug. He smelled of shaving soap and pipe tobacco. "It's good to see you, Elizabeth, did you have a good trip?" he asked.

Seattle was bustling with activity. Wartime commerce supported ship building and the Boeing Company was busy building aeroplanes. The forty-two-story Smith Tower dwarfed the next tallest building on the skyline. On the waterfront, nine parallel railroad tracks ran atop a timber trestle. The Pike Place Public Market attracted the waterfront crowd as well as residents from the hills above Elliott Bay. Well-dressed women in long woolen coats mixed with fishmongers and farmers. An arcade sheltered both shoppers and merchants from the weather.

Elizabeth accompanied Carl to the F. S. Lang Manufacturing Company store where he purchased a range for the hotel kitchen. The heavy iron stove had a polished cooking surface and large fire box for either coal or wood. He took her to several restaurant and hotel supply houses where he stocked up on cooking utensils and bedding.

Everyone seemed to know Carl from his earlier years in Seattle and all were eager to learn about his new hotel venture in Alaska. One shopkeeper threw in a complimentary toque. Elizabeth stifled a giggle when he tried it on. The white hat made him look eight feet tall.

Finally, they visited Alaska Steamship's office where Elizabeth purchased her ticket to Petersburg and Carl arranged for transport of his purchases. He offered to pay her fare but she insisted on paying the $21.50 herself. She didn't want to be beholden to anyone.

They had dinner at the New Washington Hotel at the corner of Second Avenue and Stewart. Carl entertained her with amusing stories of happenings at the hotel when he ran the kitchen. The new chef sent a complimentary dessert to their table.

"Why is Mr. Wester leasing out his hotel?" she asked Carl.

"I think he just got tired of being in the hotel business," said Carl. "He closed the Wester Annex – several apartments located upstairs in the bank building – and he's selling all of the furnishings. He's had a problem with fires in the annex the past few years. The firemen come and put out the flames, but he's had to repair damage to the flooring and replace scorched furniture. And there's been water damage to businesses downstairs – the banking room, the newspaper office and the Glacier Fish Company office."

"What is he going to do now?" she asked.

"I'm not sure. He said he's planning a trip south and might even arrive here before we go north. He owns a scow outfitted with living quarters and seems to spend a lot of time in Juneau. I don't think we'll be seeing much of him."

The next morning, Elizabeth and Carl stood dockside looking at the steamer that would take them north. The *Jefferson* was in need of paint. Rust stains ran down her hull to the water line. The two hundred-foot ship was built twenty-five years earlier and looked the worse for wear from the severe winter weather she encountered on her route. She had very little deck space and loading and unloading was accomplished with fore and aft booms. The hull was pierced with a single row of port holes and square-cut windows lined the above-deck structure. A single smoke stack jutted high above the lifeboat-rimmed top deck.

A booming voice behind them said, "Hello, Carl. I thought I'd find you here. Is this the little lady who's going to help you run my hotel?"

"Why Mr. Wester," Carl said, "yes it is. I'd like you to meet my sister-in-law Elizabeth."

"It's a pleasure to meet you, Mrs. Roger," said Mr. Wester. "I hope you'll find Petersburg to your liking."

"Thank you, I'm looking forward to it," Elizabeth replied.

"When did you get in?" Carl asked.

"Arrived on the *Jefferson* yesterday. Did you find all the supplies you were looking for?"

"Sure did. The crates are on the dock waiting to be loaded. How's the work on the hotel coming along?"

"The Anderson boys had it all torn up getting ready for new wallpaper and paint when I left," said Mr. Wester. "It should be in good shape by the time you arrive."

"Where do your travels take you next?" Elizabeth asked.

"Not totally certain. Thought I'd spend some time around Puget Sound and maybe take a trip to California to soak up some of that sunshine. Now that I've got someone dependable to run the hotel," he added, smiling at Carl.

Mr. Wester shook their hands as passengers began boarding. Carl helped move Elizabeth's luggage into her cabin. "I'll see you in the lounge after you get settled," he said, ducking out the doorway.

Elizabeth looked around the cabin that would be her home for the next four days. Two bunk beds stretched from wall to wall at the far end of the narrow room. She put her hat box and purse on the bottom bunk. A drawer beneath the bunk contained extra blankets. Wood-paneled walls and ceiling were all painted white. Two lighting fixtures were suspended between beams in the ceiling. The only furniture was a white wicker chair with a seat cushion and padded arm rests, and a small brown table draped with a white cloth. Six coat hooks were screwed into the wall and a window in the facing wall had a shade that rolled up from the bottom. A small radiator was mounted beneath the window and a thin carpet covered the bare floor.

Elizabeth found Carl in the lounge and they joined the other passengers on deck as the steamer pulled away from the pier. Travelers leaned over the railing waving and calling goodbyes to families and friends.

"Is this the same boat you took to Alaska when you moved there?" Elizabeth asked Carl.

"No, my partner and I made the trip on the *Al-Ki*."

"That's a funny name. What does it mean?"

"It's the point of land where Seattle was settled before they moved the city across the bay," he said. "A storm blew the steamer aground at Point Augusta a little north of Petersburg a few months ago, though. She's a total loss."

"Was anybody hurt?"

"No, they got the passengers and crew off safely and brought them to Juneau. What's left of the ship is covered in ice on the beach and they hope to salvage her engines in the spring."

"Do you know any of these people?" Elizabeth asked as they traveled across Puget Sound.

"Most of the Petersburg people," said Carl. "There are sixteen on this trip. This time of year, everybody's returning from business trips or visits with their families in the states. And of course, there's the crew – the ship travels with sixty to help with passengers and freight at the stops along the way. I'll introduce you around when everyone gets settled in."

The lounge was full during the afternoon. Tan wicker chairs lined the sides of the room beneath a coffered ceiling. The room was furnished with a grand piano and a fireplace hugged the far wall. Elizabeth wondered if they actually burned wood in the fireplace. She hoped not. Didn't seem safe somehow.

Carl introduced Elizabeth to several passengers. There were only three other women traveling to Petersburg. Mr. and Mrs. Norberg and their pretty daughter Alice, Mrs. Wikan and her children Marie and Rudolph, and Mr. and Mrs. Leines are all cordial and had made this trip several times.

"Do you do needlework, Mrs. Roger?" asked Mrs. Wikan.

"Why yes, I do," replied Elizabeth.

"Then you'll have to join the Red Cross and help with knitting for our boys in France. We meet twice a week at the Arctic Brotherhood Hall and yarn and instructions are provided to everyone who helps fill the orders."

"What do you knit?" Elizabeth asked.

"Each set of garments includes a sweater, a muffler, one pair of wristlets and a pair of sox," replied Mrs. Wikan. "Our more experienced knitters tackle the sweaters and sox, and the younger girls work on wristlets and mufflers. It's a chance for the ladies of the town to get together and it's for a worthy cause."

"It sounds very worthwhile," said Elizabeth. "I'll have to wait and see if I have any time to spare from the hotel."

The steamer threaded its way through many islands, crossed the Strait of Juan de Fuca and docked at Bellingham in early evening. There they took on freight for the canneries and logging camps as well as general merchandise for the merchants. They traveled up Georgia Strait into Canadian waters during the night. The rain had stopped and lights from small towns on Vancouver Island twinkled in the darkness.

Chapter 9

February 7, 1918 – Elizabeth tried to control her excitement as they left Wrangell on the last leg of their journey. The entrance to Wrangell Narrows was shrouded in dense fog. All officers were on deck as the ship slowed. Passengers spoke in hushed tones while staring through the windows into the gray soup. The pilot blasted the ship's horn every few minutes as the captain studied his pocket watch.

"What are they doing?" Elizabeth asked Carl.

"Taking soundings so we won't run aground in the fog. You see, they know how long it should take for the horn to echo off the sounding boards on the beacons."

"What sounding boards? What beacons?"

"We can't see them for the fog but the pilot and captain know where they are."

The fog finally cleared, revealing red and green channel markers showing the safe passage route. Both sides of the narrow channel were heavily wooded and a looming mountain on the Kupreanof Island side was capped with a treeless, snow-covered patch resembling a map of America. On both sides of the Narrows, smoke curled above homesites with skiffs tied out front.

"Is that Petersburg?" Elizabeth asked.

"That's Scow Bay," said Carl. "See the tall covered structure with a ramp leading into the water? That's the ways where they build scows, logging floats and small boats in wintertime and repair fishing boats during the season. Those buildings built on pilings over the water contain a cannery and a sawmill."

Petersburg finally came into view. A distant range of snow-covered mountains on the mainland provided a stunning backdrop to the town. "Devil's Thumb," Carl said, pointing to a steep-sided mountain shaped like a thumb and a forefinger. "Some prospectors have poked around up there and came back with some pretty amazing stories."

Two long docks on pilings extended out into the Narrows. Waterfront houses and businesses were also built on pilings and Elizabeth wondered how they kept their floors warm with their bare legs exposed like that. Wood-framed homes lined the hillside behind the main street. Snow covered the rooftops and vacant land between buildings. A crowd of people huddled on the dock, only half of which had been cleared of snow. Carl introduced Elizabeth to his partner, Julius Reese, waiting at the foot of the gangplank.

"How do you do?" Elizabeth said as the older man shook her hand.

"Pleased to meet you," he replied.

As he released her hand, he dragged his middle finger lazily across her gloved palm. She glanced at him sharply but he was looking away. She decided it was accidental and busied herself with gathering her belongings.

Julius had brought a sledge which he and Carl loaded with luggage and pulled up the dock toward town. A four-foot high berm of snow straddled the middle of Main Street wherever there were buildings on both sides. The snow had been shoveled onto the beach on the parts of the street that had buildings only on the land side. Several structures had living quarters above stores and offices. Others had two-story facades on the sides facing the street.

The Hotel Wester was an imposing two-story, false-fronted structure with a second-story balcony on the front. Snow-covered railings enclosed the balcony that provided protection from the weather for people walking on the boardwalk below.

The lobby was snug and warm, a welcome relief from the blustery winter weather outside. The front half of the ground floor was occupied by the lobby and dining room and the kitchen and manager's quarters were in the back. Three small sample rooms off the main corridor were reserved for traveling salesmen to display their wares. Twelve rooms upstairs had hot and cold water, steam heat, electric lights and private baths. Carl insisted Elizabeth move into the manager's quarters adjacent the kitchen. His room was upstairs at the front of the building and Julius had lodgings at a rooming house on Indian Street.

Chapter 10

February 1918 – Carl was pleased with the renovations made while he was south. Every room had new wallpaper, paint and decorative work. Three rooms were occupied, so they skipped those in their inspection, but Julius said all the improvements were finished. The men returned to the dock for the freight while Elizabeth unpacked. She had a big pot of coffee brewing when they returned.

Julius brought Carl up to date on activity around town.

"Everyone's talking about an even better fishing season than last year," he said. "The war in Europe created a big demand for seafood and Manager Kracke at the Packing Company said they expect to put up 80,000 cases of salmon this season. Several local boys had such good seasons last year that they're showing up with brand-new boats they had built in Seattle. Halibut schooners are already out fishing and the *Pioneer* was into Scow Bay with a load of 36,000 pounds. Captain Hansen got sixteen cents a pound. And Polsen brought in the first shrimps of the season on the *Cape Spencer*."

"What's going on with the sawmill?" Carl asked.

"Olaf Arness is getting ready to open it soon as weather permits," said Julius. "He'll still be running the mill at Scow Bay and a couple of logging camps for getting out saw logs too."

"The mill was shut down four years ago when it was owned by the Pacific Coast & Norway Packing Company," he explained to Elizabeth.

"I hear Jacob Otness over at the Trading Union store is the new manager," he continued, "and they're expecting an engineer and his family from down below any day now. Looks like the toughest part will be getting enough men to run the mill. Everybody prefers to go fishing. Even Deputy Marshal Kildall resigned to go fishing. I hear they're bringing in a new marshal from Ketchikan."

"They're putting in a big cold storage plant at Scow Bay," he added, "with enough ice-making capability they won't have to tow their cold-storage ship *Glory of the Seas* up from Seattle this year. Manager Nelson is trying to get everything in place by the first of May. Two of the steamship companies are picking up Scow Bay fish directly at their cannery now, so they don't have to bring it all the way into Petersburg for shipment south. Nelson's gonna keep his office in town, though."

"And how are the saloon keepers coping with the new 'Bone Dry' law?" asked Carl.

"Well, Hadland transformed his Dory Bar into a soft drink house; Brennan reopened his place as a pool and billiard room selling soft drinks and cigars; and Schelderup is moving his restaurant to the empty Gauffin Building. Charlie Mann's and Haug & Todal's are pool rooms now too. And all the old timers are exchanging home brew recipes," he chuckled.

Julius glanced sharply at Elizabeth, trying to see if she was one of those Woman's Christian Temperance Union ladies who protested the evils of alcohol. She just smiled and said nothing.

"Oh yeah," he added. "They formed a food conservation committee to enforce the rationing. John Stoft, Conrad Arness and Pastor Maakestad are the officers. When I told Stoft we'd be reopening the dining room, he said he'd stop by and let you know what the new rules are for restaurants."

Elizabeth set about keeping the hotel clean and tidy. It was an easy task with only three guests and everything freshly painted. Their guests included traveling salesmen from the Pacific Coast Biscuit Company, the Fuller Paint Company and Oak Olson from Juneau. The men invited town merchants to view their wares displayed in the hotel sample rooms.

Carl and Julius replaced the small stove in the kitchen with the new range. It took up an entire wall. Carl hung a cross-stitch sampler above the stove that read: *Cleanliness is Next to Godliness, Don't Befriend the Devil.* A two-door cooler for keeping food chilled occupied the opposite wall. The metal ice bin in the top was filled with snow as ice was in short supply since Le Conte Glacier was frozen up later in the year than usual.

Mr. Miller, editor of *The Petersburg Weekly Report*, stopped in every day to see who was newly arrived in town and join in discussions of the war, politics, fishing and logging prospects and local happenings. Other regulars included: Luther Hogue and Chris Tveten of the big Hogue & Tveten general store; Knud Stenslid of the Star Bakery; Knut Steberg, steamship agent and insurance man; Commissioner John Allen; John Stoft, banker and partner in Stoft & Refling's store; and Pete Jorgenson and Charlie Greenaa of the P. Jorgenson Sanitary Market grocery store. The dentist, Dr. Mathis, maintained his office in the hotel building and was also a frequent participant in the discussions.

Business picked up with the arrival of more steamers. Many passengers were on their way to outlying fish camps and canneries and only spent one night at the hotel as they waited for boats to pick them up. Mr. Stoft advised Carl and Elizabeth on the food conservation program for restaurants.

"Carl," he said, "this is what the government requires in order to do our part to support the war effort: Meatless Tuesday and one meatless meal each day; porkless Saturday (including fresh pork, bacon, ham or lard); and wheatless Wednesday. No bread, crackers, butter or sugar should be on the table or counter until the meal is served, unless the guest specifically requests it. Serve only two cubes of sugar on the tea or coffee saucer unless the guest requests more. And eliminate butter and animal fats from cooking."

"How much flour and sugar can I buy?" asked Carl.

"Hotels, restaurants and boardinghouses are allowed to purchase fifty pounds of sugar without a permit. Tom Elsemore is now the local food administrator and he just got a report from Washington telling us that when purchasing wheat flour, everyone must also purchase an equal amount of other cereals. That would include corn meal, corn starch, corn flour, hominy, corn grits, barley flour, potato flour, sweet potato flour, and soya bean flour. These regulations change all the time and he'll keep you informed when they do."

He left them with a poem written by an anonymous author as they pondered the impact of the regulations on the restaurant and hotel:

POEM OF THE PATRIOT

My Tuesdays are Meatless,
My Wednesdays are Wheatless;
I'm getting more Eatless each day.
My Home it is Heatless,
My bed it is Sheetless –
Have gone to the Y. M. C. A.

The Bar-rooms are Treatless,
My Coffee is Sweetless;
Each day I grow Poorer and Wiser.
My Stockings are Feetless,
My Trousers are Seatless –
By Gosh! I do Hate the Kaiser.

Carl reopened the dining room and Mr. Miller wrote a nice article about it in the *Report*. Being a Tuesday, Carl served no meat dishes and offered fresh halibut, king salmon and clams. He also kept a big pot of meatless chili simmering that was a big hit with the diners.

Elizabeth waited tables and kept an eye on the hotel lobby while Carl cooked. Julius didn't do any real work, just shot the breeze with whomever came through the door. Elizabeth no longer considered her work an easy task as they washed dishes and prepared the kitchen for the next morning's breakfast trade.

The *City of Seattle* arrived with eighty passengers for Petersburg – fifty-three first class and twenty-seven steerage. The Wakefield cannery crew was on board and they left immediately on a cannery tender for Little Port Walter on Baranof Island. Several passengers booked rooms and the rest were entertained by a show at the Dream Theatre while awaiting daylight and a favorable tide.

The steamers also brought big shipments of lumber, steam engines, boilers and cold-storage equipment for the canneries at Scow Bay and Petersburg. A donkey engine and other machinery arrived for the Arness Lumber Company. And Standard Oil steamers made several round trips to Ketchikan bringing distillate for the local agency.

A new doctor arrived in town and leased the Petersburg hospital. "We've been without a doctor to run the hospital since December when Doc Bulkley moved his practice to Wrangell," said Carl. "And they just finished installing bathrooms on the first and second floors and hot and cold running water in the kitchen. I hope this Dr. Kyvig stays longer than the other doctors we've had."

Martin Kildall, Deputy U.S. Marshal of the Petersburg district, stopped in at the hotel to introduce his replacement – Marshal Noah Howell from Ketchikan. Marshal Howell was formerly police chief in that city.

"What do you think of Petersburg?" Carl asked.

"Seems like a nice enough town," he replied. "I've just posted notices for all alien enemies who use Petersburg as their address to register at the postoffice."

"What exactly is an alien enemy?"

"Anybody from a country with which the United States is at war and who hasn't taken out their final citizenship papers," replied the new marshal. "Failure to register could result in arrest and internment."

At a mass meeting two days later, the town's fishermen and businessmen adopted resolutions protesting the importation of alien enemy fishermen and laborers. "These men are taking jobs away from American citizens," said the committee chairman. The men sent the resolutions to the governor and the United States Congress at Washington, D.C.

Charlie Greenaa burst through the lobby door with news of a drowning. "The *Volante* lost a man overboard while she was being towed to Big Port Walter," he said excitedly.

"Who drowned?" asked Carl.

"A Seattle man from Norway," replied Charlie. "He's been fishing in Alaska for several seasons."

"What happened?" asked Carl.

"It was around eight o'clock in the morning about six miles southwest of Portage Bay," said Charlie. "Several men were aboard the *Volante* as she was being towed by the *Fanshaw* and the *Carmen*. This fella climbed down into a skiff to change the towline. The skiff capsized, dumping him overboard. He'd disappeared by the time the *Carmen* got the alarm and turned back to rescue him. A man can't last long in those frigid, choppy waters. They searched for a long time but never found the body."

"What a sad story," said Carl.

"The tragic thing is," continued Charlie, "some of the men thought he might've been saved if the schooner had some lifesaving equipment on board. There were no life preservers or buoys to throw him, not even an ax to cut the line on the skiff so it might drift back to where he could reach it."

"I gotta tell you, Carl, that old schooner is spooky. This is the same schooner abandoned in a storm in Chatham Strait while under tow to Sitka two years ago. They couldn't find her after the blow and a Japanese liner reported sighting her several hundred miles out to sea."

"Four months later," continued Charlie, "she was spotted plunging in heavy weather near Banks Island and a Canadian fishing boat towed her into Prince Rupert. One mast was broken off but most of her cargo of barrels and salt was still useable. The Pacific Mildcure Company had a helluva time getting the Canadians to release her, and after paint and repairs they put her to work as a floating salting station."

"Elizabeth," said Carl, "between the bad weather and all the work you've been doing at the hotel and restaurant, you haven't had a chance to meet many of the ladies of Petersburg. The Moose Club is giving a masquerade ball Saturday night. Why don't we close the restaurant early and go? The whole town will be there."

"A masquerade ball," said Elizabeth. "Do I have to wear a costume?"

"Only if you want to. Just a few people will be in costume. Mostly it's a chance to catch up with people who've been stuck indoors all winter or spent the winter down below. I hear some lodge members are coming over from Wrangell for the affair."

Elizabeth looked forward to the dance with great anticipation. She hadn't realized how much she'd missed female companionship after working with only men for so long. She decided to wear a nice dress and change into her dancing shoes at the hall.

When Carl, Elizabeth and Julius arrived at the Sons of Norway Hall, the dance was in full swing. The Petersburg Band played loudly as Carl introduced her to several men and their wives. Everyone had a good time as the costumes were judged. Mrs. McLaughlin won first prize for costume and best sustained character. Cecil Allen took second prize for impersonating a lady.

Elizabeth took an immediate liking to the commissioner's daughter, Miss Mary Allen, who impressed her as strong-willed, capable and independent. "Alaska is a place where men are men and many of the women are too, Mrs. Roger," she said. "And if you're looking for a husband, the odds are good, but the goods are odd. Just take a look around."

The men outnumbered women four to one. Most were bashful bachelor fishermen with thick Norwegian accents and limited English. They lined one side of the room and the women sat on the other. The men disappeared regularly into a cloak room at the back of the hall and reappeared with more swagger and liquor on their breath. Several asked Elizabeth to dance but most just stood around gawking at the dancers.

She heard, "Dance, Elizabeth?" and looked up to see Julius leering down at her. She didn't want to dance with him but didn't want to cause a scene, either. It was a slow dance number and he held her so tightly that she finally gasped, "You're squeezing me too tight, Julius. I can't breathe." He relaxed his grip and shuffled her slowly around the floor. His breath smelled of liquor and chewing tobacco. She was so relieved when the dance was over. Carl didn't dance with anyone. He said he had two left feet.

Elizabeth thanked Carl for the evening as they walked back to the hotel. She had met so many nice people and promised to stop by the Red Cross work rooms to see the knitting done by the Junior Red Cross students. She might even pick up some knitting supplies for sweaters for the soldiers. One lady, Mrs. Barron, told her she was interested in working at the hotel or restaurant. Elizabeth promised to mention her to Carl. They may need extra help when the season started.

Elizabeth didn't mention to Carl or Julius that Mrs. Swanson had invited her to a meeting of the Woman's Christian Temperance Union. She didn't think the men would approve. Mrs. Jensen also invited her to a Ladies' Aid meeting. She was certain she wouldn't have time for that.

Spring rains melted the snow and volunteer firemen used the fire hose to clean Main Street of the filth that accumulated over the winter. The health officer instructed residents to clear rubbish from their properties and dump it only from docks or floats beyond the low tide line. Rubbish and tin cans were not permitted on the beach or tide flats. Le Conte Glacier remained frozen and fishermen were running out of the dwindling supply of snow for icing their fish. One of the breakfast-trade halibut fishermen was heard to mutter, "We can always dig clams. The Alaska Clam Canning Company's paying seventy-five cents a bushel and they don't need ice to can clams."

Meat restrictions were suspended for thirty days and Carl added this missing ingredient to his popular chili. Three freighters arrived with building materials for the Scow Bay cold-storage plant, coal for Hogue & Tveten's store and general merchandise for town merchants. Traveling salesmen arrived from as far away as Kansas City and San Francisco. Elizabeth visited the work rooms at the Arctic Brotherhood Hall and admired the work of the Junior Red Cross. The students had completed sweaters, baby bonnets and bootees. She also admired a beautifully knitted sweater turned into the military relief committee by Charlie Greenaa from the P. Jorgenson Sanitary Market store. She left with enough yarn to knit two similar sweaters for the soldiers.

Sergeant McLaughlin of the wireless station hurried into the lobby. "Carl," he said, "better get some rooms ready. The *Admiral Farragut* hit the rocks at the north end of the Narrows hard enough to shake the buildings on shore. We got a call that she's sinking and twenty gasboats are on their way to rescue passengers."

"Anybody hurt?" Carl asked.

"We don't know yet. Doc Kyvig's been notified to stand by just in case."

"How many passengers?"

"Almost three hundred."

Carl and Elizabeth scurried about collecting bedding and rearranging furniture to accommodate the unexpected guests as Sergeant McLaughlin left to notify Mrs. Willard at the Petersburg Hotel. Somehow, the two hotels found room for everyone and the town merchants pitched in with extra food and blankets. They covered the lobby floor and half the dining room with sleeping mats. One-hundred-thirty-seven steerage passengers were brought to town and one-hundred-forty cabin passengers remained on board when it was determined the ship's pumps could keep up with the leaks.

The passengers spent one night in Petersburg while the big steamer was towed to Scow Bay to assess the damage to her hull. In the morning, the steerage passengers were taken to Scow Bay by gasboat and the steamer once again passed north through the Narrows on her way to Juneau where her passengers and freight would be transferred to another steamer.

Seven men were elected to the town council. The vote was determined by only 146 ballots, as most registered voters were out fishing on election day. The council elected Erick Ness mayor and Hans Wick was reappointed town marshal and health officer. Elizabeth mentioned to Mary Allen that she had seen women voting at the Fire Hall.

"That's because the first territorial legislature gave Alaskan women the right to vote," Mary said. "Really, the men just wanted to impress government officials in Washington by increasing the number of voters. But everyone knows women have proven themselves in Alaska just as much as the men."

"My lady friends in Illinois have been voting for the past five years," Elizabeth replied.

"You'll be able to vote in next year's election," said Mary. "You only have to be a U.S. citizen, over the age of twenty-one, reside in the territory for one year and in Petersburg for six months."

Elizabeth didn't mention that she lacked citizenship papers. Something had been overlooked between arriving in America in the company of her guardian and reuniting with her biological father in Illinois. At the age of seventeen, it just hadn't seemed important.

Late one night, Elizabeth heard a soft tapping at her door. "Elizabeth, are you awake?" Carl whispered.

"What is it?" she replied.

"Put on your coat and come outside. There's something I want to show you."

They stepped out the back door into a cold, clear night. Elizabeth caught her breath as she looked up at a nighttime wonder of colored lights. Above their heads, pale rainbows shimmered against a velvet black backdrop. They hung in folds, like curtains draped across a grand stage.

"Aurora borealis," Carl said.

"They're beautiful," she breathed.

"And look, over there," he said, turning her slightly. "The big dipper, Ursa Major. Do you see it? Now follow those two stars at the end of the basin upward and it'll lead you directly to the north star, Polaris. It's the last star in the tail of the little dipper, Ursa Minor."

"Why, Elizabeth, you're shivering," he said, draping his coat around her shoulders. His arm brushed her breast and they stood still, gazes locked in the silent night as the northern lights danced above their heads.

Then he said, "See those three stars all in a straight row? That's Orion, the hunter. Those three stars are the belt around his middle."

"You sure know a lot about the stars," said Elizabeth.

"I've always been interested in astronomy," said Carl. "All the early explorers navigated by the stars. It's a wonder they found their way back home again."

They returned to the hotel and, as she handed him his coat at her door, he stooped, tilted her chin upward and brushed her lips with his. His kiss was as soft and sweet as she imagined it to be. She slipped into her room, closing the door behind her. Her heart was beating so loudly she feared it might awaken the guests.

The town's social life quickened with the melting of snow and arrival of more workers from the states. Three hundred people enjoyed a musical recital at the Variety Theatre. Vocal and instrumental numbers were presented by Mrs. John Allen, Mrs. McLaughlin, Mrs. Munro, Mr. Kjempness, Mr. Grevstad, and the chorus. The theatre showed the Ethel Barrymore drama, *The Awakening of Helena Ritchie.* Admission was twenty-five cents for adults and ten cents for children.

Mr. Scarborough reopened the Dream Theatre and ran shows seven nights a week with four programme changes. The opening show consisted of an Alaskan feature film, singing by Mrs. McLaughlin, violin solos by Mr. Kjempness, and a dramatic reading by Mr. Scarborough.

The Boy Scouts presented a programme of musical numbers and recitals in the Sons of Norway Hall. Receipts from two hundred people in attendance provided sufficient funds for the eleven boys to purchase uniforms.

Other entertainment included dances sponsored by the Arctic Brotherhood, Sons of Norway, the Moose Lodge and the ladies of the Red Cross. And, roller skating season started at the Variety Theatre rink which opened its doors from 7:30 until 10:00 p.m.

Although Elizabeth and Carl were too busy at the hotel to attend the events, activity at the café quickened before and after the entertainments. Carl hired Mrs. Barron to help with the increased business.

Chapter 11

April 1918 – Elizabeth served coffee to Carl and the four other men playing cards in the lobby. Julius moved the spittoon within spitting distance. A steady rain pounded outside and most of the guests had retired to their rooms. Julius winked at her as he poured whiskey into his coffee before passing the flask around the table. She felt his eyes follow her apron strings down the hallway to the kitchen. Just before she was out of earshot, Julius said, "So Carl, did you get some of that when you came north on the steamer?"

"What did you say?" Carl replied angrily.

"You heard me. What are you doing, keeping it all in the family?"

Carl's chair scraped across the wooden floor and Elizabeth turned to see him towering over his partner. Carl's fists were clenched in rage as he knocked Julius to the floor not once but three times before stepping away. The other card players all stood in bewilderment.

As Julius struggled to his feet, nobody saw him reach into his vest and pull out a gun. The first shot penetrated the ceiling above Carl's head. The second hit Carl in the right temple and he crashed to the floor.

Elizabeth screamed and rushed back into the room as two of the men tackled Julius, taking the gun away. One of the men leaned over Carl and shouted, "Is Doc Ballance staying at the hotel?"

"I'll fetch him," said another card player, bounding up the stairs.

Carl's eyes were closed, his breathing shallow, face and hair burned by gunpowder. Blood gushed from an ugly gash above his right eye. An image of Albert lying dead on the sand flashed through Elizabeth's mind as she held a towel to the wound while waiting for the doctor.

Doc Ballance hurried downstairs and rushed over to the injured man. Kneeling beside Carl, he said, "It doesn't appear the bullet pierced the skull. That's a nasty wound, though. You men help me carry him to his room where I can see to him properly."

Elizabeth sat with the men in the lobby awaiting word from the doctor. The mood was somber and nobody was adding whiskey to the strong coffee she poured anymore. "Where's Julius?" somebody asked.

"Marshal came and took him over to the jail."

"Didn't know he carried a gun."

"Didn't know either. He sure was spoiling for a fight."

All heads turned as Doc Ballance came down the stairs. "He's going to be all right," he said. "The bullet shattered on impact and exited an inch away. It's a good thing the shot wasn't from a more direct angle; it would've been fatal for sure. I removed the bullet fragments and patched him up. He's regained consciousness and he's going to have a terrible headache when the medicine wears off. He's asking for you, Mrs. Roger."

Elizabeth followed the doctor to Carl's room as the men filed out the door to spread the news of the near tragedy. A thick bandage encircled Carl's head and his color had returned. "Oh Carl, how do you feel?" she asked.

"Like I've been kicked in the head by a mule," he replied.

"I feel terrible that I was the cause of the fight."

"I've seen the way Julius treats you and also saw you didn't like it," said Carl. "Couldn't let him get away with it any longer."

"Thank you. I only put up with it because he's your partner."

Doc Ballance cleared his throat and said, "We have to let Carl get his rest, Mrs. Roger. I'll sit with him awhile longer and then we can take turns looking in on him."

Carl's eyelids were closing as he said, "Elizabeth?"

"Yes?"

"The hotel – we'll have to close the dining room until I'm on my feet."

"Don't worry about a thing. Mrs. Barron and I will take care of everything."

Marshal Wick and Deputy Howell came to visit Carl the next day. "Your partner was arraigned before Commissioner Allen this morning," said the deputy. "He claims he used the gun in self defense but waived preliminary hearing and was bound over on a $1,500 bond."

"You do understand I don't want to press charges, don't you?" said Carl. "I've known Julius for eight years. He's elderly and in poor health. I should've been able to control my temper."

"You'll get a chance to plead for clemency when you give testimony at district court," said the marshal. "The term of court begins next month in Ketchikan. In the meantime, he'll be a guest of the town jail."

Doc Ballance arrived and shooed the men from Carl's room. "He needs his rest," he said. "Mrs. Roger, I'll sit with him awhile so you can tend to the hotel."

Elizabeth and Mrs. Barron posted a notice in the window that the dining room was closed. They cooked themselves some breakfast and discussed running the hotel without Carl. Elizabeth would handle the guests and tend Carl while Mrs. Barron handled the housekeeping duties.

Carl was awake when Elizabeth relieved Doc Ballance. "I've brought you chicken soup to get your strength up," she said.

He gave her a weak smile as the Doc helped him sit up in bed. The right side of his face was badly bruised and his eye was swollen shut. He put up a weak protest before allowing Elizabeth to spoonfeed him. Soon, he was fast asleep and didn't hear the doctor tell Elizabeth he needed careful watching because head injuries could be so dangerous.

Elizabeth brought her knitting to Carl's room in the evening and worked on her second Red Cross sweater as he slept. His room was tidy, by bachelor's standards, but she couldn't keep from straightening up anyway. She organized his impressive collection of astronomy books and *National Geographic* magazines. *Here's a man who keeps informed even in this remote corner of the world.*

Elizabeth was startled into wakefulness when Carl said, "Elizabeth? You were asleep in the chair. You should go and get some rest yourself now. I'm feeling better."

"And what kind of a nurse deserts her patient?" Elizabeth said, plumping his pillow.

"Thank you for sitting with me. It's nice knowing you're here."

"There's no place else I'd rather be," she replied. "And, you're welcome."

Elizabeth and Carl talked of many things – their families, Albert, his partner Julius and his hopes for the business. Lapses in their conversation were filled with comfortable silences.

Elizabeth slipped out the door after he drifted off to sleep again, carrying his supper dishes and her knitting bag. She made a point of stopping to talk with his friends in the lobby, giving them an update on his progress. She wouldn't want the town gossips to think she was spending too much time in his room – it wouldn't be proper.

Carl recovered rapidly and moved downstairs to the lobby where his business and fisherman friends stopped by to visit. He was soon back behind the counter checking guests in and out of the hotel. Within a few weeks, the only indications of the shooting were a fading wound at his right temple and headaches that began to diminish with time.

The weather turned bright and sunny and the glacier began calving. Spectacular blue-white ice bergs drifted through the Narrows; some were deposited on the beach by the outgoing tide. The end of the ice famine spurred the shipment of fresh king salmon, halibut, cod and shrimps. Blocks of glacier ice filled the kitchen cooler. Carl reopened the dining room and ran an advertisement in the local paper:

Hotel Wester and Wester Café
Carl Roger, Proprietor
Everything of the Best in Season
When in Petersburg, Give us a Call

Local men aged twenty-one to thirty were required to register for military service with the newly-formed exemption board. The board determined which men would be classified for active duty. At age thirty-six, Carl was not among those required to register.

Fourteen Petersburg boys were drafted into military service. Carl knew most of them. The town gave a dinner in their honor at the Sons of Norway Hall and a parade marched down Main Street after the dinner. Elizabeth watched from the hotel porch as the band, the drafted men, Red Cross workers, boy scouts and a big delegation of fishermen marched by. She wondered how many of the boys would survive the war.

Carl attended the programme following the parade. The hall was filled to capacity as musical numbers were performed by the band, school children and grownups. Pastor Maakestad of the Lutheran Church gave an address to "Our Boys" and Reverend Munro of the Salvation Army appealed for contributions to the Red Cross war fund. The next day, the whole town accompanied the boys to the wharf where they boarded the post steamer *Peterson* for their trip north to Fort Seward in Haines. Draftees from Ketchikan and Wrangell were already on board. The band and many town folk on gasboats convoyed the steamer out into Frederick Sound.

Passenger and freight traffic picked up with the warmer weather. The Marathon Packing Company's floating cannery arrived from down below and was berthed at the end of the Citizen's Dock for the season. The hotel was busy with traveling salesmen, logging crews en route to the camps, and construction and cannery crews on their way to Baranof Island fishing stations at Warm Springs Bay, Port Walter and Port Armstrong.

Two men walked into the lobby and Carl exclaimed, "Why Fred, when did you get into town?"

"Just arrived on the *Humboldt*, good to see you, Carl," said one of the men, shaking hands. "This here's my brother John, all the way from Auburn, Washington."

Carl introduced them, saying, "Elizabeth, the Patten brothers."

"Nice to meet you, ma'am," they said in unison, tipping their hats.

The men carried canvas duffle bags and women's luggage. "These suitcases belong to Mrs. Roden," Fred said. "The senator wasn't there to meet the steamer and we told her we'd bring her bags to the hotel. She'll be along shortly."

"Henry made a quick trip to Juneau," said Carl. "He's expected back today."

Elizabeth left the men to talk and headed for the kitchen to bring them coffee. The brothers said they were going to build a scow and try their hand at salmon-salting this season. "A couple years ago," explained Carl, "Fred operated a floating bakery during the trolling season."

Mrs. Roden arrived a few minutes later, exclaiming, "And just where is that man of mine, Carl?"

"Mrs. Roden, welcome back," Carl said, rising to greet her. "Henry made a quick trip to Juneau where he heard there's a boat for sale. He should be back later today."

"Well then, better book me a room," she said. "You never know when he might be delayed."

Carl introduced Elizabeth as he filled out the hotel register. Elizabeth took an instant liking to Mrs. Roden who reminded her of her sister-in-law Anna in San Diego. Both women had the same no-nonsense attitude tempered with a sense of humor. After Carl showed Mrs. Roden to her room, he told Elizabeth about her husband.

"Henry Roden, now there's a story," Carl said. "He was born in Switzerland and moved to Paris to study music. When he heard of the Klondike gold rush, he went to London and bought a ticket straight through to Skagway, which he reached by steamer from Vancouver."

"He mined for several years and then decided to become a lawyer. Studied law with Judge Wickersham and was city attorney in Fairbanks and Iditarod. He became a United States citizen without ever setting foot in any of the forty-five states."

"When Alaska became a territory," Carl continued, "Henry won a seat on the territorial senate. He got to the session in Juneau by mushing a dog team from Iditarod to Valdez and taking a steamer from there. He lived in Juneau for a few years, left the senate and is now superintendent of the Republic Fisheries Company. He's also quite an expert on mining law."

Mayor Ness and the banker, Mr. Stoft, carried a heavy banner into the lobby and asked for Carl.

"Petersburg's been awarded an honor flag for our participation in the Third Liberty Loan program," said the mayor. "We're one of only two Alaska towns to receive a flag."

Mr. Stoft added, "Our $19,000 quota was oversubscribed within five minutes. We had total subscriptions of more than $33,000 including $5,000 from the president of the Alaska Pacific Herring Company."

The men attached the banner to the hotel's second-story balcony and suspended it across Main Street. Citizens pointed to the banner with pride and many visitors stopped at the hotel to inquire about it.

The fire bell rang at the fire hall as Carl was speaking with Marshal and Mrs. Howell. He whipped off his apron and joined the men running down the street to fight a fire at the federal building. Sergeant McLaughlin was already there aiming a garden hose at the blaze and the three prisoners at the jail helped save the building from total destruction.

"Was anybody hurt?" Elizabeth asked when Carl returned.

"No, nobody."

"What caused the fire?"

"They think it started in the light wires," he said, "but they're not sure. The commissioner and marshal's papers and records were mostly saved but the Howells lost most of their household goods and personal belongings. The commissioner's going to put them up at his house until the U.S. Marshal from Juneau authorizes the repair work."

Mr. Miller from the newspaper office stopped in for coffee and was soon joined by a group of fishermen "What's new in town?" one asked.

"Seems the most critical thing is the labor shortage," replied the newspaperman. "The town council sent a letter to the U.S. Public Service Reserve in Juneau advising them there's lots of good jobs available here."

"What kind of workers did they say we need?"

"Men to work in the lumber and fish business, house builders and domestic help," replied Mr. Miller. "Business is booming and several big projects lack manpower to work on them."

"I hear Olaf Arness over at the sawmill is recruiting men from Seattle, Ketchikan and Wrangell," said another fisherman. "He's running the mill with thirty men and needs about twice that number."

"And don't forget men to work on building the new Standard Oil plant south of town and the Scow Bay road," added a third. "The lack of men is also slowing down Pete Jorgenson's store expansion and John Gauffin's new building on Main Street."

More loggers passed through town on their way to logging camps. "They're getting out piling for any number of construction projects in town and at nearby canneries," Carl told Elizabeth. "They just towed a couple of log rafts for Diamond Fish Company to Warm Springs Bay where a shipment of lumber for a new dock and warehouse is waiting. Former marshal Kildall has the contract for driving piling for the dock and buildings."

"The contractors for the Standard Oil station are getting out piling for their dock and several men are busy preparing the site," he added.

"They're building a dock, warehouse and office quarters. And the Doyhof Fish Company at Scow Bay is building a new dock and approach. Olaf Arness at the lumber mill is busy cutting saw logs into lumber as fast as he can."

The Sons and Daughters of Norway celebrated the 17th of May Constitution Day with a dance at their hall. A parade of tow-headed children with freshly-scrubbed faces and new haircuts marched down Main Street. They waved red, white and blue Norwegian flags as well as American flags. The children were dressed in their *fest bunads* – national costumes. The little boys wore white cotton shirts beneath soft wool vests, woolen knickers with suspenders, black or white leggings and black leather shoes. The little girls wore long black skirts topped with red brocade bodices over long-sleeved white blouses. Starched white aprons covered their skirts and their costumes were completed with black stockings and shoes. The children looked adorable.

The children were followed by adults – also in national dress. Their costumes were more elaborate and carried designs specific to the towns and valleys in Norway where they were born. The men's woolen knee britches had tassels at the cuffs and pewter buttons adorned their black and red trimmed vests. The ladies' costumes were much like those of the young girls, but with more elaborate needle work. Delicate embroidery decorated starched white aprons and brightened the hems of their dark skirts. Brocade bodices trimmed in velvet covered lace-trimmed white blouses. Some wore black silk bonnets or scarves with floral embroidery. Others were hatless with braided hair pinned close to their heads.

The crowd bringing up the rear was dressed in an assortment of Nordic sweaters and vests, or regular street wear. The entire town was invited to the dance regardless of nationality.

"*Uff-da*," Elizabeth said quietly as they marched past. "That's too many Norwegians for me."

Elizabeth accompanied Carl to the dock where he boarded the *Jefferson* for the trip to district court in Ketchikan. The case of the United States vs. Julius Reese, charged with assault with intent to kill, maim or wound, would be heard by the petit jury when the steamer arrived with the men from Petersburg. Deputy U.S. Marshal Howell boarded with the prisoner before regular passengers were permitted to board. Four witnesses also made the journey – Dr. Ballance, town marshal Hans Wick, revenue agent Mr. Snow and Magnus Finney, one of the card players.

"I don't know how long we'll be," said Carl, giving Elizabeth's shoulder a squeeze. "I'll send word when it's over."

The party walked up the gangplank and Carl remained waving at the railing as the incoming tide carried the ship into the Narrows.

The men were gone for a week, during which Elizabeth managed the hotel together with Mrs. Barron and her daughter Lillian. Fortunately, the women weren't too busy since much of the town was either out on the fishing grounds or at the fish and logging camps. The dinning room was closed once again. Few details about the trial made their way to Petersburg until Elizabeth received a telegram from Carl saying he would be home on the *Admiral Farragut*.

Carl described the experience upon his return: "The jury examined all four witnesses and then I was allowed to tell my story," he said. "I asked them for leniency due to Julius' age, health and his condition when he fired the gun. The jury was out for twenty-four hours and brought in a verdict of guilty but recommended clemency. Julius looks terrible – he's pale and looks even older than he is."

"What will become of him?" Elizabeth asked.

"I don't know," replied Carl. "Judge Jennings will pass sentence in a few days."

On the last day of court, the judge passed sentence on several parishioners who had been tried and convicted. Julius Reese got a light sentence of three months in the Petersburg jail. Deputy Howell took some prisoners south to McNeil Island in Puget Sound and returned by way of Ketchikan to escort Julius back to Petersburg.

Five more Petersburg boys were sent to join the colors at Fort Seward. They were guests of honor at the Good Eats Restaurant where a steady parade of town folk stopped to wish them well. No sooner had their ship left than two submarine chasers arrived in port. Forty sailors wandered around town, peering in store windows and enjoying the sunny weather.

"What are they doing here?" Elizabeth asked Carl. "Do they expect to find enemy submarines in these waters?"

"They're patrolling the coast to keep the *wobblies* from interfering with putting up the season's pack and rounding up any men who may have gone to remote spots to evade military duty," he replied.

"The *wobblies*?"

"The Industrial Workers of the World, a radical union group that's caused mischief on the docks in Seattle. They're also known as the I.W.W. They're against the war and want to organize all workers to overthrow the employing class. They're big trouble."

Mr. Nelson stopped by with news that the Scow Bay cannery had put their new ice-making plant into operation.

"We can now ship fish all summer for freezing at the Tacoma plant," he said. "And we're prepared to provide ice to all fishing boats who stop at Scow Bay."

"How's the missus adjusting to living in Scow Bay?" Elizabeth asked.

"She misses living in town," he replied, "but she's a big help around the mess hall. She's putting in a vegetable garden. And now that the weather's turned nice, I'll be bringing her to town with me more often."

The town continued to thrive and the town council authorized the Standard Oil Company to connect to the water main at the city limits and extended the town light line to the new oil station as well. John Gauffin let a contract to build a two-story building on the lot north of the hotel. Hogue & Tveten built an extension to their store warehouse. Their mailboat *Trygve* took over the Baranof Island mail route while the *Americ* was south for her annual inspection.

Commissioner Allen added Deputy Collector of Customs to his list of official titles. Respected old-time businessman Sing Lee decided it was a good time to cash out and offered all his holdings for sale, including two stores with rooms above and cabins in the rear, groceries, hardware and men's furnishings. He told prospective buyers, "I am an old-timer in Alaska, alone and not now able to handle the business." He told Carl he wanted to retire to Fresno, California.

Fred Patten came into the restaurant and said, "You'll never guess what those crazy Chinamen are up to now."

"What Chinamen?" Elizabeth asked.

"You know, the cannery crew at the Packing Company."

"What's going on?" asked Carl.

"Seems two of them got into a fight and had a duel behind the mess hall, pistols and all."

"Was anybody hurt?" Elizabeth asked.

"Nah," said Fred. "They fired a dozen shots and didn't hit a thing. U.S. Marshal Tanner's in town to look over the damage to the federal building and he, Deputy Howell and Marshal Wick arrested the fools."

"If nobody was hurt, will they just let them go?" asked Elizabeth.

"Not sure," said Fred. "Turns out, the territory has a penalty of from one to ten years in prison for dueling."

Chapter 12

June 1918 – Elizabeth joined Mrs. Ballance, Margaret Roden and Anna Holt for a berry picking expedition. The women met at the hotel and trudged up the hill carrying a picnic lunch and two-pound coffee cans threaded with twine. When they reached the muskeg, Margaret sang out, "Watch your step now. You don't want to step in a hole. Some of these ponds have no bottoms."

"That's just an old wife's tale," responded Anna Holt.

The soggy, acid muskeg was dotted with stunted shore pine. They moved slowly among the ponds, accompanied by the sound of small frogs plopping into the water as they approached. Enormous dragon flies skimmed the surface, flashing iridescent blue and green. Mosquito larvae wriggled up from the murky depths and then wriggled back down again.

"See this moss we're walking on?" said Mrs. Ballance. "This is what the boys of the Junior Red Cross have been collecting for surgical dressings for the war effort. They dry the moss in a shed by the wireless station and the schoolgirls sew it into dressings."

"What are these flowers?" Elizabeth asked, pointing to delicate pink blossoms poking through the moss.

"We just call them June flowers. Aren't they pretty? And these are shooting stars and there's some cotton grass too. It's not the kind of cotton you can weave into cloth, it's probably too fine for that, and there's not enough to make it worthwhile anyway."

"And look," Mrs. Ballance continued, "low bush cranberries growing on that other kind of moss. They make a fine jelly, but it takes a lot of them."

The vegetation changed as they approached a wooded area. Open muskeg ponds were replaced by dense brush beneath tall moss-draped western hemlocks and Sitka spruce. "That's 'old man's beard'," said Anna as she pulled down a strand. "Feel how scratchy it is."

They followed a rugged trail downhill to a narrow creek encircled with three-foot high skunk cabbage, pink and white fireweed and goatsbeard. "This is Buschmann's dam," said Margaret as they carefully crossed a rickety split-rail foot bridge to the clearing on the far side.

"Peter Buschmann was the founder of Petersburg and this is where he got the water to run his cannery. Of course, we get our water from the new dam on the other side of town now."

"He committed suicide, you know," said Mrs. Ballance.

"Who?" Elizabeth asked.

"Peter Buschmann."

"Why?"

"The company he sold his Alaska holdings to paid him in stock and then went bankrupt. They say he felt responsible for the financial losses suffered by his friends who invested in the company on his recommendation."

"How sad," said Elizabeth.

They left their picnic in the clearing and climbed back up the trail to bushes heavy with plump blueberries. Using both hands to fill the cans hanging around their necks, they kept up a steady conversation so they would know where one another was.

"If you hear a growl, just back away and don't run," said Anna. "The bears like blueberries too."

"Bears," exclaimed Elizabeth. "How big?"

"They're on the small side, just black bears, but wild and unpredictable. It's best to stay away from them."

"Mrs. Ballance, how many students did you have in school this year?" asked Anna.

"We had seventy-two," she replied. "And let me tell you, it was a lot easier cleaning up after them since they installed the sanitary plumbing. You had a more difficult time of it when you were doing the janitorial work there."

"Are the same teachers coming back next school year?" asked Anna.

"I think Miss Kirchstein and Miss Burke are returning," said Mrs. Ballance. "The school board plans to hire two more. And I don't know who they'll get to teach at Scow Bay now that Mr. Swanson has decided to become a fisherman. They're going to have to get a new custodian, too. It looks like we'll be moving to Texas at the end of the fishing season."

"Oh, no," Elizabeth said. "Why doesn't Dr. Ballance open up a practice in Petersburg?"

"He's given that some thought," she replied. "But, with Dr. Kyvig already in charge of the hospital and Dr. Bulkley moving back from Wrangell, that's too many doctors for one small town. I think he'd rather try his hand at ranching anyway. It was just a fortunate coincidence he was in town when Carl was shot. And quite frankly, I'm tired of this rainy climate. It's too depressing," she added.

They finally filled their berry cans and returned to the creek where Elizabeth was relieved to see their picnic had not attracted any bears. They enjoyed their lunch while sitting on the banks of the creek, bare feet dangling in the cool water. Minnows rose to the surface to feast on golden salmon berries drifting by.

"How's Mr. Roden doing with his new fishing venture?" Elizabeth asked Margaret.

"Well, Henry's bought a new boat – the *Pilot* – for the company," she replied. "He's hoping for a good salmon season in Chatham Strait this year."

"Do you think you'll spend time at his cannery this summer?" asked Elizabeth.

"Oh, I'm sure I will," Margaret replied. "But I like it just fine here in town, too. Henry comes to town often on company business, so I can get back and forth easily."

"We'd better pack up and head back to town," said Anna. "By the way, Elizabeth, did you know there's a beaver dam just a little upstream from here?"

"There is?" said Elizabeth. "Oh, I'd love to see that."

The women waded across the creek and followed the bank around a bend, ducking through brambles and devils' club until they saw it. The beaver's dam stretched from shore to shore. Water cascaded over the top and trickled through tree branches and mud set carefully in place by the industrious creatures. "Where are the beavers?" Elizabeth whispered.

"Oh, they're here," said Anna. "They heard us coming and are probably in their lodge. See that mound of mud in the middle of the pond? That's their lodge. Look at all the wood chips scattered about from chomping down alder branches. And see those trails leading up those mud banks? They slide down those on their bellies bringing tree branches for the dam."

The small trees nearest the pond had been gnawed into pointed stumps. Dense forest covered the banks on both sides of the dam. Huge moss-covered logs laid rotting on the forest floor. Very little light filtered through the canopy above. The only sound was the trickling water as it spilled over and through the dam. Even the birds were silent. "It feels like we're being watched," said Elizabeth. "Let's leave."

They made their way downstream into the sunlight and picked up their belongings for the hike back to town, pausing in the muskeg to pick wild flowers. Elizabeth avoided those with white spit-bug foam clinging to the stems. Devil's Thumb stood above snow-frosted mountains on the mainland across Frederick Sound, its blue gray cliffs too steep to hold snow. "Do those mountains have snow year 'round?" asked Elizabeth.

"Yes," responded Anna, "but only at the very top. You know, there's a story about Devil's Thumb," she added. "Seems some prospectors explored up there and came back crazy."

"How's that?" asked Elizabeth.

"They swore water ran uphill and they were chased around a half-moon lake by hairy monsters covered in scabs and oozing sores," said Anna. "All crazy talk. Those men have never been the same since."

The four weary, sunburned ladies hiked back to town. Elizabeth set the blueberries to soak and washed up to help Carl with the dinner trade. "Did you have a good time?" he asked.

"I had a wonderful time," she responded. "And we've got enough blueberries for four big pies. Do you think we have enough sugar?"

"We get our next ration tomorrow," he said, "so there'll be plenty. Home-baked pies are sure to be a big hit."

The pies were such a success that Elizabeth became the restaurant's new "pastry chef."

"Annie Nelson's been shot and killed at Scow Bay," exclaimed Marshal Wick.

"What?" said Carl. "How can that be? I just saw her in town yesterday."

"Ole Shatter shot her through the dining room window of the Alaska Fish and Cold Storage plant," said the marshal. "He'd been on a ten-day bender in town. I picked him up twice over in the red light district and let him sleep it off overnight in the jail. But then he'd just start all over again the next day. He was crazy drunk when he got back to Scow Bay and started shooting at everyone he saw. He sneaked down the back stairs outside the mess hall building and fired through the open window. The cook and machinist were in the dining room too and saw everything."

Everyone in the lobby listened in stunned silence as the marshal continued.

"Ken Hatlan, skipper of the halibut boat *Mascot*, heard the commotion and ran to get his rifle off the boat. He shot Shatter just as Shatter was taking aim at the freezing plant operator. Shatter was still alive when they brought him to town in a gasboat but he was dead before Doc Bulkley arrived."

"How's Mr. Nelson taking it?" Elizabeth asked.

"He's all broke up," said the marshal. "Says he never shoulda' moved her there from town. They've only been living there for three months. They're real old timers, you know. Mrs. Nelson was one of only four white women in the area when they first arrived in Petersburg. And their son was the first white child to attend school here."

The coroner's jury found that Ole Shatter came to his death, " . . . by a shot fired by K. Hatlan, in defense of himself and others," and that Mrs. Nelson came to her death, ". . . by a shot fired by Ole Shatter while temporarily insane caused by alcoholism."

In the wake of the shooting, a mass meeting was held at the Sons of Norway to consider ways of riding the town of evils, especially sales of liquor in the red light district. The citizens forwarded a petition of protest to the town council who appealed to Juneau for legal advice in closing the red light district or moving the brothels beyond the city limit.

"It's a shame it takes a tragedy like this for the men of this town to do something about those houses of ill repute," said Mrs. Barron.

"Where do the girls come from?" asked Elizabeth.

"Some of them worked the gold rush up north and drifted south when the gold ran out. Now they're trying to gain respect by marrying local men. And they hold their noses up in the air like they're better than you and me. I tell you, it makes my blood boil to see how the men treat these 'sporting girls' like real ladies."

"And what about the madams?" said Elizabeth.

"What a joke that is," Mrs. Barron replied. "They'll look you straight in the eye and tell you they run rooming houses for women. And the men just wink and look the other way. If it wasn't for their sordid business, poor Annie Nelson would still be alive."

The weather on the Fourth of July was warm and sunny – perfect for a day of festivities, although the town was saddened by Mrs. Nelson's tragic death. The Sons of Norway Hall was filled to capacity to hear a patriotic address by attorney Hellenthal from Juneau. His remarks were interrupted by frequent applause.

The Petersburg band led the parade past the hotel. "Uncle Sam" and "Miss Liberty" led a group of uniformed soldiers carrying the American flag. Little girls pushed their decorated doll carriages over the plank street. The children were dressed in their Sunday best and clearly excited by the holiday.

Elizabeth and Carl were busy at the café and missed the afternoon foot races and athletic events. The highly anticipated wrestling match between Kelly and Johnson was won by Kelly. The big dance at the Sons of Norway Hall continued into the early hours of the next morning and the street in front of the hotel was noisy with revelers.

Mr. Miller and a stranger dropped by the hotel. "Carl," Mr. Miller said, "I'd like you to meet the new editor and publisher of the *Report*, Mr. Perkins."

"Pleased to meet you," said Carl as he shook the stranger's hand. "Where are you from?"

"I've been with the *Juneau Daily Empire* for the past four years," Mr. Perkins replied. "I welcome the opportunity to work with the businessmen here for the advancement of the town. Traveling men have spread the word that Petersburg is the most prosperous town on the Pacific Coast. And, I assure you, the paper will be strictly independent as to territorial politics."

"Carl's a good man to know," said Mr. Miller. "Not much happens around here that isn't discussed by the regulars in his lobby."

"I'd certainly appreciate the opportunity to check in with you regularly," said the new editor. "Although I know the newspaper business inside and out, I'm coming from a community where mining is the principal industry and I'm sure to need help getting acquainted with the needs of a town where fishing takes first place."

"Drop by anytime," Carl replied. "You're sure to get an earful."

"We're going to miss you, Lynn," he said to Mr. Miller. "When do you leave?"

"The missus and I are taking the *City of Seattle* south at the end of the month," said Mr. Miller. "We'll see my brother in Washington and visit other places along the coast before deciding where to settle down. We'll miss the people of Petersburg, but not the rain."

"Good luck to you then," said Carl, shaking the newspaperman's hand.

"Give Mrs. Miller my regards," Elizabeth added.

The town was jumping with activity. Everybody seemed to have money in their pockets and spent freely. Salmon were running and canneries were near capacity. A new federal food administrator announced higher prices to be paid for salmon, news that was happily received by fisherman and fish processors alike. Northbound steamers arrived with more mail, freight, passengers and Oriental cannery crews. Southbound steamers were laden with cases of canned salmon and boxes of fresh fish. The Coast and Geodetic Survey made Petersburg their headquarters while they undertook a pipe drag survey at the north end of the Narrows where the *Admiral Farragut* struck a boulder last April. The dangerous work was expected to take most of the summer due to the channel's swift tides.

Repairs were completed on the sawmill bridge and the water main was extended between "D" and "E" streets. Main Street was widened from the hotel to the Petersburg Packing Company wharf. The town was without lights for three days and nights while a new foundation was installed at the power house, making it ready for larger machines. The Sunde Building got a new coat of paint and a large warehouse was added to the Sons of Norway Trading Union store. Commissioner Allen became the new postmaster and his daughter Mary Allen and Mrs. McLaughlin took charge of the office. Doctor Anna Brown, the only woman doctor in Alaska, opened a practice in Petersburg. Well-known traveling entertainers W. B. Woodworth and J. A. McLaren entertained the town with a special feature show at the Variety Theatre.

Charlie Greenaa stopped in on his way to the Sanitary Market to tell Carl of a liquor raid in Scow Bay. "Deputy Howell found old man Beck's whiskey stash in the woods behind the power house," he said. "He arrested Beck and brought the barrel of whiskey to town as evidence. Commissioner Allen sentenced Beck to sixty days in jail and fined him $250."

"What happened to the whiskey?" asked Carl.

"They're going to ship it to Ketchikan on one of the sub chasers when they're back in town."

"The sub chasers are expected back?"

"Yep," said Charlie. "They're coming down from Juneau to close the red light district. The town council asked for help cleaning up the town and they're gonna send the girls packing on the first outbound steamer."

Sub chasers *309* and *310* arrived in port and the ladies of the town organized an impromptu dance in their honor at the Arctic Brotherhood Hall. The dance was well attended and everybody did their best to impress upon the young men that they were always welcome in Petersburg.

"Stay indoors, Elizabeth," Carl said. "The street is full of drunken sailors."

"What's going on?" asked Elizabeth. "I thought everyone was at the dance."

"Not everyone. It's not safe for respectable women to be outdoors."

Elizabeth peered through the hotel window and saw three sailors staggering arm in arm down Main Street. They were singing at the top of their lungs and tugging on the door knobs of each business that was closed for the night. Civilians joined the party and several loggers took turns trying to stay upright on a log they rolled down the center of the street. Elizabeth went to her room and locked the door.

Charlie was the first customer at the café in the morning. "Strange doings in town last night," he said. "Everyone says old man Beck's whiskey stash came ashore and that barrel is bone dry now. But that wasn't the half of it."

"What do you mean?" asked Carl.

"Seems while everyone was at the dance, the officials in charge of the clean up and officers of the sub chasers were over in the red-light district drinking and dancing with the girls until early this morning. Some of the town's upstanding citizens went over there and broke it up."

"Who was there?" asked Carl.

"Well, Jim Brennan over at the pool hall for one," said Charlie. "He had some pretty strong words for the navy men and they almost came to blows."

The new editor of the *Report* described the fracas in an article titled, "Officials Are In Disgrace." The article made its way to navy headquarters, and before long, Jim Brennan was arrested for sedition.

"What's sedition?" Elizabeth asked Carl

"It means rebelling against authority and disrespecting the uniform."

Mr. Brennan was taken to Ketchikan and tried at commissioner's court. The big Irishman offered no defense and was sentenced to one year in jail. He immediately appealed to a higher court and was released on a $5,000 bond. Editor Perkins published a public apology to all officials concerned, stating it was now his impression the officials were under orders from the Naval Intelligence Bureau to secure certain information required by the government before the girls disbanded.

Seven more Petersburg boys, including Charlie Greenaa, were called for active service. "Being of German ancestry," he said, "I don't know how much they'll let me do. But I'm ready to serve in any capacity." The town entertained the boys and their guests with a big dinner at the hotel. Carl closed the dining room for breakfast and lunch and enlisted Elizabeth, Mrs. Barron and Lillian to help prepare the feast.

Charlie stopped by in the morning to say goodbye.

"You be sure to write," Elizabeth told him as he gave her a big hug.

"I sure will Mrs. Roger," he promised.

Carl accompanied him to the dock where the *City of Seattle* waited to take the draftees to Fort Seward.

"Is the proprietor in?" asked the man in the lobby.

Elizabeth fetched Carl from the kitchen where he was mashing potatoes for the supper trade.

"I'm Carl Roger," he said to the stranger.

"George Edmunson with the Standard Oil Company," the man replied. "Just arrived on the *Despatch* with a shipment of steel plate for the new tanks. I've got a crew of boiler and tank makers arriving on the *City of Seattle* and want to put them up at your hotel."

"How many men we talking about?" asked Carl.

"Thirteen, including myself. The work should take a month or so."

"I'm sure we can accommodate you if you don't mind doubling up two men to a room."

"That'll be fine," said the newcomer.

As he checked in, Mr. Edmunson told Carl about the progress at the plant south of town. "The wharf is finished," he said, "and the construction crew is almost finished driving piling for the foundations for the tanks and buildings. Then they'll pour concrete for the tank's foundations. Everything should be ready when my men arrive to erect the tanks."

"You're building at the best time of year," replied Carl. "Any other time and you'd be working in rain or snow."

"So I understand," said Mr. Edmunson. "We work in all kinds of weather, but this is a real treat. Can you tell me where I can find Knut Steberg? He's just been appointed Petersburg's agent for Standard Oil and I'd like to introduce myself."

Carl directed him to Mr. Steberg's office in the Sunde Building. "Looks like we'll have a full house for a while," he told Elizabeth with a broad smile.

Editor Perkins informed Carl that the Navy Department requested all Alaskan newspapers refrain from printing any news of the movement of boats. "That'll cut down on the number of stories in the paper telling folks who's coming and going on the steamers," he said. "But it's for the safety of the maritime industry so the enemy can't figure out our ship movements."

"I'm going up to Juneau to collect my family for the move to Petersburg," he added. "We're coming back on the *City of Seattle* and I want to put them up at your hotel until work on the Gauffin house is finished. We'll move in when they're done with the renovations."

"We look forward to meeting your family," said Carl. "How many guests are we talking about?"

"My wife, daughter and my wife's sister. It should be for just a few days."

Carl was clearly pleased the new editor had selected the Hotel Wester over the Petersburg Hotel for his family.

Mr. Perkins returned from Juneau with a copy of the *Daily Alaska Dispatch* in which Assistant District Attorney Steve Ragan was credited with branding Petersburg "a hotbed of pro-Germanism" and implied that the red light district was closed due to pro-German activities.

"That's outrageous," exclaimed one of the lobby regulars. "Isn't this DA one of the men found partying with the girls that night?"

"He sure is," replied another. "And he isn't even one of the Naval intelligence officers that editor Perkins says was there on official business. I think he's afraid that will come out when Brennan's case goes to a higher court."

"But we can't stand by and let him smear Petersburg's good name this way," said the first man. "I can't think of a more patriotic town. Why, we were the first town in the country to double our quota for liberty loans and we tripled our share of the Red Cross war fund. We're the ones who requested the town be cleaned up after Mrs. Nelson's death, not because of some so-called 'pro-German' activity."

The town council adopted resolutions of protest against Mr. Ragan and forwarded copies to the highest authorities with recommendations that further misstatements of this nature be stopped.

Chapter 13

August 1918 – Mrs. Mathis waved as she crossed the lobby. "I'm helping Ray in the office today," she said.

"Doctor Mathis seems to be doing a big business," replied Elizabeth, "especially since he announced free dental work for the drafted men."

"It's his way of supporting the war effort," replied Mrs. Mathis. "He's behind in his paperwork, though, and I hope to help him catch up today."

"Will you and Dr. Mathis be returning to Seattle for the winter when fishing season is over?"

"We're staying in Petersburg this winter," she replied. "Ray is having the stumps and logs removed from our lot on the Narrows north of town. And we'd like to get as much work done as possible on our new house before the rainy season sets in. I'll see you later," she called as she disappeared down the hallway.

Another voice interrupted Elizabeth's morning chores. "Good morning, Mrs. Roger."

"Why Mrs. Ballance, how nice to see you. Aren't you working today?"

"No, the cannery's closed due to a shortage of cans," said the doctor's wife. "The Marathon Packing Company is out of cans too. We've been told to come back to work when the *Portland* arrives from the south with more tins. I can see you're busy, will you be free for coffee and a little visit this afternoon?"

"I'd like that," said Elizabeth.

Mrs. Ballance reappeared in mid afternoon and the two women retired to the kitchen for a chat. "What's it like working in a salmon cannery?" Elizabeth asked.

"It can be tiring when we have to work until two or three o'clock in the morning to get the fish in cans while they're still fresh," said Mrs. Ballance. "And it's wet work what with water running all the time. The cannery supplies rubber gloves, boots and full-length aprons. We hose down our oilskins while we're still wearing them when we break for coffee and lunch. And, we have to wear hair nets – not very becoming."

"What about the smell?" asked Elizabeth.

"You get over that after the first day or you don't come back," laughed Mrs. Ballance. "And you really get over it when you get your first paycheck. They pay very well. All the ladies and girls from town work there during the season."

"What exactly do you do there?"

"Oh, I have the best job of all," Mrs. Ballance said. "I'm a floater."

"What does that mean?"

"I fill in wherever there's a vacancy because somebody didn't come to work that day. I get to work all the positions. All positions except the fish-butchering machine, that is. That's too dangerous."

"Fish-butchering machine?" asked Elizabeth.

"It's a big machine that cleans the fish when they enter the cannery after being offloaded from the boats. The Chinese crew lines up each fish all pointing in the same direction on a conveyor belt that moves through the machine. The heads, fins and tails are all chopped off as the fish move through the machine. The bellies are also slit so the innards can be removed by water pressure. We're told the machine does the work of fifty men."

"Then the gutted fish drops to a sliming table where a crew of women runs sharp knives along the insides to remove any gut still remaining," she continued. "The cleaned fish then moves through another machine that chops it into parts small enough to fit into cans. Another crew of women, each with a scale in front of them, puts the fish into cans which they weigh before sending them down the line. They put up one pound and half pound cans. Lids are placed on the cans by another machine and they are all dumped into big metal bins that the Chinese crew rolls into boilers for cooking."

"So the fish are cooked in the cans?" said Elizabeth.

"That's right."

"What's your favorite position?"

"I like to work in the box loft where we assemble cases for shipping and make up the cans," said Mrs. Ballance. "The tins are shipped to us flat and we feed them into a machine that makes them round and attaches the bottoms. Then a conveyor moves them downstairs where they meet up with the fish to be canned. I also like to work in the egg house where we separate fish roe by rubbing the egg sacs across wire mesh screens stretched across wooden frames. The separated eggs drop into barrels which they ship south as caviar."

"I understand this is an especially good year for the canneries," said Elizabeth.

"Oh, yes," Mrs. Ballance agreed. "Both the Petersburg Packing Company and the Marathon Packing Company have put up more cases than last year and more than they expected to can this year. The Packing Company will close for the season soon and Marathon will stay open awhile longer. Doctor Ballance will stop fishing when the Packing Company closes and then we'll leave for Texas."

"We're going to miss you," Elizabeth told her.

"We'll miss the people too," she said, "but not the weather."

Tom Elsemore came into the café during the luncheon hour. "Got some new marching orders from the federal food administrator," he said. "First of all, they say it's unpatriotic to use canned goods at this time of year when fresh products are available. Canned goods must be reserved for American soldiers and our allies."

"That everything?" asked Carl.

"No, they also sent these special permits for anyone who wants to purchase extra sugar to preserve Alaskan berries and fruit."

"We could use some of those," said Elizabeth. "My lady friends and I are going on another berry picking expedition soon. We know where to find the best blueberries and huckleberries. And Mrs. Holt's backyard is full of rhubarb and wild strawberries."

"Retailers and bakers may now buy wheat flour without substitutes," Mr. Elsemore added. "Consumers must still buy one pound of substitute for each pound of wheat flour, though."

"That'll make Knud Stenslid at the Star Bakery very happy," said Carl. "And customers have been clamoring for more of Elizabeth's pies."

Not everyone participated equally in the town's prosperity. Cannery workers eating their lunches on the dock observed one fisherman so pleased with his catch that he paraded back and forth in front of the dock rather than queuing up to offload with the other boats. The cannery workers cheered as they admired his deckload of silver salmon. His hold was overflowing and fish were piled high on all decks, both fore and aft. The small boat sat low in the water, with less than a foot to spare below the gunnels. As the fisherman slowed to turn the boat around for another pass in front of the dock, his wake caught up with him, sending the boat and his record catch to the bottom. Other fishermen rescued the man and eventually got his boat refloated, but not before losing his bounty of fish.

The cannery at Waterfall on the west coast of Prince of Wales Island was destroyed by fire and over 12,000 cases of salmon were lost. Closer to home, the Ripley fish-buying scow sank at the end of the Citizen's Dock. Several barrels of salt fish and unboxed fresh fish were lost. An unsuccessful attempt was made to tow the scow to the beach but it sank again before reaching land. The scow was finally towed to the beach at low tide so repairs could be made and the fish-buying service put back in operation.

"Hello Carl," said Mr. Roden, entering the hotel.

"Henry, good to see you," replied Carl. "How have you been?"

"No complaints. I'm in town settling up the affairs of the season."

"And how was your season?"

"Even though we had a short run of fish in lower Chatham Strait this year, I'm well satisfied with the showing made by Republic Fisheries," replied Henry.

"Is Mrs. Roden with you?" Elizabeth asked.

"She is. I lost her at Hogue & Tveten's store but she'll be along shortly." Turning to Carl, he asked, "And what's new in town?"

"You probably already know the Packing Company put up a record 112,000 cases this year, and the Marathon cannery pack is over 30,000," said Carl. "Other than that, I guess the big news is the progress being made on the Scow Bay road."

"They finish it yet?"

"No, but the planking has almost reached the new Standard Oil plant and grading is pushing ahead from there. I don't think they'll finish before rainy weather sets in, though," Carl added.

Elizabeth and Carl made donuts for a meeting of the Chautauqua committee to be held in the dining room.

"Tell me again what this committee is all about?" Elizabeth asked.

"It's a group of businessmen who signed a contract to have a troupe of traveling entertainers put on a festival," said Carl. "If ticket sales aren't enough to pay for the performance, the committee makes up the difference."

"And who is on this committee?"

"People like Tom Elsemore, Earl Ohmer, Rasmus Enge, Peter Jorgenson, Johnas Olson, editor Perkins, Knud Stenslid, Chris Tveten and Luther Hogue," said Carl. "There's about twenty of us in all."

"Is this traveling group something like a circus?"

"Nothing like that," replied Carl. "Chautauqua is a traveling circuit dedicated to self improvement through lectures on literary, scientific and moral topics. This year's tour group includes sixteen lecturers, elocutionists, artists and musicians."

Carl joined the group around the big table in the dining room as Elizabeth served coffee and donuts. Miss Grace Peck, advance agent for Chautauqua, was introduced. "I want to thank each of you for sponsoring your first Chautauqua," she said. "We pride ourselves on carrying the highest type of culture from town to town, and you won't be disappointed. The troupe will arrive Monday and we're having difficulty finding sleeping quarters for everyone. So if you know of anyone who can provide room for one or more for a few nights, please contact me at the hotel."

"How many more rooms do you need?" asked Earl Ohmer.

"We've found accommodations for all but four," she replied.

"I'm sure we can find someone to put them up," said editor Perkins. "How many will be staying at the hotel?"

"In addition to myself, the manager Mr. Heinline and the superintendent Miss Gray," she said. "All other cast members will board with your generous citizens."

Carl attended the lectures on the first two days of the three-day event at the Sons of Norway Hall. He reported that the McDonalds and the Fillions gave excellent performances. "Everyone found the lectures both inspiring and instructive," he said. "You could've heard a pin drop, people were so intent on not missing a single word. Reverend Hindley, he's a war veteran, spoke about conscription and its importance to the war effort. And then he had everyone laughing about the ordinary wage earner who pays rising prices while everyone around him seems to be getting rich."

Elizabeth and Margaret Roden were entertained by the Ladies Festival Orchestra during the final evening's performance. Long hours of practice were evident in the girls' playing, singing and elocution. The appreciative crowd was rewarded with three encores.

It was generally agreed that Chautauqua was the greatest entertaining body ever to come to Petersburg. The performers thanked everyone for the hospitality as they boarded the *City of Seattle* for their next engagement, in Juneau. And the Chautauqua committee businessmen signed a contract for their return the following year.

The school term began on September 4 and the teaching staff was short two members. Mrs. Strand filled in until the arrival of the missing teachers on the first boat from the south. High school was delayed until their arrival. Miss Rita Hon arrived from Wyoming to teach at Scow

Bay and spent one night at the hotel before being taken by gasboat to her new one-room schoolhouse.

Several older students left for college in the states. Mrs. Barron and Lillian also left for the south after promising to return in the spring. Southbound steamers were filled with departing cannery crews and the families of fishermen and businessmen who preferred to spend their winter months down below. The Seattle Steamship Company raised ticket prices to Seattle to $23 for first class and $15 for second class on the steamers *Despatch* and *Portland*. The *Admiral Goodrich* ran ashore while leaving Petersburg but floated off the mud sand at high tide without damage.

A number of traveling salesmen took lodgings at the hotel and spent several days in town. Mr. Chamberlain, Oak Olson and Gus Gillis were well known in these parts and displayed their wares to town merchants in the hotel's sample rooms. Newcomers included representatives of the Juneau Hardware Company and the Union Meat Company of Portland. One man was selling a new fish-cleaning machine he claimed reduced fish wastage during canning. He had been in town earlier in the season when cannery bosses were too busy to talk with him and now, at the end of the season, many of the same men had already left for the states.

Carl was visiting with the salesmen late one evening when Elizabeth overheard Oak Olson ask him, "Tell me Carl, why is it that you live in the front of the hotel and Mrs. Roger lives in the back?"

"Oh, Elizabeth isn't my wife," said Carl. "She's my sister-in-law. We have the same last name because she was married to my brother who died two years ago."

"Oh, well, that explains it," said Olson. "She's a fine-looking woman."

"That she is," Carl agreed.

Editor Perkins joined the lobby regulars with news from the Juneau *Daily Alaska Dispatch.* Elizabeth eavesdropped from her stool behind the front desk.

"It says here a referee in the Brennan case took depositions from the landlady of the Petersburg brothel and three of her girls," said the newspaperman. "Their testimony will be used in Jim's appeal to the district court."

"What did they have to say?" asked one of the men.

"First of all," replied Perkins, "the navy intelligence man had a confidential conversation with the landlady regarding pro-German activity at Petersburg and then he left."

"And what about that district attorney fellow, Ragan?" asked another.

"Let me read you from the paper," said Perkins.

> *She swore that Steve Ragan held her on his lap for an hour and a half. That he had been drinking and, as she expressed it, he was under the influence of liquor because he was hilarious, made love and wanted to dance. She also claimed she denied Ragan any opportunity to take liberties with her and told him 'you closed these places and I am going square.'*

"And this district attorney would have everyone believe he was there on official business?" asked the first man.

"Yep, and it gets even better," Perkins continued. "Listen to what one of the girls had to say about the whiskey."

> *Ensign Ragan invited me to go to the dance. I dressed and then he walked with me to the cannery dock, where he left me for a few minutes until he went aboard the sub chaser. Returning, he offered*

> *me a drink from a pickle bottle filled with whiskey. This bottle he took to the house where it was nearly all consumed before the men left about 2:00 a.m. I am positive Ensign Ragan and his friends were intoxicated by their actions.*

"The district attorney and the ensign have the same last names," said Carl. "Are they related?"

"I don't think so," replied the newspaperman, "but this is confirmation about what happened to old man Beck's whiskey stash. This is building up to be one interesting trial."

"I sure hope that district attorney gets his comeuppance for labeling our town 'pro-German'," said Carl.

"Oh, and here's another article about Petersburg from the same paper," said Perkins. "Remember that lady from the Grolier Society who was in town last week? She was selling encyclopedias for the school children."

A few of the men nodded their assent.

"She's in Juneau now and this is what she said about Petersburg."

> *The people of Petersburg are loyal to the nation and the cause of the Allies, and I would not conscientiously be doing my duty to that community unless I made a statement in their defense. I certainly found the people of Petersburg intelligent, progressive and appreciative, as well as patriotic.*

"Hear, hear," said Carl.

Carl closed the Wester Café for the season and he and Elizabeth ran the hotel without additional help. Steamships arrived less frequently and the hotel was no longer full. Although the days turned colder and shorter, Elizabeth was surprised by an Indian summer of sunny skies and autumn colors.

"Elizabeth, how would you like to go on a picnic?" Carl asked. "Fred Patten told me I could use his dory anytime I wanted and we could row down the Narrows to a spot I know. The next steamer doesn't arrive for two days and the hotel can do without us for a day."

"Oh, I'd love that," said Elizabeth.

They were like two little kids fixing their picnic in the hotel kitchen. They packed home-baked bread, Alaskan strawberry jam, cheese – including Carl's favorite Limburger – apples, pickles, sprutbakkelse cookies and huckleberry pie. Carl added a gallon water jug and they set off for the Citizen's Dock where Mr. Patten's scow was moored.

"Hello the scow," Carl called. "Permission to come aboard?"

"Why Carl, and Mrs. Roger," said Fred, poking his head out the doorway. "Come on aboard."

"We're going on a picnic and would like to borrow your dory," said Carl, helping Elizabeth aboard.

"Sure thing. Gertie, Mrs. Roger's here," he called to his lady friend in the galley.

"Elizabeth, welcome," she said. "Would you like a cup of coffee?"

"Thank you, no. I'm told we need to catch the outgoing tide."

"Carl, where are you taking this poor thing?" she chuckled.

"Down the Narrows for the day, a little north of town," he replied.

"Fred, drop a couple pairs of rubber boots in the skiff they can wear beach combing, and don't forget life preservers," she said. "They're handy to sit on. Those seats get mighty hard."

Fred gave the dory a mighty shove and they were off. Elizabeth sat in the bow facing Carl who manned the heavy oars. He rowed through the small harbor, pointing out after-season activity. The floating machine shop on a scow near the wharf was getting a new twenty-foot addition. Citizen's Dock was getting a new addition for the storage of coal. And a crew was busy adding new piling and planking to the Petersburg Packing Company dock.

They finally cleared the harbor and the outgoing tide carried them down the Narrows toward Frederick Sound. Carl stood at the oars, facing forward. His broad chest and strong arms rippled beneath his shirt as he worked the oars. The oar locks creaked with every stroke.

Carl kept the boat close to shore and they could see starfish clinging to barnacle-covered rocks beneath the cold, clear water. Long tentacles of whip kelp rose to the surface. An occasional eagle dipped his talons beneath the surface searching for fish while seagulls scavenged for scraps on the beach.

"Look up there, Elizabeth, that's Doc Mathis' place."

"Where?" said Elizabeth.

"Up there where the men are pulling stumps with the donkey outfit."

"Oh, I see them now. How does a donkey engine work?"

"The upright tank is the steam engine that runs the winch," said Carl. "See how the outfit is tied to that big tree? They run a cable from the winch out to the stump they want to uproot and the engine reels it in. Does the work of several men. It's mostly used by loggers for getting out piling and saw logs from the woods."

"How do they take out the last tree after they've removed all the stumps?"

"Ah, that they do the old-fashioned way if they don't have anything to anchor the engine to," said Carl. "Sometimes they tie it to something on a neighboring lot, though. They're going to have a wonderful view of the Narrows when they get their house up."

A gasboat went by and they bobbed in its wake as they waved to the men on shore. The plank street built on pilings narrowed to a foot path as they continued down the waterway. Two black and white cows chewed their cuds as they watched them drift by. "That's Nette Martinsen's new place," said Carl. "Bought Alfred Swanson's property, including those two milk cows. I hear she wants to start a dairy."

Carl turned the boat toward shore just before Wrangell Narrows emptied into Frederick Sound. He pointed the skiff up a shallow creek tumbling across the rocky beach and secured it with a long rope to a stout tree. "Come this way," he said. "There's something I want to show you."

He took Elizabeth's hand as they followed the stream a short distance inland and then up an embankment to a dense stand of hemlock trees on a grassy knoll. "Now turn around and look," he said.

Elizabeth was struck speechless by the view. They looked directly across Wrangell Narrows to the tip of Kupreanof Island where a navigational beacon warned mariners of an underwater reef. To the right was the wide expanse of Frederick Sound. Off in the distance, three small forested islands seemed to float above the water. Across the Sound, blue grey cliffs rose straight up from the water's edge. Beyond the cliffs and taller still was the snow capped mountain range Elizabeth had admired from the muskeg.

"Oh Carl, this is the most beautiful spot I've ever seen."

"I think so too," he replied. "Those cliffs out there are called Horn Cliffs. They're home to Rocky Mountain goats. They're solid white with small, pointed black horns and easy to spot against those dark cliffs. If we were closer, you would see spectacular waterfalls falling hundreds of feet. In the springtime, big icebergs from the glacier scrape along the sides of the cliffs."

"What about those three little islands? Does anybody live there?"

"Those are the Sukoi Islets – one name for all three," he said. "Claude Green has a fox farm on one of them. Does quite well, I'm told."

"A fox farm?"

"Yes. He's stocked it with foxes that run wild. They can't get off the island and they have no natural predators. None except eagles, that is, and there's a bounty on them. Last year, Claude brought sixty-three pairs of eagle talons to town and sent them up to the territorial treasurer in Juneau. Got fifty cents a pair."

Carl wrapped his arm around Elizabeth's shoulder as they gazed at the spectacular view. "All the boats coming or going from the north pass this point," he said. "Look, here comes one now – it's the *Americ*."

They waved at Hogue & Tveten's mail boat and Captain Johnas Olson blew the whistle as he passed on his way to the Baranof Island settlements. "Now that the season's over, they'll only make this trip once a month," Carl explained. As they watched, the boat continued toward the distant cliffs before making a sharp turn around the tip of Kupreanof Island to avoid the reef.

They returned to the stream and followed it inland. Carl filled the water jug, leaving it in the cool water to pick up on their return. Parts of the stream were nearly covered with thick underbrush and downed trees. Footing was treacherous on the moss-covered rocks. The rapidly running water sang cheerfully as it tumbled around and over the rocks on its way to the sea. Brilliant blue birds with black crests flitted among the trees, making a noisy racket. Carl said they were Steller jays. The air was filled with the tangy scent of evergreens and rotting vegetation.

"Shhh," Carl said, grasping Elizabeth's arm. He pointed to a clearing where a young buck grazed on alder bushes. The deer sensed their presence and turned his head slowly in their direction. All stood motionless. The deer's large dark eyes regarded them somberly before, tossing his head, he bounded away on pencil thin legs.

"He's beautiful," Elizabeth breathed. "I hope no hunters find him."

"He'll be safe for this season," Carl replied. "He's a young one and they can't take bucks with horns less than three inches, does or fawns."

They rested in the deer's sun-dappled meadow before making their way downstream.

Upon reaching the grassy knoll, Elizabeth was surprised to see how much of the beach was exposed by the low tide. The dory was high and dry on the beach and the shoals across the Narrows on Kupreanof Island were fully exposed. "Oh Carl, look," she said. "A sand bar. Let's go explore it."

They passed the beached dory on their way to the wide sand bar. Receding water left several tide pools filled with small minnows, sea urchins, spider crabs and Chinese sun hats. Seaweed popped beneath their boots as they made their way across the beach. Finally, they reached the sand bar and shed their boots and Carl laughed as Elizabeth ran barefoot across the damp, smooth surface. They walked hand in hand down the length of the bar, dipping their toes in the frigid water and then out again. The air smelled salty and they shared their sandy domain with four seagulls searching for sand crabs.

Clams shot streams of water two feet into the air at the far end of the bar. When Elizabeth dug down into the hole left by the water spout, she found nothing but wet sand. "Where's the clam?" she asked Carl.

"You've got to be quick, they move pretty fast," he laughed.

"Are they safe to eat now?"

"Yes," he said. "Any month with an 'R' in it. We'll have to bring shovels and buckets next time."

They turned and strolled back to the middle of the sand bar where they had left their boots.

"Is it my imagination, or is this sand bar smaller now?" Elizabeth asked.

"It sure is," said Carl, "and look, the tide's coming back in and cut off our way back to the beach."

Elizabeth turned in a circle to see they were completely surrounded by water.

Carl just laughed and rolled up his trouser legs. Handing Elizabeth their boots, he scooped her up in his arms and plunged through knee-deep water to the beach. He carried her all the way to the beached dory where they dried their feet, slipped into their boots and walked back to their waiting picnic.

After their picnic, they sat on the blanket and admired the view. Or, at least, Elizabeth admired the view. Carl's head was in her lap and he was looking skyward.

"Elizabeth, I told you at your wedding that Albert was a lucky man, and now that I've gotten to know you, I'm certain of it."

"Why, thank you, kind sir," she teased.

"You're welcome," he laughed.

She traced the features of his face with her fingers – across his brow, down his nose, around his chin and lips. He flinched when she touched the place where the bullet had grazed his temple.

"Is that still painful? There's a hard lump there."

"I get headaches sometimes," he said. "I'll have it looked at the next time I'm in Seattle."

"There's something I've been wanting to ask you," said Elizabeth.

"What's that?"

"Well, now that men up to the age of forty-five are required to register with the exemption board, do you think you'll have to go to war?"

"Even though I have to register now," he said, "they're still only drafting men from eighteen to thirty-six years of age and they'll have to run out of them before they draft older men. Doc Bulkley already examined me and said I probably wouldn't pass the physical. There's a piece of Julius' bullet too close to my brain for him to operate. It really doesn't bother me most of the time."

"I hope you don't have to go. I wouldn't want anything bad to happen to you."

"Why Elizabeth, I think you're worried," he teased, pulling her down beside him. He removed the pins from her hair which tumbled to her shoulders. "Better," he said, kissing her tenderly.

Her arms were around his neck, their bodies close together. He ran his hands slowly down her sides and she felt him growing hard against her. They pulled apart, gazing at one another in wonder. Her heart was pounding and they were both short of breath.

"I've been wanting to be alone with you for so long," he said. "I couldn't do anything about it with the whole town watching."

"And I you, ever since you showed me the aurora borealis."

He pulled her to her feet and bent down to give her a lingering kiss. "I'm afraid we have to go back now. Look. The dory is floating free."

And indeed it was. The incoming tide had covered the sand bar and most of the beach. And the beacon across the channel was completely surrounded by water.

Carl hauled in the dory while Elizabeth re-pinned her hair and smoothed her dress. They stowed their picnic supplies together with her collection of driftwood and shells. Carl gave the skiff a mighty shove, hopped aboard and pointed the bow toward town. They glanced back at their secluded picnic spot as he rowed with the incoming tide. It was surely the most beautiful place on earth.

Chapter 14

October 1918 – Indian summer lasted less than a week and was replaced by cold, blustery rain squalls. A pile driver under tow from Dundas Bay to Ketchikan was lost in a storm and later found on the rocks of Gambier Island, a little north of Frederick Sound.

Carl read a letter from Charlie Greenaa to the regulars in the lobby. "Charlie's been assigned to the United States Guards," he said. "He says to tell the new recruits to bring an extra blanket and anything else they find useful 'cause there's plenty of locker space."

Editor Perkins announced that nineteen Norwegians had turned their citizenship papers into the local exemption board. "These men are too pro-German to fight or too yellow," he said. "They've violated their oath to abide by the principles of democracy and protect the American flag, if necessary. And they've been heard to boast that within a few months, their standing will be as good as before they turned back their papers."

A mass meeting was called at the Arctic Brotherhood Hall to discuss the presence of these renegades. Carl attended and told Elizabeth about the meeting afterward.

"The hall was filled to the rafters. I've never seen so many angry men. The first thing they did was agree that mob violence would not be used in dealing with the slackers. They passed resolutions of protest and sent them to the president, the governor, and the secretary of war."

"What did the resolutions say?" asked Elizabeth.

"First, these men should be deported as soon after the war is ended as possible. Their pictures and names should be posted in a public place so all may know of their cowardliness. And, they should not be allowed to compete for American jobs but be put to work for the government at some occupation for the pursuit of the war. I tell you, Elizabeth, nobody wants to have anything to do with these men."

Editor Perkins published a "Dishonor List" in the *Report* with the names of the nineteen men. He also published an "Honor Roll" of sixty-nine individuals who purchased bonds in the Fourth Liberty Bond program, noting that those individuals were ". . . willing to back the government with their cash, and with their lives if necessary."

The town ran out of coal and Carl turned off the steam heat to the dining room and all unoccupied guest rooms. "We'll have to get by on what we have in the boiler room," he said. "There's not a pound for sale anywhere in town."

"How could the coal dealers have run out?" Elizabeth asked.

"The boats just haven't delivered the contracted amount. The *Admiral Farragut* brought 137 sacks of Seattle coal which was rationed at four sacks to the family."

"When will we see a big shipment?" Elizabeth asked.

"I hear the *Portland* is on her way here with one hundred tons," he said. "She'd better hurry or we'll have to start burning the furniture."

Fred Patten stopped by with another story of a lost season for the owners of the barge *Neptune*. "She was anchored in Seymour Canal all season and was being towed to Seattle when they hit a southeaster off

Gambier Head," he said. "The tow lines snapped and the barge hit the rocks. Broke up in just minutes. Lost the entire season's cargo of salt herring."

"What happened to the crew?" Carl asked.

"They jumped overboard just before the barge hit the rocks and got ashore as best they could. But that's not the half of it. The barge tore the side out of one of the two gasboats towing the rig and they had to head for the beach too. The engineer stayed at his post until water reached the carburetor and the boat sank from under them. The men had to swim about a mile to reach the beach."

"Did everybody make it?" Elizabeth asked.

"Yeah, and later the boat washed up on the beach and they made her fast at low tide. They think she can be repaired. They had to spend all night on the open beach and were rescued by the other gasboat the next morning. They took them to Pleasant Bay."

Elizabeth hurried through the rain to the post office to mail a letter to Ruthie. Mrs. McLaughlin looked up from whatever she was reading and said, "Hello Mrs. Roger, an outgoing letter?"

"Yes, please, and how are you?"

"Getting ready to move to Wrangell. You've probably heard that we've been reassigned?"

"Yes, I heard."

"Now that Petersburg is connected to the cable," continued Mrs. McLaughlin, "they won't be needing a wireless office anymore."

"How does the cable work?" asked Elizabeth.

"The cable ship *Burnside* cut the underwater cable in Frederick Sound and landed an end at Sandy Beach. From there, they carried it overland to town. Now we're connected with Juneau, Sitka, Wrangell and Ketchikan."

"I guess that's progress," said Elizabeth. "How long have you lived here?"

"The U.S. Signal Corp. transferred us here three years ago and we've seen many changes in those three years. Why, Petersburg didn't even have electricity when we first arrived. And now there are new buildings and homes, a new Standard Oil station, better streets, a sewer system, an ice-making plant for the fishermen and a new road that almost reaches Scow Bay."

"We're going to miss you and Sergeant McLaughlin," said Elizabeth. "We'll especially miss your singing and piano recitals at the theatre."

"We'll miss everyone in Petersburg too. But we'll be close enough to come for visits."

"When you do, be sure to stop in at the hotel."

"We will. Goodbye for now."

The town's first war hero was a young man who died of Spanish influenza at Camp Dodge in Iowa. He had moved to Petersburg from another state and was well liked by those who knew him. His passing awakened the town to a new threat from a deadly sickness.

"Do we have any cases of Spanish flu in town?" Carl asked Doc Bulkley.

"Just two," the doctor replied. "A man they brought in from Cape Fanshaw and a native are sick, and I've got five natives under quarantine in a house on the muskeg. We also have a whopping cough epidemic among the younger school children."

Editor Perkins added, "Reverend Munro and his family were on their way south on the last trip of the *City of Seattle* and had to get off at Ketchikan until their children recovered from the whopping cough."

Travelers from the south described scenes of people wearing face masks on the streets and crowds being dispersed at movie houses and churches. They told of otherwise healthy people developing a blue tint to the face, becoming too feeble to walk, and dying the next day. Soon, Spanish influenza spread like wildfire through the neighboring towns of Ketchikan and Juneau. Both towns were placed under quarantine and scheduled court terms were postponed indefinitely.

The town council appointed a four-member health board to take precautionary measures against the spread of the flu. Governor Riggs appointed Doc Bulkley as temporary U.S. Public Health Surgeon. The health board published notices in the newspaper and distributed handbills to all businesses, schools, canneries, and churches.

"Carl, what do you think of this notice from the new health board?" Elizabeth asked.

"Some of these instructions will be difficult to follow," he said. "For example, we're supposed to keep away from the docks when steamships and gasboats are landing. That's how most of our guests arrive and then they come here and book lodgings. It's not practical that we avoid contact with them altogether unless we close the hotel, and I don't think that's a requirement."

"It also says 'All social and public meetings, including churches, schools and theatres are forbidden'," he continued. "That should keep people at home. And pool rooms are only open for the sale of tobacco and cigars if customers make their purchases and leave immediately. That will hurt their business too."

"What can you and I do to keep from getting sick?" asked Elizabeth.

"It says to keep rooms well ventilated and aired and avoid contact with other people as much as possible," reported Carl. "That's a pretty short list. I hope they know what they're talking about."

The man brought in from Cape Fanshaw was the first flu death in Petersburg. The official cause of death was determined to be pneumonia caused by exposure before he had fully recovered from the flu. Doctor Anna Brown received the sad news that her fifteen-year-old daughter attending school in Missouri was one of two pupils to die of the flu. The Red Cross work rooms were closed due to the epidemic and ladies were encouraged to do their work at home, especially the knitting of sweaters which were in great demand.

Editor Perkins arrived with news of another steamship disaster. "The Canadian steamer *Princess Sophia* sank on Vanderbilt Reef thirty miles north of Juneau," he reported. "She hit the reef about two in the morning and was so firmly lodged that she sat there for a day and a half. The weather was too rough to attempt a rescue so the rescue boats returned to safe harbor and returned on the second day. By then, the ship had shifted into deep water and sunk. All they could see was the top of her forward mast poking above the water."

"What about survivors?" asked Carl.

"There weren't any. All 350-some passengers and crew perished. Most suffocated from bunker oil released by the sinking ship. A half-starved setter dog wandered into the cannery at Auk Bay and they think it belonged to a wealthy couple on board. The sad thing is, many passengers were heading south to escape the Spanish flu at Skagway."

Carl and Elizabeth just stared at Mr. Perkins, at a loss for words.

"They've sent the *Princess Alice* north to take the bodies to Seattle," he continued.

"That's going to be one sad voyage," said Carl.

"Good news at last – the war is over," exclaimed editor Perkins a few days later. "An armistice was signed between the allied forces and Germany on November 11. The German flag was lowered from all her naval boats and the fleets of Great Britain, the United States and France accompanied the captured vessels to England."

"That's news worth celebrating," said Carl. "It's too bad social and public meetings are banned due to the flu epidemic."

"I know," replied Mr. Perkins, "but I can still write about it." And he disappeared down the street to the *Report* office to prepare articles for the next edition.

"Elizabeth, you have red dots on you cheeks – are you feeling all right?" asked Carl.

"Yes, I'm fine. Just a little light headed. Must be a cold coming on."

"Come here," he said, pulling her toward him and putting his hand on her brow. "Why you're burning up. I'm calling Doc Bulkley."

"It's nothing really," Elizabeth protested.

"I'm not taking any chances," he said. "You climb into bed and I'll get the doctor."

It was no use arguing with him so Elizabeth did as he said. The doctor was haggard-looking from attending all the sick people in town. "I'm sorry to bother you," said Elizabeth, "but Carl can be so stubborn."

"You should be glad he is," the doctor replied. "This may be more than a cold. I want you to stay in bed, get lots of rest and drink plenty of fluids. I'll look in on you tomorrow."

Elizabeth must have dozed off, because when she awoke, Carl was sitting by her bedside and a cool damp cloth covered her forehead. Every muscle and joint ached and she couldn't get out of bed if she tried. She couldn't speak without coughing. Carl saw that she was awake and offered her chicken soup. "You need this to keep your strength up," he said. She managed a few sips and closed her eyes again.

Elizabeth had wild, crazy dreams. A fortune teller repeated again and again . . . *long voyage over water and two little girls, long voyage over water and two little girls* . . . Uncle Emil and Albert tugged at her, pulling her arms in opposite directions until her shoulders and elbows ached.

She was a ballerina dressed in pink shoes, tights and a pink tutu. Carl stood in the shadows, his long arms forming a circle around her. She twirled on tiptoe, arms raised above her head in a perfect ballet movement. Carl wore a bemused expression tinged with admiration. She knew he would catch her if she should falter.

Elizabeth opened her eyes in the darkened room. Carl dozed in the chair next to her bed. He heard her stir and sat upright. "You're awake," he said. "How do you feel?"

"Like I've run a long race. What time is it?"

Pulling out his gold pocket watch, he said, "Two o'clock."

"Why is it so dark at two in the afternoon?" asked Elizabeth.

"It's two o'clock in the morning. Your fever broke a few hours ago and you've been getting some much needed rest. How about some chicken soup?"

"That sounds good," she replied.

He left the door open so he could keep an eye on her from the kitchen as he prepared the soup. She got a half a bowl down between coughing spasms before falling back exhausted.

In the morning, Anna Holt came by and helped with Elizabeth's toilette while Carl changed the bed. They had her back in bed by the time Doc Bulkley arrived. "I want you to stay in bed and continue drinking fluids for several more days, Mrs. Roger," he said. "More people die of pneumonia after the flu than from the flu itself."

Carl took excellent care of Elizabeth and she was so glad to be back on her feet after a week in bed. The Red Cross sent a party of doctors and nurses north on the *Spokane* to assist in controlling the outbreak and Governor Riggs sent the naval collier *Brutus* north with additional doctors and nurses to assist local doctors.

More than three hundred cases of influenza developed throughout town and three small children died within hours of one another. Finally, no new cases were reported to the health board and it was thought there would be no more. Steps taken to enforce the quarantine and the orders of the health board were credited with stopping the spread of the disease.

Charlie Greenaa wrote from Fort Seward that only five recruits had died from the Spanish flu. The boys were looking forward to being discharged but knew they would all still be there for Christmas. The town took up a collection and shipped a community Christmas box to the boys from Petersburg.

Elizabeth attended a bazaar at the Sons of Norway Hall with Margaret Roden, Anna Holt, and Gertie Friedman. It felt good to be out again. The hall was lively with people enjoying the luncheon and fish pond and admiring the many hand-crafted articles for sale. The Ladies' Aid applied the proceeds from the event to assist in paying the mortgage on the church.

"Carl," said Elizabeth upon returning from the bazaar, "let's decorate the lobby for Christmas. We could put a small tree in that corner by the window, drape the registration desk in garland and bake some Christmas cookies for our guests and visitors."

"You watch the hotel and I'll go for the tree," he said, heading out the door. He returned a few hours later with a perfectly-proportioned pine tree and an armload of spruce boughs.

"There's no shortage of trees on this island," he laughed. "The most difficult part is deciding which one to chop down."

In no time at all, the lobby was transformed into a festive room scented by evergreens. Elizabeth decorated the tree with red ribbons from her sewing box and Carl set out candles he found in the pantry. They moved into the kitchen, donned cooks' aprons and were soon up to their elbows in cookie dough.

"It's good to see you laughing again, Elizabeth," said Carl. "I was so afraid I was going to lose you."

"You'll not be rid of me that easily," she teased.

That evening after their guests retired, Carl took Elizabeth's hand as they sat side by side in the flickering candlelight. "I love you, Elizabeth," he said. "Will you marry me?"

She caught her breath before replying, "I love you too, Carl, and I'd be proud to marry you."

He cupped her chin in his hand, kissing her deeply. She felt like she could fly. This wonderful man wanted to marry her! He picked her up and whirled her around the lobby before setting her down. "There's just one thing," he said.

"What's that?"

"This bullet in my head – I want to have it removed before we marry. Doc Bulkley says there's a doctor in Seattle who may be able to remove it."

"But why wait?" she exclaimed. "I'll take you just the way you are."

"The surgery's very risky because the bullet is so close to the brain," said Carl. "There's a chance something could go wrong and I won't have you saddled with an invalid."

"When would you go?"

"I'm thinking of taking the steamer south next month. Of course, you would have to run the hotel while I'm away. We could be married as soon as I return."

"I'll be so worried for you."

"I'll be in good hands," said Carl. "The Seattle hospital has a new machine called an X-Ray that can take a picture inside your head. They'll be able to see exactly where the bullet is before they operate."

And so it was settled. Elizabeth's emotions ranged from bliss to anxiety and back again as she went about her daily chores. Their friends were happy for them and they no longer needed to hide their affection.

"Why Elizabeth," said Mrs. Mathis upon hearing the news, "Ray and I were saying just the other day how well suited you two are for each other. And you won't even have to change your name."

"Thank you, I hadn't thought of that. I'll just be so glad when the surgery is over."

For Christmas, Elizabeth gave Carl an olive green sweater vest she had knitted with a very fine yarn. He slipped it on over his long-sleeved shirt. "It fits perfectly," he said. "How did you know my size?"

"I did a little snooping while you were recuperating and measured a sweater in your closet."

"This is for you," he said, handing her a small box from the Wheeler Drug & Jewelry Company.

It contained a jade ring with an Alaskan gold nugget mounted in the center of the dark green stone. The gold band was adorned with two gold leaves. "Carl, it's beautiful. I love it, but so extravagant!"

"We had a good season," he said. "And now that we're getting married, I can give you such gifts without setting tongues to wagging."

"Merry Christmas, my love."

"Merry Christmas."

Chapter 15

January 1919 – The Moose Lodge invited the entire town to a free "Hard Times Dance" at the Sons of Norway Hall on New Year's Eve. Everybody was instructed to wear old clothes. Elizabeth and Carl joined the crowd laughing at the antics of Dictator Jacob Otness as he presided over the "Yustice Court" where those who were inappropriately dressed were given a chance to explain themselves.

Everyone was caught in various offenses, ranging from wearing a white collar to contempt of court to having their hair combed. Those with unsatisfactory explanations were invited to enrich the treasury with donations ranging from two bits to a dollar and a half. Even the U.S. Marshal and the newspaper editor were fined. At the stroke of midnight, everyone stood and welcomed the new year by singing the "Star Spangled Banner."

A midnight supper of sandwiches, cold meats, fruit salad, cake, pie, waffles, fruit, nuts, tea and coffee was served in the lodge rooms upstairs. Dancing continued until well after Elizabeth and Carl had walked back to the hotel.

"Hello everybody, I'm back," a voice announced from the doorway. The men in the lobby all rose to welcome Charlie Greenaa home from Fort Seward.

Everyone talked at once while shaking the young man's hand and thumping him on the back.

"When did you get back?"

"Are you home for good?"

"You look like you could stand to gain a few pounds."

"We've been wondern' when they were gonna let you out."

Elizabeth hurried in from the kitchen upon hearing the commotion. Charlie stood tall in his uniform, grinning from ear to ear. Carl put his arm possessively around Elizabeth's shoulders. "Elizabeth and I are to be married," he boasted.

"Aw, you stole my girlfriend while I was away, you old fox," Charlie said, lifting Elizabeth off the floor for a big hug. He set her down with a wink and turned to the men clustered around him.

"Didn't think we were ever going to get home," he said. "We had to take the steamer all the way south to Ketchikan and then catch the *City of Seattle* back to Petersburg. Some of the other boys are with me too. Boy, it feels great to be home." The men followed Charlie out the door and trooped over to see Peter Jorgenson at the Sanitary Market.

Shrimp processor Earl Ohmer and Carl were deep in conversation in the corner of the lobby. Earl's attire of riding breeches, leather leggings and ten-gallon hat always amused Elizabeth. *A cowboy without a horse. How bizarre.*

"The boys got caught in rough weather at the entrance to Thomas Bay," Earl said. "It looks like they dropped anchor in deep water and tried to reach the beach but never made it. I've sent the *Kiseno* to join the search but we haven't found any sign of them yet."

"What happened?" Elizabeth asked after Earl left.

"Three men from the Van Vlack shrimping outfit at Thomas Bay are missing," said Carl. "They've been running a shrimp and salt salmon plant on barges there all summer. Their families are moving to town while they wait for word. Earl is hoping for better weather so more boats can join the search."

The Van Vlack women – two wives and a sister – moved into the hotel while the search continued. It was a somber group that awaited word of their husbands and brother. The search was called off after two weeks and most of the family left for their homes in the south.

Elizabeth and Carl peered out the window in the wharfinger's office at the *Admiral Watson* tied to the Citizen's Dock. "What happened to her windows?" asked Carl

"A big wave took out two windows in the main deck social hall crossing the gulf," replied wharfinger Allen.

Although larger than the *Jefferson* that brought Elizabeth to Alaska, she didn't have a good feeling about this ship. Wind-driven rain washed over her black hull as a handful of southbound passengers prepared to board.

"Don't worry," said Carl. "I'll wire you from Seattle as soon as I know anything. A few of the boys will be looking in on you and Charlie Greenaa's just a few doors down if you need anything."

"I'll be fine," Elizabeth said. "Take care of yourself and hurry home to me. I love you."

"I love you too."

After a quick kiss, he joined the passengers climbing the slippery gangplank in the deepening gloom. Elizabeth put on a bright smile to hide the tears as Carl waved from the deck of the departing ship.

The café was closed until the start of the new season and the hotel was practically empty. There wasn't much to do but keep it heated and cleaned. Carl's friends still congregated in the lobby in the afternoon and Elizabeth supplied them with coffee. Wharfinger Allen joined the group four days after the *Watson* sailed to tell her the ship encountered another mishap on her way south.

"She broke her crankshaft crossing Queen Charlotte Sound," he said. "Luckily, two other ships reached her before she drifted ashore and they towed her the rest of the way to Seattle. Just wanted you to know, Mrs. Roger, so you wouldn't worry none about Carl."

"Thank you, Sam, I appreciate it."

Elizabeth received a wire from Carl: "Arrived safely. Dr. Horton to do surgery tomorrow at Providence Hospital. Don't worry. Love, Carl."

Anna Holt stopped by to introduce her son recently arrived from the south. The men in the lobby monopolized him as soon as they learned he had been a gunner's mate on the *Martha Washington* during the war and made several trips through sub-infested waters in the Atlantic.

Anna pulled Elizabeth aside. "What do you hear from Carl?"

"Only that he's having the surgery," said Elizabeth. "Oh, I'm so worried, Anna."

"I'm sure he's in good hands," said Anna. "Waiting is the hardest part."

A wire finally arrived from Dr. Horton: "Carl Roger resting comfortably after two and one-half hour surgery. Confined to hospital for two weeks."

Elizabeth was so relieved that she ran across the street to Hogue and Tveten's to show the wire to Anna. "I told you everything would be all right," Anna smiled, giving Elizabeth a hug.

Suddenly, the winter weather was no longer oppressive. The church bell rang at noon every day so all could set their clocks to the correct time. With each ringing of the bell, Elizabeth counted off one more day until Carl's return.

A shipment of Gideon Bibles arrived and Elizabeth placed one in each room. The Petersburg Hotel did the same. The Gideons sent fifty additional Bibles to Seward purchased with donations collected in Petersburg.

Town bachelors held a dance at the Sons of Norway Hall. It was the last dance before the halibut fleet was to leave for the fishing grounds. All Red Cross knitting was stopped except for work in progress. The work rooms remained closed as the supply of knitting material ran out some time ago.

Henry Roden returned from Seattle to begin preparations at the Republic Fisheries' new cannery at Saginaw Bay. He didn't stay at the hotel this trip, rather with Mrs. Roden who was teaching school in Petersburg this term. Doctor Bulkley and his family moved to Kodiak where he assumed the position of company physician with a large fishing concern, leaving Petersburg without a doctor once more.

The Ketchikan term of court, postponed on account of the influenza epidemic, convened and the grand jury dismissed the charge of sedition against Jim Brennan. Everyone congratulated the proprietor of Brennan's Pool and Billiards for standing his ground against the outrages charges made by the assistant district attorney from Juneau. Even the jury could see the official had labeled Petersburg "pro-German" to cover up his own indiscretions in the red light district.

Elizabeth hurried from the kitchen when she heard the insistent ringing of the lobby bell. It was the town busybody, Mrs. Christensen. "Hello Mrs. Roger," she said, "I'm collecting for the Rechickening France Committee for the magazine."

"The what?" asked Elizabeth.

"The Rechickening France Committee. I'm the local agent for *McCall's Magazine*, you know. Each ten-cent piece I collect is used to buy one egg which is hatched to furnish a chicken to be placed in the barnyard of a poor French peasant who lost everything during the war."

Wisps of brown hair escaped the flowered head scarf knotted tightly beneath her chin. Her dark eyes darted about the lobby, searching for improprieties.

"Everyone who contributes to this worthy cause gets a membership in the Poultry Club of the American Committee for Rechickening France," she added.

Elizabeth gave her a dime to get rid of her.

The town lost power, again. The light plant rationed power from 6:00 to 8:30 a.m. and from 3:00 p.m. until midnight. Ladies were encouraged to refrain from using electric irons altogether. Without lighting, the streets were in total darkness most of the time.

Charlie Greenaa stopped in and said, "Looks like we're going to have to change our opening hours at the store until this fuel oil famine's over. Everyone's forced to get their work done in late afternoon and at night when the power's on."

"Do you think this will last very long?" Elizabeth asked.

" 'Fraid so," said Charlie. "The steamer with the town's oil shipment wired over from Wrangell asking if we could take a full shipment of 340 barrels. Since the town's tanks only hold 240 barrels, some square-headed genius on the town council said 'No,' so the steamer offloaded everything at Wrangell. We won't have another shipment for three weeks."

"And if they still bring more than we can store?" asked Elizabeth.

"We'll take it all and put any excess in the tanks at the Petersburg Packing Company. They should've thought of that in the first place."

Town merchants adjusted their operating hours to stay open later at night. The newspaper was late getting out; the Citizen's Steam Laundry worked nighttime hours; even the Bank of Petersburg stayed open late. Those merchants who were early risers appeared grumpy in the mornings due to lack of sleep from working well into the night. The few guests at the hotel took everything in stride and got by with oil lamps during the hours when power and light were withheld.

Elizabeth stood on the dock awaiting the arrival of the *City of Seattle* from the states. Carl's wire said he'd be aboard and several other Petersburg residents had also booked passage. The big ship finally made an appearance and was soon tied fast to the dock with the gangplank lowered.

Several of the town's prominent businessmen stepped off the boat, including the owners of the laundry, a pool hall, sawmill and a logging camp. Also on board were a former town marshal, former city councilman and the skipper of a Packing Company tender. Carl brought up the rear looking wan but smiling from ear to ear. He wore a small bandage above his right temple.

He smothered Elizabeth in his arms whispering, "It's so good to be home." He handed her a small package as they walked arm-in-arm up the long dock to Main Street.

"What's this?" Elizabeth asked.

"Open it."

The package contained a rough, flat metallic object about the size of a dime.

"It's the slug Dr. Horton took out of my brain," Carl said. "He said if it had been left unattended much longer, it would've killed me for sure. And I wouldn't have had it looked at if it weren't for you."

"Then I'll treasure this always. How are you feeling now?"

"Better than I've felt in a long time. Now, let's put a wedding together!"

They were married at the home of Doctor and Mrs. Mathis on Carl's thirty-seventh birthday. Commissioner John Allen performed the ceremony, but not before his daughter Mary played the "Wedding March" on the piano. This was one of the commissioner's last official acts before resigning his commission.

The forest ranger's wife, Mrs. James Allen, Anna Holt and Margaret Roden were also in attendance. The happy group enjoyed delicious refreshments after the ceremony. Elizabeth thought about her wedding nearly five years earlier and decided she preferred the genuine friendships in this small Alaska town to the hollow spectacle of a big wedding among strangers.

Their friends escorted them along the boardwalk back to the hotel. A Canadian steamer glided down the Narrows, taking advantage of a high tide to use the faster, inside route on its way south. The captain gave three blasts of the whistle as he sailed past the town. The ship was lit up like a Christmas tree almost as bright as the stars dancing overhead.

Carl insisted on carrying Elizabeth over the threshold into the manager's quarters that were to be their new home. He deposited her on the bed bathed in moonlight streaming through the small window. "I hope you don't miss having your family from Evanston here for our wedding," he said.

"Not at all. In fact, I think I prefer having you all to myself."

They undressed and slipped beneath the covers. Her head fit perfectly in the hollow of his shoulder as she ran her fingers across his smooth chest. Carl had a slow hand and she shivered with pleasure at his caresses. The bedsprings creaked in cadence and for a fleeting moment Elizabeth was glad they were on the ground floor. Then, she had no thoughts at all, just the all encompassing feeling of sheer joy.

They laid entwined while their hearts stopped racing. "You're exhausting," he teased.

"You take my breath away," Elizabeth replied.

"Carl, I understand you had a front row seat for the labor union strife in Seattle," said editor Perkins.

"That I did," Carl replied. "From my hospital window, I saw thousands of men march down Stewart Street on their way to police headquarters. They were singing I.W.W. songs and chanting, 'The Bolsheviki are all right.' Caused quite a stir and they came very close to shutting down the city. They tied up every car on the Puget Sound Electric Company and many of the better restaurants closed for fear of being struck. The strikers wanted to shut down all the industries and reopen them under the management of labor."

"Why was the strike called off?" asked one of the lobby regulars.

"The labor union bosses came to their senses after Seattle's mayor threatened to deputize ten thousand civilians to protect life and property," said Carl.

"And what about the strike organizers?"

"Turns out, one of the organizers was sent to Seattle from Siberia to incite a revolution. He'd been in this country less than a year. All the I.W.Ws were rounded up and sent on a special train to New York where they will be deported to Europe. Good riddance, I say."

"We've had a little labor organizing in Petersburg while you were away," said editor Perkins.

"How's that?" asked Carl.

"A group of men got together and formed a Deep Sea Fisherman's Union. They have their own union hall and meet every Tuesday. They even opened a town library and somebody donated a set of encyclopedias."

"Unions must be the latest rage then," said Carl.

March roared in like a lion. Fierce winds and rain delayed Hogue & Tveten's mail boat *Trygve* on her return from the Kake run. Because of the especially rough trip, the men stayed in port an extra day before setting out again.

Carl slapped his wet hat against his thigh before entering the lobby. "I was just over to the steamship office," he said. "Sounds like they're expecting a busy summer."

"What did they have to say?" Elizabeth asked.

"Northbound steamers are sold out three months in advance. Hundreds of people are being turned away from Seattle steamship offices every day."

"Has Alaska finally been discovered, then?" asked Elizabeth. "Or are there just not as many steamers as before?"

"They're filling them with returning cannery crews and all those people who left last fall looking for better jobs," said Carl. "Instead, they found lower wages in the states, so they're coming back. The boats are also filled with discharged enlisted men who want to try their luck in Alaska. All these traveling people will be good for the hotel, that's for sure."

Editor Perkins informed the men in the lobby that Charles Sulzer had ousted Judge James Wickersham as Alaska's Delegate to Congress. "Sulzer won by a margin of only thirty-three votes," he said.

"So the judge will be leaving Washington?" asked one of the men.

"Not likely," replied Perkins. "If I know Wickersham, he'll contest the election and probably win, too."

"What's going on with the legislature in Juneau?" asked another, puffing on his pipe.

"Seems the territory's requesting Congress pass a law prohibiting the killing of whales in Alaskan waters," responded Perkins.

"That'll put the whaling station over at Port Armstrong out of business," said Charlie Greenaa.

"For sure," said the first man. "But you have to ask yourself. What returns the most profit? An occasional whale or all the herring you can catch when the whales force the herring close to shore?"

Elizabeth gathered from the grunts and nods that the men preferred the latter.

Steamers carrying freight and passengers arrived from the south with greater frequency. Cannery bosses and pile driving crews were the first to arrive. Seafood processors prepared for a busy season rebuilding their plants, adding more canning lines and extending operations to include other types of seafood. The *City of Seattle* arrived with 254 passengers, including crews for outlying canneries. The *Admiral Evans*, wrecked at Hawk Inlet over a year ago, made her first trip north after being completely rebuilt from the main deck up. The town took on an almost festive air as newcomers and old-timers alike bustled about preparing for the season.

"Elizabeth, you'll never guess who I saw over at the post office this morning," said Carl.

"Who?"

"Julius Reese. He's back in town after spending time in Seattle. It was good to see him again. He wants to stop by and congratulate us on getting married."

"You're a very forgiving man, Carl Roger," said Elizabeth. "He almost killed you."

"He never really meant me any harm. It was just the booze that made him shoot at me. He was so relived when I told him the doctor removed the last piece of bullet from my brain, I thought he was going to cry."

"He's lucky you're such a good friend," said Elizabeth. "I'll try to be civil to him."

The very next day, Julius appeared in the hotel doorway. He looked quite presentable in a dark business suit, hat in hand. His hair had turned white and he somehow appeared shorter than Elizabeth remembered.

"Julius, come on in," Carl said, beckoning him to a chair. "I think you know everyone."

Before acknowledging the other men, Julius crossed the lobby to where Elizabeth stood behind the counter. Extending his hand, he said, "Mrs. Roger, I hope you'll accept my apologies for my bad behavior the last time we met. I also want to congratulate you on marrying my former partner. Carl is a very lucky man."

He looked so miserably sincere that Elizabeth softened as she accepted his apology. "And what brings you back to Petersburg?" she asked.

"Well, I looked all around Puget Sound and didn't find anything to my liking, so I've decided to make my home here. Petersburg's a growing seaport and I always liked the people."

"And," he continued, "I brought the newlyweds a little token of my esteem." He handed Elizabeth a box he'd kept hidden behind his back.

Elizabeth was chagrined accepting his gift, but there was no graceful way out of it with the men in the lobby looking on. "Why Julius," she said, "you didn't have to get us anything."

"But I wanted to," he replied. "Jim Wheeler told me you'd been admiring these in his shop window, so I hope you like them."

The package contained two delicately shaped bone China cups and saucers. Tiny blue forget-me-nots were hand painted on a milky white background. "Wheeler told me that's the official flower adopted by the territorial legislature," he said.

"They're beautiful," said Elizabeth. "Thank you so much, and thank you for your thoughtfulness. Carl and I will enjoy many cups of coffee in these on special occasions."

Julius rejoined the men and Elizabeth took his gift to the manager's quarters, hoping he would retain his more civilized demeanor.

Elizabeth missed her menses for two months and dearly hoped it meant she was in a family way. She hadn't thought too much about missing the first month, given the excitement of Carl's successful surgery and their wedding. And she'd never been that regular anyway. But missing a second month together with morning nausea must surely mean a baby was on the way. With no doctor to consult, she confided in Anna Holt.

The older woman clapped her hands in glee. "When did the nausea begin?" she asked.

"About three weeks ago," said Elizabeth. "It's worse first thing in the morning and when I catch a whiff of a strange odor."

"Oh Elizabeth, you're going to have a baby. You must tell Carl right away, eat soda crackers and drink ginger tea for the morning sickness."

That night in bed, Elizabeth turned to Carl and said, "You're going to be a Daddy."

"What? Oh, Elizabeth, that's wonderful," he said, hugging her tightly and then releasing her quickly, fearing he'd been too rough.

"I won't break," she laughed. "What do you hope for – a little girl or a little boy?"

"It doesn't matter, as long as he or she is healthy," he said.

"I think a baby girl would be nice," Elizabeth sighed.

"As long as she looks just like her mother," he said, cupping her chin for a kiss. And then, "Elizabeth, I don't want you to have a baby in a town with no doctor. I couldn't stand it if anything should happen to you."

"What do you suggest?" she asked.

"When you get closer to your due date, but still able to travel, you should take the steamer south to your family in Evanston and have the baby there where they have good doctors."

"But you wouldn't be with me for the birth."

"I know," said Carl, "but I would give that up for the comfort of knowing you were in good hands. And you could return to Petersburg as soon as the baby is old enough to travel."

The prospect of seeing her family again was appealing. And Elizabeth was a little worried about having a first child at the age of thirty-two without a physician in attendance. She agreed to write to Mamma and Papa with the news when she was a little further along.

They were jolted awake when the building started to roll from side to side. "Quick," said Carl. "It's an earthquake. Stand in the doorway."

They clutched the sides of the doorway to the kitchen and watched in amazement as dishes flew from the cupboards and shattered on the floor. The tremor lasted about a minute but they waited a little longer before venturing into the room to survey the damage.

"Looks like just a few pieces are broken," Carl said. "I'll see to the guests while you sweep up this mess."

An aftershock sent Elizabeth and her broom back to the safety of the doorway, but it wasn't as frightening as the first shaking. She put the coffee pot on as guests filed into the kitchen. Like Elizabeth, several had never experienced an earthquake before.

"Morning folks," said a gregarious young man. "I was coming home from the big dance when I was almost knocked on my keister. And I didn't even have a nip of the home brew they was passing around the cloak room. Saw your light on. Is that coffee you got brewing?"

The young man joined the guests as everyone recounted the events of the night. Elizabeth never did get his name. Carl returned and reported everything was in order with the other guests and just a few pictures had jolted off the walls in the lobby.

Chapter 16

April 1919 – "Afternoon, Mrs. Roger, is Carl about?" asked Charlie Greenaa.

"He had to run an errand but should be back shortly," she said. "Charlie, I was just reading this nice letter you wrote in the *Report* thanking everyone for patronizing the Sanitary Market while you were in the service."

"Just wanted everyone to know how much appreciated their business is. And we'll be able to do a much better job at the store now that we're back to full staff."

"And I see the new town council elected your boss as mayor," Elizabeth continued.

"Pete's the right man for the job," said Charlie. "They got a lot of work ahead of them, what with getting us a better light plant, widening Main Street, installing a better sewer system and building enough houses for all these newcomers. Just hope I don't have to address him as 'Hiz Honor'," he laughed.

Carl joined the other merchants in restarting the town's Commercial Club. New officers included the druggist, the manager of the lumber mill, the bank's cashier and the owner of the largest mercantile store.

"Why do we need a commercial club?" Elizabeth asked Carl.

"To do the things the town council doesn't do to bring new business to town and keep the community growing," he replied.

"And what is the club going to do to bring in new business?" continued Elizabeth.

"Well, we've drafted a resolution to dredge Wrangell Narrows and sent it to all elected officials in the territory and our delegate in Washington."

"How will dredging the Narrows be good for business?" she asked.

"It'll let steamers that are too big to go through the Narrows stop here and avoid the longer, more dangerous trips in the open waters around the outside of Kuiu Island. Some smaller steamers can only use the Narrows when the tide is in, so it will help them to have deeper water too. We also hope the towns to the north will get behind our resolution because the steamers will reach them more quickly and at less cost if they can use the Wrangell Narrows route."

"How often will the Narrows have to be dredged to keep it open for large ships?" asked Elizabeth.

"That's the funny thing about these waters," said Carl. "Money will only have to be spent once for dredging. After that, the tide will keep the channel clear."

Doctor Mathis returned from Wrangell where he'd been practicing dentistry for several weeks and reopened his office at the hotel. He brought news that the Wilson-Sylvester sawmill was up and running again after burning down last year. The town had almost died when it lost its chief industry. Also arriving on the steamer from Wrangell was Doctor Upton who was considering moving his practice to Petersburg. The town had been without a doctor for five months. Carl still insisted that Elizabeth have their baby in Evanston, pointing out that none of the medical men stayed very long and there was no guarantee there would be a doctor available when the baby came.

Fred Patten returned from the south for the fishing season and stopped by the hotel for a visit. "I tell you, Carl," he said, "I've half a mind to go into fox farming instead of fishing."

"Why is that?"

"There's lots of money to be made in fox pelts," said Fred. "Why, did you know, that fella running the Sukoi Island fox ranch north of town just got $185 a pelt for thirty-eight blue fox pelts he shipped to London? And he got another $110 a pelt for the ten blues he shipped to St. Louis."

"That's a lot of money," Carl said.

"You bet it is. And it's a good way to make a living. Build a little cabin, plant a vegetable garden in the summer and live off the land and the sea in the winter."

"How does he raise the foxes?" Elizabeth asked. "Does he have sheds full of cages? And what do they eat?"

"Nah, they run wild on the island," said Fred. "Can't get away 'cause it's too far to swim to the mainland. He's got over a hundred breeding pair. They dig dens and hole up in the wintertime and come out to eat the feed he puts out on the dock. In winter he feeds them mostly fish he's caught for them. And in summer, he adds some cooked cereals to their feed. They also eat rodents and anything else they catch in the woods. He takes the pelts in the wintertime when they're at their prime. He's getting large litters of pups too and expects an even bigger fur shipment next winter."

"Sounds like a good business to get into," said Carl. "Do you really think you're going to try it?"

"Sure would like to," said Fred. "A fella can make a real fine living as long as the price of furs holds."

"The Cleary brothers just sent a shipment of lumber and supplies to build smoke houses, living quarters and store houses at their new fox farm on Strait Island," he continued. "And another group of greenhorns just got a permit to place stock on Channel Island about fifteen miles from Wrangell. The thing is, the water's so shallow over there that it sometimes freezes up in the winter and all their livestock can escape across the ice to the mainland. Guess they don't know about that."

"Isn't somebody going to tell them?" asked Elizabeth.

"Nah, we'd rather wait and watch all the fun."

The Baltimore Grill offered a one-dollar dinner on the last Sunday in April. The latest manager and his wife arrived from the south where he had been a caterer. Elizabeth and Carl stopped by to see what the competition had to offer before Carl reopened the Wester Café for the season.

The dinner began with shrimp salad or chicken with rice soup. Five entrees were offered: fried steel head trout, fricasseed chicken with rice, pot roast with corn fritters, roast chicken and dressing or roast pork and applesauce. Entrees came with vegetable, mashed potatoes or stewed corn. Dessert was sliced pineapple cake with coffee, tea, chocolate or Postum.

"Carl, how can they possibly offer such an extensive menu for only one dollar?" Elizabeth asked.

"They can't," said Carl. "This is just a one-time occasion designed to get people in the door. If they only charged a dollar for this menu every day, they wouldn't stay in business for long."

A young Chinese cannery worker stood in the hotel doorway wringing his hands. "Please," he said, "marshal here?"

Deputy Cornstad rose and walked toward him. "Something wrong?" he asked.

"You come quick . . . China house . . . 'ver bad."

The two men ran through the rain toward the Packing Company dock, followed by several of the lobby regulars.

Carl left Elizabeth in charge and joined the crowd forming at the steps to the Chinese mess hall. He finally returned after what seemed like hours, shaking his head and muttering under his breath.

"What's going on?" Elizabeth asked.

"A brutal murder," he said. "The wife of the Chinese foreman of the Packing Company. There's blood everywhere."

"That pretty little Mrs. Mar Kim?" Elizabeth said.

"Yes, and her three-year-old daughter."

"What?" said Elizabeth. "Who did it?"

"They don't know yet," said Carl. "The man who watches the children while Mrs. Kim prepares the noon meal found them lying in a pool of blood on the mess house floor. It looks like they were beaten to death with a hand ax."

"But why?"

"They don't know that either," said Carl. "She was still wearing her rings and locket, so robbery wasn't the motive. Mar Kim is heartbroken. He says he didn't know he or his wife had any enemies and there's been no trouble with the Chinese cannery crew this summer. A coroner's jury has been empaneled to make an investigation."

The town buzzed with news of the tragedy. Mar Kim was highly regarded by the locals and an effective boss of the Chinese cannery crews. When their little boy was born in Petersburg last fall, his birth was announced as the first full-blood Chinese baby to be born in Alaska.

After the coroner's jury completed its investigation, the Japanese bookkeeper of the Packing Company was taken into custody by newly appointed U.S. Commissioner M. S. Perkins and special deputy Peter Cornstad and held on an open charge.

Mar Kim took the bodies of his wife and daughter south for burial. He also took the baby boy to leave with relatives in the south. He said he expected to return to Petersburg in about three weeks.

"Have you heard the news?" asked editor Perkins. "Our delegate to congress, Charles Sulzer, died at his copper mine in Sulzer."

"What happened?" asked Carl.

"We don't have the details yet, just that he died suddenly," said the newspaperman and new commissioner. "He was only forty years old and hadn't even taken his seat in Congress yet."

"Does this mean that Judge Wickersham will now take his place?"

"No," said Perkins. "The judge still intends to contest the last election that Sulzer won by thirty-three votes. I think Congress now has to call a special election to fill Sulzer's seat. Wickersham says he won't run in that election – he still thinks he can prove chicanery in his contest with Sulzer and get in that way."

Carl awakened Elizabeth at 3:00 a.m. for a day of shrimping at Thomas Bay. Their footsteps were muffled as they walked through the dark, fog-shrouded town to the Citizen's Dock.

"There you are," said Earl Ohmer. "The boat's all warmed up and ready to go."

All that could be seen of the boat was a mast poking above the end of the dock.

"Tide's out," said Earl. "Mrs. Roger, you can either climb down the ladder or we can lower you in the supply bucket with the winch."

"I'll take my chances with the ladder, thanks."

The wooden ladder stretched straight down into total darkness where the *Kiseno* was tied to the pilings. The bottom part of the ladder disappeared into the black water. Carl positioned himself on the ladder and motioned Elizabeth to climb on. They crab-stepped down into the wet darkness in tandem, passing pilings encrusted with barnacles and mussels. Near the bottom, Carl stepped onto the boat's railing, lifted her off the slippery ladder and deposited her on deck. Earl scrambled down the ladder with no effort at all.

Earl helped the deckhand cast off and the skipper pointed the bow into the Narrows, heading north. Houses along the shoreline were dark at this early hour, the rocky beach exposed by the low tide. Sitting at the galley table, Elizabeth noticed the cupboards and cabinets had locks on them and metal railings criss-crossed the galley stove top to hold the coffee pot in place during rough weather.

Carl left the men smoking their pipes in the dimmed pilot house and made his way down the companionway to the galley. "Elizabeth," he said, "it'll take a couple hours to reach the shrimp grounds. Why don't you climb into a bunk and get some sleep while we're under way?"

She pulled a rough sleeping bag up to her shoulders and let the engine's rhythmic cadence lull her to sleep. The sleeping bag smelled of salt air and engine grease.

Elizabeth awakened to the aroma of pancakes, bacon and eggs frying on the galley stove. It was light out as the men lowered the trawl into the cold deep water. Elizabeth hadn't paid much attention to it in the darkness but now she could see the trawl was a log as long as a light pole draped with netting. On each end of the log was an iron horseshoe-shaped affair to keep the net open as the log was dragged along the bottom. The boat listed sharply to one side as the trawl was suspended over the railing and then righted itself when the trawl was lowered beneath the water.

The deckhand took wheel duty while everyone else enjoyed breakfast. The boat crept forward, slowly dragging the trawl along the muddy bottom. Breakfast was delicious but the coffee was twice as strong as any Elizabeth had ever had. The men didn't object when Elizabeth insisted on washing the dishes.

The fog lifted, revealing a sunny day and calm seas. Seagulls followed the boat, waiting for the trawl to be raised. The skipper dropped a metal bucket over the side and hauled it aboard by the rope attached to the pail's handle. "Mrs. Roger, if you want to use the head, you can use this water for flushing," he said, placing the bucket of water on the floor of the tiny facility.

"Why thank you," said Elizabeth.

Elizabeth closed the door behind her and stood facing a funnel shaped, rusty commode. From deep within the plumbing she could hear the ocean lapping at the outlet pipe at the ship's water line. There was barely room to turn around and there was no way she was going to sit on the cold, smelly contraption. She took care of her chores standing over it, bracing against the walls to keep her balance as the boat rocked in the swells. She supposed the men used the railing when a woman wasn't on board. In fact, they were probably doing just that while she was in the head. She smoothed her clothes and emptied the bucket of sea water into the gaping hole.

Elizabeth and Carl stood on the deck, backs against the cabin wall, as the men prepared to raise the trawl. The boat tipped dangerously toward the side where the trawl would appear as wet rope fed through squeaking pulleys. Dripping with brown kelp and green seaweed, the trawl broke the surface just as Elizabeth was certain the boat would tip over, spilling them all into the cold water. The men lashed the trawl alongside and used a long-handled dip net to transfer the catch onto a sorting table in the center of the deck. Then, they lowered the trawl and began another hour-long drag for more shrimp.

Elizabeth and Card donned rubber aprons and thick rubber gloves as Earl instructed them in sorting shrimp. The wriggling pink mass contained not only shrimp but every other sea creature the trawl retrieved from the bottom. "These are spots," said Earl. "They're the biggest shrimp and there won't be very many of them. See these two white spots on their back? They go into this tote on my right. And these are sidestripes. They have long white stripes on their sides. They go into this other tote. We get higher prices for spots and stripes. And all the other shrimp go into the other totes. The small salad shrimp will be separated at the cannery."

They set to work, exclaiming on all the strange creatures mixed in with the shrimp. Hundreds of screeching seagulls swarmed around the boat, diving for scrap fish they tossed overboard. Earl pointed out spiny-finned Irish Lords and straight-spined sea horses with yellow mustaches. One tiny fish was perfectly round like a small grey ball. It had bumps on its surface like a pineapple and when placed in a bucket of water, swam in circles before adhering to the side of the pail with some sort of suction appendage. They caught many legged starfish and prickly sea urchins. They discarded all but the largest Dungeness crabs and one good sized halibut. When one wooden tote was full, the men lugged it by rope handles to the poop deck and returned with an empty. Elizabeth wondered how the raised deck at the stern of the boat got its name, but she wasn't about to ask.

Many shrimp had clusters of brownish-orange eggs attached to their abdomens. Earl explained that all shrimp began life as males and then transformed into females for the remainder of their lives. Elizabeth wasn't sure if she believed this or if he was just pulling her leg.

Their labors were interrupted by the toot of a boat whistle and they looked up to see the *White Bear* passing their shrimping operation. "Jack Hadland's boat," said Earl. "Looks like he's got a big party on board."

"Oh, I remember now," said Elizabeth. "That's Mrs. Roden and her seventh and eighth graders. She mentioned they were going to have a class picnic at Thomas Bay today." Everyone waved and Elizabeth had the honor of pulling the whistle cord in an answering hello.

Earl drew another bucket of sea water, tossed in several scoops of sidestripes and placed the entire affair on the galley stove. They shed their oil skins and sat in the sun on the poop deck, enjoying the beautiful day as they continued to drag the trawl across the bottom. Bald eagles ventured out from the mainland in search of easy fishing. A few dazzling blue-white ice bergs drifted by with seagulls perched on their melting ridges.

"Are the fishing boats ever damaged by the ice bergs?" Elizabeth asked.

"Very seldom," said Earl. "Everyone knows that two thirds of the berg is under water and good skippers give them a wide berth. These ones are pretty small. Sometimes you'll see a seal or two hauled out on the ice."

Earl retrieved the steaming bucket of boiled shrimp from the galley stove. He poured off the water and placed the bucket on the deck. "Here's how you do this," he said. "First, you grab a shrimp, twist off the head and throw the head overboard. Then you pinch the tail like this and that forces the shrimp meat out of the shell. Now plop it in your mouth for the most delicious treat you've ever tasted."

Elizabeth and Carl followed his example and feasted on the succulent delicacy requiring no salt or butter, seasoned entirely by natural salt water. The shrimp tasted heavenly and they all made pigs of themselves. "These are the finest shrimp in the world," Earl said. "The shrimp you get from the Gulf of Mexico have a sand vein that has to be removed unless you want to bite down on grit. But these cold water northern shrimp have no sand vein and much more flavor."

"How do you process them at the cannery?" Carl asked.

"We give them a first cooking and pass them over to a line of pickers, mostly native women and Philippinos," said Earl. "Boy, can they pick shrimp. They get paid by the pound and their fingers just fly. Shrimp are easier to shell after they've been cooked a little. Next, we give them a second cooking and then re-clean them to remove any pieces of shell or whiskers. Then we pack them in five pound cans which we either keep in ice or cold storage and ship them south to market."

"How many shrimp do you process each day?" asked Carl.

"We prepare about a ton of shrimp for market every day," replied Earl. "That's about what the boys at the Van Vlack Company process too. We're using the quarters they used last year on the approach to the Citizen's Dock and they've moved to a warehouse the Marathon Packing Company used last summer."

They made two more sets before the men lashed the big trawl to the railing and headed for port. The deck was piled high with totes filled with pink shellfish. Cannery workers were waiting at the dock and began offloading the day's catch even before Elizabeth and Carl had left the boat. The tide was in and they could step right off the boat onto the dock. They thanked Earl, his skipper and deckhand for a very enjoyable day and walked back to the hotel with a gunny sack full of freshly caught shrimp.

The town bustled with activity. Carl reopened the Wester Café and attracted a large lunch and dinner crowd. "Just look at this advertisement in the *Report*," Elizabeth said, pointing to an ad for the New York Restaurant. "It says, 'Everything of the best in Season.' That's our slogan for the Hotel Wester and Wester Café."

"I guess Sammy Nakamoto approves of our slogan," Carl replied.

Christian Wester arrived on a steamer filled with seasonal workers. Elizabeth and Carl hadn't seen him since that morning in Seattle when they were leaving for Petersburg. "Congratulations on your marriage, Mrs. Roger," he said. "And I understand you're starting a family."

"Why, thank you."

Elizabeth blushed when he told Carl, "You don't waste much time young man."

The two men moved to a corner table and spoke, heads together, in hushed tones. Later, Carl told Elizabeth about their conversation.

"Chris is well pleased with the business we're doing," he said, "but he's here to see if he can scare up a buyer for the hotel and café."

"Why would he want to sell if we're doing so well?" asked Elizabeth.

"I guess he's been away so long that he got used to the easy living down below and just wants to cash in his Alaska holdings," said Carl. "He asked if I would be interested in buying the business."

"What did you tell him?"

"That I might be interested if he would front me a loan. He said he might be inclined to do that."

"What would happen to us if he sells to somebody else?" asked Elizabeth.

"That depends. If he sells to an absentee owner like himself, they would still need to hire a manager to run things. If he sells to somebody who also wants to run the operation, we would probably be out of a job. We may have to join Fred Patten in setting up a fox farm on an island somewhere," he joked.

"What are you going to do?" asked Elizabeth.

"I'm going to take Chris up on his offer if the price is right. This is our home now and we're here for the long haul."

The summer months seemed to race by. Elizabeth no longer suffered from morning sickness and marveled each time she felt the baby move. Carl said she positively glowed.

The Petersburg Readywear Store opened in the Gauffin Building. The proprietor, Mr. Bender, stocked it with clothing and shoes for ladies, men and children. Shortly thereafter, the Stoft and Refling store filed to dissolve their business, offering all merchandise at reduced prices for cash only. Elizabeth wondered if the two events were related.

The Fourth of July was a rainy affair. A collection taken up among the merchants paid for prizes to winners of the sporting events and supplies for a vaudeville show and dance at the Sons of Norway Hall. The main sporting event, a tug-of- war between the loggers and fishermen, was won by the loggers.

Elizabeth eavesdropped on the men in the café as they discussed salvaging the steamer *Mariposa*.

"She went ashore on Strait Island nearly two years ago," said one of the men. "The salvage outfit being towed to the site plans to live aboard while they take the cargo out and then refloat her."

"What's her cargo?" asked another.

"Copper ore from the Kennecott mine and the ship's donkey engine."

"If the salvage crew is going to live aboard, they'll have one leg longer than the other by the end of summer," said the first man.

"Why is that?"

" 'Cause the stern is under water," he replied. "Only the bow is livable."

Commissioner Perkins joined the men. "The governor just assigned a cruiser and another sub chaser to Alaskan waters to suppress the epidemic of fish trap piracy," he said.

"It's about time," said one of the men. "Why, you take your life in your hands being a trap watchman these days. All you can do is stand by while the trap is being robbed, otherwise you'll get shot."

"I hear fish pirates fired over a hundred shots into a cannery tender in Chatham Strait, standing the tender off until they finished lifting a trap and making their getaway," said another.

"The skippers of the *Marblehead* and sub chaser *239* are under orders to show no mercy to anyone caught stealing fish from a trap," replied Perkins. "They hope this will curb the thievery."

The manager of the Arness Lumber Company joined the men with news of a big lumber contract. "Just got a wire from Olaf Arness," he said. "He's landed a big contract to deliver rough timber to Australia. The Aussies want three million feet this season, six million feet next season and ten million feet each year for five years after that."

"That'll put Petersburg on the map as a major lumber producer," said Commissioner Perkins. "Can the loggers produce that much timber?"

"Olaf plans to double the size of the mill and put on a double shift immediately," said manager Otness. "He's in Seattle buying equipment and hiring more men. The payroll will be good for the town, that's for sure."

"How does he plan to get the lumber to Australia?" asked one of the men.

"The cut logs will be rafted to Scow Bay where oceangoing steamers anchored in the stream there will load the timbers over the sides of the ships," replied Otness.

"What do the Aussies want the timber for?" asked another man.

"They'll re-saw the timbers and make them into butter boxes," said Otness. "They need a nonresinous wood for that and spruce is the ideal timber. They've been getting their wood from Finland, but that source of supply has been cut off since the war."

"That's a lot of butter boxes," said another man.

Earl Ohmer walked into the café with a fistful of cigars. "Loyla just had the baby," he said proudly. "A boy. He's so big he'll be down ordering the shrimp pickers around the cannery in no time."

Carl smiled at Elizabeth across the room as everyone congratulated Earl.

Elizabeth, Approximately Four Years Old, Norra Ljunga (Jönköping, Sweden) circa 1891

Elizabeth's Wedding, Evanston IL, April 6, 1912
Bottom Row: Elizabeth and Albert, Far Left
Top Row: Uncle Emil and Julia, Far Right

Papa's Family, Evanston, IL circa 1916
Bottom Row: Ruth, Mamma, Paul, Papa, Alice
Top Row: John, Elmer, Julia, Helen Ida, Elizabeth, Karl, Clarence

Steamship Arrival, Petersburg, Alaska 1890-1920

Alaska State Library, William R. Norton Photograph Collection

W. H. Case, P226-371

Petersburg Independence Day Celebration, circa 1910-1917
"Fat Man's Race" Finishes in Front of Hotel Wester
Photo Courtesy of Jim Brennan

Elizabeth as "Fox Island Princess," circa 1922

Elizabeth's Girls – Betty and June, circa 1924

Carl, Elizabeth and First Grandchild, Lester White
at the Log House, circa 1945

Chapter 17

August 1919 – Mr. and Mrs. Roden came into the café for a late dinner. Afterward, Margaret and Elizabeth visited while the men retired to the kitchen for home brew and Limburger cheese.

"Henry's going to return to practicing law in Juneau," said Margaret.

"I thought he was busy with the cannery at Saginaw Bay," Elizabeth replied.

"They're expanding the cannery but don't expect to be ready for canning before the 1920 season," said Margaret. "They'll stay with salting operations this season, but that doesn't require much of his time."

"Why doesn't he open a law office in Petersburg?" asked Elizabeth.

"He's so well known in Juneau because of his work with the senate and there's more business there. Plus, he's got an opportunity to take over the law practice of an attorney who recently passed away. He'll have a partner too, a young man named Dawes."

"And what about you?" asked Elizabeth.

"I've already agreed to return to teach fifth and sixth grades in the fall. The school board is looking for space for us since the rooms used last year are not available. There will be five teachers in all, including the new principal who will also teach seventh and eighth grades."

"Is the condition of the school buildings really as bad as everyone says?" asked Elizabeth.

"Probably worse," said Margaret. "We're teaching one hundred pupils in three different buildings with poor lighting, bad sanitary conditions and inadequate gymnasium and playground facilities. We do the best we can but we really need that new school house the town council keeps talking about."

"And where does that stand?"

"Last I heard, it's a question of getting Congress to give the town permission to issue bonds for building a school house and hydro electric plant. I think they're just waiting for Congress to act. Be sure to tell Carl to vote for the bonding bill whenever they hold a special election."

"I will," said Elizabeth. "What are you planning to do over the summer?"

"Go to Juneau and set up housekeeping for Henry. We've lived there before, you know. It's a busy place, especially when the legislature's in session."

Anna Holt pulled Elizabeth aside at Hogue and Tveten's where she was shopping for pink yarn for baby clothes. "Elizabeth, I've decided to move up north," said Anna.

"Where will you go?"

"I've heard good things about Valdez and decided to move there. My son Alden is moving south to locate in the Puget Sound area. But I prefer less civilized surroundings. Even Petersburg is getting too crowded for my tastes."

"What will you do there?" asked Elizabeth.

"I'll find a job like the one I have here or maybe work for the post office there," said Anna. "I'm told it's in fjord country like Petersburg and also has an ice-free port so steamers can bring in supplies year-round. And they get a lot less rain."

"I will miss you but wish you the best of good luck," said Elizabeth, giving her friend a hug.

"Oh, I'll write," said Anna. "And I want to hear everything about that new baby you'll be bringing home."

"You'll never guess what they want the town merchants to do now," said Carl, returning from a Commercial Club meeting.

"What?" asked Elizabeth.

"Let a committee review our books to make sure we're not making an obscene profit," he fumed.

"Why?"

"It's part of President Wilson's hunt for fraud and profiteering in connection with the high cost of living. Anyone found guilty of profiteering will face criminal charges. Councilman Tveten, Pete Swanson with the fisherman's union and Mrs. Erickson will investigate local merchants and stores. Another committee will investigate seafood markets and the local canneries."

"What do we need to do?" asked Elizabeth.

"Not very much," said Carl. "Just open the books to the committee when they come by. I'm sure they're not going to find any evidence of profiteering among local merchants. In fact, some things sell cheaper here than in Seattle. I'm just disgusted that everyone in this town already knows everybody's business and this will make it even worse."

The profiteering committees conducted their investigations during two weeks when the power was off while machinists realigned the engines and generator at the power plant. Carl seated them at the corner table next to the front window where the light was best. Chris Tveten quickly reached the conclusion there was no evidence of profiteering at the Hotel Wester and Wester Café and told Carl they hadn't found any wrongdoing among the other merchants either.

Three weeks of good weather brought out every painter in town. Two coats of red paint were applied to all the buildings of the Petersburg Packing Company. The Bank of Petersburg was painted an attractive grey with white trim before the painting crew moved on to Brennan's building. Several residences also received new paint and the whole town took on a new and prosperous appearance.

Elizabeth and Carl were busy at the hotel despite a slower than hoped for fishing season. Among the guests was Miss Marjorie Mason, advance agent for Ellison-White's Chautauqua. Editor Perkins published a glowing editorial of the traveling Chautauqua movement, claiming it stood next to the press in molding public opinion and next to the church and school in its work for the common good. This year's sixteen-member troupe included the Cravens Concert Company, the Serbian Tamburica Orchestra and storyteller and orator Captain Wood Briggs. The Cravens family sings, performs drama and plays the cornet, saxophone, piano, violin and xylophone. The Captain delivers lectures on "The Making of a Man." Elizabeth and Carl sold tickets at the hotel along with the other merchant boosters of Petersburg's Chautauqua Committee. Elizabeth was disappointed she would miss the September event.

Another hotel guest was well-known traveling salesman Sidney Jacobs, representing Premium brand hams and bacon for Swift and Company. Carl let him use the kitchen range to demonstrate his products for town merchants. Several other guests awaited passage on congested southbound steamers. Elizabeth was glad she'd arranged her mid-August passage several months earlier.

Elizabeth left Petersburg on a beautiful fall day that was picture postcard perfect. Carl waved from the dock as the *Admiral Evans* headed out into the Narrows. Seagulls floated high above in the gentle breeze. Everywhere Elizabeth looked was blue – blue sky, blue water, even snowless blue mountains above the tree line. The town appeared tidy and prosperous with the Packing Company's bright red buildings, newly painted homes and businesses, and sparkling white fishing boats bobbing in the harbor.

They sailed past the Arness lumber mill, idled for several weeks while the owner completed his Australian lumber contract, and the newly painted tanks of the Standard Oil plant. Scow Bay soon came into view. Elizabeth could almost smell the new lumber on the facing of the cold storage plant. Signs of civilization soon were replaced by deserted beaches piled high with driftwood timber. Thick pine forests loomed over the beaches. Bald eagles perched on the broken limbs of beached logs, gorging on spawning salmon plucked from shallow creeks. She wondered why they're called "bald" when their heads were covered with white feathers? Several young eagles squabbled over a spawned-out salmon, their mottled grey feathers in stark contrast to the majestic markings of the adult birds.

"Hello Mrs. Roger, how are you?" a girl's voice asked behind her. Elizabeth turned to see the two girls who ran the Good Eats Café this season. Silly girls of the younger set who never missed a dance at the Sons of Norway. One was named Margurite and the other was Hilda. Elizabeth wasn't sure which was which.

"Why hello," said Elizabeth. "Are you two going south?"

"Yes," the tall one answered. "We closed the restaurant and are heading home after our Alaskan summer adventure."

The short one added, "We had a great time and now we're looking into the activities going on in the social hall." And with a wave and a giggle, they disappeared into the crowd.

The ship was crowded with passengers from Juneau and other northern towns. Many seasonal cannery crews were aboard – having given up hope for a fall fishing season. Elizabeth wondered where they'd put the Wrangell and Ketchikan passengers they would pick up as they traveled south.

Despite the crowded conditions, the new above-deck accommodations were beautiful and everything shined with new paint and varnish. The below-deck compartments smelled musty, not surprisingly considering all but the pilothouse had been submerged at high tide after the steamer hit the rocks in Hawk Inlet last year. Or maybe it just seemed musty to Elizabeth because of her condition, or because she knew more about the ship's history than most passengers. Either way, Elizabeth was glad to have main-deck accommodations.

They had smooth sailing all the way to Seattle where Elizabeth boarded the Great Northern Railway to Chicago. Although she missed Carl terribly, she found herself enjoying this time alone with their unborn child. She thought of the baby as a girl and she kicked sometimes when Elizabeth sat very quietly. Elizabeth thought the baby didn't like trains. The four day journey across the northern plains was very different from Elizabeth's last trip in the dead of winter. Autumn colors painted the mountains, wheat fields were newly harvested, and the dairy cows appeared fat and content.

Uncle Emil met her train in Chicago and they got caught up on the ride to Evanston. At fifty-seven, he looked a little paler and his hair was thinner, but he was still the dapper gentleman who took such good care of Elizabeth back in Sweden.

"So you found Alaska to your liking, Lisa," he said.

"Oh, yes. The country is indescribably beautiful and the people are honest and hard working, with just the right number of odd characters thrown in for variety."

"And you're happy with Carl?"

"He's the best," said Elizabeth. "He's got a gentle way about him and a nice sense of humor. He's a good businessman too and nobody takes advantage of him. He's two years younger than Albert, you know. Alaska is a young man's country. And I'm lucky his work doesn't take him out on the fishing grounds. Fishermen's wives have a hard lot, never knowing if their men will be lost at sea. The weather can be very unpredictable."

"I'm glad to see you happy, then," he said, squeezing her hand. "Get prepared for a houseful of people. You've got two new nephews, including Julia's baby born just three weeks ago."

Papa's house was full of relatives with small children. Only Ruth and Clarence still lived at home. Elizabeth's other brothers and sisters dropped by to say hello and she marveled at how much their children had grown. Karl's three children by his former wife were the eldest and Elizabeth met his new wife, Johanna. John's one-year-old boy looked just like him. Elmer's little girl was two years old. She was just an infant when Elizabeth last saw her.

"Just look at you, Lisa," said Ruthie. "You left here a widow with an uncertain future and now you're the wife of a successful businessman and starting your very own family."

"It is rather remarkable, isn't it," said Elizabeth. "I had no idea it would all turn out this way."

Julia invited Elizabeth downstairs to see the new baby. "We named him Darwin Chester Rudd," she said. "His middle name is after his daddy. Here, you can hold him. I didn't want to bring him upstairs because there are too many people and I don't want him to get sick."

"Oh Julia, he's beautiful. Perhaps I can help you with him while I'm waiting for my baby to be born?"

"You sure can," she replied. "With a three and four-year-old, my other boys keep me busy. And, it will be good practice for you. Tell me Lisa, do you want a boy or a girl?"

"I'm hoping for a little girl."

"So was I," said Julia. "In fact, see that baby crib over there? I painted it pink in hopes we would get a girl. It didn't work for us, but I'll give it to you and maybe you'll have better luck."

"Why, thank you."

"Have you chosen a name for the baby?" continued Julia.

"Betty Jane if it's a girl and John Carl if it's a boy," said Elizabeth. "John is Carl's father's name."

While Elizabeth and Julia talked about babies, everyone else discussed the events of the summer. Elizabeth gathered that local politicians were campaigning on promises of lowering the high cost of living. A dirigible had fallen through the skylight of the Illinois Trust & Savings Building in Chicago, killing thirteen passengers being transported to the White City Amusement Park. Twenty-seven bank employees were injured when flaming debris fell through to the banking floor below. And Chicago was hit with five days of race riots when a Negro boy drowned after being hit by a stone thrown by a white boy at the 29th Street beach. Thirty-eight people were killed and more than five hundred injured. The racial conflict ended when 6,000 National Guard troops were deployed to put an end to the violence.

The Chicago paper showed a picture of General Pershing leading the American Expeditionary Force up Pennsylvania Avenue. Vice President Marshal, representing the president, received the general's salute. Elizabeth missed the conversations of the men in the hotel lobby and could almost hear them discussing the picture and pointing with pride at the men from Washington and Alaska taking part in the parade.

Elizabeth wrote to Carl every day after helping with the cleaning, cooking and caring for Julia's baby. Carl wrote less often and his letters were filled with news of happenings around town.

He wrote that Elizabeth would have enjoyed the Chautauqua performers. He and the other businessmen of the committee renewed their contract for the 1920 season. He hired a girl to help in the kitchen, paying her $15 a week with board. The local cannery expected to reach their contract pack of fall fish and the town was still busy. Julius Reese was appointed acting marshal when Marshal Cornstad resigned. Julius' first official act was to post notice that water would be shut off for an entire day while repairs were made to the water system. The town marshal was instructed to shoot all dogs without a license. The mayor's wife and their three children left for the south and she expected to locate in Texas. Mayor Jorgenson tendered his resignation to the town council but they failed to consider it. The three boys arrested for robbing the post office, Wheeler's drug store and the Trading Union store last summer were released on their own word by Judge Jennings and awaited further word from the Department of Justice in Washington. School teachers arrived from the south for the new term. Margaret Roden joined them from Juneau and sent her best wishes.

Elizabeth stood quietly before Albert's grave at Memorial Park. Hers were the only flowers at his gravesite.

"Oh, Al, so much has happened since I lost you," she said. "Your brother Carl and I are now married. He's a good man and takes good care of me. Although you and I were not blessed with children, part of you lives on in this child I carry. I look back on our life together with love and sadness. My new life in Alaska is filled with new people and the challenges of living in a sometimes hostile environment. I'll always love you and cherish our time together."

A faint breeze rustled the autumn leaves in the deserted cemetery. A wisp of hair caressed her cheek. She felt as though someone was staring at her and looked around but no one was there. Elizabeth retraced her steps to the exit feeling as though a weight had been lifted from her shoulders.

Carl wrote that Henry Roden had the misfortune to be appointed defense counsel for the man accused of murdering Mrs. Mar Kim and her daughter. Henry stopped in Petersburg on his way to court in Ketchikan. The district attorney from Juneau who filed the trumped-up sedition charges against Jim Brennan was shot and killed on Front Street in Ketchikan. People said the logger responsible for the shooting had been acting queer all summer. The town council restricted power usage after 4:00 p.m. and encouraged ladies to stop using their electric irons, again. The council toured Blind Slough looking for a suitable location for a hydro electric plant.

Fifty native children from nearby towns accompanied an Indian boarding school agent to Oregon where they were promised a free education. Doctor Upton relocated to California, leaving Petersburg without a doctor close to the time they would have needed one to deliver their baby. Mr. and Mrs. Russell York arrived to take over the Citizen's Steam Laundry across the street. Carl wrote that Elizabeth would like them.

He also reported an outbreak of smallpox among the natives. "I am so thankful you are far away from this," he wrote. "It would be terrible if you got sick in your condition. I am fine, so don't worry about me. Governor Riggs sent us a marine surgeon who placed the town under quarantine and prohibits public gatherings. It was time to close the café for the season, anyway."

Of course, all Elizabeth could do was worry until his next letter.

Elizabeth was getting big and clumsy. Her ankles were swollen and she practically waddled when walking. She knitted an entire baby's wardrobe – bonnets, booties, mittens, sweaters and baby blankets. She was so certain of a girl that she used pink yarn for most of the items and green or yellow for the rest.

Carl's next letter contained good news – the quarantine had been lifted and steamers were once again taking on Petersburg passengers. Eight cases of smallpox were found among the natives and three among the whites. All the school children were vaccinated and no deaths resulted. A fire destroyed the Samuelson family home near the power house. Two of their children discovered the fire when returning home from the picture show. Carl joined the men fighting the blaze but by the time they got the water on, all they could do was save the surrounding buildings. A collection was taken up and volunteer labor secured to build a new house for the family near the Standard Oil Company plant.

High seas and hurricane force winds had forced the mailboat *Americ* to lay at Kake for many hours with three anchors out and engines running full speed ahead to keep from being washed ashore. The big tug *Edward Schenk* wasn't as lucky and big waves drove her four feet up on the rocks above the high tide line. Despite a vigorous defense that the case was based on circumstantial evidence, Henry Roden and his partner lost the case against the man accused of murdering Mrs. Mar Kim and her daughter. The jury found the man guilty and sentenced him to life in prison. The men who started the fox ranch on Channel Island recaptured all but three of their animals and moved their ranch to Entrance Island when the waters surrounding Channel Island froze up. A new wintertime mail boat was put in service between Ketchikan, Wrangell and Petersburg and Rasmus Enge completely remodeled the Variety Theatre.

On Thanksgiving Day, Elizabeth's family had an early dinner of roast turkey with gravy and dressing, candied yams, mashed potatoes, fresh vegetables, molded salads, and home-baked bread. In addition to Mamma, Papa and Uncle Emil, her brothers Paul and Clarence and sisters Alice and Ruth were seated at the table. Her married brothers and sisters spent Thanksgiving with their families and visited in the afternoon to share in the pumpkin and mincemeat pies that Alice, Ruth and Elizabeth baked for the occasion. Only Helen Ida was missing – she and her family lived more than two hundred miles away in Findlay, Ohio.

Everyone was in a holiday mood and had many questions about Elizabeth's life in Alaska.

"So tell us, Lisa," said John. "How much snow do you get up there?"

"Sometimes it reaches the eaves and sometimes our winters have very little snow. Carl writes that this year is very mild and we'll probably have a worse winter in Evanston and Chicago than in Petersburg. The rest of the year is mostly rain, the drizzly foggy kind that keeps the vegetation so green. And in the summer, sunshine and warm temperatures make the rest of the year tolerable."

"How many people live on your island?" asked Elmer.

"Around two thousand during the season and a few hundred in the wintertime. The fishing and logging seasons run from about May until

September when the town is filled with cannery crews recruited from down below and burley loggers who come in from the logging camps from time to time."

"Where do you do your shopping?" asked Alice.

"Mostly through mail order catalogues," Elizabeth laughed. "But we do have some stores and Carl maintains sample rooms at the hotel for traveling salesmen to show their goods when they come to call. We have a couple general stores selling everything from groceries to fishing gear. We have two hotels – ours is in the center of town and the Petersburg Hotel is up the hill – a bank, newspaper, post office, a school with five teachers, a couple of drug stores, several restaurants and two bakeries. We also have a courthouse and jail, customs office, fish canneries, shrimp cannery, machine shops and a sawmill. It's one of the most prosperous towns in Southeastern Alaska."

"And what kind of fish do they catch?" asked Paul.

"The year starts with halibut fishing in January," said Elizabeth. "It's the most dangerous kind of fishing because the weather is so rough at that time of year. They either freeze the halibut in cold storage or ice it down and ship it fresh on southbound steamers. Then there's herring – I don't know too much about that. They pack it in barrels or salt it down, I think. Salmon season starts next and the fish are brought to the canneries on big tenders that buy the fish directly from fishermen on the fishing grounds. Some fishermen sell directly to the canneries too. Salmon season lasts until fall and employs many people in the canneries and at the fish camps. Oh, and then there's shrimping; the shrimp are brought in for canning or freezing too. I think they fish for shrimp most months except when they spawn. Carl and I spent a day on a shrimp boat in May."

"Boy, I'd like to see all that," said Clarence. "Do you think a greenhorn could get work in a cannery?"

"They do every summer," Elizabeth responded. "They'll show you what you need to know to do the job and they pay pretty well too. Don't expect to get a job on a fishing boat, though. Skippers usually hire only experienced fishermen or family members."

"So, Clarence, when are you leaving for Alaska?" teased Paul.

"Wouldn't you be surprised if I did go?" Clarence retorted.

"Lisa, what is there for womenfolk to do there?" asked Alice.

"The women work shore jobs right alongside the men," said Elizabeth. "They put in vegetable gardens, pick berries and put up preserves, work in the canneries or at the stores, and raise their boys to work on their father's boats. The big social events are dances at the Sons of Norway Hall, going to the picture show, knitting for the Red Cross or getting involved in church activities."

Feeling tired, Elizabeth soon retired to her room. It's just wasn't possible to explain to these people the sheer grandeur of the country and the feeling of accomplishment that came with thriving on the remote island. They'd have to experience it firsthand to understand fully.

Betty Jane entered the world on December 3 at St. Francis Hospital where Elizabeth was attended by Dr. Rudersdorf. "Here she is little mother," he said, placing the baby in her arms. She was a good-sized baby, weighing seven and half pounds, with blue eyes and a crown of hair the color and consistency of corn silk. Elizabeth loved holding her and breathing in her sweet baby scent.

Elizabeth wired Carl with the good news and did her best to regulate the press of relatives who came to see her. Julia exclaimed, "See, the pink crib worked for you! She's just a perfect little doll."

Carl wrote that he distributed cigars all over town. He sent a clipping about the birth of their little girl from the *Petersburg Weekly Report:*

Word is received from Chicago that Carl Roger, proprietor of the Hotel Wester, is the father of a baby daughter, born in that city on December 3rd. Mrs. Roger, who left here some time ago for her former home is reported to be doing nicely and will return here after several weeks.

Carl also wrote that the town was very quiet on account of so many people gone south for the winter. The special election for the new school building and hydro electric plant passed with sixty-one yeas and two nays. Margaret Roden was very pleased with the prospect of a new school building and sent congratulations about the baby. She can't wait to see her. The town ran out of coal and the *Redondo* arrived just in time with a new shipment from Seattle. Carl was called by the fire bell to help put out a blaze at the Sons of Norway Trading Union store. The chemical engine failed and the fire spread while the men were securing water. The store was a total loss and only the snow and ice on nearby rooftops saved a large part of the town from total destruction. The volunteer fire department was completely reorganized and Earl Ohmer became the new Fire Chief.

The weather turned bitter cold following the birth of the baby. A storm system moved up the Ohio Valley, plunging temperatures from the upper twenties to one degree above zero in just a few hours. A few days later, the temperature dropped to eight degrees below zero. Snowfall was kept to two or three inches by gusty winds. Newspaper accounts said below-zero temperatures stretched from the Mississippi River to the Rocky Mountains. Nobody seemed to believe Elizabeth when she told them Carl reported Christmas weather in Petersburg of fifty degrees with snow receding half way up the mountains.

The cold weather brought another wave of influenza to the Chicago area. More than two thousand cases were reported in one day. Health officials warned against wet and cold feet and tagged houses where influenza cases were reported. Due to a shortage of nurses, the health commissioner petitioned the governor to allow student nurses to work at area hospitals. Elizabeth was worried the baby would get the flu but Julia said she thought, since Elizabeth already had it, she'd passed her immunity to the baby. Elizabeth kept outsiders away from the baby just the same, wishing for the day when Betty would be strong enough to travel.

Chapter 18

February 1920 – Elizabeth and the baby were finally going home. "Home" had such a nice ring to it. Elizabeth loved being with her family for the past few months but she missed Carl so much and her home was with him. The baby was the picture of robust good health. And for such a little thing, she certainly required a good deal of luggage. Uncle Emil, Clarence and Ruthie saw them comfortably settled on the train and waved goodbye from the platform. Elizabeth held Betty up to the window and waved her tiny arm as the train pulled away from the snowy depot.

An elderly porter took an interest in Elizabeth and the baby. "Afternoon Ma'am," he said. "You'll be traveling all the way to the coast with us?"

"Yes, I'm going to join my husband," she replied.

"And how old is the young'un?"

"She's just two months."

"Well, if there's anything I can do to make your trip more comfortable, just call for 'Ole Willie.' "

"Why, thank you," said Elizabeth.

She reread Carl's last letter as the train moved along. He wrote that he missed her terribly and couldn't wait to see their little girl. The town was still quiet with so many folks south for the winter. Those who remained spent too much time drinking and paid little heed to the prohibition laws that became effective on the first of the year. The Fire Department no longer used a long ringing of the bell to call the men to drill since it frightened timid women and some of the property owners. A new nurse was in charge of the hospital and she taught classes in home nursing. Gasboats used to deliver winter mail were not up to the task and some mail arrived frozen into a solid mass – addresses illegible, wrappers off, and water soaked. Mr. Bender combined the Stoft & Refling store, Petersburg Readywear store and Petersburg Mercantile stores. Sad news was received in town that Doc Ballance had passed away in San Pedro. Elizabeth mailed a condolence note to Mrs. Ballance and their three children before leaving Chicago. She felt almost guilty to be so happy when her friend was having such a hard time.

The train sped west through the same icy, snow-covered terrain Elizabeth witnessed on her first trip to Seattle two years earlier. She was grateful for the cozy compartment where she had privacy for nursing the baby. The kindly porter paused in his rounds several times a day, alerting her to the next stop so she could cover the baby from cold drafts brought aboard by new passengers. By the second day, he was bringing her meals from the dining car and watching the baby while Elizabeth used the facilities.

"She sleeps like an angel," he said. "Just like my little girls used to."

"How many children do you have?" Elizabeth asked.

"Six in all. Three boys and three girls. 'Course, they're all grown now and the girls are giving me grand babies. Don't get to see them often enough, though, with all this traveling."

"Where do you call home?" asked Elizabeth.

"The missus and me have a little place just outside Chicago."

"And how long have you been working for the railroad?"

"Been railroading about twenty years," he said. "Gonna get my gold watch and retire soon. Gonna miss all the interesting people, though."

On the last day of the trip, Willie pointed at the tracks climbing the eastern banks of the Cascades. "There was a time," he said, "when we had to climb to the summit on those switchbacks. Then they built a tunnel right through this here mountain."

"Did that make the trip much shorter?" Elizabeth asked.

"A little shorter," he said, "but mostly it made it safer for winter travel and we don't need snow sheds to protect the tracks from avalanches no more."

Soon, they descended into the Puget Sound area where the weather was surprisingly mild. The small amount of snow on the ground was mostly slush. Fresh air entering the car at Everett did not contain the northern plains' bone chilling bite. At Seattle, Willie helped Elizabeth claim her luggage and flagged down a porter to take it to the ship.

"This here's my friend Andy," he said. "Andy, I want you to take Mrs. Roger and her baby direct to the Pacific Steamship Company dock and wait while she collects her ticket. Ma'am it's been a pleasure making your acquaintance. You and your little one have a safe journey to Alaska now."

He refused the tip Elizabeth tried to give him and waved goodbye as they jostled down the street with Julia's baby crib and the rest of the luggage. Elizabeth collected the ticket waiting for her at the steamship office and some of her luggage was added to freight being loaded aboard the *City of Seattle* for a morning departure. The ticket agent directed her to a small hotel across the street where she booked a room for the night.

The big ship left promptly at ten the next morning. There were more than one hundred passengers on board, including seventeen for Petersburg. Most were newcomers, but Elizabeth recognized three of Petersburg's leading businessmen. Erick Ness, manager of the Sons of Norway Trading Union store, was on the Chautauqua Committee with Carl. Mr. Kracke, manager of the Petersburg Packing Company, was also on the committee. Knut Steberg was a banker and agent for the Pacific Steamship Company. He also handled property sales and insurance from his office in the Sunde Building. Mr. Ness crossed the lounge to where Elizabeth sat with the baby in her lap.

"Mrs. Roger, it's good to see you," he said. "Is this the newcomer Carl's been waiting for?"

"Why yes, this is Betty Jane," Elizabeth said, moving the blanket so he could get a better look. The other two men smiled down on them somewhat awkwardly.

"She's the spitting image of her mother," he said.

The men made polite conversation about the mild winter weather and asked about her stay in Evanston. "Carl wrote me about the fire at the Trading Union," Elizabeth told Mr. Ness. "I was sorry to hear about it."

"That was an unfortunate accident," he replied. "The important thing is that nobody was hurt and it didn't spread to other buildings. We're working on getting the store back in business."

The three men had their heads together throughout the four-day voyage. They appeared to be working on some sort of business deal. She forgot about them when the ship entered the south end of Wrangell Narrows. She was almost teary eyed at the sight of the beautiful mountains, thick forests and pristine waters. She wondered if those were the same eagles she had seen sitting on the beach when she left six months earlier. She was surprised to find this country had such a hold on her that she truly felt she was coming home.

Carl stopped his pacing on the dock as the three men helped Elizabeth down the gangplank, one holding her elbow and the other two carrying her luggage. "Here are your girls, Carl," Mr. Ness said. "Delivered safe and sound."

Carl shook hands all around before the men left so he could get a look at his new daughter in private. "How does it feel to be a Daddy?" Elizabeth asked.

"Well, would you look at that," he said, as Betty curled her tiny hand around his finger.

"Here, you can hold her, she won't break," Elizabeth said, passing the baby to him. He held her as carefully as a basket of eggs, his face wreathed in a beatific smile.

"And how's the little Mother?" he asked, giving Elizabeth a big kiss.

"So happy to be home with you again."

He handed the baby back to Elizabeth and arranged for the luggage to be delivered to the hotel. "You brought a baby crib?" he asked.

"A gift from my sister Julia. I'll tell you the story behind it later."

They joined the other passengers walking up the dock toward town and entered the hotel lobby. Only a few of the regulars were there – the others were still at the dock meeting the steamer. After a few pleasantries, Carl led the way down the long corridor to the kitchen, passing the doorway to the manager's quarters. He marched out the back door, down the steps, across the yard and into the small house behind the hotel. There he stopped, turned around and said, "How do you like it? A hotel's no place to raise a family and the owner was happy to rent it to me."

"Oh Carl, what a nice surprise. I love it."

Elizabeth set about unpacking between bouts of nursing the baby while Carl returned to the hotel. The sparsely furnished house had a living room in the front and a small kitchen and large bedroom in the back. And, wonder of wonders, it had indoor sanitary plumbing rather than a "shack in the back." A small service porch tacked onto the rear of the house led to a clothesline tied to a tree.

Carl reappeared several times to handle the heavy lifting and marvel at the baby asleep in her crib, oblivious to the activity going on around her. "I told your lady friends to give you at least a day to get settled before they come calling. Hope that's all right with you."

"Thanks. I could use a little time to catch my breath."

That night, Elizabeth caught him staring at her full breasts as she nursed the baby. After she put the baby in her crib, he led Elizabeth to bed saying, "Come here, Mother."

"Why Daddy, I always suspected you weren't a leg man," Elizabeth giggled as he cupped her breast in his big hand.

They tumbled into bed and made sweet, sensuous love before drifting to sleep. Carl stirred when the baby began to cry. "What's the matter?" he asked.

"Nothing," said Elizabeth. "She's just hungry. I'll take care of her. Go back to sleep."

"How often does she wake up during the night?"

"Only every three or four hours."

"And how long does this go on?" he groaned.

"Just for a few more months. It's perfectly normal. Go back to sleep."

Mrs. Mathis and Margaret Roden came to see the baby. As they visited over coffee and pastries, they brought Elizabeth up to date on their activities. "Margaret," Elizabeth said, "how's that new school building coming along?"

"It isn't," replied Margaret. "The state school superintendent was in town recently and he stood before the city council and informed them that $25,000 wasn't enough money for the school. He especially encouraged them to include a gymnasium and assembly rooms."

"But I thought the town already had approval to float a bond to pay for the school and a hydro electric plant," said Elizabeth.

"They did, but now they're going back to ask Congress to double the size of the bond."

"How long do you think that will take?"

"I have no idea," said Mrs. Roden, "but if there isn't some progress by the beginning of the next school year, I'm seriously considering giving up my teaching job and moving to Juneau to be with Henry."

"I'm leaving for Juneau on the next steamer," said Mrs. Mathis. "I've been feeling so poorly all winter that I've decided a change of scenery is in order."

"What do you think is the matter?" Elizabeth asked.

"I just feel so cooped up and cut off from things on the outside," Mrs. Mathis replied. "And Ray's been so busy with his dental practice now that he's sharing his offices at the hotel with that new Dr. Johannesson."

"And what did the new doctor have to say about your condition?" continued Elizabeth.

"He could find nothing wrong, but he's just been discharged from the Army Medical Corps and I doubt he's had many female patients."

Margaret and Elizabeth exchanged glances. Their friend's malaise was probably more a case of cabin fever than a medical condition.

When Carl came home for dinner he said, "Remember you told me that Erick Ness, Knut Steberg and Mr. Kracke had their heads together all the way north from Seattle?"

"Yes."

"Well, today they announced that the Packing Company store, wharf, warehouses and floats are being transferred to the Trading Union.

"So that's what they were working on so hard."

"Yep," said Carl. "The co-operative Trading Union has more than a hundred shareholders and both Knut Steberg and Erick Ness will serve on the board of directors."

"Will Erick continue as manager of the store?"

"No," said Carl. "Carl Swanson from the Packing Company store will be the new manager."

"And what about Mr. Kracke?"

"He's transferring to the Packing Company's Seattle office as soon as the store sale is completed," said Carl.

Elizabeth established a routine whereby she spent the mornings cooking, cleaning and tending the baby while Carl ran the hotel. Elizabeth helped out at the hotel in the afternoons after putting the baby down for her nap. It was good to listen to the conversations of the lobby regulars again.

"Knut Steberg tells me that Alaska is the only part of the Pacific Coast to get distillate from the Standard Oil Company this season," said one of the men.

"I hear a fifty-fifty mixture of gasoline and kerosene might work in the gasboats when distillate disappears altogether," added another. "Standard Oil's also increasing the price of gasoline and fuel oil. Prices are so much higher on the East Coast that West Coast petroleum is being shipped east, leaving us with a fuel shortage. At this rate, there might not be any profit in fishing this season."

"Prices are going up for everything," agreed the first man. "Even Enge is raising the price of a picture show to forty cents for adults. How's the tourist business shaping up this year, Carl?"

"It's expected to be pretty good," replied Carl. "A New York booking agency tried to purchase all the berths on one of the steamers for a summer cruise. The steamship company had the good sense to turn them down so there would be room for locals, though."

"Sounds like they're sending a big group," said the first man.

"Yep," replied Carl. "The Shriners are making a tour of Alaska this summer. The steamship company is putting most of them on one ship and the overflow on another. They're going to run the steamers close together so both ships will be in port at the same time."

"What about Canadian steamers stopping in Petersburg?"

"They've received our petition inviting them in but turned us down for now," said Carl. "They said their capacity is seriously taxed in the summertime and they don't want to affect business with ports they've been serving for so long."

March may have come in like a lamb, but it went out like a lion. Wind-driven rain lashed the town for several days. The Petersburg Lumber Company's logging outfit was caught in a heavy storm while being towed to Pillar Bay. The tow lines snapped several times and the camp was driven ashore near Cape Bendel. It sat on the beach for two weeks before being towed to its destination. The big pile driver of the Packing Company's Washington Bay cannery broke loose in another storm and was recovered fifty miles away from where she was anchored. The driver was upside down with the donkey and hammer still attached and other parts were recovered five miles away in Chatham Strait. Ruthie wrote that even Chicago experienced the worst blizzard of the winter with heavy snowfall and sub-zero temperatures.

The men in the lobby were discussing something called the Volstead Act.

"So this Volstead Act allows a man to have liquor in his own home?" asked one of the regulars.

"Yep, as long as it's for his own use or for his guests when entertaining," replied another. "And nobody has the right to search your home unless you're selling the liquor."

"That sounds like something we can live with," said the first man. "What's the problem then?"

"Nobody knows if the Volstead Act applies to Alaska and whether or not it replaces the territory's 'Bone Dry' law passed a few years ago."

"What if the 'Bone Dry' law is the one that applies?" asked the first man.

"Then they can search your home for liquor and throw you in jail if they find any."

"Let's hope the federal law rules then," said the first man. "Doesn't seem right that a man can't have a little snort in his own home."

The conversation turned to fur trading when local fur buyers Andy Anderson and Luther Hogue of Hogue & Tveten's store joined the men.

"Trappers in this section had the best season in history," said Andy. "Anyone with time to secure traps and set a line made comfortable stakes on account of the high prices for furs."

"I estimate between $50,000 and $80,000 worth of furs were handled by Petersburg buyers during this past season," added Luther. "Few people realize how much money changes hands and how much is released for trade during a trapping season."

"What kind of furs are you seeing?" asked one of the men.

"I got several of those rare blue foxes caught on Kuiu and Kupreanof Islands," said Andy.

Luther added, "I don't have any exceptional furs like that but I'll still have about $20,000 worth to display at the fur sale in San Francisco this spring."

A fuel shortage shut down the power plant and the stores had a run on sales of kerosene lamps and candles. Mayor Jorgenson posted notice that the plant would be down between the hours of 8:00 a.m. and 4:00 p.m. on Tuesdays, Thursdays and Saturdays until further notice.

"At least we have heat," Carl said. "We'll stay warm with coal to run the boiler at the hotel and feed the kitchen stove in the house."

"And who needs light anyway," Elizabeth added, "when dining by candlelight is so much more romantic?"

"Ah Mother, they threw away the mold when they made you," Carl laughed.

Editor Perkins joined the group in the lobby with big news. "They're planning a big paper and pulp mill at Thomas Bay," he said. "With Petersburg the nearest town, it means more revenue and year-round jobs for everyone."

"How certain is this?" asked one of the men.

"Well, a fellow came into the commissioner's office and filed a location notice for record to use waters from Cascade Creek to power the plant and then left for the south to confer with his employers," said Perkins. "Our information is that money has been raised and necessary arrangements have been made with the Forestry Service. And a work boat with the first crew of men is ready to leave Seattle any day now."

"We sure could use an alternative to commercial fishing, given the poor fishing season that's shaping up so far this year," said Charlie Greenaa.

"I hear tell that smaller timber, not too old, is what mills need for papermaking," said Earl Ohmer. "And it seems there's plenty of that around. How big do you think this mill's going to be?"

"From what I gather," replied the newspaperman, "there's an initial outlay of between $2 million and $5 million depending on the size of the plant. Much of that would be spent in Petersburg for construction of buildings and other incidentals. Once they're up and running, they'll probably employ upwards of two thousand men in all departments. And being located only fifteen miles from Petersburg, they'll do much of their business through our cable station, merchants, steamer stop and what have you."

"That would give our town growth and prosperity while the rest of the country is running downhill," said Carl.

Carl and Elizabeth relaxed in the evening after dinner. The power and light plant had received more fuel and lights were back on again. Elizabeth knitted a sweater for the baby and Carl smoked his pipe while reading one of his astronomy journals.

"Listen to this, Mother," he said. "It says here that Marconi has issued instructions to all available wireless stations to listen intently on April 21 when the planet Mars is closest to Earth to pick up any signals that Mars may sound to establish communication with us."

"Who's Marconi?" asked Elizabeth.

"He's that inventor, Italian I think, who won the Nobel Prize for his work in developing wireless telegraphy."

"Do you think they'll hear anything?"

"Hard to say, but it's interesting, isn't it, that someone as smart as this fellow thinks it's worth trying?"

One hundred and sixty-four residents voted in the general election and Tom Elsemore, cashier at the Bank of Petersburg, replaced Pete Jorgenson as town mayor. Cannery workers arrived with each new steamer and dispersed to outlying fish camps and canneries. The Petersburg Packing Company announced plans to put up 200,000 cases of salmon at their two locations this season. The mail boat *Americ* began her summer schedule calling at canneries, logging camps and fishing stations. Carl reopened the dining room and the lobby regulars moved to the corner table by the window. Leonard Heys reopened the Baltimore Grill and kept it supplied with fresh eggs and vegetables from his ranch across the Narrows. Bert Haug purchased and opened the Petersburg Restaurant.

Mrs. Mathis stopped by for an afternoon visit. "I can't get over how well you look after your trip to Juneau," Elizabeth said.

"They have better doctors there," said Mrs. Mathis. "Whenever we get good ones here, they just don't stay very long. Seems they only stay as long as there's good fishing and hunting and then they're off to some other town. Practicing medicine is just how they finance their other activities. It's a good thing the Hospital Association hired those two nurses to run the hospital. At least we can count on them to be here when needed."

"What do you think of the new doctors in town?" asked Elizabeth.

"I haven't been to them as yet and Ray hasn't expressed an opinion," said Mrs. Mathis. "Doctor Rowley and his wife are both physicians and surgeons, you know, and their practice in the new Gauffin Building appears to be growing. They're from New Zealand. I do like having a woman doctor in town. When I'm in Wrangell, I always see Dr. Anna Brown-Kearsley. She's the best."

"And what have you heard about this Dr. Carothers from Chicago?" Elizabeth asked.

"Ray tells me he's having trouble getting a license to practice here because Petersburg already has two doctors," said Mrs. Mathis. "He needs to take the territorial medical examination and until he does, they've issued him a temporary permit to practice in Kake. And since Kake is in the same division as Petersburg, he can practice anywhere within the division, including in Petersburg."

"It seems we either have too many doctors or none at all," Elizabeth replied.

The town was without light and power again due to a lack of fuel oil. Operating hours at the light plant were restricted to one o'clock in the afternoon until daylight. And, the city water was shut off while repairs were made to the dam and dirt cleaned out of the water main. Elizabeth refilled the kerosene in the hurricane lamps and set out buckets to catch rain water. Residents grumbled about the situation while old timers chuckled that everyone had gone soft.

"Mother, look who just arrived from Juneau," said Carl, leading Henry Roden through the front door.

"Why Henry, it's so good to see you, and you too, Margaret," Elizabeth laughed as Mrs. Roden peeked around Henry's coat tails.

"You're looking well, Mrs. Roger," said Henry. "I just had to stop in and see the new addition to the family I've heard so much about."

"She's right here in her playpen," said Elizabeth. "Betty's five months old now and she surprises us with something new every day."

Margaret picked up the baby and handed her to Henry, whereupon Betty began to wail.

"There, there honey," Margaret said, "you're just not used to this funny looking man, are you?"

"Guess I have that effect on all women," replied Henry.

They put the baby back in her playpen and everyone gathered around the kitchen table for coffee and a visit.

"What brings you to town?" asked Carl.

"I'm on my way to the Ketchikan district court to appear for the defendants in a rioting case," said Henry. "Can't say much more about it than that. And, I wanted to make arrangements for Margaret to join me in Juneau as soon as the school term is over."

"Is it true what we heard, that the man who shot Assistant District Attorney Steve Ragan isn't going to stand trial?" asked Carl.

"Looks that way," said Henry. "The man was adjudged insane and unfit to defend himself on the charge of first degree murder. The jury deliberated for just a few minutes."

"I'm afraid Petersburg doesn't have much sympathy for that district attorney fellow after labeling us 'a hotbed of pro Germanism' during the war and charging poor Jim Brennan with sedition," mused Carl. "Practically ruined Jim, having to put up everything he owned to make bond and defend himself. And after all that, the charges were dropped. Still, nobody wished the guy dead."

"Never underestimate the power of a greater hand to right an injustice," replied Henry.

Chapter 19

May 1920 – "Nels Nelson came in from Scow Bay today and described all the activity going on out there," said Carl.

"And what did he have to say?" Elizabeth asked.

"Well, they're working on the road again. Got thirty or thirty-five men and a logging donkey working this time. They still don't know if they'll finish before winter sets in though. And they're almost finished building the fish by-products plant. They'll extract oil from fish offal and herring and sell the residue stateside as stock feed."

"That sounds like it could be smelly," said Elizabeth.

"I'm sure it is, but it's the smell of money," replied Carl. "And they're almost finished with their new cold storage plant. It's built to handle over a million pounds of fish and a thousand tons of ice. And they're rebuilding the Mountain Point Packing Company that burned down a few months ago."

"Did they ever find out what caused the fire?"

"No, the men were just finishing dinner when someone ran in and shouted something was burning. By the time they got out the door, the main building was in flames. The entire structure burned down within fifteen minutes. They're going to rebuild all the buildings this year and install machinery next year when they'll be up and running again. All in all, it seems Scow Bay is making better progress than Petersburg right now."

"Mother, I need you to watch the place while I'm away this morning," said Carl. "I'll move the playpen into the kitchen so you can watch the baby and the lobby at the same time."

"Where are you going?"

"Got some business to tend to down at the post office. Hopefully, I'll have a surprise for you this afternoon."

Well, that sounded mysterious. But Carl wouldn't tell Elizabeth anything more before he slipped out the door. She divided her time between guests in the lobby and the baby in the kitchen. She could see a crowd of men down the street in front of the post office but couldn't make out what they were doing.

Carl finally reappeared a few hours later waving a piece of paper and Elizabeth followed him into the kitchen. "Remember where we had a picnic last summer at the north end of the Narrows?" he asked.

"Of course."

"Well, now we own it," he grinned. "And one day, we'll build a proper house there."

"Oh, Carl, how is this possible?"

"The town site trustee just held a public auction for the sale of unclaimed lots," said Carl. "He sold 66 lots out of the 280 that were available. The rest will be deeded to the town. Nobody else bid on our lot – they all thought it was too far out of town – so I got it for $50."

Carl danced Elizabeth around the kitchen while the baby watched in wide-eyed wonder.

"Did it take a lot of our savings?" Elizabeth asked.

"It put a dent in them for sure," said Carl. "But it's an investment in the future. All we have to do is pay property taxes while we save enough to build. And one day, as the town grows north, that property won't seem like it's very far away at all."

The men in the lobby were discussing the country's state of affairs.

"Seems like this country's going to hell in a handbasket," said one.

"Why do you say that?" asked Russell York from the laundry across the street.

"Just open your eyes and what do you see?" replied the first man. "Pacific Mildcure closed all their stations, claiming even last year was unprofitable. Other mild curing operations are shutting down too, owing to low prices paid for fish and an export market hampered by the exchange situation."

"That's just one type of processing," said Russell. "What about canned salmon and halibut?"

"It's too soon to tell what's going to happen to the salmon pack, but it seems unlikely they'll pack more than last year like they hoped," said the first man. "Local fish buyers disappeared from the trolling grounds this spring so trollers had to ship their fresh fish direct to southern markets through the new Petersburg Co-operative Association over Alaska Fish and Cold Storage's dock at Scow Bay. And they still have to bring their fish to the dock. Why trollers can't even sell their fish in Ketchikan 'cause the cold storage plants there give first position to halibut boats."

"What about logging?" asked Russell. "The mill seems to be keeping busy."

"They're still only sawing logs for local consumption," said the lobby regular. "You never hear about that big Australian contract anymore, do you? Seems it fell through about the same time Arness Lumber Company became the Petersburg Lumber Company. Two piling camps have already quit work for the season and they've towed their floats and engines to town along with a big raft of logs for the mill. We're told the mill expects to double its output next year. It's always 'next year' with these fellas."

"What do you think about the power plant increasing rates by 15 percent?" asked Carl.

"It's a damn outrage. The engines are too small for this size town and one engine is out of commission half the time. As long as they have to operate the plant on Pearl Oil, you can bet more increases in the cost of light and power are right around the corner. And I hear they've put price controls on sugar down in the states. Carl, you probably know something about that."

"Yes," said Carl. "The Department of Justice just limited profits on sugar to one cent per pound for wholesalers and two cents per pound for retailers. They'll prosecute anyone for profiteering that they find in violation of those prices."

"See? The country's going to hell in a handbasket," concluded the first man.

Editor Perkins was upset. "Just got the official results of the government's 1920 Census of Population," he sputtered. "And can you believe it – they took the count in the dead of winter when thousands of people were away visiting in the south and Petersburg got credit for only 880 residents?"

"That sounds awfully low," said Carl. "I thought it was around two thousand."

"It is, in summertime," said Perkins. "And that's what we told Congress when we requested permission to float a bond for a new school building and hydro electric plant. Why, this undercount is going to be with us for the next ten years. It'll be impossible to attract new business here if everyone thinks we're just a small town. It's a tragic joke, that's what it is."

"What about the neighboring towns?" asked Carl.

"They counted 864 year-round residents at Wrangell and 397 at Kake," said Perkins. "Both are serious undercounts too. All I can say is it's a good thing Congress doesn't read these reports because they just approved our request to double our bonding bill to $150,000."

Carl changed the name of the hotel to the Hotel Arctic.

"We're nowhere near the Arctic," Elizabeth said.

"I know," said Carl, "but it impresses the tourists and gives the impression that we're a new, going concern. Chris Wester said it was time for a new name when we reached our sales agreement. I just didn't get around to it until now."

Carl ran a new ad in the *Petersburg Weekly Report:*

Hotel Arctic
When in Town, Stay With Us
First Class Rooms, Reasonable Rates
Carl Roger, Proprietor

Mrs. Mathis joined the committee preparing a welcome for the touring Shriners. The committee decorated the Sons of Norway Hall for a buffet luncheon where fresh shrimp salad was to be the main dish. Two days before the steamers arrived, she took Elizabeth down to the hall to show her the decorations.

The ladies stepped through the doorway of the big room and Elizabeth stopped in her tracks, stunned. The walls were hung with bear skins, goatskins, deerskins, fox skins and mounted heads. Deer and moose antlers were mounted above each window.

"Where did all these furs come from?" Elizabeth asked.

"Borrowed from people's homes," said Mrs. Mathis. "The men are especially proud of these tables made from local lumber. Each table is constructed from one board nineteen inches wide and thirty-four feet long. And each board is entirely free of knots. Well, Elizabeth, what do you think?"

Elizabeth was still speechless. Mrs. Mathis looked at her and wailed, "I know, it's awful, isn't it? The committee wouldn't listen to reason. You're a city girl like me and we know the Shriners and their wives are wealthy, educated people. Why, they're going to think we're barbarians."

"Oh, it's not as bad as all that," Elizabeth finally sputtered. "Maybe they'll think it's charming."

The first group of 250 Shriners arrived on the *Spokane* at one o'clock in the afternoon and the second group arrived three hours later on the *Jefferson*. The visitors were treated to the luncheon at the Sons of Norway Hall, provided with commemorative brochures touting the features of the town and entertained with musical pieces performed by Miss Mary Allen, Josephine Halgeson and Frances Roundtree.

The Shriners took over from there with their Shrine Band providing dancing music and several concert pieces. The Shriners Quartet also sang several numbers. The travelers came from as far east as Massachusetts and as far south as Georgia. Included in their numbers were the mayor of Portland and the Supreme Imperial Potentate for North America. In recounting the affair, Mrs. Mathis declared the Shriners the most distinguished group of men and women ever to visit Petersburg. She was particularly saddened to see the steamers pull away from the docks and continue their voyage north to Juneau.

"One of the guests is accusing the hotel staff of thievery," said Carl.

"What happened?" Elizabeth asked.

"You know that Mrs. Jacobsen, who's been with us for the past few days?"

"I don't really know her, but I know who you mean."

"Well," said Carl, "she claims jewelry and money disappeared from her room and she's blaming it on hotel employees."

"What's missing?" asked Elizabeth.

"Two rings – one diamond and the other cameo – a gold nugget watch fob and two twenty-dollar gold pieces. She claims everything is worth about $585."

"That's a lot of jewelry to be carrying around," said Elizabeth. "Who does she think took it?"

"She doesn't accuse anyone specifically but claims the housekeeping staff must have taken the items from her luggage."

"And what does Mrs. Henderson have to say?"

"Oh, she's in tears. She swears up and down she didn't take anything from the woman's room and has never before been accused of being dishonest."

"I can't believe she would do anything wrong either," said Elizabeth. "For all we know, this Mrs. Jacobsen travels from town to town collecting money by making false accusations. What are you going to do?"

"Nothing at the moment," said Carl. "She's threatening to file suit against me if she doesn't receive payment before she leaves on the next northbound steamer. I'm not going to pay her one thin dime unless she can provide proof of wrongdoing on the part of the hotel staff. Just one of the unpleasant things about dealing with the public, I guess."

With the Fourth of July falling on a Sunday, Chief Earl Ohmer and his Fire Department boys planned a three-day celebration beginning on Saturday, July 3. Merchants contributed generously to the fund for prizes and materials for the festivities. The hotel was full and the town alive with people from outlying fish camps, fox farms and logging camps. Out-of-towners stopped to admire Georgette and Crepe de Chine waists in Hogue & Tveten's windows. Elizabeth thought $25 was outrageous to pay for a blouse. Business houses and the bandstand on Main Street were decorated with evergreens, bunting and flags. A big arch made of evergreens and highlighted with paper lanterns straddled Main Street. Made by the boys at the cannery, it carried the words, "Alaska" and "By Loyal Filipinos." The sun came out on Saturday and temperatures quickly reached the low eighties.

The sound of approaching music drew everyone to the front of the hotel. The Kake Band marched by and performed a short concert. The entire population of Kake had arrived on five big boats to participate in the festivities. The Kake Band supplied music at a dance at the Arctic Brotherhood Hall later in the evening while another dance took place in the Sons of Norway Hall for the benefit of the Hospital Committee.

"Do you want to go to the baseball game in the morning?" Elizabeth asked Carl.

"It could be good," said Carl, "but what about the baby?"

"I'll stay here and watch her and the hotel. You should go. It's really for the men."

It didn't take much coaxing for Carl to join the crowd hiking the boardwalk across the muskeg to Sandy Beach for the first real game of baseball ever played in Petersburg. He was in good cheer when he returned a few hours later. "We won," he announced. "We beat the native boys from Kake by thirteen to five. Everyone had a good time and the Kake boys were good losers. They said they'll get back at us during tomorrow's sporting events."

"Why was the game scheduled at nine o'clock in the morning?" Elizabeth asked. "That seems awfully early."

"We had to finish the game before the tide covered the ball field," said Carl.

In the afternoon, a large number of townspeople boarded fishing boats for a picnic at Browns Cove on the mainland. They waved at the passengers on the southbound *Spokane* that arrived just as the picnickers left port. Before long, the strains of another marching band called everyone outdoors to witness the returning Shriners, preceded by their band, marching up Main Street to the bandstand. The plank street resonated with their marching feet. Each Shriner was dressed in full regalia with topcoat and fez. Children ran excitedly alongside the impromptu parade.

They congregated at the bandstand and presented a programme of distinguished speakers, more music by the band and vocal pieces by exceptional singers. Carl and Elizabeth took turns holding the baby as they watched from the hotel porch.

"This is a surprise," said Carl. "Nobody on the entertainment committee knew they were coming."

One Shriner read the Declaration of Independence. The mayor of Portland gave an address on "The Flag and Our Duty To It, and What It Stands For". The Shriners and their wives led the gathering in singing "America" and the Shrine Band closed the programme with "The Star Spangled Banner".

The big parade started at ten the next morning, July 5. The Kake Band had the honor of leading the parade followed by the American Legion boys, school children and others. Once again, Carl and Elizabeth had an outstanding viewing position from the hotel porch. They were unable to leave the hotel unattended to participate in the patriotic exercises that followed in the Variety Theatre but enjoyed several sporting events taking place on Main Street in the afternoon.

"So do you think the Kake boys redeemed themselves for losing the baseball game?" Elizabeth asked Carl.

"They did all right, thanks to their women. They won the women's 100 yard dash, the ball throwing contest and the women's nail driving contest."

"I'm going to walk down to the dock and see the start of the race between the *Americ* and the *Jugoslav*," he added. "It's thirteen miles round trip from the Citizen's Dock to a stake boat at Browns Cove, so they'll be gone awhile and I'll be right back."

The *Jugoslav* beat the other boat by more than two minutes. Activity lessened on Main Street as everyone went home to prepare for the big dance at the Sons of Norway Hall. Dancing continued until 3:00 a.m. and everybody agreed the celebration was a complete success.

A native girl from Kake walked past the house as Elizabeth stepped outside to hang the laundry. Elizabeth tossed pebbles at a large flock of ravens impeding her path to the clothesline. The big black birds stopped pecking at the dirt and hopped out of her way. "Don't do that," said the girl. "Those are my ancestors."

Elizabeth was so astonished that she blurted out, "Then why can't you fly?"

The native girl burst into tears and ran down the street.

Later, Elizabeth told Carl about the encounter. "Remember when you told me about the Tlingits and their Raven Clan?" she said.

"Sure."

"I thought you meant they simply worshiped the raven," said Elizabeth. "Before today, I didn't know that they actually believe they are reincarnated as ravens."

"I didn't know that either," said Carl. "I wonder if that's really true or if that's just what that girl believes."

Charlie Greenaa celebrated his birthday with a dance and dinner party at the Hotel Arctic. Carl prepared the midnight luncheon that included his famous individual salads. Charlie saw Elizabeth peeking through the back door to observe the goings on and insisted on a dance.

"I can't leave the baby, Charlie, but I just wanted to wish you a Happy Birthday," she said.

"Nonsense," said Charlie. "Olaf, trot over to the house and sit with the baby while I dance with her mother."

He danced Elizabeth around the dining room until they were both laughing uncontrollably. Elizabeth hadn't danced so hard since before she and Carl were married. He finally released her and she hurried through the kitchen, gave Carl a quick kiss, and relieved Olaf of his babysitting duties. Elizabeth was asleep when Carl finally came to bed. In the morning, he told her the party broke up in the wee small hours. "That Charlie," he said. "He kept everyone so entertained that they can't wait until his birthday next year. He told me that the Sanitary Market is about to announce an agreement with Carl Swanson over at Point Agassiz to sell local dairy products."

"How will that work?" asked Elizabeth.

"You place your order with Charlie at the Sanitary Market," replied Carl. "Swanson makes deliveries by boat three days a week and you pick up your order at Charlie's store."

"What kind of dairy products will they handle?" asked Elizabeth.

"Milk, cream, butter, cottage cheese and eggs."

"It would be so nice to have those items locally," Elizabeth replied. "By the time the steamers arrive from Seattle, the milk is sometimes sour and every other egg is rotten."

The weather stayed unseasonably hot and sunny the entire month of July. Temperatures between 85 and 90 degrees drew everybody outdoors. Carl and Elizabeth arranged a picnic on their property out the point. Carl loaded their picnic supplies and the baby into a wheelbarrow and they hiked to the end of the plank street and continued along the footpath paralleling the beach until they reached their scenic knoll.

"Look at that view, Mother. Have you ever seen anything so pretty?"

The Sukoi Islets were blue green with thick forest; they could see all the way across Frederick Sound to Horn Cliffs, and the calls of seagulls, crows and blue jays carried far in the still summer air.

"Which of those islands did you say has the fox ranch?" Elizabeth asked.

"Not quite sure myself," said Carl. "Used to be Claude Green's place but now a fellow named Chastek has it. He calls it the Hercules Fox Ranch."

"We'll put the front of the house right here," he continued, "with a big window so we can admire the scenery and watch the passing boats." Carl paced off the dimensions of their future home while Elizabeth watched over the baby as she crawled through the grass.

"Carl, look what Betty found. It's a strawberry. Why, there are hundreds of wild strawberries hidden in the grass."

"That's sure to be a sign of good luck," he said.

Elizabeth picked an apron full of the small, sweet berries to add to their picnic.

Not everyone was pleased with the hot weather. The lobby regulars bemoaned a lack of fish buyers.

"I hear Ripley Fish Company stopped buying salmon and halibut altogether until the hot spell is over," said one of the men.

"Yep, just too hot to keep the fish for the fresh fish trade," replied another.

"Seems the canned fish business isn't doing as well as hoped, either," added the first man. "The Mutual Packing Company's floating cannery passed through the Narrows heading south yesterday. They said the salmon run in Icy Straits was a failure and none of the canneries reached their expected packs."

"Mayor Elsemore just returned from a trip to the East Coast and said people down below are talking about a recession," he continued. "Farmers need loans for fall plantings, only the country banks don't have any money. So the country banks are trying to borrow money from the city banks to finance the farmers. If farmers don't get their crops in the ground, there'll be a food shortage too."

"Goes to show, times are tough all over," added another. "How's that pulp and paper mill coming along at Thomas Bay?"

"Seems to be mostly talk so far. They keep sending engineers to assess the site. I hear they're building one at Juneau too and that one's further along. It'll be interesting to see if they can pull it off, given the rising transportation costs."

"Mother, come look at the Navy ships," said Carl.

Elizabeth arrived at the hotel doorway in time to see three grey torpedo boats slowly thread their way through Wrangell Narrows. They passed in single file as townspeople watched the procession from the waterfront. "What are they doing here?" Elizabeth asked.

"The first destroyer is carrying the Secretary of the Navy, Secretary of the Interior, Commander of the Pacific Fleet and the Governor of Alaska," said Carl. "Wharfinger Parks tells me they're on their way westward to inspect progress on the government railroad and some naval coaling stations."

Residents waved from the shore and some of the sailors waved back as the big ships gained Frederick Sound and turned north for Juneau.

They were visited by another big ship several days later – the U.S. Naval Destroyer *Moody*. The ship docked overnight and the visiting officers were given a tour of the Petersburg Packing Company cannery. The new ship was 310 feet long and the bow and stern extended well beyond the width of the Citizen's Dock.

The hotel was full most of the summer. Two representatives from the Dynes Company spent several days compiling a directory and tourist guide of the area. Carl and Elizabeth assisted them in identifying local points of interest before the men continued north to gather information on other southeastern towns.

Several tourists were stranded in town when the steamer *Spokane* was sent to drydock in Seattle to repair hull damage. Every berth on the ship, both north and southbound, had been sold out and the Pacific Steamship Company was forced to cancel the bookings. Many guests had come north on earlier boats and were booked to return on the *Spokane*. While the tourists were inconvenienced, the extra business was good for the hotel. Several extended their stays while working out other travel arrangements.

Doctor and Mrs. Mathis returned from several weeks in Wrangell. "Doctor Mathis just informed the city council that smallpox has been raging in Wrangell for the past several months and it's only a matter of time before it's brought here," Mrs. Mathis announced.

"Have there been any deaths?" Elizabeth asked.

"Not that we know of. However, you can't be too careful."

"What's the city council doing about it?" asked Elizabeth.

"They voted to supply free vaccinations to anyone desiring them as a precaution and Dr. Carothers offered to vaccinate everyone free of charge."

"Have you been vaccinated?" Elizabeth asked, glancing at the baby.

"Oh my, yes," said Mrs. Mathis. "We travel back and forth so often, we wouldn't want to take chances."

When Elizabeth repeated the conversation to Carl, he said, "Yes, I heard. I didn't want to worry you. The council also purchased a pest house on the muskeg that they'll keep boarded up in case they ever need to quarantine somebody there."

"Doesn't the latest remodel at the hospital include space for contagious diseases?" asked Elizabeth.

"Yes, it does," said Carl. "They converted the old woodshed into two rooms for that purpose. There are no occupants in those rooms at the moment, but I understand the hospital has been full ever since those two nurses took over. Seems they've had their hands full recently with an insane patient too."

"What happened?" asked Elizabeth.

"They arrested a stranger in town, and he was adjudged insane in commissioner's court and ordered to Morningside. But, he faked an illness and was taken to the hospital where he created a disturbance among the other patients. The nurses had to use a club on him before help arrived."

"Sounds like we have tough nurses," said Elizabeth.

A loud humming noise brought people running into the street. "Look up," cried a bystander.

An aeroplane flew down Wrangell Narrows from the north, circled the waters in front of town, and returned over the same course it followed coming in. For many, it was their first sight of a flying plane.

"It's one of the planes from the New York-to-Nome air squadron," said Carl. "Four planes are making the 9,000 mile round trip and they're supposed to land at the mouth of the Stikine River near Wrangell for supplies. I wonder where the other planes are?"

They later learned that the planes had become separated in heavy fog but reunited at Glenora at the headwaters of the Stikine. The supplies awaiting them at Wrangell were shipped up river to the waiting planes.

"Mother, do you remember Captain Nord from the *Jefferson*?" asked Carl.

"How could I forget him?" said Elizabeth. "He was so nice to me on my first trip to Alaska. Invited us up to the wheelhouse and everything."

"Well, according to wharfinger Parks, the Alaska Steamship Company just made him the first Commodore Captain of their fleet. He's been with them for twenty-six years and when the *Jefferson* was first built, brought her on her first trip north. He presently skippers the *Alaska* and that steamer will now fly the commodore's flag."

"The steamship company is lucky to have such a man," Elizabeth replied.

Chapter 20

September 1920 – The regulars in the lobby wore long faces. "The cannery quit processing fish for the season," said one of the men, "and they only put up 54,000 cases for their effort."

"How's that compare with last year's pack?" asked another man.

"They had 85,000 cases last year and considered it a bad year," said the first man. "I tell you, it's gonna be a long hard winter for a lot of folks."

"You may be right, especially now that town merchants have stopped issuing credit. Why most folks charge their groceries and essentials all winter long and then pay the stores after fishing season starts in the spring. Not this winter."

"Who stopped issuing credit?" asked the first man.

"You name it – Hogue & Tveten, Petersburg Meat Company, The Trading Union, Sanitary Market and the Petersburg Mercantile Company. All accounts are due and payable on the tenth of the month and no further credit extended until payment in full. And, they're all charging 10 percent on overdue accounts."

"Why the change?"

"Luther Hogue says their wholesale dealers down below are insisting on cash or no more than thirty-day credits due to the tough financial conditions throughout the country. So they have to pass that on to the general public. He also said the country is no longer in a recession, but a full-fledged depression."

"We just heard from the Ellison-White Chautauqua group that they're canceling their Alaska tour this season," added Carl. "They claim they've never made a profit on the Alaska circuit and they won't be back until they've settled their unpaid bills. Sounds like everybody is scaling back."

"Listening to the men in the lobby can be downright depressing," Elizabeth told Carl later. "Do you think things are really as bad as they say?"

"We're clearly in for some belt tightening, but we'll manage," said Carl. "There's plenty of fish for the catching and clams for the digging. And there'll be venison and ducks as soon as hunting season starts. I don't want you to worry, Mother. In fact, you should listen in the next time editor Perkins drops by. He can find signs of progress that others overlook."

The boys from the Petersburg Packing Company held a farewell dance at the Sons of Norway Hall. Mary Allen claimed it was one of the best dances of the year. "They served sandwiches, cake and coffee in the club rooms upstairs at midnight," she said, "and the dancing downstairs only stopped when the light plant shut down."

"What's the collection jar for?" Elizabeth asked.

"The Fire Department is collecting for the Near East Relief Fund for starving orphans," said Carl. "And they've placed literature and subscription lists around town. According to the literature, it costs $60 a year for each orphan. Petersburg's quota is $300 to support five orphans for one year."

"People here are very generous, even when they haven't much themselves," said Elizabeth.

"In addition to collections around town, Petersburg girls are selling tickets to a big dance at the Sons of Norway to benefit the children," Carl added. "And the Fire Department and Jim Brennan each adopted an orphan."

"It says in this brochure," said Elizabeth, "that the orphans range from babies to sixteen-year-olds and they wander the country eating grass roots and garbage. Those admitted to the orphanages established by Congress only get three spoonfuls of rice a day. How tragic."

When the campaign was over, the town transmitted $517 to the relief organization to support the starving orphans of Armenian war victims.

Ed Locken joined the men in the lobby. "We just closed the lumber mill for the season," he said. "One logging camp is still working, though, getting out a supply of logs for our spring start up."

"How did you do this season?" asked one of the men.

"Not bad, considering we got a late start due to the reorganization," said Locken. "We cut between four and five million feet of lumber. Most of it went for the Petersburg-Scow Bay road but we did send two shipments south. This was the first year we shipped lumber out of town."

"What do you hear about the plans for the pulp and paper mill at Thomas Bay?" asked one of the men.

"We're not involved with that directly, but the last engineer that came to town said he was looking at it from every angle and the Forestry Service was being especially helpful."

"We sure could use another source of income," said the first man. "We're too dependent on commercial fishing."

Wharfinger Parks joined the group. "The southbound *Jefferson* is due in a few hours," he said. "She's carrying a million-dollar cargo."

"What could be so valuable?" asked one of the men.

"Five safes of gold dust from claims in the Interior are going south before the Yukon freezes up," said the wharfinger. "She's also carrying thousands of dollars of furs, including one bale valued at $30,000. And she's finally taking out large shipments of fresh fish from Southeastern."

"Let's hope she has a safe trip to Seattle, then," said another man.

The lobby regulars spent much of October arguing politics. Elizabeth gathered that Grigsby and Sutherland were among the candidates for Alaska's Delegate to Congress and Henry Roden was running for the territorial legislature. Beyond that, most of the discussion was lost on her. Carl didn't share his political opinions. He believed doing so could be bad for business.

Elizabeth was more concerned with the situation at the light and power plant. "The new engine is sitting on a scow next to the plant," said Carl, "waiting for the machinist to dismantle the old engine."

"Are we going to be without light and power for very long?" Elizabeth asked.

"The town will be dark for two weeks or so," said Carl. "The business district will have power from the smaller engine they're leaving in place, although it will only be running during the evening hours."

"I'm glad we live in the business district then," said Elizabeth.

That evening, as they lay warm beneath the quilts, Elizabeth told Carl they were expecting another baby.

"Are you sure?" he said. "How far along are you?"

"A couple of months," said Elizabeth. "I waited until I was certain before telling you. I know this isn't the best time to be expanding our family."

"Nonsense," he said. "Anytime is the best time. How do you feel?"

"I feel fine. So you're happy about this then?"

"Of course I am," said Carl. "Don't worry so much. Everything will work out. When do you think the baby will come?"

"Sometime in June, I think."

"Ah, a summertime baby," said Carl. "That's perfect."

"Daddy?"

"Yes, Mother?"

"I want to have this baby in Petersburg. We have good doctors here now and it's too expensive to travel to Evanston like I did with Betty."

"Are you sure?" he asked. "The two Doctor Rowley's moved to Juneau a few months back."

"We still have Dr. Johannesson and Dr. Carothers is getting his Alaska medical license," said Elizabeth. "The hospital has been modernized and the two nurses in charge are doing an excellent job running it. No, now that I know what to expect, I think it would be best to have the baby here."

"Whatever you think, Mother."

The light and power plant was shut down totally when it was discovered that the old engine needed repair before it could be put on line with the new engine.

"The men are relining the generator and putting a bushing in the old engine," said Carl. "We'll be without power for a few days. It's a good thing they're doing this after the tourist season and before winter sets in."

"What's wrong with the old engine?" Elizabeth asked.

"The town outgrew the old one and needed a bigger engine," said Carl. "The city council thought it best to get it installed before winter. Of course, if Pearl Oil stays in short supply, it won't really matter what size engine we have. They won't run without fuel."

Just when it seemed the situation couldn't get worse, the men shut off the town's water.

"And how will this be an improvement?" Elizabeth asked Carl.

"They're moving the overflow for the dam from the top of the hill to the bottom of the hill," he said. "That's so the fire department can control water pressure in the main whenever they're fighting a fire."

Everyone except Mrs. Mathis seemed to take the lack of power and water in stride. "I don't know if I can take another winter under such conditions," she said. "I'm really trying to convince Ray to move back to the states."

"Knud Stenslid tells me he and his partner are going to excavate Steberg's lot over on 'E' Street," said Carl one day.

"What does that involve?" asked Elizabeth.

"They'll hydraulic out the dirt and prepare the site," said Carl. "It's a big lot – 45 by 100 feet – and Steberg plans to put up a two or three-story brick building in the spring."

"How is it a former baker has the skills for this type of work?" asked Elizabeth.

"You'd be surprised what Knud can do," said Carl. "Why, when he expanded the Star Bakery a few years ago, he built the oven with enough bricks to build a small house. He only leased it out because he was tired of being the only merchant in town at work at three in the morning."

With the dining room closed for the season, Carl decided to lease it out to Dr. A. B. Jones who arrived from Juneau to open his practice.

"I passed through Petersburg a few weeks ago on a hunting trip and liked what I saw," he told them. "My wife will be here for a few weeks and then she's going east to collect our daughter and bring her here as well."

Mrs. Jones, Mrs. Mathis and Elizabeth got acquainted over coffee. "And how old is your little girl?" Elizabeth asked.

"She's thirteen," replied Mrs. Jones. "Too young to travel alone, although she doesn't think so. She's going to school in Boston and will transfer to the Petersburg school."

"I understand you're going to take a new route east, bypassing Seattle altogether," said Mrs. Mathis.

"Yes. Over the Canadian National Railway."

"Where do you make connections?" asked Mrs. Mathis.

"First, I take the steamer to Wrangell, the *Jefferson* I think," said Mrs. Jones, "where I transfer to a Canadian Princess ship. The Canadian boat takes me south to Prince Rupert where I connect with the railway. The railroad runs all the way across Canada with spurs crossing the border at Chicago and New York. I'll take the spur to New York and from there to Boston."

"I'll have to consider that route the next time I travel to Chicago," said Elizabeth. "Why you'll bypass the crossing of Queen Charlotte Sound too, which can be the roughest part of the trip."

A disturbance on Main Street brought the ladies to the hotel window where they observed a man beating his wife with a beer bottle. He struck her above the left temple, shattering the bottle and cutting her face in several places. Marshal Howell arrived on the scene and disarmed the man of an open razor. Doctor Jones rushed to the woman's aid while the marshal took her drunken husband into custody.

Mrs. Mathis turned to Mrs. Jones and said, "Welcome to Petersburg."

"I heard the *City of Seattle* is taking $63,000 worth of foxes south," said Carl.

"That must be a lot of pelts," Elizabeth replied.

"These aren't pelts, they're live foxes," said Carl. "The Hercules Fox Company over on the Sukoi Islets added thirty foxes to those already on board from Skagway and the Interior. Chastek is shipping twenty blues and ten silvers to his farm in Minnesota. And Andy Anderson just received twenty-eight foxes from the westward that he's placing on islands in this area."

"Do you think the fox trade will continue to be a growing business?" Elizabeth asked.

"It's hard to say," said Carl. "Fred Patten tells me fur prices for marten and muskrat are dropping in the London market. It's anyone's guess if that'll extend to fox furs."

The election was over and most of the men in the lobby approved the results of the race.

"It's now up to Harding and Coolidge to fix this mess that fool Wilson got us into," said one of the men. "General bankruptcy and ruin are certain in this depression unless they find a way to protect farmers from the present price situation. And whatever hurts the farmer finds its way down the line to every man, woman and child in America."

"And who would have predicted that Alaska's entire territorial legislature would be elected on the Republican ticket?" said another, to no one in particular.

"It looks like Dan Sutherland's our new Delegate to Congress," continued the first man. "Made you wonder, though, when his remarks at the Variety Theatre were received in dead silence on his campaign stop here. He did get some applause when he mentioned the work the United States marshals and their deputies were doing, though."

Later, Elizabeth asked Carl how Henry Roden had fared in the contest for the territorial legislature.

"He didn't have much of a chance, running as a Democrat," he said.

"Maybe he should have changed parties," Elizabeth suggested.

Carl just chuckled, "It really doesn't work that way."

The town turned quiet with more people leaving than arriving. The Baltimore Grill closed for the season, one of the two nurses at the hospital left for her Wrangell home, the city council ordered the light and power plant to run twenty-four hours a day and reported the water dam to be in good shape for the winter. And a new Lutheran minister arrived to fill the vacancy left by Reverend Maakestad.

Carl was outraged when home brew was actively brought under the prohibition law. "Can you believe it?" he fumed. "It's bad enough you can't have hard liquor for your own consumption, but to keep people from making home brew? Why, half the population of the town won't make it through the winter without it."

"What change did they make in the law?" Elizabeth asked.

"They're prohibiting all sales of hops and malt except to bakers and manufacturing confectioners who have to prove their supply is confined strictly to their needs to carry on their business."

Secretly, Elizabeth thought this was a good thing, but she held her tongue. At least Carl kept his home brew crock in a back room at the hotel so their clothing and home wouldn't smell of beer.

Betty was one year old. The weather was too cold and rainy to take her outdoors so Elizabeth dressed her in a party dress and took her over to the hotel where the lobby regulars fussed over her. Carl bounced her on his knee and the baby loved being the center of attention.

Two of Elizabeth's lady friends came to call in the afternoon – Gussie York from the Citizen's Steam Laundry and Mary Allen from the post office. Elizabeth served a chocolate birthday cake covered with white seven-minute frosting and a single candle in the middle. She put Betty down for a nap when the excitement of the day finally caught up with the baby and returned to the kitchen just as Gussie was saying, "I noticed the lights are out in Dr. Mathis' office. Have they gone to Juneau or Wrangell again?"

"No," Mary Allen replied, "Mrs. Mathis finally convinced the dentist to take six months off and they've left for the states. I'm forwarding their mail. I hope they come back, but he clearly likes it here better than she does. Elizabeth," she continued, "you have the most adorable little girl, and this cake is delicious."

"Why thank you," said Elizabeth. "She can scoot across the floor almost as fast as I can run and she's started pulling herself upright on the furniture. She could start walking any day now. And, Betty is going to have a little brother or sister soon."

"No," said Mary Allen. "Why that's wonderful. You don't even show. When are you expecting?"

"Sometime in June I think."

"And are you going to your old home in Illinois like you did with Betty?" asked Gussie.

"Not this time. This baby's going to be born in Alaska. Carl and I are looking forward to raising our family here."

Editor Perkins joined the men in the lobby. "Well, the cat's out of the bag," he said. "Erick Ness is starting up a shrimp and crab plant. He and his partner secured quarters on the approach to the Public Dock and they've got carpenters busy putting the space in order."

"What does he have in mind?" asked one of the men.

"They're going to ship picked shrimp in five-pound cans and cooked crab to the Seattle market," said Perkins. "They're calling the concern the Ness Fish Company."

"Who they got fishing for them?" asked another man.

"They're going to use a hired boat for the first few months and put on more as soon as business warrants," replied the newspaperman. "Given the general lack of jobs, they're offering employment to about twenty people to start, giving preference to white men and women and those with families."

"How's Earl Ohmer feel about the new competition?" asked another man.

"He says there's room for everyone. His Alaskan Glacier Sea Food Company now has six boats shrimping for him and he's putting up between four and six tons of shrimp a day."

Elizabeth listened in as she mopped the lobby floor.

"I know people around here grouse about the bad year," continued Perkins, "but we've got a lot going for us too. Shrimp fishing is good enough to attract a second processor. The sawmill had a successful season under new ownership. Trapping and fur farming are very lucrative. More new houses were built in Petersburg than ever before. The Scow Bay road is nearly completed. Scow Bay got a new reduction plant and their cold storage plant is nearly completed. The city power plant has increased capacity, deposits at the Bank of Petersburg are higher than ever before, and I increased the *Report* from four to six pages. Given the failure of the salmon processing industry this season, I think we've come through in fine shape."

"And maybe we've got the right team in Washington now to get the country out of this dammed depression," echoed another man.

The city council instructed all users of motors of three horse power and over to shut them off between the hours of 4:00 and 11:00 p.m. daily. The city electrician was authorized to shut off electrical power to offenders without further instruction from the council. Although the new rules were not a hardship for Elizabeth and Carl, she continued to be amazed by the inability of the new power plant engine to make any real difference in the delivery of electrical power.

The annual Red Cross roll call was conducted during the week before Christmas. No house-to-house canvass was made. Rather, lists and supplies were placed in various business houses for all to sign up and leave their dollar. The treasurer collected the donations on Christmas Eve and hotel guests and visitors filled the collection jar almost to the top.

Doctor Jones got an unexpected patient when a badly beaten and bloodied fisherman staggered into the lobby. The doctor administered first aid and enlisted several men to help move the injured man to the hospital. Upon his return, he told Carl what happened.

"The fisherman says he was resting in his bunk on his boat tied up to the wharf when another man boarded the boat and tried to throw him off," said the doctor. "They fought for a while and then a second man came up behind him and knocked him out with an iron bar. They threw him onto the wharf and another boat cruising the area passed a line to the two men and towed the boat out into the Narrows."

"Did he get a look at the two men?" asked Carl.

"He said they were strangers to him but gave the marshal a description as best he could recall. Sam Gauffin and several men took the *Lorraine* and went looking for the stolen boat. They know they headed north and the marshal wired warrants to all deputy marshals in the First Division. It's not likely they'll get very far."

"And how's the injured party?" asked Carl.

"He's in pretty bad shape but no broken bones," said the doctor. "How he managed to crawl uptown after regaining consciousness, I'll never know. I expect he'll be spending several days in the hospital."

After hearing this story from Carl, Elizabeth showed him a letter from her sister Ruthie. She wrote that a band of thugs overran the city and was committing street attacks on women in Evanston. Policemen armed with rifles were patrolling the streets in autos and hundreds of detectives disguised as women patrolled the streets with revolvers in their hand satchels. "We're afraid to go out even in broad daylight," Ruthie wrote. "This lawlessness has got to end."

Mary Allen promised to stop by and show Elizabeth her costume for the New Year's Eve Masquerade Ball hosted by the Moose at the Sons of Norway Hall. She was dressed as a yellow butterfly with chiffon wings stretched over a wire frame.

"Why Mary, you look beautiful," said Elizabeth. "You're sure to win first prize."

"Do you think so?" she said. "I can't wait to see what everyone else is wearing."

"Promise you'll stop in tomorrow and tell us all about it?"

"I will, but not too early," Mary laughed. "I expect to be up late tonight."

As she glided happily up the street, Carl turned to Elizabeth and said, "Are you sure you wouldn't rather be going to the dance? I could stay home with the baby."

"Not at all," said Elizabeth. "I don't think it proper in my condition and without an escort. I'd much rather welcome in the new year with just you and little Betty."

Elizabeth and Carl spent a quiet New Year's Eve at home. Elisabeth worked on a new handbag for the summer tourist trade while Carl revised the plans for their new home for the millionth time.

"Mother, where would you like the kitchen?" he asked.

"What are my choices?"

"It needs to be in the rear of the house so we can have a large front room with a view," he said. "Do you want it on the side nearest the creek or on the side closest to town?"

"Let's put it on the side nearest the creek. We can still see a piece of the Narrows from the kitchen table beneath the window."

Elizabeth looked over his shoulder at the two-story log house taking shape in his drawings. "How will you get the logs to the site?" she asked.

"We'll float them down the Narrows from the mill. Once we get them on the beach, we'll drag them up the hill with a donkey engine and block and tackle. Then we'll have to season the logs."

"How do you do that?" asked Elizabeth.

"First, we'll use only the best red cedar logs cut in the fall after the sap goes down," he replied. "Then we'll lay them out on a couple of other logs to season by rotating them 180 degrees for several months. It'll be easier to peel off the bark after they've shrunk a little. When we're ready to build, we'll lay the sill logs on the ground and build up from there, joining the logs together with lock joint notches."

"Show me the room layouts again," said Elizabeth. "I love thinking about where to place the furniture."

"When you walk through our front door," he said, "you step into a small coat room where you can leave your coat and boots. When you leave the coat room, you can either climb the stairs to the second story, walk straight ahead to the lavatory, or turn left and enter the front room. This room extends to the far wall of the house and has a large window overlooking the Narrows. A heating stove in this room backs up to a chimney that extends right through the second floor and out through the roof. You can't see the chimney though, because it's hidden behind the walls. From the front room you can either walk into the spare room which we'll use for visitors, hanging laundry and anything else you want, or walk into the kitchen."

"Now, the kitchen stove backs up to the same chimney used by the front room heating stove," he continued. "The kitchen sink is right next to the stove. And a door leads from the kitchen outside where we'll have a woodshed, clothesline and pantry for keeping foods cool."

"And what about upstairs?" asked Elizabeth.

"Well, upstairs will be all one large room with beds tucked beneath the eaves and lots of closet space on the walls. The chimney from downstairs occupies the center of the room and helps heat the upstairs. Since heat rises, we'll also get warm air coming up the stairwell from down below."

"Oh Daddy, I can't wait to move in."

"That," he laughed, "will depend on when we've saved enough money to start building. In the meantime, we can enjoy the site and you and Betty can pick strawberries."

Mary came by the next afternoon full of stories about the masquerade ball. "You were right," she exclaimed. "My costume won first prize for best-dressed lady."

"Didn't I tell you?" said Elizabeth. "Tell me about the affair."

"The hall was decorated in evergreens and colored streamers and they had a five-piece orchestra," said Mary.

"Oh, there were clowns, highwaymen, southern belles, dandies, nurses, French diplomats and a British ambassador," she continued. "And there was a wild Zulu cannibal with enormous earrings and pointy false teeth. He won the prize for most comical character. Mrs. Hans Wick was a wise owl passing out checks drawn on the bank of good wishes. And Barbara Gauffin was the Queen of Hearts with the other cards of the deck displayed on her costume."

"And then there was a curly-haired little girl in a pink summer frock with pink sash and pink stockings," she laughed. "You'll never guess who she turned out to be when the masks were removed."

"Who?" asked Elizabeth.

"None other than Joe Hill of Joe and Jack's Place," laughed Mary Allen.

"There's something to be said," said Carl, "for a community where people of character pull together with good cheer and camaraderie to welcome in the new year despite a disappointing season."

Chapter 21

January 1921 – Carl tried not to worry Elizabeth, but she could see he was concerned about the lack of business. The lobby regulars seemed to take perverse pleasure in bemoaning the dark state of business conditions.

"Luther Hogue just got back from Seattle," said one, "and he says to expect further rises in the price of cotton goods, rubber goods and paper of all kinds. He says market conditions are unsettled, is the word he used."

"People claim the salmon canners are hopelessly broke unless they can market last season's pack still sitting in warehouses," added another. "Even the Wakefield outfit is selling some of their canneries."

"There's always halibut fishing," said Carl.

"True, if you can survive the weather. The *Baltic* just got back from the banks where the weather was so foul she lost eight skates of gear. A Ketchikan boat lost all her gear and returned to port empty. Furthermore, nobody can afford to buy all new gear for halibut fishing and pay for a place to stow their nets until salmon season."

"Say, did you hear about that Ketchikan boat that was offloading herring and a flock of starving seagulls flew right down into the hold?" asked the first man.

"No, what about it?"

"The birds so gorged themselves that they couldn't fly out again. The crew had to place a plank so they could walk out."

Carl looked downcast when he came home for lunch.

"Well Mother," he said, "just when I thought conditions couldn't get any worse, Doc Jones informed me today that he's closing his office at the hotel and moving to Wrangell. We really need the rent to keep the hotel going until things improve."

"Can you rent the space to another doctor?" Elizabeth asked.

"I don't see how. Doc Carothers is comfortably situated at the hospital and we never know when a new doctor may step off an inbound steamer."

"What are we going to do?"

"I need to make a quick trip south and talk to Chris Wester about delaying payments on the hotel until these crazy business conditions improve," said Carl. "It's not the sort of news you put in a wire or a letter. Do you think you and Mrs. Henderson could run things here for several days while I'm away, and in your condition?"

"Of course we can," said Elizabeth. "I'm only four months along and feel fine. When would you leave?"

"I checked at the steamship office," said Carl, "and the southbound *Admiral Watson* is due here on February 18 and leaves Seattle again six days later. I'll send Chris a wire to let him know I'm coming."

The baby began teething again. She already had four front teeth on top and four on the bottom. She chewed on anything she could get her hands on to relieve the pressure and drooled constantly. Elizabeth was on constant alert to see she didn't put foreign objects into her mouth. Betty's first words had been "dada, maaa," and "uh-oh." She also communicated in baby talk while pointing to something she wanted. She clearly understood much more than she could express. She mastered saying "no" with authority and kept Elizabeth and Mrs. Henderson smiling and entertained with each new discovery.

The men in the lobby reviewed the latest edition of the *Petersburg Weekly Report.*

"Looks like Perkins is putting his new linotype machine to good use," said one of the men. "He's expanded the paper to six pages. You wouldn't think there's enough going on around here to fill two more pages."

"You'll notice he's printing a new weekly report from Kake on the extra pages," replied another.

"So what's the news from Kake?" asked the first man.

"Well, let's see here. Seems 124 votes were cast in their town election. Billy Grant has two fine wolf hides and he'd like to see the law changed so he can collect the bounty by just sending the hides to Juneau rather than appearing in person. Natives from Killisnoo brought in many furs and moccasins for trading. And most of the people left town for their fish camps, leaving only two students enrolled in the government school."

The bell above the door rang as Henry Roden stepped into the lobby. He gave Elizabeth a hug after hanging his wet coat and hat on the coat rack.

"Why Mrs. Roger," he said, "you're looking well."

"Thank you, Mr. Roden. What brings you to town?"

"Just got in on the steamer. I'll be spending a few days here on business. How's Carl?"

"He had to make a quick trip to Seattle. He'll be so disappointed he missed you."

"Ah, that's too bad. Is my usual room available?"

"That it is."

Henry scooped up the baby and joined the men in the lobby while Elizabeth sent Mrs. Henderson to his room with fresh towels.

The men told Henry about the disappearance of the wreck of the *Mariposa*.

"That old steamer's been sitting there on Strait Island for more than three years," said one of the men. "We pass her every time we travel down Sumner Strait. And then, last Wednesday it was, we pass the island and the wreck was just gone. Slipped into the sea at last, I imagine."

Henry spent three days in town before catching a gasboat to Juneau. Elizabeth reminded him to give Mrs. Roden her best and to tell Margaret to come visit soon.

Carl returned on the *Admiral Watson* on a cold, wintry Sunday. The temperature was below freezing and it was too cold to snow. A fracas broke out between some passengers and the purser while the ship was in port. Carl said the men had been spoiling for a fight ever since leaving Seattle and managed to escape down the gangplank just as the free-for-all got underway.

They finally got time alone after Carl had seen to the hotel and exchanged news with the men in the lobby.

"What did Mr. Wester have to say?" Elizabeth asked.

"He was very understanding. Said with the whole country in a depression, everybody is suffering. But he really wants to get his money out of the hotel and will take any reasonable offer from the first man who comes along."

"Does he think we should be doing better?"

"No, no," said Carl. "We went over the books together and he could see that business just isn't at the level it used to be. Of course, he wants me to get back to making regular payments as soon as possible but we shouldn't be surprised if he sells the business out from under us if he gets a good offer. He had some ideas about the dining room. Thinks we could make more money by renting the space for some other purpose, like the arrangement I had with Doc Jones. He doesn't think enough people are eating out to make the restaurant business profitable right now."

"While you were away," said Elizabeth, "Leonard Heys reopened the Baltimore Grill and Sammy Nakamoto reopened the Petersburg Restaurant."

"There you go then. It'll be interesting to see how they do."

"What are we going to do?"

"We'll continue to advertise and hope business improves this coming season. And once it does, we'll be able to send Chris full payments again. Most of all, Mother, you're not to worry. Everything will work out."

Spring rains replaced the cold weather and activity quickened around town. The Trading Union extended the Public Dock; work was started on a new Union Hall and Public Library Building, and on a parsonage for the pastor of the Lutheran Church.

Carl was successful in leasing out space in the dining room.

"George Nelson and his partner are going to open a first class gentlemen's resort in part of our dining room," he told Elizabeth.

"George Nelson, the barber?"

"Yep. They're calling their place the 'Arctic Club' and they'll have cigars, candies, soft drinks, tobacco and cigarettes. They're also putting in card tables. And George is moving his barber chairs from the new

Gauffin Building to a side room next to the club to provide privacy for children who come in for a haircut."

Fast on the heels of installing the new tenants came word that the hotel guest who claimed her jewels went missing from her room last summer had filed suit against Carl in District Court.

"Now what?" Elizabeth asked Carl.

"I don't really know," he said. "According to these papers, the woman claims her valuables were taken from her room through the negligence of employees of the hotel. It's not clear if she's accusing the employees of theft or failing to secure her room so someone slipped in and robbed her. I mentioned this incident to Chris Wester and he advised just waiting to see if a court agrees she has a claim. At some point, I may have to testify or maybe she'll just drop the whole thing."

"That was more than eight months ago," said Elizabeth. "I can't believe she still thinks she can squeeze money out of you when she has no proof of wrongdoing."

"It takes all kinds," said Carl. "We'll just wait and see what develops."

Editor Perkins told the men in the lobby that he was enthusiastic about business prospects. "Even if we have a slow salmon season this year," he said, "it looks like shellfish processing will take up much of the slack."

"How do you figure?" asked one of the men.

"First of all, the new Ellson and Malcolm shrimp and crab cannery is putting up their first pack this week. They're marketing shellfish under the 'Gold Dollar Brand.' And, of course, we have the Ness Fish Company and the Alaskan Glacier Sea Food Company that are now starting up again. Add to these two more shrimp canneries entering the field – the plant they're building on the beach south of Standard Oil and Dobbins Packing Company's floating shrimp cannery. That brings the total to five shrimp-packing plants employing between 150 and 200 people."

"But do any of them pay a living wage?" asked one of the men.

"At twelve cents a pound for picked meat, a good picker can make several dollars a day," replied Perkins.

Mrs. Mathis was among the passengers arriving from the south on the *City of Seattle.*

"It's so good to see you, Elizabeth," she said. "What's this? Could that be a new little Roger I see beneath your apron?"

"You have such poor manners," Elizabeth laughed. "Yes it is; I'm expecting sometime in June. And it's good to see you, too."

She gave Elizabeth a hug and the two women caught up on the news as Carl took her luggage to her room.

"Is Dr. Mathis with you?" Elizabeth asked.

"No, Ray had some business to finish up before heading north. I decided to come without him and get the house ready."

"You'll be staying at the hotel?"

"Just for a day or two, at most. I want to take a handyman out to the house in the morning to check the pipes and get the place heated. Did you have a cold winter?"

"It was below freezing a few weeks ago but Carl says the worst is over."

"I just hope none of the pipes burst. We drained them well before we left in the fall but even a little water left in the pipes can cause damage in a freeze."

"We didn't expect you back quite this early in the season."

"To tell you the truth," said Mrs. Mathis, "I was bored to tears in San Francisco. Conditions down below are so dismal that nobody's giving parties and having fun. I decided there would be more things to do here."

"Well, now that you're back, I'm sure the town will be much more lively. The Sons of Norway Hall has been filled with dancers almost every weekend. And the Moose Lodge is forming a women's group called the Mooseheart Legion."

"Oh, goody."

Elizabeth stood motionless, transfixed by the big moose head displayed in Hogue & Tveten's window. A sign next to the display said the record head belonged to Andy Anderson and the horns measured sixty-nine inches from tip to tip. The hideous head with brown glass eyes was the most frightening thing Elizabeth had ever seen and she was certain she would suffer nightmares in which it played a prominent role. Carl laughed at her reaction and said the Moose Lodge was considering buying the trophy for their lodge rooms.

Carl and Fred Patten paid a visit to the room in the back where Carl mixed his home brew.

"Fred, what have you been up to?" asked Carl.

"Spent the last two seasons out at Port Alexander and made a good living with mild curing," said Fred. "If you ever get tired of the hotel business, you should consider moving out there and opening a restaurant. It's a nice little town; they even have their own one-room school house."

"That sounds more attractive than you know," Carl chuckled. "Are you going to work mild curing again this season?"

"Doesn't appear like there'll be much of a season this year," said Fred, "so I've decided to sell my scow. It's a good scow, all housed in with good living quarters and fitted up for mild curing. I'll even throw in the anchor and chains."

"How much you want for it?" asked Carl.

"Six hundred and fifty dollars. It's anchored out at Port Alexander right now."

"You've put a lot of work into that scow," said Carl.

"Yeah, but it's no place for a woman. You know I've been keeping company with the dressmaker Gertie Friedman?"

"Everyone knows that," said Carl. "You going to make an honest woman out of her?"

"I haven't exactly asked her yet," replied Fred, "but I hope to."

Carl raised his glass. "*Skoal*, you old rascal. I'll hold off on the congratulations until you actually do. Elizabeth will be so pleased."

Wharfinger Parks joined the men waiting their turn in George Nelson's barber chair. "You hear about the *Zilla May*?" he asked nobody in particular.

"What about her?" responded one of the lobby regulars.

"She was carrying 20,000 pounds of halibut to Prince Rupert and went aground on Strait Island."

"The same island that took out the steamship *Mariposa* a few years ago? I thought there was a light on that reef now."

"There is," said the wharfinger, "but it was snowing and the man at the wheel miscalculated the distance."

"Anybody hurt?"

"They were very lucky," replied Parks. "All thirteen men got off safely after losing three dories in the wind and high seas. They spent two nights in a makeshift hut on the island before being picked up by a gas boat and brought to Wrangell."

"How's the boat?"

"The cabin was washed away," said Parks, "but they're going to try to raise her to salvage the engine."

"Isn't there a fox farm on Strait Island?"

"There is," said the wharfinger, "but the man there had a peculiar notion of hospitality and provided the men with only a few utensils and very little food."

Mrs. Mathis stopped Elizabeth on the street to say her husband was due to arrive on the *Admiral Watson*. "Ray had to spend a few more days in Seattle than planned," she said, "to stock up on personal items lost with his luggage."

"The steamship company lost his luggage?" Elizabeth asked.

"Even worse," said Mrs. Mathis. "He shipped his personal baggage from San Francisco on the *Governor*. Everything was lost when the ship sank after colliding with the *West Hartland* off Point Wilson."

"I heard about that," said Elizabeth. "Most of the passengers were able to climb aboard the other ship or make it to the lifeboats."

"I'm so thankful Ray wasn't aboard," said Mrs. Mathis. "I think we'll travel together from now on. Baggage can always be replaced."

One hundred and nineteen votes were cast in the municipal election on April 5. Elizabeth and Carl's good friend Russell York of the Citizen's Steam Laundry was elected one of six city councilmen. The new mayor was Ed Locken, superintendent of the Petersburg Lumber Company. This was the first year the mayor was selected directly by the voters rather than being appointed by the city council.

Mayor Locken and editor Perkins were discussing pulp and paper mill prospects with the men in the lobby.

"I understand two eastern paper companies have made application for water power development in the territory," said Perkins. "They're looking for sites for pulp and paper mills."

"It takes a lot of water to run a pulp mill," responded Locken, "and I don't think paper prices are high enough to justify development, once you consider the high transportation costs to the states."

"Even the Federal Power Commission is examining water power sites," said Perkins. "And one of the biggest sites is at Cascade Creek in Thomas Bay. The forestry department is building a three-mile trail from tide water, up Cascade Creek to Swan Lake. The trail will assist with the survey work."

"They're on a fool's errand," said Locken. "Just look at what's happening at the new pulp mill at Speel River up by Juneau."

"What's going on there?" asked one of the regulars.

"It's only been operating for three months and they've just shut it down," replied the mayor.

"Why?"

"High freight costs and low pulp prices," said Locken. "Their wharf is groaning under the weight of a rain-soaked load of pulp awaiting shipment south. But the mill operators can't come to terms with the steamship companies so they closed the plant."

"So you think getting into the pulp and paper business at this time is a bad idea?" asked Perkins.

"Absolutely," said Locken.

The men of the town went crazy for basketball. Carl attended all the games and practice sessions at the Sons of Norway Hall. After practicing amongst themselves, the Petersburg boys invited teams from Wrangell and Kake to town for friendly games. They defeated the Kake team easily, but the Wrangell team was another matter.

"We lost to Wrangell by a score of fifty to twenty-two," said Carl.

"They must be pretty good," Elizabeth replied, "or else the Petersburg boys need more practice."

"Nah, we just need better equipment," he said. "Our boys train with an old dead ball and when they play with the Wrangell ball, which is fast, their shooting goes to pieces."

Warm spring weather brought out members of the Petersburg Fire Department and Boy Scouts to build a baseball park and playground at the top of the "F" Street hill. The men threw themselves into clearing and surfacing the new park. Everyone was asked to report with shovels to the site or the sawmill each Sunday. Several cars hauled sawdust and slabs from the mill to the ball park. The city council approved a roadway connecting to the site so cars could dump material directly onto the diamond. The firemen raised funds by sponsoring a big Baseball and Playground Dance at the Sons of Norway Hall to cover their expenses. Everyone looked forward to the first game at the new site.

"It looks like we're losing one of our renters," said Carl.

"What's happening?" asked Elizabeth.

"George Nelson just sold his share in the Arctic Club to his partner and is moving his barber shop to the Gauffin Building."

"Does that mean they're closing the Arctic Club?"

"No, E. J. Heacock will continue to run it," said Carl, "but it will be smaller when Nelson moves his two barbers' chairs out."

"Why did they break up the partnership?" asked Elizabeth.

"All George said was he needed more room for the barber shop."

"Seems like he's going to a lot of trouble," said Elizabeth. "He wasn't located at the hotel very long."

"Sounds fishy to me too," agreed Carl. "The men probably had a falling out. George doesn't seem all that stable somehow. Anyway, we'll probably never know the real reason."

Charles West, agent for the Alaska Steamship Company, informed the lobby regulars that steamship companies operating in Alaska had discontinued the sale of tickets to the territory until after May 1.

"Why is that?" asked Carl.

"That's the date maritime union crews expect to tie up the ships and walk ashore if they haven't come to terms with the Shipping Board," replied West.

"What does the Shipping Board want?" asked one of the men.

"A 15 percent wage reduction, abolition of overtime pay and only two deck watches instead of three, among other things."

"I can't see the maritime workers agreeing to such terms," said Carl.

"If they don't, they'll all be out of jobs," responded West.

The strike went into effect as scheduled, idling all boats on the Pacific Coast and many on the East Coast.

"What does it all mean?" Elizabeth asked Carl.

"It means we'll have no more steamships until the strike is over," he responded. "No more freight and coal deliveries, no more mail service, and no passenger service. And no fresh fish will be shipped south. This is very bad for Alaska."

They watched in amazement as the strike impacted the town. Grocery stores sold each family only what was needed for immediate use, not allowing anyone to stockpile supplies at the expense of others. Communication between towns was by gasboat. The Canadian steamer *Princess Mary* arrived in Wrangell with eleven days worth of mail for southeastern Alaska. Outgoing Petersburg mail was sent to Wrangell on the *Princess Pat*. Shrimp and crab canning and fresh fish buying came to a standstill due to the inability to ship. The lighthouse tender *Cedar* took the officers and witnesses to the court session in Ketchikan. The northern towns of Valdez, Cordova and Seward were even worse off, having run out of butter, eggs and fresh vegetables completely.

Finally, Charles West came into the lobby with promising news.

"I just received a wire from the Seattle office," he said. "The freighter *Redondo* was out westward when the strike was called and now she's laying in Juneau. They've just ordered the ship south and told me to wire Juneau if we had any southbound freight. I wired right away that we have fresh and mild cured fish, passengers and mail. The ship should be here around noon tomorrow."

A cheer went up in the lobby and several guests returned to their rooms to pack while merchants adjourned to their stores to write business letters and prepare other mail for shipment. The next day, the hotel guests walked down the Public Dock to the wharfinger's office to await the steamship. The sun was shining and everyone was in high spirits.

An agent for Swift and Company was the first guest to return to the hotel.

"What happened?" asked Carl.

"The steamship kept on going," said the traveling salesman. "We were all standing on the dock and the ship sailed right past at full speed and within a stone's throw of the dock. The men on board shouted, 'Keep your blankety-blank old freight.' Begging your pardon, Mrs. Roger," he said, tipping his hat. "Why, I thought the wharfinger was going to have a heart attack right there on the dock, so red in the face he was."

The town adjusted to the unpredictability of steamship sailings and travelers arranged passage on gasboats or journeyed to Wrangell to connect with the Canadian steamers. The light and power plant was shut down between 3:00 and 9:00 a.m. to save fuel and manpower expense. The weather was warm and clear and the town burned wood as a substitute for coal. Elizabeth's family really didn't suffer from the shortage of food, as merchants were generous with rations to families with children.

Finally, the steamship agent informed the lobby regulars that the *Admiral Watson* was on her way north from Seattle. "She was delayed for ten hours getting her cargo aboard," he said. "She's loaded to the water line with foodstuffs for every town in southeastern and southwestern Alaska and carries 255 passengers."

"Does this mean the strike is over?" asked one of the men.

"No," the agent replied. "They imported strike breakers from the East and Gulf Coasts. And they had plenty of law enforcers at the dock making sure she got away with no violence."

Elizabeth was now huge with child and Carl treated her as if she would break. Her ankles were swollen and she was uncomfortable in any position. Carl wouldn't let her lift heavy objects and insisted on sending their personal laundry to the Citizen's Steam Laundry along with the linens for the hotel.

"Carl didn't see me when I was this far along with Betty," Elizabeth told Gussie York, "so he's much more nervous about this than I am."

"Enjoy the special treatment while it lasts," Gussie chuckled. "All too soon, things will be back to normal and you'll be doing laundry on the wash board and hanging it out to dry on the clothesline again."

Chapter 22

June 1921 – Elizabeth awoke cold and wet in the middle of the night. Carl was snoring softly. She made her way to the lavatory and changed into dry underwear before rousing Carl.

"Carl, wake up. My water broke."

"Wha . . .? When . . .? Are you all right?"

"Yes, but it's time. I'm going to rest here while you get Mrs. Henderson and notify Dr. Carothers that we'll meet him at the hospital."

Carl was wide awake, almost comical in his haste to dress and get moving. "Are you sure you're all right?" he asked again.

"Yes, I'm having a few contractions but they're pretty far apart. Hurry now."

The rest of that June night was something of a blur. Elizabeth remembered bright stars hanging above the sleeping town as they walked the two short blocks to the hospital. Carl carried her bag and his arm was strong around her waist. He wanted to carry her or awaken a friend with an automobile, but Elizabeth wouldn't hear of it. The hospital lights blinked on as they approached the large, white building. Elizabeth remembered Dr. Carothers' smiling face, painful contractions coming faster, the nurse moping her brow as Elizabeth strained to deliver this child, and finally, a tiny voice crying in protest at the abrupt entrance into a new world.

"Here she is, Mrs. Roger," said the doctor. "A beautiful baby girl."

Elizabeth took the squirming infant and looked at Carl, who was beaming from ear to ear. "You did good," he whispered.

They named the baby June Alice. Carl bought out all the cigars at the Arctic Club and distributed them to his friends between visits to the hospital to see "his girls."

"I didn't know they came so small, red and wrinkled," he said.

"That's because you didn't see Betty until she was two months old," said Elizabeth. "In fact, baby June looks just like Betty when she was born. I wonder what Betty is going to think of her new sister?"

As Elizabeth lay in the hospital waiting to be discharged, she thought back to the words of the old fortuneteller, Madame Cézanne. "I see a long journey over water," she had said, "and I see two little girls in your future."

Elizabeth rubbed her eyes. *Amazing how all that came true.* And she wondered what lay ahead for her family in this remarkable country.

Betty was very curious about her new sister. Elizabeth pulled the blanket away from the baby's face and Betty peered at her with eyes opened wide.

"This is you new baby sister, Betty. Her name is June. Can you say June?"

"Dune," said Betty.

"No," said Elizabeth. "June."

"Dune," repeated Betty. "Dune-ah."

"Well there you have it," laughed Carl. "The baby's name is Duna."

Caring for a newborn and an eighteen-month-old took some getting used to but within a week Elizabeth had established a routine of feedings, bath time, playtime and household chores. Her lady friends came to see the new baby at the little house behind the hotel. They thoughtfully brought gifts for both girls so Betty wouldn't feel displaced by the new arrival.

Mrs. Mathis was her first visitor. She brought along Dr. Mathis' sister and her friend who were visiting from Los Angeles. "And how do you like our little town?" Elizabeth asked the ladies.

"Oh it's just beautiful," enthused the dentist's sister. "I've wanted to come to Alaska ever since Ray decided to practice here. We hope to stay for several weeks and visit Juneau before we return to California."

"And how is Dr. Mathis?" asked Elizabeth. "We used to see more of him when he had his office in the hotel building."

"Ray's doing just fine," replied Mrs. Mathis. "He's opening his office on Front Street this week."

The ladies took their leave when the baby started to cry for her next feeding. Their lifestyle in Los Angeles seemed as foreign to Elizabeth as hers must have appeared to them.

The "yoo-hoo" at the front door was Mrs. Gauffin. "Barbara, come right in, it's good to see you," Elizabeth called.

"Hello Elizabeth, and look how Betty has grown since I've been away." She picked Betty up from the floor where she'd been playing with her toys and carried her to the kitchen as Elizabeth put on the coffee pot.

"I heard you were back," said Elizabeth. "How was your trip and how are your folks?"

"The folks are as good as can be expected," said Barbara. "They're getting up in years, you know. That's why I spent such a long time away.

It feels so good to be home again. And what have you been up to while I've been away visiting in Washington?"

"Not too much, although I did have a baby," said Elizabeth.

"You're joking."

"No, really, I did have a baby."

Elizabeth held her finger to her lips and took Barbara into the bedroom where Duna was fast asleep in her bassinet. "Why Elizabeth," Barbara whispered, "you never fail to amaze me. This really is a baby."

Elizabeth felt very clever as they continued their visit over coffee.

Henry Roden also visited while passing through town on his way to and from the Ketchikan court. He and Carl discussed the goings on in that town. "The Ketchikan Pioneers filed a resolution with the legislature to amend the law concerning pioneer pensions," said Henry.

"What's their point of view?" asked Carl.

"As it now stands, a pioneer who has been a resident of the territory for ten years or more may receive a $12 monthly pension if he is deserving but must first put ownership of his property – whether cabin, land or mining claim – in the hands of the territory. Ketchikan folks feel this places undue hardship on deserving citizens."

"That's a big price to pay for such a small pension," said Carl.

"Exactly," Henry agreed. "And to deny an old timer with limited earning capacity the free use and enjoyment of his property just doesn't sit well with folks. They say it reflects no credit on the great Territory of Alaska."

"What do you think the legislature will do?" asked Carl.

"It's hard to say," replied Henry, "but I hope they amend the law."

"It looks like we're going to have a salmon season after all," said Carl a few days later.

"Why do you say that?" Elizabeth asked.

"The Petersburg Packing Company has decided to put up 90,000 cans of fish, using their oversupply of cans from last season."

"That should make the lobby regulars happy," said Elizabeth.

"You said it," agreed Carl. "They've all taken off to mend nets and overhaul their boats. The cannery is going to release the pack after the supply stored in warehouses down south is sold. No Chinese contract is in place on account of the short season, so a crew of forty Japanese is arriving on the *Spokane* tomorrow."

"Daddy, who's that strange man?" Elizabeth asked, peering out the window. "He's been wandering up and down the street gawking at everything. Some people stop and shake his hand so he must be known here."

"That's Andy Anderson's partner at the True Blue Fox Ranch on Walter Island," said Carl. "Andy finally persuaded him to come to town for the Fourth of July. He hasn't been among this many people in two years. He says he's taking in the sights and trying not to get lost."

The Independence Day celebration spanned three days. Festivities began with a big dance at the Sons of Norway Hall on July 2, a baseball game on July 3, and the parade and sporting events on July 4, followed by another big dance in the evening. Spirits were not dampened by cloudy weather and the constant threat of rain. The Petersburg team won the baseball game with Kake on the new ballfield by a score of fourteen to five.

The town changed its focus from basketball to baseball and team members adopted a certain swagger. They challenged a team of Japanese workers from the cannery and trounced them soundly. The men in the lobby recounted one particular play with great relish: "There goes Russ York after a long fly ball," said Charlie Greenaa. "He's watching the ball as it goes farther and farther and doesn't notice a chuckhole that wasn't filled in and plunges up to his armpits. By the time he hauls himself and the ball out of the mud, the cannery worker is sitting calmly on the bench after making the rounds of the bases."

At this point, Russ added, "And we won eighteen to three."

The coal famine was finally broken when the freighter *Redondo* arrived with several hundred tons of Nanaimo coal from Vancouver Island. Practically every business house and residence was entirely out of coal and delivery cars from Hogue & Tveten and the Trading Union were kept busy filling orders that had stacked up during the famine. The West Coast steamer strike was settled and crews went back to work without having won many concessions.

Elizabeth stayed close to home caring for the girls and Carl kept her up to date on goings on about town.

"Editor Perkins was in today," he said, "and he says things are looking up and we're almost out from under the cloud of this depression."

"What makes him so sure?" asked Elizabeth

"He said opening salmon prices are much higher than expected," replied Carl. "The local cannery is going to buy 10,000 more cans and thinks they can reach a pack of 100,000; work on the Scow Bay road has resumed with the arrival of four horses from down below; and the Reduction Company plant has started processing fish fertilizer. He's just full of enthusiasm."

"What do you think about this, Mother?" said Carl from the doorway.

"What is it?" asked Elizabeth.

"It's a Royal Electric Vacuum Cleaner. I'm the new sales agent for Petersburg. The salesman is leaving this machine with me to use around the hotel and demonstrate to anybody who might want to buy one. He'll pick up the orders on his way through town on the steamers and ship the machines from Seattle. Here, let me show you how it works."

Betty scampered to the sofa when he turned on the noisy contraption. She watched soundlessly as he passed the machine over the floors. Elizabeth had to admit, it did a good job in a fraction of the time it took her to sweep.

"The company's paying for advertisements in the local paper telling everyone to come see it at the Hotel Arctic," said Carl. "You can use it around the house, too."

Carl showed Elizabeth a book titled *Alaska Mining Law* written by Henry Roden. "Our friend is quite the expert on mining laws," he said. "This book covers territorial and Federal laws and contains the forms a miner needs to protect his claim. And look, it's small enough that a miner can carry it in his coat pocket when he's out prospecting."

Elizabeth had an opportunity to compliment Henry on his publication during his next visit to town. "My sole purpose was to provide the miner with something to guide him when out in the mountains making discoveries so he may secure the benefits from his efforts," said Henry.

During nine days of warm, clear weather at the end of August, Elizabeth took the girls in the buggy on daily walks along the boardwalk. The town was busy again and steamers were coming and going with shipments of live foxes, fresh fish and excursionists. The Lotus Pool Room installed new card tables, Mr. Missick reopened his dry-cleaning store, the New York Café was under new management and Mr. Elfstrom displayed his latest jewelry inventory. A large party of Wrangell people spent a day visiting around town. Myrtle Cornelius stopped to fuss over the girls. She and her twin brother Bert had arrived recently to help their uncle Luther Hogue with the Hogue & Tveten store. A nurse by training, Myrtle helped her uncle during his recovery from recent surgery in Seattle. She said her brother was working in the store's accountancy department.

A beautiful Indian summer enveloped the town. The few trees that were not evergreens turned shades of red and gold. Townspeople spent weekends at the baseball park rooting for the home team against crews from the cable ship *Burnside* and revenue cutter *Bothwell.* The Petersburg boys traveled to Ketchikan where they were soundly beaten but treated royally. The young people of town held dances at the Sons of Norway and Arctic Brotherhood halls every weekend. Five school teachers, including a new principal, arrived for the school term. One Saturday morning, Fred Patten and Gertrude Friedman were married in a ceremony performed by Commissioner Perkins. Everyone congratulated the well-liked couple, although Fred's bachelor friends labeled him a "Benedict."

Carl was one of eighteen local businessmen to put up $900 to engage the traveling Chautauqua troupe. Since each committeeman would be assessed for his share of any deficit, all the merchants were busy selling tickets to the three-day event.

"Do you think the committee will sell all their tickets?" Elizabeth asked.

"No doubt about it," he replied. "People have a little jingle in their pockets now and since Chautauqua skipped Alaska last year, everyone is eager for good entertainment and thought-provoking lectures."

Mrs. Henderson stayed with the girls while Carl and Elizabeth attended the opening programme. The "Old Fashioned Girls" performed several excellent musical numbers and Captain Norman Allan Imrie delivered a lecture on "Problems Confronting Uncle Sam and John

Bull." While Elizabeth was not well versed on the Irish question, she was certain his lecture would be the subject of discussion among the lobby regulars in the morning. Everyone agreed this was the best Chautauqua company ever seen in Petersburg.

Carl burst through the door shouting "Mother, something terrible just happened."

"Carl, calm down. What is it?"

"George Nelson just shot Nels Peterson over at the Lotus."

"Our George Nelson," said Elizabeth, "who had his barber shop at the hotel?"

"Yes," replied Carl. "He walked across the street from his barber shop, entered the pool room, walked to where Nels was playing cards and shot him with a revolver he fired from his pocket. After he shot him, he said, 'You son of a bitch, you have laughed at me long enough.' "

"Is Nels all right?" asked Elizabeth.

"No," exclaimed Carl. "He jumped up and ran to the door holding his right side and Nelson followed him around the corner of the Petersburg Restaurant trying to get off another shot. Peterson collapsed between John Thompson's machine shop and the Citizen's Laundry. They put him in a car and rushed him to the hospital but he didn't make it."

Everyone was stunned by the news and idle tongues claimed jealousy was the cause of ill will between the two men who had to be separated when they got into a fight at a recent dance. While waiting in line at the post office, Elizabeth overheard two girls claim that Nelson had been very attentive to Mrs. Peterson for several months and had stated numerous times that he intended to marry her.

The *Report* published the findings of the coroner's jury: "We find that Nels Peterson came to his death at about 5 o'clock p.m. Sept. 17, 1921 as the result of a revolver wound inflicted at the hands of George Nelson.

The shooting having taken place in the Lotus Ice Cream Parlor, which is operated by Bert Haug."

The Deputy U.S. Marshal from Wrangell took George Nelson north to Juneau to face a charge of first degree murder.

Henry Roden and Carl were discussing politics. Henry said the new governor was now settled into his position at Juneau. "At least the waiting is over," he said. "I understand President Harding got pretty tired of all the infighting among the candidates trying to destroy one another. He finally selected Scott C. Bone."

"What do you know about the man?" asked Carl.

"He's the former editor of the *Seattle Post Intelligence* and should know more about Alaska than most candidates from the outside. Equally interesting is the selection of Arthur Shoup as District Attorney and Major George Beaumont as U.S. Marshal. Shoup has stated his intention to wipe out gamblers and bootleggers and enforce the prohibition laws."

"Surely he doesn't intend to prosecute the citizen who makes home brew to share with his friends and for his own consumption," said Carl looking at the half empty steins sitting before the two men.

"Let's hope not," chuckled Henry. "I think he's really after the bootlegger who charges outrageous prices for intoxicants he sells to the husband or father who spends the household money on booze. And, of course, those who sell liquor to the natives. We've never had an administration serious about stopping the liquor trade before."

"What do you know about our new Deputy U.S. Marshal Fred Handy?" asked Carl.

"He moved here from Ketchikan, as you know, but before that he was Deputy Marshal at Haines when Shoup was the U.S. Marshal. So I would expect him to follow Shoup's lead in seeking out and prosecuting bootleggers."

Witnesses in George Nelson's murder trial sailed for Juneau on the *City of Seattle*. They included City Marshal Hans Wick, Councilman Russell York, Commissioner Perkins, Dr. Carothers and five others. The men were to remain there until the trial concluded.

"I hear George Nelson tried to commit suicide in the jail at Juneau," said one of the men in the lobby.

"How can you commit suicide in jail?" responded another. "They even take away your shoelaces."

"Somehow he climbed to the top of his cell door – about ten feet up – and flung himself backward onto the floor and against the bars of his cell," said the first man. "He was trying to break his neck. He suffered a gash on the top of his head which they bandaged and then shackled him to a bed in the center of the room."

"What happens next?" asked another man.

"They're giving the defense time to put their case together," said the first man. "I understand Judge Wickersham is one of the defense attorneys and they just subpoenaed Nels' wife, Helga Peterson, Mrs. Skog and Mrs. Hill from Petersburg. The ladies are to take the first boat north."

A loud knocking at the door interrupted their dinner and Carl opened the door to Deputy U.S. Marshal Handy. "Elizabeth, stay here," he said, following the Marshal across the yard to the hotel. A small crowd parted in front of the hotel as Carl's five-gallon fermentation crock was loaded onto a truck. Carl returned an hour later, red faced and as angry as Elizabeth had ever seen him.

"I've been charged with the sale of intoxicating liquors concealed on the premises," he sputtered. "I'm to appear in commissioner's court on Wednesday."

"Oh, Carl, how awful."

"I've never sold so much as one drop of liquor, ever," Carl ranted. "And if they think they're going to charge every man who makes home brew for his personal use, they'll have to arrest every man in town and build a bigger jail. That new marshal is out to make a name for himself."

Carl appeared in commissioner's court on Elizabeth's birthday. Commissioner pro tem Jacob Otness heard the charges in the absence of Commissioner Perkins who was in Juneau for the Nelson murder trial. Three other establishments had been raided and those proprietors were also tried. Marshal Handy acted as prosecuting attorney at all four trials.

Carl pled "not guilty" but was found in violation by the jury of twelve and fined $100 plus costs. Another man was fined $500 plus costs. And Leonard Heys was found in violation of the "Bone Dry" law for selling a drink to a prohibition enforcement officer and fined $200. Only then was it learned that the friendly stranger who purchased the drink from Heys had come to town to gather evidence about the liquor traffic.

Gussie York comforted Elizabeth. "There, there Elizabeth," she said. "Everybody knows Carl is an honest, upstanding businessman. Nobody who knows him thinks lesser of him and you shouldn't feel ashamed that his name is in the paper in connection with this affair. That new marshal's just trying to make his mark. I predict he won't last long in Petersburg."

"Oh Gussie, I can't even talk to Carl about it," said Elizabeth. "He's still so angry. I can't decide if he's more upset about the $100 fine, the slur on his good name or losing his favorite crock pot."

The liquor raids furnished the main topic of conversation around town for a few days but soon were replaced by developments at the Nelson murder trial in Juneau. Nelson's attorneys first attempted an insanity defense and then tried to have the case dismissed on the basis of improper jury selection. The judge denied both defenses and Nelson entered a plea of "not guilty." Four days later, the jury found him "Guilty without capital punishment." He was sentenced to life imprisonment at hard labor in the Federal Penitentiary at McNeil Island. Witnesses in the case returned to Petersburg after a twenty-eight-day absence.

"Hello Elizabeth, remember me?" called a familiar voice from the doorway.

"Why Anna Holt, I thought you'd dropped off the ends of the earth. It's so good to see you again. What brings you to Petersburg?"

"I've moved back, and it's Anna Rincke now."

"That's wonderful," said Elizabeth. "Come in and tell me all about it."

"I'm on an errand for the store and can't stop long."

"What store, and what happened in Valdez?" asked Elizabeth.

"Hogue & Tveten's dry goods department, of course. I arrived at just the right time when they had an opening. My new husband owns a jewelry store in Valdez but I convinced him to give Petersburg a try. I can't wait for you to meet him."

"Carl and I will be looking forward to it," said Elizabeth. "Let me know when you have more time to get together."

"I will. Take care."

Carl was in his element. The Freemasons reserved the hotel dining room for a banquet in honor of Mr. and Mrs. Bert Cornelius and Doctor and Mrs. Carothers. Bert had just returned from the south with his new bride and the doctor was relocating to Seattle.

The table was set for thirty Masons and their ladies. The centerpieces were cornucopias filled with ears of colored corn and winter squash and the dining room was decorated in a fall harvest theme. Carl was in full regalia with bright white apron and chef's toque. Mrs. Henderson and Elizabeth served and cleared and every dish from the kitchen was greeted with praise.

Among the usual assortment of traveling salesmen stopping at the hotel was a lady selling hand-colored Alaskan photographs. She was married to the editor of the *Whitehorse Star* in the Yukon Territory and her photographs were breathtaking. She ran an advertisement inviting customers to view her pictures at the Arctic Hotel. She provided a little competition to the *Petersburg Weekly Report* which also sold Christmas cards at this time of year. After spending several days in Petersburg, she continued north to Juneau.

Temperatures plunged to near zero. Not a flake of snow had fallen and the ground was completely frozen. The creeks feeding the water system had frozen up until reaching the vanishing point. With no water in the mains, the power plant was shut down and every house in town was without water.

"Daddy, what are we to do?" Elizabeth fretted. "There's no snow to melt for water and no rainwater to collect. We can manage without lights but not without water. And thank goodness we don't have a coal shortage too or we'd all freeze to death."

"Don't worry, Mother," he said. "City officials are putting emergency measures into effect and the men are hauling water from the sawmill creek and delivering it by car. If we boil the water and everyone is careful not to use more than absolutely necessary, we'll be just fine."

The cold spell finally broke and the rains returned. While the town's water dam was refilling, Elizabeth caught rainwater in every bucket they had, heated it on the kitchen stove and bathed two very dirty little girls.

Laundry was next and then she gave the house a thorough scrubbing. She vowed to never complain about the rain again.

The men in the lobby were discussing the town's medical facilities.

"You heard that the shareholders of the hospital want to deed it to the town for the price of one dollar?" asked the first man.

"Yep," said another. "And they should take them up on it too. Most other towns own their hospitals."

"Seems the hospital owes about $5,000 and the Ladies Auxiliary just can't raise enough money from dances to pay it off," said the first man.

"How'd they get so far in debt?"

"Most of it was for that new heating plant they bought last spring," replied the first man. "Can't run a hospital without one of those. Seems we got a new supply of doctors since Doc Carothers left too. Doc Jones from Wrangell took over his practice and even got Carothers' modern new X-Ray machine. Doctor Pigg is opening a practice here after several years in the medical branch of the army. And, say, Carl, isn't that fellow staying at the hotel a doctor too?"

"You mean Doc Rogers," replied Carl. "Yes, he's also planning to practice here."

"Any relation?"

"No," said Carl. "He spells his name with an 's.' He tells me he's from New York and was last practicing in Hyder."

Carl leased space in the hotel to the Petersburg Lodge of Moose to serve as their new lodge and club quarters.

"It's a good source of steady income during these slow winter months," he told Elizabeth. "I'm sorry to be the one to tell you, but they'll probably want to hang that big moose head you like so much on one of the walls."

"*Uff-da*, that's an ugly trophy," said Elizabeth. "Will they be having their weekly meetings here?"

"Yep," replied Carl. "The men meet every Tuesday night and the Women of Mooseheart Legion meet the first and third Tuesdays of each month. They're celebrating their new quarters with a card party and supper in honor of the women. The men won't let the women do any of the work for this party."

"Do you mean to tell me the men will prepare and serve the midnight luncheon?" asked Elizabeth.

"That's what they want the ladies to believe," said Carl. "Actually, I'll be running the kitchen while everyone is playing whist."

Everybody was happy that the season turned out far better than expected. The excess supply of canned salmon had been used up and the fish were now in short supply, ensuring good prices for the fishermen. A halibut boat called at Petersburg loaded with 100,000 pounds of halibut caught in only three days on the banks. Petersburg men held nearly half of the permits issued by the forestry department for fox farms on islands in the Tongass Forest. Knud Stenslid waved from his new one-ton Ford truck that arrived on a recent boat. It was equipped with pneumatic tires and he planned to use it in his new general hauling business. And U.S. Deputy Marshal Fred Handy returned to Ketchikan to be replaced by a new deputy marshal.

Chapter 23

January 1922 – Despite stormy weather, area fox men were busy coming to town for supplies and moving foxes among the islands. Fred Patten stopped in on his way through town.

"Is Mrs. Patten with you this trip?" Elizabeth asked.

"No, the weather's too rough and she stayed behind to keep the foxes fed. I hear the logger at Totem Bay lost his boat in the high easterly winds last week," he said, turning to Carl.

"Did it go adrift?" asked Carl.

"The winds drove it ashore and the rocks chewed it up," said Fred. "It's a total loss except for the engine. I'll be glad when this cold, stormy weather's behind us."

"How do you like the fox ranching business?" asked Carl.

"I like it fine," Fred replied. "Me and the missus got a cozy cabin out at the Brothers Island ranch and we're learning everything there is to know about fox raising. Came to town to put in for our own farm on an island out by Cape Fanshaw. The Department of Agriculture recalled all outstanding permits and they're replacing them with new ones, you know."

"I heard about that," said Carl. "What's the difference between the old and new permits?"

"The new permits are on an experimental basis for three years," replied Fred. "You can't kill any game or birds to feed the foxes, and you can't disturb any native artifacts that may be on the island like burying grounds or totem poles. The rent's the same, though, $25 a year."

"What happens after three years?" asked Elizabeth.

"Oh, you can get extensions up to fifteen years."

"Seems everyone's getting into the act," said Carl. "Loggers, merchants, the transfer and hauling man, and even the local dentist are in the fur business now. Doctor Mathis is even buying raw and dressed furs. He has trappers set their prices and mail the furs to him. He returns whatever he doesn't accept and pays transportation costs both ways."

"And how's that working out for him?" asked Fred.

"Too soon to tell," said Carl.

"I bumped into Andy Anderson walking down the street," Fred continued. "He's leaving on a fur buying trip among the trapping camps. He tells me the big Hercules Fox Company out on Sukoi Islands has now transferred to the new owners. They raised some fine foxes out there, I'll tell you. I'd love to have some of that stock."

Carl and Fred joined the men in the lobby and Elizabeth crossed the yard to the little house to prepare dinner. What a hard life Gertie must be having. Stuck out there on that island with very little contact with other people. Elizabeth wondered if she were ever lonely for female companionship and missed the little luxuries everyone in town took for granted, like a constant source of light and power and indoor plumbing. Once again, Elizabeth thanked her lucky stars that Carl preferred a more civilized life.

Carl joined the Moose Lodge. "I may as well," he said. "With the lodge room at the hotel, I'm spending most of my time preparing their midnight luncheons anyway. It's also good for business and their membership drive just brought in twenty-seven new members."

"Who else has joined recently?" Elizabeth asked.

"Doctor Jones, Doc Rogers and Mayor Locken, to name a few," said Carl. "All good men."

Elizabeth didn't know which group she enjoyed working with more – the men of the Petersburg Lodge of Moose or the Women of Mooseheart Legion. They had many joint card parties with singing around the piano, dancing and solos sung by the school principal's wife. Elizabeth's friend Barbara Gauffin was the Recorder for the women's group and even editor Perkin's wife was an officer. Elizabeth helped Carl prepare the luncheons while Mrs. Ryde, who worked at the hotel during the busy summer months, watched the children.

The men in the lobby gave editor Perkins a hard time about stepping down as United States Commissioner.

"Two years is long enough," said Perkins. "It became a much bigger job when they established the Petersburg Recording Precinct and I have a newspaper to run."

"I hear commissioner's court was pretty busy while you were in charge," said the new U.S. Deputy, "Mac" MacGregor.

"We settled many minor cases and originated two capital cases," replied Perkins. "Convictions were secured in the higher courts for those and two men are now serving life terms at McNeil Island for them – one for the murder of Mrs. Mar Kim and her baby and the other for the murder of Nels Peterson."

"I hear Oscar Granquist who does the books for the Packing Company and the Trading Union will be the new commissioner," said Charlie Greenaa.

"That's right," replied Perkins. "He served in France during the war, is strongly supported by local Republicans and will make a fine officer."

"Mother, look outside at that steamer tied up at the dock," said Carl.

"That ship's almost as big as the whole town," Elizabeth replied. "What is it?"

"It must be the steamer *Queen* the wharfinger was telling me about. It's the first time she's ever called at Petersburg. She's over three hundred feet long and draws more than twenty-one feet. There was quite a bit of speculation as to whether she could land at the local docks. I think I'll take a walk down the dock for a closer look."

"I wonder if that's the ship Charlie Mann has been waiting for with his shipment of Polar Cake and carbonized ice cream for his pool hall?" Elizabeth mused.

"His what?"

"You know, Polar Cake," said Elizabeth. "It's the new confection that's very popular in the states. It's a brick of ice cream dipped in hot chocolate and re-frozen. Supposed to be delicious."

"Leave it to Charlie to always be up to date," laughed Carl.

Doctor Rogers returned from Ketchikan where he had filled in for another doctor while he went south to get married.

"I see that a badly-burned trapper was brought to the hospital while I was away," he said.

"That would be Oscar Parks," said Carl. "I don't know the particulars."

"According to nurse Warner," said the doctor, "the trapper was living on his boat which was frozen in for the winter about five miles from the Pybus Bay cannery. He started his morning fire with some priming oil. Then a five-gallon can of gasoline caught on fire, filling the cabin with flames. By the time he got the cabin door unlatched, the fire had burned all the clothes off his body. He jumped from the deck onto the ice which broke under his weight and sank in the water, putting the fire out. Then he managed to climb back aboard and put out the fire in the cabin."

"Was there somebody nearby to come to his aid?" asked Carl.

"Nobody," replied the doctor. "He wrapped a blanket around his naked body and launched his dory but the ice was so thick he couldn't row and had to break it with an oar. Took him several hours to reach the cannery. They heard him hollering about a half mile out and two boats put out and towed him to shore. They gave him first aid treatment and 'San Juan' Smith brought him to town the next day. He's suffering from burns and exposure."

"Is he going to make it?" asked Elizabeth.

"Looks like it," said the Doc. "He's in a lot of pain but he's getting good care at the hospital."

Mrs. Ryde stayed with the girls while Carl and Elizabeth attended the big masquerade dance put on by the Petersburg Fire Department. Elizabeth looked forward to wearing one of the beautiful dresses in her closet that Carl kept buying from traveling salesmen staying at the hotel. She selected a crème and navy jersey dress cut in the new relaxed waist style that didn't require a corset. Carl looked handsome in a dark suit and tie and a starched, white shirt with French cuffs.

Carrying her dancing slippers and wearing their winter coats, they hurried through the rain beneath a big black umbrella to the Sons of Norway Hall. The Petersburg Jazz Band played as masked couples whirled around the floor. Close to a hundred people were masked and just as many, like them, were not.

Judges awarded prizes donated by town merchants. Everyone laughed as some prizes were totally inappropriate to the winners. Mary Allen, as best dressed gent, received a case of Pearl Oil courtesy of Mr. Steberg and the Standard Oil Company. Barbara Gauffin received five pounds of coffee from the Petersburg Meat Company for her performance as best lady waltzer. Harold Dawes, as best colored comedian, received a carton of cigarettes donated by the Arctic Club. Charlie Greenaa won a box of candy from Charlie Mann's pool room for his costume as second comical lady. Third comical lady, Gussie York, was awarded a cake from Lersten's Bakery. The Citizen's Steam Laundry awarded a month of free baths for the dirtiest character and the Petersburg Cooperative awarded twelve handkerchiefs to the masquerader with the longest nose.

Carl and Elizabeth climbed the stairs to the luncheon waiting in the dining room after the prizes were awarded. Everybody enjoyed doughnuts donated by the Star Bakery and in general, ignored the cold rain swirling around outdoors. They said their goodbyes after the luncheon as dancing resumed and continued until the small hours of the morning.

"Daddy, I had a wonderful time," said Elizabeth, as they fell into bed. "I hope you did too."

"Of course, how could I not?" he said. "I was with the prettiest girl at the dance."

Basketball, basketball, basketball. The lobby regulars talked nonstop about the rivalry with Wrangell. They knew every player on both Petersburg and Wrangell teams and attended every game as well as the Petersburg practice matches.

"We shoulda won that game Saturday," said Charlie Greenaa. "The Fire Department boys have never trained so hard and we were ahead thirteen to seven at the end of the first half."

"The Wrangell boys are in better condition, lighter and quicker," said Russ York. "After all they're high school kids."

"We were tied at the end of the game but couldn't hold on for eight minutes of overtime," moaned Charlie. "The game was so intense, even the Wrangell rooters had a hard time keeping off the court. We'll get our revenge next weekend at Wrangell, though."

Elizabeth asked Carl about the games when the teams returned from Wrangell.

"You don't want to mention it to any of the men," he cautioned. "They beat us again – by a score of fifty-nine to nine. Even the Petersburg school team got beat by the Wrangell school team."

"Oh, my."

"And then, to make matters worse," he continued, "the two boatloads of rooters that went along got caught in that easterly gale and snow storm on the way back and most of the ladies were seasick. I hear some of the men were green around the gills, too."

Heavy, wet snow took down the power lines and the town was without light and power for seventeen hours. Councilman York reported that the linemen had found eighty-one breaks in the line. The hotel guests took the inconvenience in stride – Fuller Paint's traveling salesman and the Standard Oil Company engineer spent their time at Brennan's Pool Room.

Mr. Henderson, the Superintendent of Territorial Schools, was invited to dinner at Mayor Locken's home. He bitterly condemned the local school buildings in a talk before the pupils, stating that the buildings were the worst in the territory.

And their favorite guest, Henry Roden, joined Elizabeth and Carl for supper by lantern light at the little house. Henry was euphoric about winning a case in the San Francisco court on behalf of the McDonald logging interests. He was in town on two smaller cases and entertained his hosts with tales of his travels.

"Carl, you got any guests going south on the *Queen*, you better get them down to the dock early," said wharfinger Gauffin.

"What's going on?" asked Carl.

"They got a greenhorn skipper this trip who's afraid to dock at the wharf," said Sam. "He doesn't like the tide in the Narrows and thinks it's too shallow. He's anchored in Frederick Sound and we're supposed to transfer passengers and freight by gasboat."

"I'll let everybody know. What about all the fresh fish in port?"

"The fish buyers won't touch it – too hard to transfer the catch to the steamer," replied the wharfinger. "Guess the fishermen will have to take their catch to other towns and try to sell there. They're not a happy lot, I'll tell you. The steamer's going to take the outside route to Wrangell. You wanna bet they put Captain Glasscock back in charge on her next trip?"

"Sounds like that would be a safe bet," said Carl.

An epidemic of chicken pox swept the town, sickening most of the children in the lower grades. Elizabeth kept the girls indoors and hoped the fact they were not yet of school age would keep them from being exposed. Her efforts were in vain, however, as first Betty and then Duna came down with the disease.

Betty developed a fever and tummy ache before breaking out in spots. Duna had a milder case and Mrs. Ryde speculated that a nine-month-old probably still carried some immunity passed down from her mother. They gave the girls oatmeal baths and trimmed their fingernails to keep them from injuring themselves scratching the itchy red welts.

It broke Elizabeth's heart to see them suffer and she looked forward to seeing this sickness run its course.

Carl reported the city council was finally working on getting a new school built. "The territorial school superintendent shamed them into it," he said. "Everybody except Earl Ohmer voted to hire a Seattle company to draft plans for the new building. All of the schools will be under one roof."

"Was Earl against it?" Elizabeth asked.

"Nope. He wasn't there. He's home with the chicken pox."

"Mrs. Ryde," called Carl, "Deputy MacGregor would like to speak with you. Elizabeth, you'd better come too."

They crossed the yard to the hotel where the deputy stood stiffly, hat in hand. "Ma'am," he said, "I'm sure sorry to have to tell you, your son Henry passed away at St. Ann's Hospital in Juneau earlier today."

"You must be mistaken," said Mrs. Ryde, "my son is the foreman at the Libby cannery in Yakutat."

"Yes, ma'am," said the deputy. "There was a gasoline explosion at the cannery Monday night and he was badly burned. Three men brought him to Juneau on the gasboat *Rolfe*. They did everything they could for him, but he passed away an hour after arriving at the hospital."

"Oh, Elizabeth," she wailed, "he's only thirty years old."

Carl and the deputy stood by awkwardly as Mrs. Ryde sobbed in Elizabeth's arms. Finally, she raised her head and asked, "What will they do with his body?"

"Whatever you prefer," responded the deputy.

"Then I want to take him home to Seattle for burial."

"I'll let the hospital know," said the deputy. "I'm very sorry, Mrs. Ryde."

"Thank you."

Mrs. Ryde took the first boat south and her son's body was shipped to Seattle on the *Queen*.

Carl filled Elizabeth in on the details of the accident. "He was trying to start a gasoline engine and the can of priming oil in his hand caught fire when the engine backfired," he said. "Then some cans of gasoline standing nearby exploded and he sustained terrible burns on his legs, face, arms and hands. The fire almost destroyed the cannery but the crew got it under control. He couldn't sit, so he stood the entire trip to Juneau but was so weak by the time they got there they couldn't save him. He would've been maimed for life if he'd lived."

Mr. Sales and his crew of boiler makers arrived on the *Spokane* and took lodgings at the hotel. They were there to erect two new tanks at the Standard Oil Company's plant on the south end of town. Mr. Sales had been involved in the original construction of the plant three years earlier. Other hotel guests included Assistant District Attorney Howard Stabler and Judge William Holzeheimer.

Elizabeth asked Carl about the two lawyers.

"They're here in connection with the Tom Mooney case," he replied. "The judge is from Ketchikan and he's defending Tom and the district attorney from Juneau is representing the government."

"What's Mooney's offense?" asked Elizabeth.

"He's charged with having liquor in his possession and the local jury found him guilty," said Carl. "He was fined $300 and given a thirty-day jail sentence in the Petersburg jail but his attorney appealed and he's now free on bond. The proprietors of two gentlemen's clubs put up a $1,000 bond for him."

"But did they find any liquor?" asked Elizabeth.

"They did," said Carl, "but Tom's attorney claims evidence was secured illegally because the deputy marshal boarded his boat without a search warrant. Now it's up to the district court judge in Juneau to rule on the appeal."

The men in the lobby were discussing the new season's seafood processing prospects. "Two big shellfish plants were just towed over from Wrangell," said editor Perkins. "The floating shrimp packing plant of Coulson and Brown is tied up at Citizen's Dock and the floating crab packing plant of Dobbins Packing Company is moored at the Public Dock."

"How many men do they expect to hire?" asked Russ York.

"The shrimp cannery needs sixty or seventy pickers and the crab cannery expects to hire about thirty, not including the crab fishermen. Dobbins says it's his policy to hire exclusively white help if possible. They'll bring a new big payroll for the town."

"Why did they leave Wrangell?" asked Charlie Greenaa.

"George Brown tells me the high Stikine winds blowing off the river made it impractical and too expensive to operate," said Perkins. "They won't have that problem in the Narrows."

"Earl, how do you feel about more competition for shrimp?" asked Russ.

"There's plenty of shrimp for everyone," replied Earl Ohmer. "Besides, they get their shrimp from Duncan Canal and we get ours from Thomas Bay. I'm more concerned about what a big pulp and paper plant will do to the shrimping grounds at Thomas Bay. What's the latest news on that?" he asked, turning to editor Perkins.

"The Forest Service just finished the foot trail on Cascade Creek so men can get in there to see if there's enough water power to run a plant," replied Perkins. "And, as I understand it, a group of San Francisco men applied for a permit for a $10 million pulp mill. No word yet if they got approval or even if they have the capital to finance it."

"That'll change the nature of the entire region from shrimping and fishing to timber and pulp," grumbled Earl.

"I see the advance crew of the Mitkof Packing Company is getting ready for the season," said Russ, changing the subject. "They just sent the last of the 1921 pack south on the *Admiral Nicholson* and the men are busy preparing trap web and making cans. They say they're expecting a good run of fish this year."

Town merchants also prepared for a busy season. Chris Swanson and Henry Dahl opened a new grocery store. The front entrance of the Star Bakery was moved to a corner of the building and Mary Allen and Blanche O'Dell opened a new establishment – the Totem Pole.

"Mary, your new shop is lovely," Elizabeth exclaimed.

"Mrs. Roger, come in and let me show you around."

A modern soda fountain occupied the cozy ice cream parlor in the former post office. The shop was furnished in the mission style with old rose wall hangings, curtains and shades.

"We carry ice cream, sodas, sundaes, sherbets, cakes, sandwiches and coffee," said Mary, proudly. "And look, here's the best part," she said, leading Elizabeth to a corner alcove containing a piano and settees. "I play every evening and keep up on my piano practice at the same time."

"Everyone loves to hear you perform," Elizabeth told the former postmistress. "And how nice to have an establishment women and children can enjoy. The men have their pool and card rooms but there's very little that can be enjoyed by everyone. I'll be a frequent customer."

The social season lingered on with basketball games and dances as the town awaited better fishing weather. The Sons and Daughters of

Norway held a benefit dance for the starving people of Russia. The Women of Mooseheart Legion gave a "Hard Times Dance" at the Sons of Norway Hall. Admission was fifty cents but there was an additional tax on anyone attired in good clothes. The ladies also gave a card party and luncheon for newly-initiated members in the club room at the hotel. A new organization was formed – Pioneers of Alaska, Petersburg Igloo Number 26.

"What are the Pioneers of Alaska?" Elizabeth asked.

"They're a fraternal organization of old timers – men of good moral character," said Carl. "They work for the betterment of their communities and the territory as a whole. I don't know how long you have to live here to qualify, but Pete Jorgenson, Sam Gauffin and editor Perkins are all officers of the new Igloo."

"But why are they called igloos?" said Elizabeth. "There are no igloos in Southeastern."

"The men's groups are called 'Igloos' and the women's groups are called 'Auxiliaries'," replied Carl. "Just the way they were set up originally, I guess. They've acquired the old Arctic Brotherhood Hall and are renovating the building for their lodge meetings. They're going to invite the whole town to a house warming when they get the place fixed up."

Chapter 24

May 1922 – Winter weather was reluctant to release its grip on the region. Wharfinger Gauffin told the lobby regulars that the gasboat *Taku II* had a rough trip coming north from Ketchikan.

"They've got a boatload of high school students on board bound for a school meet in Juneau," he said. "They left here this morning but had to turn back due to rough weather in Frederick Sound. They're going to try again in the morning."

Editor Perkins added, "The *Trygve* just got in from her mail run and they reported one of the worst wind storms in years in the Chatham Strait section. The halibut boats had to lie in harbor for three days. I hope the worst is over by the time the school kids get there."

"The *Einar Beyer* just cleared the customs house bound for Seattle," added the wharfinger. "They had a hard time putting into Big Port Walter with equipment and supplies on account of damage to the dock from the ice. They've got fourteen men making repairs and he placed orders for additional pilings with the McDonald logging outfit before heading south."

Their work completed, the Standard Oil Company's crew of boiler makers vacated the hotel. The oil company's big new tanker *Charlie*

Watson delivered distillate, gasoline and Pearl Oil, filling every tank at the plant before proceeding north to Juneau. As the boiler makers departed, the Bureau of Public Roads crew arrived to resume work on the Petersburg-Scow Bay road. The crew chief told Carl he'd be moving from the hotel to the big scow and camp headquarters when it was towed from its winter location at Scow Bay to the creek closer to town. The lobby regulars discussed the move as Elizabeth tided the room.

"Did you see them moving their big camp outfit?" asked Russ York of no one in particular.

"I heard it got away from them and drifted down the Narrows," replied Charlie Greenaa.

"Yup," said Russ, "Took out that big pile dolphin in its travels before they could recapture it. Took two tow boats to reel it in. They should've waited for slack tide before trying to move anything that heavy."

"I hear West and Woodward got the contract for hauling gravel from the pits for the road surface," added Charlie. "They're going to bring in the tractor from their fox ranch at Big Johns Bay to haul the gravel trailers."

"How long have they been working on this four-mile road?" asked Carl.

"Six years that I know of," replied Charlie.

"Do you think they'll finish it this year?"

"I wouldn't put any money on it," Charlie answered.

Henry Roden spent several days in town compiling a case against the Marathon Packing Company for failure to pay the watchman at their Cape Fanshaw plant. Carl invited him to dinner and he brought Carl and Elizabeth up to date on activities in Juneau.

"Judge Reed dismissed the case against Tom Mooney," he said. "He ruled the evidence was illegally secured when the deputy marshal stepped aboard Mooney's boat without a warrant, even though Mooney told him to go ahead and search."

"That's what a lot of people in Petersburg thought too," said Carl, "even though the local commissioner's court found him guilty. Two Petersburg merchants felt so strongly about it, they put up a $1,000 bond to set him free on bail while he appealed to the Juneau court."

"The grand jury also handed in their final report of the court term to Judge Reed," continued Henry, "and did they ever give him an earful about the actions of the federal prohibition enforcement officer and his men."

"What did they have to say?" asked Carl.

"They recommended the prohibition officer stop the practice of burning cabins and their contents when the cabins were found to contain equipment for making booze. They could find no authority in law permitting such practice without any sort of judicial hearing or order."

"So if a man was found to be making home brew in his cabin, they would burn down his home?" asked Elizabeth.

"That's right," said Henry. "They went even further and recommended the prohibition bureau be abolished in Alaska and the money spent for two fast patrol boats on the Canadian border."

"Good for them," said Carl. "I don't know anybody who doesn't agree that the prohibition enforcement bureau has gone too far."

"I guess you heard that George Nelson died at the McNeil Island penitentiary," continued Henry. "He's been hopelessly insane for several months and died of a stroke."

"Yes, we heard," said Carl. "And to think, just last year he was cutting hair and giving shaves right here in the hotel. He was a good barber, too."

"Such a sad story," Elizabeth added. "I always thought he was a little odd and he was certainly smitten with Mrs. Peterson."

"It turns out Judge Wickersham was right when he was defending Nelson and wanted to have him declared insane during the trial," said Henry. " 'Course, he probably still would've had the stroke."

Henry left for Juneau as soon as Deputy MacGregor returned from serving an attachment on the Marathon Packing Company plant at Cape Fanshaw. He promised to bring Margaret for a visit in the summer.

All the snow had melted from nearby mountains by the time Petersburg and Scow Bay schools closed for the summer. The Hume cannery at Scow Bay donated refreshments and provided a boat for a student picnic celebrating the close of the school year. It had become quite fashionable to travel to Scow Bay for social affairs. Although Carl and Elizabeth were too busy with the hotel to attend, Mrs. Mathis and Barbara Gauffin declared the store building of the Alaska Fish and Cold Storage Company there to be an excellent dance hall.

"I think the best dance was the private party given by the Masons," said Mrs. Mathis. "I've never arrived at a dance by gasboat before."

"It was a nice change from the Sons of Norway Hall," agreed Barbara.

"After the dancing, we had a midnight luncheon and returned to Petersburg on the same boats that took us there," continued Mrs. Mathis. "Oh, and we had special entertainment too."

"What was that?" Elizabeth asked.

"There's a couple who live there who are professional stage dancers known as 'Million & Donovan'," said Mrs. Mathis. "They put on a special dancing exhibition that was just wonderful."

"I liked their Rose Dance best," said Barbara. "It's kind of a fancy waltz. They also did a soft shoe routine and a Spanish dance. Everyone was very impressed."

"How on earth did such people end up in Scow Bay?" Elizabeth asked.

"That's a good question," replied Mrs. Mathis. "There seems to be a number of interesting people living there."

Carl accompanied the other members of the Commercial Club and city officials to the dock where the revenue cutter *Mojave* was moored. Assistant Secretary of Commerce C. H. Huston and a party of government officials were on board making a tour of the Alaskan coast.

"It was an impressive group of men," Carl said. "In addition to the commerce secretary, the heads of the Bureau of Fisheries, National Museum, Public Health Service and Geological Survey were all on board."

"Where are they going?" asked Elizabeth.

"All the way to the Pribilof Islands to investigate the salmon and fur seal industries. And then the secretary and a few of his party are going to Japan and around the world."

"And what did they think of Petersburg?" asked Elizabeth.

"It was raining too hard to give them much of a tour, but they had to be impressed with our gifts of fresh Alaskan shrimp donated by Earl Ohmer and a case of canned crab from the Dobbins Packing Company," Carl chucked.

Numerous fox ranchers were in and out of Petersburg getting supplies, transporting live foxes or responding to editor Perkins' letters to bring about a fox farming association. The former owner of the Sukoi Island fox ranch arrived from the south to secure stock for his new ranch in Idaho. Mr. and Mrs. Smith arrived from their fox farm at Pybus Bay and spent several days in town. The Smiths had made their home on their forty-foot boat the *San Juan* for the past nine years and Elizabeth wondered what kind of a woman could adapt to such a lifestyle. Fred Patten was another Pybus Bay fox rancher visiting town. This time, he brought his wife.

"Gertie, it's so good to see you," said Elizabeth. "How have you been?"

"No complaints, although it feels good to be back in civilization again," she said. "I figured I'd better come to town to make sure Fred buys the things I need to make our new place at Fanshaw comfortable. If I left it up to him, he'd return with grub and fishing gear but no yardage goods for window curtains or paint for the living room."

"When are you moving in?" asked Elizabeth.

"Probably next month sometime," said Gertie. "Fred still has some things he wants to finish at Pybus Bay. Say, Elizabeth, why don't you come out and spend a week when we get settled? I'd love to have some female company and Fred is away fishing for fox feed half the time."

"Oh Gertie, I'd love to, but there's the girls and the hotel."

"Carl can survive without you for a short vacation," said Gertie. "If the girls were older, they could come too, but I'm sure you can find someone to take care of them while you're away."

"It does sound tempting," said Elizabeth. "Let me talk to Carl and I'll let you know."

Carl related the news from Pybus Bay over dinner. "Fred says the Admiralty Packing Company at Pybus is in trouble with the government for shipping what they call 'adulterated' salmon last year. The Department of Agriculture found some cans to be stale, tainted or putrid."

"That sounds disgusting," said Elizabeth.

"He also said that Kirberger over on Hound Island near Kake will be selling up to one hundred pairs of blue fox after September 1," Carl continued. "He's asking $300 a pair for them."

"Speaking of foxes," said Elizabeth, "Gertie invited me to spend a week at their new ranch this summer."

"What about the girls?" said Carl.

"I was thinking maybe Barbara Gauffin would look after them," said Elizabeth, "if you can spare me from the hotel, that is."

"We can work something out," said Carl. "You don't get much opportunity to get out of town like your lady friends. Let's wait and see what Mrs. Gauffin has to say."

The weather turned nice with clear, sunny days and only occasional bouts of fog and rain. Petersburg and Wrangell American Legion boys organized a joint picnic at Mason's Place twenty miles down the Narrows. The *Americ* left port with the early birds at 8:00 a.m. followed by the *Eunice, Lorraine, Sherman* and *Odin*. By noon, the town was practically deserted.

Elizabeth took the girls for a walk down the boardwalk, stopping to say hello to Doc Rogers working on his new quarters in the Gauffin Building. "We're going to miss you at the hotel," she told him.

"It's about time I had a proper medical office," he said, handing each girl a lollipop. "There's plenty of doctoring work here and I like the townsfolk."

"Will your family be joining you?" Elizabeth asked.

"I've sent for my mother and my two boys who are now out of school for the summer," replied the doctor. "I've rented a house for them and they should be here in about two weeks."

"Will the boys attend school in Petersburg in the fall then?" asked Elizabeth.

"The youngest will," said the doctor. "Cecil will be a senior in high school and I'm considering enrolling him in school at Ketchikan. I don't think the Petersburg schools are up to standard in the upper grades. That will probably change when they get the new school house built though."

"I understand the city council bought the lot above the cannery for the new school," Elizabeth said.

"That's right," said the doctor. "They're getting bids to clear it and build a new street from the end of First Street to the site. And they just approved preliminary plans for the building. They should have it up and ready just about the time these two enter school." Betty and Duna giggled when he tousled their hair.

It was a tired, noisy group of picnickers who filed into the lobby at the end of the day. "The Wrangell crowd didn't get there until two in the afternoon," said Charlie Mann. "They came on two big gasboats and brought an enormous scow. The weather was fine and everyone had a good time dancing on the scow and getting acquainted."

"Tell Carl about the sharpshooter contest," said Mayor Locken.

"We were ahead in the rifle shooting contest but then Charlie Greenaa's stray shot lost the match by one point," said Mann.

"Not true," said Charlie. "I put two bullets in the same hole."

The town celebrated the Fourth of July over three days. On Saturday night, the American Legion gave a big ball in the Sons of Norway Hall. On the morning of July 4, the Legion sponsored a street carnival. Afternoon sporting events were followed by a baseball game between Petersburg and a mixed native and Filipino team. Petersburg won with a score of fifteen to thirteen. In the evening, the Fire Department gave a dance in the newly-renovated Pioneer's Hall. The hall was still torn up for repairs, but the crowd wanted a first hand look at the new lodge and enjoyed itself nonetheless.

Carl and Elizabeth were busy with out-of-towners and traveling salesmen coming and going between entertainments. Several sporting events – tug of war, foot races, sack races and a "fat man's" race – took place on the plank street in front of the hotel. The girls were excited by the festivities but too young to participate.

The *Spokane* arrived from the south the next morning with a cargo of fireworks that had been delayed in shipment. Many Petersburg children had never seen fireworks before and they "oohed" and "aahed" when the display was set off from the approach to the Citizen's Dock.

Mayor Locken, editor Perkins, Russ York from the Citizen's Laundry and Johnas Olson from the Trading Union were discussing business conditions with Carl. "You wouldn't know it to look around town," said Mayor Locken, "but the two big strikes down below are tying up commerce from coast to coast."

"The strikers turned down all plans proposed by the government and President Harding and his cabinet are taking a hands-off policy, letting the strikes be fought out to a finish," said editor Perkins.

Russ York added, "Between the railway strike in the east and the coal mine strike in the west, the trains can't run for lack of shopmen and fuel. I understand a large number of trains have been withdrawn from service."

"It's a good thing the *Redondo* recently brought us one hundred tons of coal and this being summertime, we won't be needing more for quite awhile," added Mayor Locken.

"The strikes don't appear to be slowing the excursion trade," said Carl. "Steamers are turning people away and the hotel is full with tourists, traveling salesmen and fox men passing through town. I've even had to refer some guests to the Petersburg Hotel, much as I hated to."

"We've noticed some slowing in shipments of merchandise from the south," said Johnas, "but we received our big summer order on the *Redondo* too, so the store's in pretty good shape for the time being. And the small hand cannery at the Trading Union dock has already put up a pack of 1,800 cases of first class reds. How are the other canneries doing?"

"The Mitkof cannery has 15,000 cases packed and the Hume cannery at Scow Bay has 4,000 cases up," said editor Perkins. "Both canneries are far ahead of where they were last year at this time. And it helped that steamship companies reduced freight rates on cannery supplies coming north and canned seafood traveling south."

"And don't forget that Dougherty and his San Francisco partners just received their permit from the Federal Water Power Commission to develop water power for a pulp mill right next door at Thomas Bay," said Mayor Locken. "He's requesting the Forest Service allocate him two and a half billion feet of timber in that vicinity."

"That's a billion with a 'b'?" exclaimed Russ.

"That's right," replied the Mayor. "They're looking at a $10 million investment."

"That's a lot of toothpicks," said Russ.

The steamship *Spokane* arrived with a boatload of conventioneers from the Western Confectioners' Association. The party had been expected since a communication arrived from Governor Bone's office several months earlier and the town was prepared with entertainment and dancing for the travelers. Unfortunately, it was raining hard when the ship arrived and members of the Commercial Club quickly escorted the visitors through the rain to the Sons of Norway Hall where music was waiting and a dance was started at once.

The visitors were served a luncheon of shrimp salad in the upstairs lodge rooms and dancing continued until the boat left with the midnight tide. The group included many leading western and Pacific coast businessmen in its membership and they all expressed their appreciation for Petersburg's hospitality.

The first official act of Commissioner Clifton, superintendent of Petersburg schools, was to hold an inquest into the death of an eleven-year-old native boy at the Willard logging camp at Totem Bay. Mr. and Mrs. Willard arrived in Petersburg in the morning to inform Coroner Granquist of the tragedy.

Carl learned the boy was literally blown to pieces by an exploding gasoline drum being used as a boiler for steaming boat boards. "The boy was helping his father steam boards for a boat he was building for Mr. Willard," Carl told Elizabeth. "They turned off the valve from the boiler to the steam chest, put some pieces of wood into the chest for steaming and returned to the boiler to turn the valve on again. The boiler exploded when they were within a few feet of it. The boy was directly in front of the boiler and took the full force of the explosion. They say the remains were unrecognizable."

"That's terrible," said Elizabeth. "Was the father injured too?"

"Badly bruised and burned on the lower parts of his body," said Carl, "but he'll live. The Willard's were away at Port Beauclerc when it happened and left immediately for town to report when they returned."

"Such a tragedy," Elizabeth replied. "It seems there's danger in even the simplest tasks in this country."

"Come to the dance with me Saturday night, Elizabeth," said Mrs. Mathis. "Ray is in Ketchikan on business and I don't feel like staying home alone. Carl wouldn't mind if we two old married ladies went without escorts, would he?"

"It's not that," said Elizabeth. "We're in our busy season at the hotel and I don't have anybody to stay with the girls. It would be nice to catch up though, it seems you and Dr. Mathis are rarely in town anymore."

"I think we've spent as much time in Wrangell as in Petersburg this year," Mrs. Mathis agreed. "And Ray has been busy with his fur buying business and his Snow Pass fox farm. Plus, he's been making trips to Juneau to take degree work in the Masonic Lodge."

"What about your house guests, Dr. Mathis' uncle and his wife?" suggested Elizabeth. "Won't they be going to the dance?"

"They would have but they wanted to see more of Alaska and are making the round trip to Skagway on the *Spokane*," replied Mrs. Mathis.

Elizabeth took a rain check on the dancing invitation and they agreed to get together when Dr. Mathis was back in town. The next day, Elizabeth learned that Mrs. Mathis had been painfully injured when the bench on which she was sitting with several other women collapsed, trapping her foot and ankle underneath. She was taken to her home by auto to recover under the care of Doc Rogers. Elizabeth brought her a casserole and found her bright and chipper, basking in the additional attention with her leg propped up on a pillow. Mrs. Mathis said she was only temporarily inconvenienced and she would be dancing again in no time.

Chapter 25

August 1922 – Elizabeth was off to see the foxes. Barbara was taking care of the girls and Fred arrived to take Elizabeth to his fox island to spend the week with Gertie. Carl claimed he could handle the hotel without her for a few days.

Elizabeth felt like a girl just released from school as Fred started the engine and cast off. They waved goodbye to Carl standing on the dock in the early morning mist and headed down the Narrows. The water was flat calm without a ripple. Sunlight touched the mainland mountain range as they passed the site where Carl and Elizabeth would be building their home. Fred agreed it was a first rate location with a first rate view.

They turned north at Prolewy Beacon and entered Frederick Sound. Soon, the Sukoi Islets were on the port side and Fred told Elizabeth about the fox raising operation there. "Several men made their fortunes in the fur business there," he said. "Claude Green started it all and then he sold to Mr. Chastek and the Hercules Fox Company and then he sold to Grover Cleary and his partners of the Sukoi Island Fox Company. Seems once a fox man always a fox man, though. Green has a fox ranch in Idaho. Mr. Chastek still has an interest in a fox ranch in Minnesota and his stock recently won several prizes in a competition held in

Michigan. In fact, the Aurora Fox Farms at Point Agassiz has two pairs of silver pups for sale that are related to the Hercules prize winners. They're asking $1,200 a pair. We'll be stopping at Point Agassiz to pick up some supplies for the missus," he added.

White frosting snow dripped down the treeless sides of the steep mainland mountains in the bright sunlight. The cloudless sky reflected the deep blue of the ocean. Or was it the other way around? Seagulls danced overhead and other boats were met with a whistle and a wave. The seas turned choppy but the little boat muscled its way through the swells without effort. The dock at Point Agassiz came into view and they were greeted by Mr. Swanson of the Point Agassiz Dairy.

"Good morning Fred, how are you?" he called out.

"Good morning to you, too, Carl," replied Fred. "Gertie told me to stop in and pick up some eggs and dairy."

"You came to the right place," said Swanson. "And is that Mrs. Roger you have with you?"

"Yes it is Mr. Swanson," Elizabeth laughed. "I'm going to visit Gertie and learn about raising foxes."

"Let me help you ashore," he said holding out his hand. "And you must come and see the newest little Swanson."

"I'd love to," replied Elizabeth. "How's the little one doing?"

"Oh, she's a fine big lass," said the proud father.

"And Mrs. Swanson?" inquired Elizabeth.

"Aurora is well too," he said, leading them up the dock to the house. "Come in and say hello."

A small herd of black and white Jersey cows followed their progress while chewing their cuds. Mrs. Swanson was delighted to have visitors although Fred said they must be on their way as soon as supplies were loaded. The baby was asleep in her bassinet, fingers curled and arms raised to her head. "She's beautiful, Aurora," Elizabeth whispered. "How old is she now?"

"Almost five months," said Mrs. Swanson. "She's a good baby. We named her Inez."

"A pretty name for a pretty girl," Elizabeth replied.

The Swansons walked them back to the boat. The former school teacher's wife was several inches taller than her husband. Her broad face was set off by dark braids pinned to the top of her head in the Scandinavian style. They waved as Fred's boat put out to sea and Elizabeth wondered about the tiny gravesite on the hillside behind them.

"Nice people," said Fred. "It sure is handy to have a place where we can get fresh eggs, milk and butter without going into town. Just isn't practical to have chickens on a fox island and we do like a change from goat's milk."

Fred pointed out the entrance to Thomas Bay as they motored past. "So this is where they plan to put the pulp and paper mill," said Elizabeth.

"Yep," said Fred. "Cascade Creek is just beyond that point to the right. It's fed by water from Swan Lake back in the mountains and there's another lake above that. That's where they plan to get the hydro electric power to run the mill."

"Why is the water so milky?" Elizabeth asked.

"That's glacier melt from Baird Glacier back in there at the head of the bay," said Fred. "You can't see where it reaches tidewater from here. Thomas Bay produces some of the best shrimp and crab anywhere. It'd be a shame to kill it all off with runoff from a paper mill."

When they passed the wide opening to Farragut Bay, Fred pointed out Read Island where Pete Jorgenson had his fox ranch. At Cape

Fanshaw, fishing boats were tied up at the cannery off loading fish. "Sometimes we put in here to pick up supplies from the cannery store during the season," said Fred. "There's a watchman who lives here year 'round but it's pretty well deserted in the wintertime."

They rounded the cape and Fred pointed out Storm Island dead ahead. There was another, bigger, island between Storm and the mainland. "That's Whitney Island," said Fred. "Andy Anderson is building a fox farm there and I hear he's going to stock it this fall."

Both islands sat in the crescent of Fanshaw Bay. "Why is it called Storm Island?" Elizabeth asked.

"Not exactly sure, but I think it's because the fishing boats anchor on the leeward side when there are storms in Frederick Sound and Stephens Passage," said Fred. "The western side of the island takes a pretty heavy pounding during foul weather."

Gertie waved from the house when she heard the motor. She helped tie up the boat when they sidled up to the short dock before giving Elizabeth a big hug. "I finally got you out of town," she said. "You're going to become a real frontier woman here. Isn't she Fred?"

"Whatever you say, Ma," he laughed.

Gertie had been baking bread and the house smelled wonderful. She proudly showed Elizabeth around the snug cabin that contained ample evidence of her sewing skills. Cafeteria style curtains hung in the kitchen windows and a beautiful handmade quilt adorned a daybed in the living room. Elizabeth presented her with the lace doilies and a lace table runner she had crocheted for her.

The single story cabin contained a kitchen with a coal and wood stove, living room with a field stone fireplace and two bedrooms. "We have running water fed from a cistern in the back," said Gertie, pointing to the hand pump at the kitchen sink. A large metal tub with a scrub board served as both bath and laundry. The outhouse contained a thick *Sears, Roebuck* catalog. "Fred says we'll really appreciate that fur-lined seat in the wintertime," she laughed.

Over dinner, Fred brought Gertie up to date on all the news from town. "They're getting close to forming that Southeastern Alaska fox farmer's association," he said. "I may need to make another run to town this week to attend that. Might stay overnight if it runs late."

"Stay as long as you want," said Gertie. "Elizabeth and me are just going to relax and enjoy the summer weather. There's not too much to do with the livestock at this time of year anyway."

"How many foxes do you have?" Elizabeth asked.

"About thirty at last count," said Fred. "It's a small number but we're just getting started. They have their pups in the spring, as many as thirteen to a litter. Some of the foxes are so tame, they'll come right into the house if you don't keep the door closed. Can make quite a mess of things too."

The household awakened early in the morning and Fred left for a day of fishing. "Gotta put up enough smoked fish to keep the foxes fed over the winter," he said before shoving off.

Gertie planned a picnic at the north end of the island. She and Elizabeth first toured the other buildings – a smoke house, wood shed, storage shed, feeding houses and combination machinery shed which housed the lighting plant and a stall for the single goat. By now, Elizabeth had met some of the furry, blue-grey foxes roaming the island. "It's best not to make pets of them," explained Gertie. "They may end up as a stole around some New York debutante's neck."

"Oh, that's so sad," said Elizabeth. "How are they killed for their pelts, or do I want to know?"

"First of all, none of these will become pelts," said Gertie. "We're raising strictly breeders. Still, I don't want to be attached to any we may sell. When they do take the pelts, though, they fix the feeding house door to close automatically when the fox enters. Once trapped inside, you reach in with these wooden tongs and grab them around the neck. Fred says it's quick – about the same as killing a chicken by wringing its neck."

They picked their way over the rocky beach to the north end of the island. Driftwood, seaweed and kelp littered the beach at low tide. Foxes collected mussels, limpets and hermit crabs from the tide pools and scurried into the woods with their prizes. "Where are they going?" Elizabeth asked.

"To bury their catch," said Gertie. "They'll dig it up and eat it only after it's totally putrid. Disgusting, really. They have dens all over the island," she added, "especially under tree stumps close to the feed houses."

The interior of the island was thick with two-foot high fiddle head ferns, skunk cabbage and huckleberry bushes beneath storm-stunted spruce trees. Moss-covered stumps and dead trees littered the ground.

The women spread their picnic on a flat rock and basked in the sun. There was a slight chop on the Sound and the ocean breeze felt cool and refreshing. "What's that glinting in the sunlight across the water," Elizabeth said, pointing.

"That's Five Finger Lighthouse," said Gertie. "It's about three miles away. Sometimes, you can hear the whales spouting as they pass between us and the lighthouse."

"Why is it called five fingers?" asked Elizabeth.

"There are five islands, although some are only visible at low tide," said Gertie. "Some say they look like bony fingers reaching out of the water to snare unwary mariners. That lighthouse has kept many a vessel from running aground. The summer mail boat leaves mail there for the fishermen and people on the fox islands."

They returned to the cabin by way of the western side of the island, picking up bits of smoothly polished driftwood in unusual and beautiful shapes. Gertie spotted two eagles and said Fred would have shot them if he were along. Eagles and weasels were the foxes only predators.

Fred had returned from fishing and the women helped clean the salmon for smoking or drying. "Fred catches them and I clean 'em," laughed Gertie.

The weather was sunny and beautiful all week. The women spent their days beach combing, exploring the island on foot and by rowboat, keeping the feeding houses stocked, tending to the goat, cooking and doing household chores. In the evenings, they played cards or sewed – Gertie on her foot treadle sewing machine and Elizabeth with her knitting and crochet needles. Whenever Fred was away overnight, Gertie worked on his surprise Christmas gift – a plaid flannel shirt with sturdy flat-felled seams. Elizabeth knitted sweaters with matching mittens for the girls.

Elizabeth found life on the island vastly different from living in town. There was no need to spend too much time on one's appearance and attire since there was no one around to notice and the foxes didn't care. The latest fashion in ladies footwear was not as important as having rugged shoes and boots capable of traveling over rocky beaches and through thick forests. It was easy to understand why many townspeople viewed fox ranchers and their families as primitive and backward.

Gertie took Fred's Kodak camera along on their last beach-combing expedition before Elizabeth returned to town. He used the camera to photograph foxes to show to prospective buyers. "Elizabeth," said Gertie, "let's do something totally crazy and take pictures of each other dressed in ferns like island princesses. Then we can give the pictures to our husbands. Fred and Carl will get a big kick out of it."

"Why not?" Elizabeth giggled. "We have complete privacy and there's nobody here to see us."

They constructed "grass" skirts and leis made completely of ferns. Elizabeth let her hair down and it covered her torso almost to her waist. Gertie tucked a flower behind Elizabeth's right ear and they took turns posing barefoot on a beach boulder with Whitney Island in the background. Elizabeth felt ridiculous with her bare arms and ankles exposed. "The men are going to love these," Gertie laughed.

Fred, Gertie and Elizabeth left for town early the next morning. Low clouds hovered over Frederick Sound and there was a damp chill in the air. "That could have been the last of our summer," said Fred, over the hum of the engine.

They finally arrived at the Public Dock and walked through town to the hotel. Carl was both surprised and happy to see them. "I didn't know when to expect you," he said. "How was the fox island?"

"Oh, I had a grand time," said Elizabeth. "Fred and Gertie took good care of me and the weather couldn't have been better. I missed you and the girls, though."

"I'll take this film over to Norwood's and order duplicates," said Gertie. "Elizabeth will soon have pictures of the things she did on the fox island to show you, Carl." The men looked at Elizabeth and Gertie quizzically when they burst into laughter.

Several traveling salesmen had been guests at the hotel while Elizabeth was away. One had established an agency for Ford parts through the Trading Union. Carl's least favorite guest, the territorial organizer for the Woman's Christian Temperance Union, signed up thirty members in Petersburg before moving on to Juneau. "You'd think the WCTU would be satisfied with Prohibition and leave it at that, but here they are still meddling," he growled. "They're all Bible thumping busy bodies, if you ask me."

"We're expecting a couple of boatloads of excursionists soon," he added. "The *Queen* left Seattle with 203 passengers and the *Admiral Watson* will follow with 117 passengers. Both steamers are fully booked."

"Then I got back just in time," said Elizabeth. "Do you think many will want to stay over in Petersburg?"

"Let's hope so," he said.

Chapter 26

September 1922 – The lobby regulars gathered around U.S. Deputy Marshal "Mac" MacGregor and Bill Norwood as the men recounted a harrowing tale of their trip to Le Conte Glacier.

"We took my skiff with the Evinrude to get some pictures of the glacier," said Bill, "and arrived at the glacier early in the afternoon. The weather was fine, not a cloud in the sky and no wind to speak of."

"Bill got out of the boat on a small rocky ledge," said Mac, "and I cruised the face waiting for some ice to fall off so he could get a good picture. Sometimes, vibrations from the motor will cause the glacier to calve."

"I had the camera trained on Mac," said the former school teacher, "when a small berg broke off the underwater shelf and came up beneath the boat. It threw Mac and the boat up in the air and then the boat slid off the berg. How it remained upright, I'll never know."

"The boat filled with water, soaking our food and camping gear and one oar was washed away," continued Mac. "I bailed some of the water out with a frying pan but couldn't get the engine started. The tide carried me a long way down the bay before I finally managed to paddle to the beach with the one oar and bail out the boat."

"In the meantime, I'm marooned on the rock shelf for several hours with no sign of Mac coming back for me," said Bill.

"I started paddling back to Bill," continued Mac, "but I was working against the current and it took me several hours to get within sight of him."

"And then," said Bill, "the glacier started calving and I'm in danger of being washed off the ledge by the waves from the big bergs that split off from the glacier. To make matters worse, the tide started coming in. When it reached my waist, I decided I couldn't wait any longer and had to do something. A small berg drifted by and I put my camera in my boots and tossed them onto the ice. I hopped onto the berg and stretched out spread-eagle like to keep the berg from tipping over. The berg drifted toward the rapids in the narrow part of the bay. Luckily, Mac had finally worked through the fast water with the boat."

"I sure was glad to see Bill drifting my way on his ice berg," said Mac. "I took him and his boots off the ice and together we managed to restart the engine. We headed for the beach and were so exhausted that we slept on the sand for two hours."

"You two were lucky to get out of there alive," said Carl.

"That's not the half of it," replied Bill. "When we woke up at daylight, we were surrounded by large bergs that had drifted in. These ice bergs were huge – bigger than any steamer that ever docked in Petersburg."

"What did you do?" asked Russ York.

Mac replied, "The engine had quit again, so with the one oar, we carefully poled the boat through the ice for nearly three hours. We went through places where ice hung over our heads for fifty feet or more. We worked in complete silence, afraid the vibration from our voices would cause the ice to drop on us."

"When we finally reached open water," Bill continued, "we made a paddle from one of the seats and paddled all day until the *Sunland*, who just happened to be passing at the right moment, picked us up and brought us to town."

"I tell you," declared Mac, "that glacier is no place for greenhorns."

The glacier almost claimed another victim when a visiting cinematographer's boat was caught in an ice jam as he tried to secure some good pictures. He managed to escape in a skiff and a later visit to the glacier to locate his boat and $1,000 moving picture camera turned up nothing. Several days later, the abandoned boat and his outfit were found intact in the kelp at Ideal Cove.

Applause echoed from the Moose Lodge room in the hotel. "What's the excitement all about?" Elizabeth asked Barbara Gauffin.

"We just learned that the Women of Mooseheart Legion won the prize for the greatest increase in membership among all the chapters in the territory," she said. "Isn't it exciting?"

"What's the prize?" asked Elizabeth.

"An all expense paid round trip for one delegate to the big convention at Mooseheart. Etta Worth, as Senior Regent, is going to represent us. She leaves on the next southbound trip of the *Spokane*."

"That's quite an honor," said Elizabeth. "Isn't Mooseheart somewhere near Chicago?"

"Yes, on a former farm about forty miles west, I'm told," said Barbara. "It's a home and school where dependent widows of Moose members can go to live with their children. The children get a good education, including vocational training. It's all supported by the Moose Lodge."

"What a wonderful experience for Mrs. Worth," said Elizabeth. "I hope she intends to make a report on what she sees when she returns."

"I'm sure she will," said Barbara. "And we can't wait to hear what she has to say."

The advance agent for Chautauqua arrived on the *Spokane* and Carl helped convene the local committee to arrange for this year's entertainment. Five performances of music, comedy, song and lectures were planned and the twenty-four committee members got busy organizing ticket sales. Mary Allen was the first woman to serve on the committee.

The traveling troupe arrived on Friday and spent the day in practice at the Variety Theatre. The entertainment was well received, although a little expensive. Season tickets were $4.40 and single performances were $1.35. Half of the performers traveled on to Juneau as the others completed their presentations over the four days of the event. Carl attended a lecture on the solar system while Elizabeth minded the hotel.

"How was the lecture?" Elizabeth asked.

"Not what I expected," said Carl. "He lectured on becoming citizens of the universe rather than narrow citizens of our own particular part of the world. And then he pointed out that many things in the Bible are borne out by science. If I wanted to hear a lecture on the Bible, I'd go to church more often. I don't think I'll participate in next year's committee."

Residents took to the streets to observe the arrival of the first flying machine ever to land in Petersburg. The hydroplane *Northbird* was moored in the harbor.

"Fellow who owns it flew from Seattle to Ketchikan where he's been doing aerial surveys for the forest service to locate water power sites back in the mountains," said Charlie Mann. "They've already located several lakes that don't appear on any maps."

"The flight over from Wrangell only took twenty-one minutes actual flying time," said Russ York.

"The pilot and machinist are staying at the hotel," added Carl. "They expect to be here about a week to take passengers up for observation trips, weather permitting."

Later, Elizabeth asked Carl if he had any interest in taking an airplane ride.

"It may have appeal for some," he said, "but I can think of better ways to spend my money."

The salmon season drew to a close and two big ships, the *Coolcha* and the *Queen*, arrived to load the last of the catch.

"I've never seen the *Coolcha* before," said Elizabeth. "And she's been in port a long time."

"She's a motor ship under charter to the Alaska Steamship Company," said Carl. "Editor Perkins tells me she's loading salmon from the Mitkof Island Packing Company, the Mountain Point cannery at Scow Bay and fish meal fertilizer from the by-products plant. Between the cost of taking on ship supplies, the money spent by the crew and paid out for long shoring, they've spent about $2,500 in Petersburg."

As soon as the *Coolcha* pulled away from the dock, the steamer *Queen* took her place and spent another twenty hours loading cases of salmon from the local cannery.

"The *Queen* is taking the Japanese foreman of the warehouse crew and twenty Orientals south," said Carl. "The cannery is still putting up chums and cohoes and when that's finished in a week or so, they'll send the rest of the cannery crew south on the *Admiral Watson*."

"It sounds liked the cannery had a good season," said Elizabeth.

"Almost 100,000 cases," replied Carl. "Everyone's pleased with that. The Hume cannery at Scow Bay closed the season with 27,000 cases and the Mountain Point cannery put up about 6,000 cases. And to top it off, the railroad strike down below is over so the season's catch can get to market."

"Do you think we'll have a new school building by the time the girls reach school age?" Elizabeth asked.

"I'm sure of it," said Carl. "The city council just awarded the contract for the building to a Seattle company for $37,000 and they've finished clearing the site and building the new street that connects to it."

"But they can't build during the winter, can they?" said Elizabeth.

"They'll probably start in the spring," replied Carl. "The plans call for a concrete building two stories high with a half basement. They're planning on nine class rooms and a large gymnasium."

"In the meantime," Elizabeth added, "the school teachers arriving for the new term will have to put up with the old buildings. One of the teachers, for the third and fourth grades, I think, and that nice girl from Hogue & Tveten's accounting department have taken the Ness cottage for the school term. I don't know where the others are lodging."

"They'll come knocking on our door before winter's out," chuckled Carl. "Those little cottages aren't built for winter weather."

Knut Steberg told the lobby regulars that the *Queen* had a rough trip south. "She was southbound from Ketchikan," he said, "running dead slow in the fog and struck a rock on White Cliff Island."

"How bad was the damage?" asked Carl.

"They floated her thirty-nine hours later and transferred the passengers to the Union Oil tanker *Ventura* who took them to Prince Rupert," said Knut. "Freight and baggage from the forward hold were also taken to 'Rupert on the *Admiral Rodman*. When they got the *Queen* there, they decided there wasn't any damage so they loaded everyone back on board and headed for Seattle again."

"Those passengers got an adventure they weren't expecting," said Charlie Greenaa.

"Yep," replied Knut. "And I understand Captain Glasscock threw quite a reception in the dining salon just before reaching Seattle to thank the passengers and crew for their behavior during the stranding."

"Did you hear about the Canadian steamer *Princess Louise*?" asked wharfinger Gauffin.

"No," said Charlie, "What about her?"

"She was coming south from Haines to Juneau and got into such a blow on Lynn Canal, she had to return to Haines and wait it out," said Gauffin. "By the time she left Haines the second time, there was two inches of snow on the ground."

"Sounds like an early winter," said Carl.

"Morning Marshal," said Carl as Deputy Marshal MacGregor entered the lobby.

"Carl, Mrs. Roger," said the affable peace officer, tipping his hat.

Russ York said, "I hear you've got a couple of Kake men locked up in your private boarding house."

"That's right," replied the marshal. "The native police sent a boat over for me. One man is charged with moon shining and the other, Oscar Ka-sheets, is charged with being drunk and disorderly, evading arrest and assault and battery."

"That Ka-sheets can be a mean son of a gun when he's drunk," said Charlie Mann.

"He was at large when I got there," said the marshal. "Seems he was arrested for being drunk and placed in the town jail. He kicked the side out of the jail and then went looking for the officers and members of the town council. He beat them up one by one as he came across them and the native officers were afraid to re-arrest him."

"Did he give you any trouble?" asked Carl.

"Nah," said the marshal. "Came as quiet as a lamb."

The Pioneers of Alaska held a house warming in their new hall and invited the entire town for an evening of dancing. More than two hundred people attended and enjoyed a delicious midnight luncheon of beans, dog mulligan, Alaska strawberries and other things dear to the hearts of the pioneers. It was necessary to reset the tables three times to serve everybody.

Miss Edna Osten performed several numbers on her violin accompanied by Mary Allen on the piano. The ladies were recalled again and again. Mrs. Clifton, the principal's wife, performed several vocal solos and was also recalled until forced to decline.

Editor Perkins, as secretary of the Igloo, delivered a few remarks of dedication. He traced the history of the Pioneers and said their one object was for the betterment of the community and the territory. He said the Pioneers dedicated their structure to the future enjoyment and good fellowship of the people of Petersburg.

Anna Rincke told Elizabeth that her son, Alden, was getting married. "His bride is arriving on the *Admiral Watson* and they plan to be married as soon as the steamer arrives," she said.

"And where is she from?" Elizabeth asked.

"Anna is from Washington. She has the same first name as mine. We've exchanged correspondence although we've never met. They're going to make their home in Petersburg."

"Are they planning a big wedding?" asked Elizabeth.

"No," said Anna. "Just a small ceremony before Commissioner Clifton. I'd love for you to come."

"I'd be honored to," said Elizabeth.

The young couple walked directly from the steamship to the commissioner's office where his mother, Elizabeth and a small group of friends waited. Following a brief ceremony, the wedding party adjourned to the Pioneer's Hall where the Elks were hosting their first big dancing party. Elizabeth excused herself and returned to the hotel.

Anna recounted the events the next day. "The hall was decorated in the Elks colors of royal purple and white," she said. "Dancing music was furnished by a pianist from Wrangell, Cecil Rogers on the violin and a drummer."

"Doctor Rogers' son Cecil?" asked Elizabeth.

"Yes," replied Anna. "He may still be a high school boy but he's quite good musically."

"Anyway," she continued, "they separated the dancers into four groups and we competed in a burlesque college meet. The men 'put the shot' with potatoes, the ladies competed in 'throwing the discus' with paper pie plates and the more dignified people propelled themselves across the floor on rugs in the boat race. It was hilarious."

"Just before dinner was served in the lodge rooms upstairs," she continued, "Edna Osten performed solos on the violin and Mary Allen accompanied her on the piano. And Mrs. Clifton also sang two solos."

"I heard those ladies at the dedication ceremony for the hall," Elizabeth reminded her, "and they were wonderful. Such talent."

"Alden and Anna slipped away after dinner and the dancing continued until four o'clock this morning," Mrs. Rincke continued.

"That's quite a day for your new daughter-in-law," said Elizabeth. "She arrived on a steamship, saw her new home and met you for the first time, got married, and attended a party of strangers behaving like children. I sure hope she has a sense of humor."

"You don't last long up here without one," agreed Anna.

The first snow of the season appeared on the mountain tops along Wrangell Narrows on October 19. It disappeared a few days later but was considered a harbinger of an early winter. "San Juan" Smith passed through town with eighty pairs of foxes he was delivering to buyers on various fox islands. The Mountain Point Cannery in Scow Bay changed over from processing salmon to clams. And Mrs. Willard shot a bear while out deer hunting. The wife of the Totem Bay logging camp operator reported that the skin was in excellent condition. The lobby regulars were impressed with her marksmanship.

Their evening meal was interrupted by a jolt followed by the sound of an explosion. Carl and Elizabeth grabbed the girls and ran into the street where people were pointing at smoke rising across the Narrows. "It's the Knutesen Brothers' sawmill," somebody shouted. Several boats left immediately for the scene to offer assistance.

Everyone waited anxiously until a small boat finally returned with word that the boiler had exploded and no one was hurt. Soon, the lobby was filled with men describing the accident. "The boiler was thrown seventy-five feet," said Earl Ohmer. "Lumber, bricks, iron roofing, rocks and boiler bits are scattered everywhere. It even blew out the windows in the big house."

"But no one was hurt?" said Elizabeth.

"Nope," replied Earl. "The boys were in the house just finishing supper. In fact, one of the boys had just remarked he was going to fix that leak in the boiler the next day when it exploded."

"What do they make over there?" asked Doc Rogers.

"It's a three-man operation," replied Earl. "They just finished the season sawing street planking for the town."

"This could cut into their profits," remarked one of the lobby regulars.

"Pete Knutesen said they were going to put in a new boiler before next season anyway," said Earl, "and this saves them the trouble of removing the old one first."

Captain Hadland was telling the lobby regulars about his experience with the *White Bear* on the Petersburg-Juneau mail route. "We were just coming out of Sumdum," he said, "when I took the wheel off Woody Spit. It was about eleven o'clock at night, black and foggy, and the tide was running about five miles an hour."

"The waters south of Juneau are filled with ice bergs this time of year," interrupted Sam Gauffin.

"Yep," replied Hadland, "and a big berg broke off from the bottom, lifting the boat about seven feet out of the water. The *Bear* slid along the face of the berg just as it started to slip over on one side and it split open, leaving the boat resting safely on the water between two walls of ice rising six feet high on each side. Believe me, it didn't take us long to get out of there."

"How much damage to the boat?" asked Doc Rogers.

"Just a few scratches below the waterline," said Hadland. "If it hadn't been for the fact that the ice sloped steeply with no jagged points, the boat would've been smashed and all aboard drowned."

"How big was the berg?" asked Russ York.

"Too dark to tell for sure," said the captain, "but it was a huge one. I can tell you I've never heard of a similar experience in all my years on the sea, that's for sure."

"There goes the *Northbird*," said Carl.

"Where?" said Elizabeth, looking up in the sky.

"Out there in the Narrows, on the *Alf*," he replied.

The southbound gasboat moved slowly past the town, a big load of covered cargo on deck.

"What happened?" asked Elizabeth.

"Jack Hadland on the *White Bear* towed it into Juneau when they had engine trouble a little south of Midway Island," said Carl. "The pilot thought he could get the engine repaired there but the boom broke while lifting the plane from the water to the machine shop dock. Broke two panels of the wings."

"And they couldn't repair the wings?" said Elizabeth.

"Nope," said Carl. "Had to send east for new ones. So they dismantled it and are taking it back to the hanger in Ketchikan."

"Somehow it seems so sad to see a flying machine all in pieces like that," Elizabeth remarked.

"Goes to show just how rough this country can be on man and machine," agreed Carl.

The whole town buzzed about a big gold strike on the Farragut River about thirty miles from Petersburg. "It's the famous 'Lost Rocker' claim," said Carl. "The white men who took out gold thirty years ago were murdered and the lone survivor refused to go back. Prospectors have been searching for it for years. It was first worked by Russians forty-five years before that."

"Who found it?" asked Elizabeth.

"Fellow named Morrison," said Carl. "He says he rebuilt the old stone cabin and old rocker left by the original prospectors. He also found an old dam built of yellow cedar in a side creek that furnished water for the rocker. Brought back pictures to prove it too. He filed eight claims and plans to start working them in the spring."

Elizabeth listened in as editor Perkins related the history of the claim to the lobby regulars. "According to legend," he said, "about thirty years ago, a white man was found drifting about in an Indian canoe in Frederick Sound. He was half starved, nearly crazy and had two sacks of coarse gold with him. They took him to town and cared for him but he refused to return to the place where he found the gold. He claimed himself and two others had discovered rich gold deposits on a river some distance from the beach. They built a dam, a rocker and a stone cabin. One day, he returned to camp and found his companions murdered, seemingly by Indians. He took the gold and crossed three mountain ranges, coming out at tidewater near an Indian village where he stole a canoe during the night. He managed to escape and drifted about until being rescued."

"I've heard about this," said Johnas Olson, "and men have been trying to find the 'Lost Rocker' ever since."

"About five or six years ago," continued Perkins, "Sing Lee grubstaked a fellow who spent two months in the Farragut Bay country and came back with two bags of gold, one coarse and one fine. He never returned to the diggings and never told anyone where he found the ore."

"How much gold do they think is still back there?" asked Charlie Greenaa.

"Morrison said he'll be disappointed if he takes out less than a million dollars worth," replied Perkins. "He says there's no doubt in his mind he'll be able to get the gold out."

Later, Elizabeth told Carl, "I'll bet Henry Roden would be interested in this discovery, him being such a mining expert."

"I'm sure he would," agreed Carl. "This country is full of rich mineral deposits. The trick is getting them out. Just look at the discoveries we've heard about this year alone. There was the nickel ledge that the Hofstad boy discovered on Baranof Island, lead silver ore found near Wrangell, and barite discovered at Duncan Canal. I wish Mr. Morrison well, but the real test will be how much gold he actually recovers."

Chapter 27

October 1922 – Captain Hadland and the *White Bear* played a role in another tragedy while on the Petersburg-Juneau mail run. "As I was passing Grand Island southbound," he told the lobby regulars, "I was hailed by Robert Barclay who operates a fox ranch there. He wanted me to transport a family of natives who were shipwrecked on his island."

"What happened to them?" asked Doc Rogers.

"The party of five natives and four children was crossing Taku Inlet bound from Juneau to Taku Harbor," said the captain. "A Taku was blowing off the glaciers and heavy seas broke in a window and flooded the engine. They couldn't get it started again and the boat smashed against the rocks on Grand Island."

"When I had the *Americ* on the mail run," said Johnas Olson, "crossing the inlet was usually a rough trip. Was anybody hurt?"

"An elderly woman was drowned," said Captain Hadland. "The boat sank stern first and she was unable to escape. Another woman crawled through a window she broke with her hand which was badly cut. One of the men was caught by a wave and thrown against the rocks. He's badly bruised and probably has internal injuries."

"What about the children?" asked the doctor. "How old are they?"

"They ranged from two to twelve years old and they made it ashore safely," replied Hadland. "The party stayed at the scene all night searching for the missing woman's body but gave up at daylight and made their way to Barclay's fox ranch."

"And what about the boat?" asked Carl.

"It's a small one without a name and it's a total loss," said the captain. "The family lost their winter grubstake, trapping outfit and all their clothing. The only thing they salvaged from the wreck was one rifle. I took them across Stephens Passage to Taku Harbor where they were taken in by relatives."

Elizabeth chatted with Anna Rincke while shopping at Hogue & Tveten's. Anna reported that the newlyweds were settling in and the store had a new millinery department. She said they could now make winter hats to order or remodel your old ones. And Miss Hofstad, the store's accountant, and her two school teacher friends had moved from the Ness cottage to the Swendsen house. "Guess they found the cottage to be too small," said Anna.

"And what grades do the school teachers teach?" asked Elizabeth.

"I believe Miss Oliver teaches fifth and sixth grades and Miss Borgaard teaches third and fourth grades," said Anna. "Miss Oliver taught at Wrangell last year, you know. That's where she met our Miss Hofstad whose parents live there too."

"How nice that the three young ladies have so much in common," Elizabeth replied. "I admire the good example they're setting for our young people."

Wharfinger Sam Gauffin reported that several halibut boats had been caught unawares by a big storm that swept the Yakutat fishing banks. "I'm told it was the worst storm in history and many fishermen gave up hope of ever reaching safe harbor," he said. "It came out of nowhere and the only thing that saved them was the fact that the huge seas and the wind were running together"

"I heard that several boats had all their fishing gear washed overboard by the heavy seas," added Earl Ohmer. "I'm thankful my shrimpers fish on inside waters."

"The halibut boat *Sentinel* was out in the open when the storm came up and all they could do was keep the boat facing open water with the engine running for six days," continued Sam. "They darn near ran out of oil, too. One of the crew went out on deck during a lull in the storm and tried to stow the gear in the hold to keep it from washing overboard. But the storm came up suddenly again and a big wave washed over the boat all the way up to the rigging. All the crew could do was batten down the hatches with the man inside to keep the water from flooding the hold. Fellow was trapped down there for twenty-four hours until the storm let up enough for the crew to get him out."

"What shape was he in when they finally rescued him?" asked Doc Rogers.

"Cold, soaked in bilge water, facing hypothermia," said Sam. "He'd puked his guts out while being tossed around in the dark. He's going to be OK, though."

"How many men does the boat carry?" asked Carl.

"Six, including the captain," replied Sam. "After weathering the storm, they put into Juneau for supplies and headed right back out again. That's one tough way to make a living."

The mountains facing Wrangell Narrows gradually turned white and the first snow of the season fell on the streets of Petersburg on November 10. Many residents prepared to go south for the holidays. Those staying over the winter looked forward to an active social season of dances, bazaars, concerts, *julebukking* and ice skating parties. Elizabeth hosted a tea party for her lady friends Anna Rincke, Gussie York, Gertie Patten and Mrs. Mathis.

"Isn't it nice that you're all going south on the same steamer?" said Elizabeth.

"And I'm so glad it's the *Spokane* and not the *Jefferson*," said Mrs. Mathis.

"Why is that?" asked Elizabeth.

"The *Jefferson* dropped her propeller on the last trip to Seattle and the *Spokane* was one of two ships that came to her rescue," said Mrs. Mathis. "They towed her to Ketchikan and that big new ship, the *Medon*, towed her all the way to Seattle from there. I just think the *Jefferson* is too old and in bad repair for winter service."

"Gussie, tell us about your big trip," Elizabeth prompted.

"It's the trip of a lifetime," Gussie said enthusiastically. "I'm taking the train all the way to New York, stopping at all the major cities along the way. From there I take the ocean liner to Sweden. And, I'm returning through the Panama Canal."

"How long has it been since you've visited the old country?" asked Anna.

"Twenty years," said Gussie. "In fact, Elizabeth, I'll be going through the town where you grew up and I'd be happy to say hello to your aunt for you."

"Oh, would you? I wouldn't want to cut into your time with your relatives."

"It's no trouble at all," Gussie laughed. "I'll be gone for three months and we'll probably all be sick of one another long before then."

"I'll write a letter tonight for you to give her then, and enclose pictures of the girls," said Elizabeth. "Aunt Emma will be thrilled."

"And Gertie, you're going to leave Fred to manage the fox island without you this winter?" asked Anna.

"He insists he can manage and I'll be back after the holidays," said Gertie.

"What will he be doing while you're away?" Elizabeth asked.

"He'll be keeping the feeding houses stocked and working on a new skiff he's building," replied Gertie. "I'm really looking forward to the foxes having their pups in the spring. We'll leave containers of food and water at the mouth of each den so the mothers can remain with the pups instead of foraging for food. Fred says we'll get better quality pups and more of them that way since the dens won't be left open to predators."

"Ray is raising foxes too, at Snow Pass," said Mrs. Mathis. "But he's hired a man to tend the operation over the winter."

"And is Dr. Mathis going south at this time too?" Elizabeth asked.

"No," said Mrs. Mathis, "he wants to help organize the fox ranchers later this month and will come south after the big meeting. We plan to be away for two or three months."

"Well, Elizabeth," said Anna, "it appears you and I will have to hold down the fort this winter while these three world travelers are away."

The hotel was full of fox farmers in town for the big meeting at the Pioneer's Hall. Fifty-nine men came from as far away as Sitka, Wrangell, Juneau and Ketchikan and included government officials as well as ranchers. Some of the men stayed on their boats tied up in the harbor.

"What's the purpose of the fox farmers association?" Elizabeth asked.

"They want an organization that will promote all areas of fox farming," said Carl, "such as improving breeding stock, exchanging information and getting protection against poachers. The fox islands are so widely scattered that it takes too long for everyone to get the news. This way, the association will get information out to everyone at the same time."

Petersburg fox men in attendance included Dr. Mathis, two loggers, a grocery store merchant, a fur buyer and the proprietor of the local theatre. The meeting lasted well into the evening and the men elected a board of directors and temporary officers to serve until the next meeting. Editor Perkins was made one of the temporary officers. Membership dues were set at $6 per year. The men began dispersing the next day, some returning to their ranches immediately and others lingering in town for a few days stocking up on supplies.

The body of a young Irishman was brought to town from Kake and a coroner's jury empaneled. Russ York told the men in the lobby about the strange story. "This fellow and three partners came across from Security Bay Tuesday night when the weather kicked up," he said. "Three of the men anchored their small boats behind Hound Island but this lad struck the rocks above the town. His boat was undamaged so he anchored on the flats in front of Stedman's ranch."

"We had some weather that night," said Johnas Olson.

"As the storm increased," continued Russ, "two natives crossed the flats to ask if the Irishman needed assistance. He said he was all right so they left. By eleven o'clock that night, a small hurricane was blowing and all the boats in the harbor were in trouble. Everybody was busy looking out for their boats and forgot about the fellow out on the flats. In the morning, the man's partners went looking for him but there was no sign of the boat."

"Had it drifted off in the storm?" asked Doc Rogers.

"That's what they thought at first," said Russ, "but when the tide went out they found the boat filled with water on the flats and the Irishman's body lashed to the mast."

"Had there been foul play then?" asked the doctor.

"The rope was tied around his waist with a knot in the front," said Russ, "so he could have untied himself at any time. And, the boat only drew three feet of water so he could have easily drifted in and reached the beach."

"And what did the coroner's jury decide was the cause of death?" asked Johnas.

"Death by drowning," said Russ. "What else could we conclude?"

Fire Chief Earl Ohmer told Carl that the firemen had just revived the homesteader who lived across the Narrows.

"What happened?" asked Carl.

"He had just come to town in his skiff and fell overboard while stepping from his boat to the float," said Earl. "The tide was running strong and swept him down toward the Public Dock. He couldn't swim with his heavy clothes and rubber boots on, so he just managed to kick himself along the bottom and get his nose above water occasionally."

"That water is cold," said Carl. "How did he get out?"

"Some natives just happened to see him in the water and pulled him out," replied Earl. "He was about all done in and wouldn't have lasted much longer. He was chilled to the bone but we managed to get his circulation restored."

"Did somebody call the doctor?" asked Carl.

"That old timer doesn't have much regard for the medical profession," laughed Earl, "but I think that flask of brandy we gave him is just what the doctor would have ordered."

"Did you hear what Pete Swanson caught when he was out fishing?" said Russ York to the men in the lobby.

"No, what?" responded Carl.

"A 150-pound lump of ambergris," said Russ. "He thinks he may be a very wealthy man."

"What's ambergris?" Elizabeth asked.

"It's a fatty substance from the digestive system of sperm whales," said Russ. "They just expel it naturally and it's found floating on the sea or washed up on the beach. It's used in perfume manufacturing and is quite rare."

"I hear the going rate is about $30 an ounce," said editor Perkins. "Let's see, at sixteen ounces per pound, that would work out to about $72,000. No wonder Pete's excited."

"He'd best not count his chickens too soon," said one of the men. "The old timers who've had a look at it said it's only whale blubber. They said ambergris is crusty and waxy, dark grey or black and has a sweet earthy odor. This stuff is soft, pale white with black streaks and it stinks."

"No, no," said another man. "Ambergris is soft and white when it's first expelled by the whale. It only turns dark and starts smelling good after it's been exposed to the elements for many months or even years."

"At any rate," continued Russ, "he sent a sample to a laboratory in Seattle, so I guess he'll soon know for sure."

The men in the lobby were worried about the disappearance of the Kake mail boat. Wharfinger Gauffin reported that the *Loomis* had just arrived in port and reported the *Trygve* missing. "Three boats, the *Americ, Sherman* and *Ranger,* started for Kake at once to search for her," he said.

"What did the captain of the *Loomis* have to say?" asked Russ York.

"He said Paul Adams, a Kake native, was a passenger on the *Trygve* when it left Kake for Petersburg. They were bucking a hard Taku when the crank shaft broke. Adams took the skiff and rowed seven miles to Kake where he got the *Loomis* to go to her rescue. The *Loomis* took the *Trygve* in tow and started for town but they couldn't make any headway against the wind so they anchored for the night behind the point above Kake. The next morning, there was no sign of the *Trygve*. That's when the *Loomis* came to Petersburg to raise the alarm."

"What do they think happened during the night?" asked Doc Rogers.

"Hard to tell," said Sam. "One theory is that the *Trygve's* anchor dragged into deep water and she went adrift again."

The whole town waited anxiously for word of the mail boat's whereabouts. Finally, a maritime parade was spotted progressing down Wrangell Narrows. The *Americ* led the parade with the *Trygve* in tow, followed by the other rescue boats.

Sam completed the story: "The rescue boats found the *Trygve* anchored at Kake. After going adrift the second time, the captain rigged a small sail out of a blanket and drifted before the wind to Keku Point. As they got close to land, Paul Adams again took the skiff and rowed seven miles to Kake a second time and got assistance to tow the boat to Kake."

"Thankfully, everyone is safe," said Doc Rogers.

"And Bert Cornelius over at Hogue & Tveten's just gave me a 'thank you' letter to publish in the next edition of the *Report*," said editor Perkins. "He thanks all who assisted in searching for the mail boat when she was reported lost and Paul Adams in particular."

Charlie Greenaa said to Carl, "You remember my partner Pete's son?"

"The young fellow who ran your floating store at Port Alexander last summer?" replied Carl.

"That's him," said Charlie. "He spent some time down below after the season ended and now he's back to spend the winter at the fox farm at Farragut Bay. He was out goose hunting with Pete's hired hand and his gun accidentally discharged, hitting the other man in the upper arm near the shoulder."

"Is he all right?" asked Carl.

"Looks like," said Charlie. "They bandaged it as best they could; young Jorgenson swam across three sloughs to get help and the *Americ* brought the wounded man to the hospital. The man is expected to recover without any permanent damage."

"How's Pete's boy holding up?" asked Carl.

"Oh, he feels just terrible. He visits the patient in the hospital every day and can't do enough for him. The man's a quiet sort who keeps to himself and doesn't have many acquaintances."

A week later, Doc Rogers announced that the patient had died.

"How can that be?" said Carl. "We heard it was just a flesh wound."

"It was," replied the doctor, "but he developed lock jaw and the hospital had no serum with which to treat the disease. We wired Ketchikan and the revenue cutter *Smith* was sent north with the medicine at once. We administered the serum and did everything possible, but without success."

Carl's prediction came true when the school teachers gave up their bachelor quarters in the Swendsen house on account of frozen pipes. Miss Borgaard and Helen Hofstad moved into the hotel and Miss Oliver secured a room with Mayor and Mrs. Locken in their quarters above the bank.

Elizabeth enjoyed having the young ladies live at the hotel and they made a big fuss over Betty and Duna. "Any time you want a baby sitter, Mrs. Roger," said Miss Borgaard, "you just let us know."

Elizabeth thanked them for their offer, knowing full well it was likely they also would be attending any social function she might consider. Most of the young people in town rarely missed a dance. The young ladies insisted on helping with Betty's third birthday party. Miss Borgaard was especially good with young children and played with the girls until they were exhausted.

It seemed everyone was in the holiday spirit, attending one party after another. The Civic Club of Scow Bay gave a fancy work sale and dance in the Nelson store building. Free boats left from the Citizen's Dock. The Sons and Daughters of Norway gave a big bazaar at their hall, netting $900 for their building fund. The Kjerulf Glee Club also gave their first annual ball at the hall. The Camp Fire Girls entertained the public with a programme at the Variety Theatre and a double header basketball game was played between Petersburg and Wrangell.

The men in the lobby reflected on the past season and speculated about next year. "Seafood processing got back to normal this year," said editor Perkins. "And now that the cannery men are out of the hole, next year will be even better."

"The Mitkof cannery is already gearing up for next year, installing a new foundation and pilings under both the cannery and wharf," said Sam Gauffin.

"And the fox raising business is really taking off," added Charlie Greenaa. "The new fox men's association is coming down hard on poachers and getting convictions too."

"The excursion business is so lucrative that the Alaska Steamship Company has commissioned a new million-dollar passenger liner," added Carl. "They're even converting the *Medon* to handle passengers."

"There should be plenty of construction work next year too," continued Perkins. "The $10 million pulp mill at Thomas Bay is likely to break ground, we'll be building a new school house, the Petersburg-Scow Bay road may finally be completed, and the town's water works needs to be over hauled. Next summer's activity has never been equaled, I'd say."

Betty and Duna played in the snow in the vacant lot next to the Sanitary Market. They looked like rosy-cheeked cherubs bundled up as they were in snowsuits, knit caps with earflaps, mittens and rubber boots. Betty was trying to build a snowman and Duna was too little to be very helpful. When Elizabeth showed her how to build a baby snowman from two snowballs, Duna shrieked with laughter. Elizabeth looked up at the sound of a boat whistle and waved to the *White Bear* towing two rafts of logs up the Narrows. Carl and Captain Hadland waved back from the pilot house. "Look, girls, there goes Daddy with our new home," she said.

When Carl returned home for dinner, he was as excited as the girls had been when playing outdoors. "We got the logs there just as the tide was going out," he said. "They're tied down as high on the beach as possible."

"How many logs are there?" Elizabeth asked.

"Seventy in all," said Carl, "some longer than others but all pretty much the same size around."

"Oh Daddy, I can hardly wait to see our home go up."

"Me too, Mother. It's about time we had a proper home for our family. 'Course, we'll have to wait for spring to actually begin building."

"What is the next step?" asked Elizabeth.

"We'll drag the logs up the hill with the donkey engine and lay them out on blocks to season over the winter," said Carl. "In the spring, we'll clear the trees and bushes and start building. May have to pull some stumps too. In fact, if we don't get too much snow, I can start chopping down trees this winter. I hope you'll be happy living out of town."

"Oh, I will," said Elizabeth. "You'll be going to town to the hotel every day and I can bring the girls in whenever I want. It's not as remote as living on a fox island."

That night in her dreams, Elizabeth saw Carl and their girls all snug in their new log house. Passing steamers blew their whistles and they waved back at the excursionists. A herd of deer clattered down the beach, crows called from towering hemlocks and the rain fell softly on the roof.

Epilogue

The little town on Mitkof Island continued to grow since Elizabeth's time. Her two girls still live in Petersburg. Her grandchildren, great grandchildren and great, great grandchildren reside in Alaska, Washington, California, Hawaii, Colorado and Virginia.

The log house that Carl built still stands on the grassy bluff overlooking Wrangell Narrows and the pristine waters of Frederick Sound. It's occupied by a new generation of Alaskans now.

Logging and the fox islands are but a memory and the pulp and paper mill at Thomas Bay was never built. Commercial fishing and tourism are the town's main industries. The fishing season still attracts an influx of transient workers to staff the canneries each summer.

Descendants of Elizabeth and Carl's contemporaries run the city council and many of the businesses on Main Street, renamed Nordic Drive. A new thirty-three room hotel stands on the site of the former Hotel Arctic. The new hotel was built around an interior door from the original Hotel Wester. The 17th of May is still celebrated with costumes, dancing, smorgasbords, salmon bakes and sporting events. Everyone is a "Norwegian for a day" and the town's moniker is "Little Norway."

Residents live close to nature and wildlife is still plentiful. Deer, moose, black bear, wolves, porcupines, eagles, hawks, waterfowl and game birds all share the island. The weather is a constant presence, with some rainfall on most days of the year. Vegetation is lush and green and the air is as sweet and pure as when Elizabeth arrived in the winter of 1918.

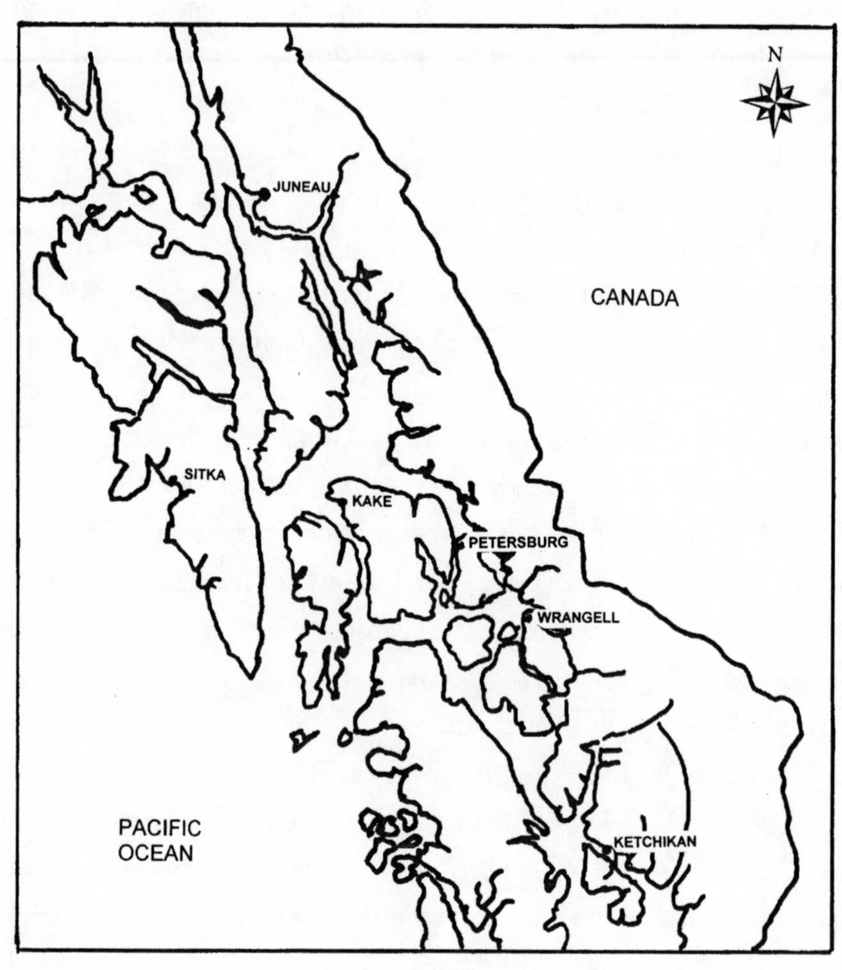

Southeastern Alaska

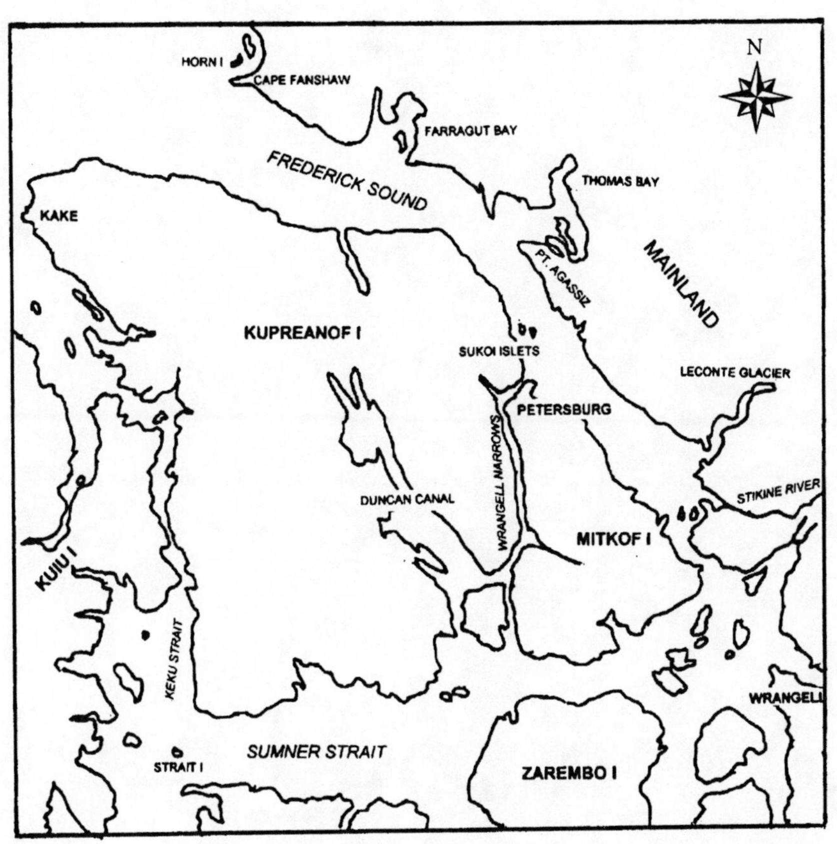

Petersburg Area

Acknowledgments

I am grateful to many people for their assistance in compiling this novel, especially my husband Randy – the consultant who was always "in" whenever I needed help. Thank you to Elizabeth's girls June White and Betty Pederson for sharing their reminisces and vintage photographs. Elizabeth's grandchildren Hoopie Davidson and her husband Bill, Bill White and his wife Donna, Janice Mikkelsen and her husband Kaare, Jean Curry and her husband Clyde and Roger Pederson all shared their memories and directed me to nautical, botanical and historical information. And thank you to Elizabeth's niece Marge Kellogg and niece-by-marriage Janet Rudd for their stories of Elizabeth's siblings.

I'm also indebted to the staffs of the College of the Desert Library in Palm Desert, the Alaska State Library in Juneau and the Clausen Memorial Museum and Public Library in Petersburg for providing authentic background information on the social, economic and political conditions of the early 1900s in southeastern Alaska and nationally.

Finally, I'd like to thank the ladies of *The Desert Woman* in Palm Desert for their encouragement and inspiration.

Selected Bibliography

"Alaska Steamship Changes Men." *The Progressive* Ketchikan AK 9 May 1917

"Amtrak Empire Builder." *TrainWeb, Inc.* 4 Dec 2005 <http://www.trainweb.com/routes/route_07/rg_7old.htm>

"Amtrak Southwest Chief Route Guide." *TrainWeb, Inc.* 4 Dec 2005 <http://www.trainweb.com/routes/route_03/rg_3old.htm>

"Balboa Park Guide to What's New." *City of San Diego Park and Recreation Department.* San Diego CA Mar & Apr 2006

"Canadian National Railway." *Wikipedia Foundation, Inc.* 14 Sep 2008 <http://en.wikipedia.org/wiki/Canadian_National_Railway>

"Chicago is Alarmed by Influenza Spread – Nearly 400 New Cases and Four Deaths Reported – Pneumonia Takes Sixteen Victims." *The New York Times* NY NY 16 Jan 1920

"Chicago Race Riot of 1919." *Wikipedia Foundation, Inc.* 25 Aug 2008 <http://en.wikipedia.org/wiki/Chicago_Race_Riot_of_1919>

"Chicago, Illinois." *Wikipedia Foundation, Inc.* 18 Nov 2005 <http://en.wikipedia.org/wiki/Chicago_Illinois>

Cole, Dermot. "Alaska Gets a Legislature." *Alaska History & Cultural Studies, Alaska Humanities Forum.* 30 Apr 2006 <http://www.akhistorycourse.org/articles/article.php?artID=135>

"Daily Doings in District Court: Petit Jury Sworn in and Examined to try Rhyde Case Today." *The Daily Progressive-Miner* Ketchikan AK 19 May 1917

"Daily Doings in District Court: August Rhyde of Petersburg Declared Guilty by Jury Sunday at 2 p.m." *The Daily Progressive-Miner* Ketchikan AK 21 May 1917

DeArmond, Bob. "The Life and Times of Henry Roden, Pioneer Miner, Lawyer, Legislator." *Juneau Alaska Empire* Juneau AK 13 June 1966

"Evanston History." *Evanston Public Library.* Evanston IL 1 Mar 2005 <http://www.epl.org/community/history.html>

Farwell, Captain R. F., USNR. *Captain Farwell's Hansen Handbook for Piloting in the Inland Waters of The Puget Sound Area, British Columbia, Southeastern Alaska, Southwestern Alaska, Western Alaska.* Seattle WA: L & H Printing Company, 1951

"Five Finger Islands, AK." *Lighthousefriends.com* 24 May 2008 <http://www.lighthousefriends.com/light.asp?ID=825>

"Fred Harvey." *Wikipedia Foundation Inc.* 6 Nov 2005 <http://en.wikipedia.org/wiki/Fred_Harvey>

Galloway, Neil. "Echoes of the Past, The Old Timer." *Alpine Historical Society.* Alpine CA Sep 2004

"History of the City of San Diego, 1900-1929." *The City of San Diego.* 9 Feb 2006 <http://www.sandiego.gov/citizensassistance/facts/history.shtml#1900s>

"History of Five Finger Lighthouse, Frederick Sound, Alaska." *Juneau Lighthouse Association.* 24 May 2008 <http://www.5fingerlighthouse.com/pages/history.html>

"History of the Marine Fireman's Union." *The Official Website of the Pacific Coast Marine, Firemen, Oilers, Watertenders and Wipers Association.* 2008 <http://www.mfoww.org/history.htm>

"The History of Mooseheart Child City & School." *Mooseheart Child City & School, Inc.* Mooseheart IL 2007 <http://www.mooseheart.org/History.asp>

Keen, Harold. "Explorer's Death Revives Memories of Historic Swedish Event, Recalls Arrival, Celebration for Crew of Vega." *The Tribune Sun* San Diego CA 5 Aug 1940

Leete, Jeremy. "The Taming of the Rock." *Vancouver Island Abound Outdoor Pages*. 30 Oct 2007 <http://www.vancouverislandabound.com/tamingof.htm>

"List of epidemics." *Wikipedia Foundation, Inc.* 11 Nov 2005 <http://en.wikipedia.org/wiki/List_of_epidemics>

Maxwell, Jeffrey Scott. "What is Chautauqua? - The Complete Chautauquan." 3 Mar 2002 <http://www.members.aol.com/AlphaChautauquan/what.html>

Miller, Lynn W. ed. *Petersburg Weekly Report* Petersburg AK 1 Jan. 1916 thru 19 July 1918

Miller Rubin, Bonnie. "Chicagoans Flock to Marshall Field's For Memories." *Los Angeles Times* Los Angeles CA 26 Dec 2005

Moore, Geoffrey H. "Recessions." *The Concise Encyclopedia of Economics*. Liberty Fund, Inc. 11 Nov 2005 <http://www.econlib.org/library/Enc/Recessions.html>

Newman, Scott A. "Dearborn Street Station." *Jazz Age Chicago*. 19 Mar 1997 <http://www.chicago.urban-history.org/sites/transpor/dearborn.htm>

Newman, Scott A. "Marshall Field and Company." *Jazz Age Chicago*. 12 Jan 1997 <http://www.chicago.urban-history.org/sites/d_stores/fields.htm>

"Panama-California Exposition, San Diego, 1915-1916." *San Diego Historical Society*. San Diego CA 16 Jan 2006 <http://www.sandiegohistory.org/pancal/sdexpo35.htm>

"Past Attorney's General." *The State of Alaska Department of Law*. 30 Apr 2006 <http://www.law.state.ak.us/department/ag_past.html>

Perkins, M. S. ed. *Petersburg Weekly Report* Petersburg AK 26 July 1918 thru 29 Dec 1922

"Pioneers of Alaska." *Fairbanks Genealogical Society.* Fairbanks AK 3 Oct 1999 <http://www.ptialaska.net/~fgs/research/clubs/pioneers.htm>

"Pioneer Profiles: A History of Petersburg Settlers 1898-1959." *Pioneers of Alaska Igloo 26 and Auxiliary 10.* Sand Dollar Press, Port Townsend, WA 2004

"President Wilson Suffers a Stroke, 1919: A Presidential Crisis the Nation Knew Nothing About." *EyeWitness to History.* 2002 <http://www.eyewitnesstohistory.com/wilsonstroke.htm>

"Princess Sophia (steamer)." *Wikipedia Foundation, Inc.* 9 June 2007 <http://en.wikipedia.org/wiki/Princess_Sophia_(steamer)>

Rasmussen, Cecilia. "Flu Epidemic of 1918 Sent Chills Through State." *Los Angeles Times* Los Angeles CA 20 Nov 2005

"San Diego and Cuyamaca Railway, San Diego, Cuyamaca and Eastern Railway." *San Diego Railroad Museum.* June 1968 <http://www.sdrm.org/history/sdc/index.html>

"San Diego's Ocean Beach." *The City of San Diego.* 26 Jan 2006 <http://www.sandiego.gov/lifeguards/beaches/ob.shtml>

"Seattle General Strike of 1919." *Wikipedia Foundation, Inc.* 10 Sep 2006 <http://en.wikipedia.org/wiki/Seattle_General_Strike_of_1919>

Scheutz, Halvard. *Medlemmar Av Släkten Scheutz.* (Biographical Notes of the Scheutz Family). Timra, Sweden 1 Jun 1974

"Spanish Flu." *Wikipedia Foundation, Inc.* 26 May 2007 <http://en.wikipedia.org/wiki/Spanish_flu>

"Timeline of San Diego History, 1900." *San Diego Historical Society.* 26 Feb 2006 <http://www.sandiegohistory.org/timeline2.htm#1900>

"U.S. Business Cycle Expansions and Contractions." *National Bureau of Economic Research.* 11 Nov 2005 <http://www.nber.org/cycles/cyslesmain.html>

"Wars and Conflict: Summary of World War One." *BBC.* 1 Jan 2001 <http://www.bbc.co.uk/history/war/wwone/summary_01.shtm>

Wheeler, Keith. *The Alaskans.* Alexandria VA: Time-Life Books, Inc., 1977

Wilma, David. "Flu Epidemic Hits Seattle on October 3, 1918." *The Free Online Encyclopedia of Washington State History.* 1 Jan 2000 <http://www.historylink.org/essays/output.cfm?file_id=2090>

"Wingfoot Air Express Crash." *Wikipedia Foundation, Inc.* 10 October 2007 <http://en.wikipedia.org/wiki/Wingfoot_Air_Express_Crash>

LaVergne, TN USA
15 December 2009
167117LV00011B/94/P